Every Woman Loves A Russian Poet

Every Woman Loves A Russian Poet

by
Elizabeth Dunkel

DONALD I. FINE, INC.
New York

Library of Congress Cataloging-in-Publication Data

Dunkel, Elizabeth.
Every woman loves a Russian poet / by Elizabeth Dunkel.
p.   cm.
ISBN 1-55611-156-8
I.   Title.
PS3554.U4688E94   1989
811'.54—dc20   89-45336
CIP

Manufactured in the United States of America

10 9 8 7 6 5 4 3 2 1

DESIGNED BY IRVING PERKINS ASSOCIATES

"I Like It Here" by Clay Boland. Copyrighted 1950 by Elkan-Vogel, Inc.
Copyright renewed 1977 by Clay Boland Jr. Lyrics reprinted by permission of
Boland Music Corporation.

For my friend
Barbara Eliason Dunkel

Contents

NEW YORK

PARIS

NEW YORK

PARIS

NEW YORK

PARIS

NEW YORK

New York

Kate Loves No One

Sunday 3:00 a.m.
January 21, 1983

KATE ODINOKOV WAS lying in bed crying. She ached to feel the arms of a man around her. It had been so long. What was it, going on two years now? It felt like twenty. She was sure she would never have sex again. Her body felt dead. She tried to remember the smell of a man's desire. What she would give to drown in that intoxicating urgency of a man as he reached for her in the dark.

Had anyone ever felt so miserable? No, she was sure no one had. She was beyond the point of merely wanting sex; no, her loneliness and hunger were so great, it scared her. That made her cry even harder. Oh, the pain of an unloved life. Why had fate dealt her this hand? Was she really so unlovable?

She ran her hands along her naked body as she lay under the puff of a down duvet on this freezing January night, trying to imagine her hands were those of a man caressing her, maybe even exploring her for the first time. What would it feel like to make love to Kate Odinokov?

Although she always wished she had a dancer's lithe form, on the whole, she had made peace with her body and liked it. She knew it was a good, strong one. A Modigliani body, one long-ago boyfriend had called it. Big thighs, she knew that meant. She circled her hands around her strong hips, tapped them a few times, then felt her rounded tummy in between. Slowly, she traveled down the softness of the flesh inside her thighs to the sinewy, tougher texture of her calves. Moving her hand back up to her ribs, she outlined them one by one and finally slid her

11

hands onto her breasts. She lingered there gently massaging them, trying to understand the sense of magic and awe that men had for these curiously soft mounds of flesh, but it was beyond her. She had been told by every man she had ever been with that she had "great breasts." What does that mean? she'd ask. To her they were just garden-variety breasts. The response was always the same and never original enough to satisfy her: they were not too big, not too small, they were, well, just right. She figured that men should know; after all, breasts were more for their enjoyment, not hers.

Of course, she felt too chubby. But she knew that feeling too fat was part of being a woman; in fact, she could not name one single woman who didn't think she was okay just the way she was. "Brown and round" was how someone once described her, much to her chagrin, and now, at the age of thirty-three, brown and round is what she had become reconciled to. She comforted herself by declaring, "I am an unconventional beauty." It sounded good. There were many famously beautiful women who were unconventional beauties. Name one, she challenged herself. Okay. Isabella Rossellini, for one; Charlotte Rampling, for two.

She rolled over and wrapped her arms around herself. What a waste of a body! Does someone up there keep track of all the these sexless nights so I can get credit for them at some future date? Pity the poor man who finally ends up in my bed. I will be so voracious I will eat him up and exhaust him to death.

This is unfair! What have I done to deserve this? What do I have to do to get a date around here? Even her friends couldn't understand why she didn't have a man. There was no logic to it, Kate argued, and that's precisely what made it so horrible and inexplicable. It was simply a symptom of the curious times they were living in. There was no one thing she was or wasn't doing. It never occurred to her in a million years that she would end up this way, feeling totally left behind by life. Being single at her age had gotten to be just plain exhausting. There was no everyday sweetness in her life, not even hi honey, how was your day? She went out into the nasty city and battled it every day and came home at night to her cat. The ups and downs were wearying; they took their toll. She felt like an emotional yo-yo. She could feel incredibly high from a success at work or go to the Museum of Modern Art and see something beautiful and inspiring, only to walk home passing couples holding hands and kissing or new parents out with the stroller. She knew she should be thankful for what she had, everyone was always telling her that, but even so, she'd plunge into a desolate funk.

But where were all the men? Was she not looking in the right places? Other women met men at work; she didn't. Other women met men at their beach houses; she didn't. The bar scene scared her; besides, she was sure the kind of man she wanted wouldn't be hunting for her in a bar. It was New York's fault, then. This was a city about making money, long hours, success and fame. Men were too tired for love, they had their minds on other matters. She thought of how every morning she would get up, take that hot steamy shower, grind those coffee beans, make a cup of café au lait, taking care to heat up the milk, enjoy her bread and butter, blow-dry her chestnutty, baby-fine hair, put on her makeup, spritz herself with perfume, swish out of her apartment, stand on the subway platform and look at those maddeningly handsome and thoroughly constipated Upper East Side men with their heads buried in *The Wall Street Journal*. There were days when she just wanted to scream, "Look at me!" She imagined she heard "Girls Just Want to Have Fun" blasting through the station while she danced around the frozen men. To make matters worse, the few single men that existed were spoiled, for New York was filled with the most gorgeous, accomplished, single women who swarmed around them.

None of her married friends could even think of a man to introduce her to. There was not one single man at her office. She couldn't understand why. She supposed it was because she was arriving at the age when everyone was married, and if they were single they were about to get married or they were gay. She felt shut out of life because slowly, one by one, all of her girlfriends married and moved on to renovating their country houses and having babies, while she was still trying to get a goddamn date.

Weekends were when she felt most hopeless about her life. Tonight had been yet another Saturday night spent alone, sipping brandy and watching dumb television in bed while all of Manhattan reveled without her. During the week she was fine; she loved her job. Her days at the chic, downtown advertising agency where she was a copywriter were filled with breakfast, lunch and dinner with colleagues, clients and suppliers. There were meetings, presentations, photography shoots, recording and editing sessions. If she was so successful and well liked at work, how could it be that she was so unlucky at love? She was admired for her talent and charm. "How can such a great person like you be alone?" her colleagues clucked in sympathy. "You'll find someone," they promised. The line Kate hated the most was, "It's just that you're so special and you need someone special." She tried not to let her sadness show. A man wouldn't want a sad sack, she reasoned, and so, despite her private fears, she was known to be a perky person. And she was.

But then came Friday. The couples went to their country houses and the last few of her unmarried friends who lived with their boyfriends did romantic things like go out for brunch, hold hands on movie lines and take long walks in Central Park. They often invited her to join them and she did. She wasn't a recluse; she did lots of things by herself, too. She enjoyed going to museums and movies and the New York City Ballet. She occasionally took classes or went on a walking tour of some unloved part of the city.

But it came to the point where enough was enough. I'm only human, she would sigh to herself. She was so tired of searching. How she yearned to live a "normal" life, freed from this compulsion of trying to connect. And so, lately, it wasn't uncommon for her to spend entire weekends alone, starting with "Dallas" on Friday night and finishing with "Masterpiece Theatre" on Sunday night and in the interim hearing only the sound of her own voice talking to Boo the cat. No wonder she was half-crazed when she showed up at the office Monday morning.

She now lay in bed, terrorized in the darkness, while the insulting street noises found their way into her bedroom. There was the horrifying clammer of the huge semis rumbling down Second Avenue heading for the Fifty-ninth Street Bridge. Delivery vans idled outside the all-night delis as they made their drops of the next morning's fresh milk and bread. The newspaper trucks would be along at any time now. Drunken couples yelled and carried on as they stumbled to their cars for the trip back to New Jersey, their sexual laughter drifting up to mock her. Familiar thoughts of despair rose up to torture her like an evil chant: I will never be loved. I will never find someone to love. There must be something wrong with me. I will always be alone.

She checked the tiny travel clock, the one that gave out such delicate beeps in the morning. Four o'clock. Great. She moaned and flopped all the way over to the other side.

Kate wondered what her shrink, Dr. Manne, was doing at this hour. That was a dumb question; he was asleep, of course. Yes, she had felt so miserable that she had actually started therapy to figure out what was wrong with her and why she wasn't meeting men. And if it was to be her fate to live a loveless life, well, then therapy would help her cope with this reality. It had been a very difficult thing for her to do, see a therapist. In her family, going to a shrink was something other people did; it was for crazy people, not people like Kate. But that's how bad it had gotten. She hit bottom and knew she sounded like a broken record to her friends. It was the only place left to turn.

She sighed. Dr. Manne. So sweet, so gentle, so wonderful, so . . . exasperating! This was unfair, too. Why did she have to have the most handsome shrink in all of New York City? She tried to summon up his face, asleep in the embrace of some unknown woman. No. She shook her head. She preferred to think he was single. He wouldn't tell her whether he was married or not. Some days she thought he was and some days she thought he wasn't.

With the winter crystal moonlight seeping in through the window, she continued to recite her litany of doom. Her inner voice became authoritative. I will never meet a man. Besides, I am over the hill. Men today want young things. What is wrong with me? Am I too needy? Does that scare men away? No, I think I am probably just the opposite. There, that's it. I come off as too strong and independent, and very successful. That's what scares them away.

American men are hopeless, she decided. They don't know how to flirt. European men are much more relaxed; their sexuality is a natural part of them, whereas American men seem to have a compartment called sex. Sex was something American men did. It wasn't integrated into who they were. Maybe I should try to get transferred to a foreign country. Well, that could take months, so maybe I should just move myself.

It was time to try an objective approach. I am no slouch, she defended herself. To an outsider her life would probably seem glamorous, and when she really thought about it, there were people who would probably envy her. She was an accomplished cook and entertainer. Her apartment was decorated like a charming country cottage in the sky. She wasn't one of those women who put off living until she met a man. No, her place was a home, where her life was really lived. There were real stuffed chairs and couches and coffee tables and expertly placed lamps creating appealing pockets of light and conversation nooks. There was a piano, which she practiced every day. There was a pine dining table where she served herself Sunday dinners. There was china and crystal.

And then there was the mistress of her life, her cozy calico cat, Boo, who made the place seem full of fun and rich with cat mystery. Boo was her confidante. Every day Kate would come home from work and tell her everything.

She was smart. She had a Phi Beta Kappa key from college and a master's degree in English with honors. She had a busy and rewarding job. She earned a decent salary. She had a housekeeper who came to clean every other week and she kept fit by swimming and saunas three times a week. She belonged to the New York Public Library. She dressed well and loved zooming into Bloomingdale's and slumming in SoHo boutiques. She rode her bicycle in Central Park. True, she had no roller skates. So what was the problem? Why hadn't she had a date in months?

These are sick times we live in, that's why. Herpes and a host of new sexual diseases cropping up every day. AIDS. Divorces, triangles, single parents, personal ads, surrogate mothers, abused children. She was tired of reading those stupid alarming articles in *New York* magazine about the dwindling age/conception curve, the new mini–baby boom, last-chance babies, in vitro fertilization, sharing men, and the latest in social female trends: marrying down, which meant the crop of men had dwindled to the point where it was now actually chic to marry your plumber. She was mortified when she saw a whole section of books at Barnes & Noble about loneliness, how to catch a man, loving the wrong man, loving men too much, not loving men enough, and worse, how to live alone creatively. The Free School even offered courses in "How to Flirt" and "The 99 Best Places in Manhattan to Meet a Mate." Looking for love had become an epidemic. Being a single woman in Manhattan was disgusting. No, worse, it was a cliché! And she, Kate Odinokov, had become one of the statistics! Then came that drastic story in *Newsweek*, the one that showed a woman's chances of getting married if she was over thirty. And her chances weren't good. Well, that just did her in.

What's the use and what good is crying if no one can hear you? She pounded the bed. Well, that was one thing she liked. Her Japanese futon and the down duvet. Then she remembered the brawny, redheaded woman who delivered the futon to her apartment several months ago and how surprised she had been that it was a woman and not a man making such a bulky delivery.

"You ever slept on one of these?" she asked in a thick Australian accent when Kate opened the door to let her in.

"No," Kate said, stepping back to give her room to maneuver the cart into the apartment. "Why do you ask?"

The rosy-cheeked woman smiled broadly at her. "You're going to die and go to heaven tonight. It's incredible," she said, wheeling the futon past her. Turning around she added, "You'll see," and raised her eyebrows in a mischievous manner. "Where do you want it?"

Kate led the way to the bedroom and pointed to the spot where she wanted the frame set up. She leaned against the door and watched as the woman took a knife from the tool kit slung around her waist and started to slit open the plastic covering. Then she wondered if she should be helping her.

"Futons are especially comfortable for two people," the redhead offered. "You get a good night's sleep because you can't feel the other person turn over."

Kate sighed. "Well, it's just me, it's always been just me." Even though that wasn't true, she had boyfriends in some distant past, it sure felt that way.

The woman looked up at her for a moment and then continued working. After a while she said, "You could try women, you know." She said it as if she was tossing a Frisbee into a wind.

Would it fly? And would Kate catch it? She froze, not knowing how to respond. Was this a proposition or what?

The woman looked up at Kate to see how she was taking this information, then bent her head back down to the futon and continued prattling on matter-of-factly. "When I couldn't find a man, that's what I did. I took a woman." She paused. "And I love it."

"Ummm," Kate said uncertainly. She wanted to be polite, but it was getting a little awkward in here.

"You get comfort, support, affection. . . ." the redhead continued. She didn't say sex, but Kate knew that would be next.

"Ummm," Kate mumbled again, and glanced at her watch nervously. "Oh, I forgot. I have to call my office. We have this major shoot tomorrow." She smiled apologetically and left the room. She hoped she had sounded normal and casual. She picked up the phone, dialed weather and talked to the recording until she waved the futon lady out with a smile. "Jesus! New York is unbelievable," she said, and collapsed on the couch.

But tonight she recalled this boisterous, contented woman setting up her futon and was envious of her ease and happiness. At least she had a companion. . . . She shook her head. This is ridiculous. Surely taking a woman as a lover couldn't possibly be the solution for her! She had never been attracted to a woman. She shuddered. But then she thought, could it be that she didn't have a man because she was, unknown to herself, secretly gay? Kate, take hold of yourself, she charged. You are not a lesbian. This is pathetic. Has it come to this? Is that the only choice left for happiness, companionship, sex—becoming gay? This is sick, this is really, really sick. I'd rather kill myself.

Suddenly her mind went blank. There was a frightening stillness. Her thoughts had run out and left her no other solution.

If I can't have a man, then I will have to kill myself.

She ran down her by-now-familiar litany of methods. Pills. She didn't have any. Okay, jumping out the window then. Too grisly. The thought of stepping out the window and falling through the night . . . what would she think about in those last moments as she stood on the ledge, staring at the street below? And what if she changed her mind on the way down? And then lying on a dirty New York street, being found by strangers? She thought of John Berryman jumping off the ferry boat to Nantucket and shook her head.

Okay, next. Hanging? That was kind of old-fashioned and she didn't think she could pull it off. She didn't have a rope, and besides, she didn't know how to tie the proper knot. Then she remembered that people nowadays did it with leather belts—or was it bathrobe ties? Maybe she should reconsider this method. Then she realized there was no place in her apartment from which to hang.

A knife! She shuddered. No, she didn't have the courage for that. It was too bloody and violent. No way.

She thought about Virginia Woolf walking into the ocean and drowning herself. . . . Kate was impressed. Now that took real determination. It seemed romantic. She thought about that one for a while, then decided no, Jones Beach was too far away, and besides, it was January.

Visions of Anne Sexton came to mind. She died with the smell of tuna fish on her hands. It was as simple as that. On an ordinary day she was making a tuna-fish sandwich for her lunch, and at one particularly dangerous, in-between moment, she lost it. She was chopping an onion —or was it celery?—when she decided enough was enough. She put down the knife, put on her jacket and went out to the garage as if she were dashing downtown to pick up some Hellman's. But instead, she closed the garage door, sat in her car and turned on the ignition. Well, Kate didn't have a car, or a garage for that matter, so that ruled that method out.

Well, that left only one way. The oven. It had been the method of choice for Sylvia Plath, and if it was good enough for Sylvia, it would be good enough for Kate Odinokov. No violent ending here, rather, a gentle, sleepy way to go with enough time to back out if sentiments changed. Yes, the oven would do quite well.

She sat up abruptly and looked at her sweet calico cat lying curled up in the tightest ball imaginable on her bed. Boo didn't budge but opened her eyes, stared back at her and then closed them again. But who will take care of my little Boo? Unable to brush away her heartbreaking sadness, she leapt out of bed, believing she could not live another minute longer. If this was going to be her loveless life, she wanted no part of it. Just as one might check out of a motel, Kate Odinokov was going to check out of life.

Boo, seeing her mistress jump up, yowled with delight, thinking it was good old breakfast time. She tangled herself up in Kate's feet as she stumbled into the kitchen. Thrown off momentarily by the meowing cat between her legs, Kate automatically unscrewed the big glass jar, scooped out some dry cat stars and tossed them into Boo's French dish. This familiar action distracted her for the crucial moment.

Saved by the Boo.

Kate paced the living room, trembling as she listened to Boo loudly crunching her bonanza breakfast. Then she wandered back into the bedroom. It was now 6:00 A.M. She stared at the bed and decided she couldn't go back to sleep. What sleep? She hadn't slept all night. She put on her most comforting clothes, the soft gray cotton parachute pants and a heavy wool sweater, threw on her leather jacket and her paisley jacquard scarf from Paris and fled the scene of her sadness.

She rode the elevator impatiently and stepped into the lobby, surprised to find the doorman not there. Probably sound asleep in the basement. She pulled open the heavy door and was greeted by a chilling gust of wind. Well, January was certainly feeling frisky. She drew the jacket closer to her and enjoyed the icy, early-morning air on her face. The bars on Third Avenue were just finishing their Saturday-night cleanup, the sleepy employees finally putting out the trash and going home. The city was a no-man's-land at this hour on a Sunday morning. She walked briskly past Lenox Hill Hospital rebuking herself. Shame on you for feeling sorry for yourself. That's where real life and death are going on at this very minute! The newspaper kiosks on Lexington Avenue were open, displaying the fat Sunday papers. The delis were sending coffee fumes out into the street. She walked past them all with great purpose, looking, she supposed, like a woman with a mission.

Whenever Kate started thinking about suicide, when things got that bad and she began having serious thoughts about what it would really be like to kneel on the linoleum and put her head in the oven and how high she would have to turn on the gas and how long it would take, that's when she made herself get up, get out and take a walk on Madison Avenue.

It never failed her. She took a deep breath as she surveyed the empty street spread out before her. Madison Avenue was always there, glorious and restrained; it could always be counted on. Within minutes of strolling past the deluxe, chockful shop windows, she always had the same realization. I could never kill myself: I love clothes too much.

She stopped in front of Givenchy and started when she saw her reflection in the window, staring with wonder at the display, her furled brow seriously considering everything she saw, critiquing and analyzing the fanciful lines of the ballgowns. She took a deep breath and sighed, strolling on pensively. Does this mean I'm shallow? she asked herself in a horrifed tone. That I'm a silly, vulgar person and all it takes is a new bauble and I'll go blithely on my way?

No! She argued back valiantly. Let's be serious. I'm battling for my life here, and if this is all it takes to keep me alive, then why quibble? I'll take it! In cases like this, one should be grateful for small things. This is not shallow at all, this is a triumph of my will.

Her inner voice softened. But it is such a slender thread, she mused. To slip in and out of life so easily. She shuddered. How delicate is our hold. She exhaled and continued down the street prayerfully, thinking, it's true that people decide to leave life over things unimaginable to others. At what moment did Virginia Woolf decide not one minute more of *this* (of what?) and stride out of her house and into the ocean? For what *reason* did Anne Sexton throw her hands up? So, Kate decided vehemently, it matters not what makes sense or brings light into that dark and fatal moment. Just grab it and hold on tight.

As she walked she imagined that most depressed people would get even more depressed window-shopping on Madison Avenue, gazing at things they could never afford, for life-styles so different from their own.

The opulence, the beauty and impracticality of the clothes, the gorgeous antiques and extravagant jewels would probably disgust most people and throw others into a frenzy of despair even greater than before. But for Kate, it was exactly the opposite. The sight of beautifully crafted objects inspired her. It put the idea of perfection within her sight, if not her grasp.

Take the supple leathers and superb craftsmanship of Brigitte Cassegrain, she said, automatically slipping into advertising copy as she took a stance in front of the elegant French saddlery boutique. I know for a fact that a handbag from Brigitte would definitely soothe some rough spots in my life. Yes, somehow, swinging one of her pocketbooks from my shoulder would make me believe there is order in this world—the order of people reaching perfection in their calling. Brigitte Cassegrain was put on this Earth for a reason.

To walk the crude streets in the buttery leather shoes of that charming Italian, Tanino Crisci, or those flirtatious Fratelli Rossetti, why I would feel I must be all right, things must be okay if I am shod as lovingly as this!

She stared deeply into the windows of Sonia Rykiel. Heavenly, she sighed. I know the world would treat me better if I were dressed in a two-piece cashmere knit dress by Sonia, accessorized perhaps with one of those rhinestone-studded belts. I would feel like a woman with a past, a mysterious creature from another era. As she stood in a trance, to her great surprise, the Sonia Rykiel mannequins came alive, moving and swaying to some private, unearthly music. Kate looked around on the street to see if anyone else was watching and could confirm what she was seeing. But no, she alone was privy to this curious dance. She turned back to the window where the mannequins were cooing and beckoning to her, sashaying about in some sort of feminine conspiracy. What did they want her to do? What was their message? Kate backed away. If only she could enter their world.

She moved on to the next boutique. Oh, that brilliant colorist Kenzo! Kenzo would make me feel bright, young, fresh, ready to kick up my heels with insouciance. She proceeded down the street slowly, giving each store window an evaluation, stopping finally in front of a boutique, where she bowed with reverence in homage to the master: Yves St. Laurent. She stood in a swoon, dissecting the perfect suits and the society ladies' tea dresses, trying to imagine the feel of the ultrafine fabrics on her skin. She noted the painstaking details on the collars and cuffs and suddenly heard the strains of that rousing army commercial that urged the television viewer to join up so they could "Be, all that you can be!"

"I understand," she said aloud. "I do understand now what it means to be all that you can be." Her eyes devoured the heightened purity of Yves's style and the uncompromising quality that resulted from the search and realization of perfection. And it was all manifested in a tea dress. It took her breath away; it was too much. She felt weak. She moved on to Giorgio Armani.

She turned around, ready to walk back home. The street was a cathedral, soaring and solemn, and she felt like a millionaire, having it all to herself. Suddenly she felt gorgeous, young and full of possibilities. She swung around and was filled with the giddy joyousness of being alive. Goodness, sometimes it was exhausting being Kate Odinokov. Couples didn't have any idea how hard it was being alone in life, making your way day by day, swinging between hopefulness and despair.

Forget the major issues, she thought, it is the small things in life that keep me hanging on. Take potato chips, for example. For potato chips, the most delicious snack food in the world, I will live. Cheese, too, is a cause célèbre for staying alive. Wasn't one of her favorite activities to step into Dean & DeLuca and survey the oozy cheeses, plump, moist, juicy cheeses, moldy, smelly ones, or those impertinent young goats bathing in olive oil. Runny, smooth, always perfect cheeses.

Or, take rice. There is no better reason for living than rice. She had struggled for months trying to answer the question that New Yorkers liked to pose: if you could eat only one thing forever, what would it be? Finally, the answer appeared from an unexpected corner of her heart. Rice. Lowly rice. It could be plain boiled rice with a pat of butter and salt, or rice in the seductive guise of a creamy, steaming risotto, blended, of course, with one of those glorious cheeses from Italy.

She walked on. Italy! How can I kill myself when there exists such a place as Italy! In her heart she knew God had created Italy so that people in despair would have their own personal country of hope. Okay, okay, I'll live, but just get me to Italy! Oh, for the marvelous land of abundance and gentleness, where only the most delicious foods pass your lips, only the most beautiful art is enjoyed by your eyes, where you live in the most beautiful buildings and where you wear only the most beautiful clothes.

She found herself in front of Fraser Morris, the elegant caterer of

Madison Avenue. Talk about perfect. She watched the chefs, up so early in their pristine white coats, setting up the window for the brunch strollers who would appear in a few hours. She looked at the glistening fruit tartlets in their various shapes, so seductive in their glazed state, flirting with her. She smiled back. And those beautiful miniature brioches, so hilarious in their silly shapes, as if they were saying, "Hi ya honey!" That raucous baked Virginia ham had no shame. And how thoughtful of those delicate, baby asparagus to be resting so languorously in that tangy vinaigrette.

Okay, Kate, what else? Let's get real. Okay. There's nothing quite so comforting as settling yourself in front of your television and watching a great old movie. Especially if you've made yourself a nice bowl of crunchy, Parmesan popcorn or a mug of creamy hot chocolate with gooey, miniature marshmallows floating in it. Kate loved watching old movies for the women in them. She felt they had a lot to teach her about being a woman. She marveled at Marlene Dietrich's self-confidence in her own beauty, intelligence and power of seduction. She seemed to have the thing known as "feminine wiles." Kate wasn't sure that feminine wiles existed today, but from watching these movies she had learned to carefully manicure her nails short and red.

Garbo and Hepburn were sultry and exasperating with men in a way that the men seemed to love. Why was it that men in the movies seemed to love a challenge? Complicated women appealed to men back then. But not today. No, today's men had no sense of the chase. How could they? Today's women were ready to plunk themselves down for them like change for the Sunday *Times.*

"Hi," Kate said, smiling at the Algerian who always clucked at her from his perch inside the newspaper kiosk. She helped herself to the hefty paper. She popped into her neighborhood deli next door, her local, she liked to call it, and picked up a loaf of fresh French bread. Oh goody, café au lait and tartines, she plotted, escalating her language to suit her sense of the occasion. "Good morning," she said cheerfully to the doorman, who was surprised to see her out so early. Something about his look disturbed her, and while she rode the elevator she realized he thought she had been out all night and was just coming back. Well good, let him think that.

She undid the three locks and let herself into the apartment, which she had left in such a different state of mind just a short while ago. She threw the paper down in the entrance hall and slapped her hands in disgust from the black newsprint that had already soiled them. She went into the kitchen, put the water on to boil and ground up some coffee beans. Then she went into the bathroom, slipped off her clothes and stepped into the shower.

Minutes later she emerged a new person. Her face was pink and healthy from the combination of her early-morning walk and the steamy shower. Instead of her usual white terrycloth robe she decided to treat herself to the black silk kimono she kept for . . . for what? Special occasions? Men? She brushed the thought from her head; she wasn't going to let that bother her. She had had a bad night, that's all. Everything would be fine. Things happen to you when you're ready, love would find her when she least expected it, that's what everyone always said. She felt composed and tranquil, ready to take on the world again with all the energy and delight she was known for.

She made the coffee, poured in the steaming milk and took the tray to the living room and settled on the couch. Whoops, she forgot the *Times*. She jumped up, retrieved it from the entrance hall and dropped it on the floor next to her with a thud. Sipping her café au lait, she gazed at the front-page headlines, then flipped through the sections and without thinking pulled out the second part of the first section, the society pages. She let her fingers do the walking and automatically ended up at the wedding announcements. She read them one by one, taking in all the details of these privileged lives. She stared at the pictures of the happy brides and burst into tears.

Kate Meets Boris

THE NEXT FRIDAY Kate left the office about three and went home drained. She had put in a hard week of early-morning meetings for a new business pitch that had taken place today at eleven. The agency desperately wanted this new wine-cooler account. She stood up in front of the prospective client and jazz-rapped her way through a jingle she had written: "It's the cooler cooler, it's the cooler that's hot. It's the cooler that's got what the others do not." She even did a little dance, complete with finger snapping and a twirl at the end, and made just enough of a charming fool out of herself that everyone loved it, loved her, loved the energy of the agency.

She thought about the nice nap she would have as the subway racketed her back uptown. "I'll do the grocery shopping later," she informed the bum who was slumped next to her. She breezed into her apartment-building lobby and automatically shuffled over to her mailbox. Today was the *New Yorker* day. A bonus! A letter from her brother, a linguistics professor spending his sabbatical year from Penn roaming about Europe in search of dead languages.

In the elevator she read how he had been playing Frisbee in Paris, in the Jardin du Luxembourg, when he heard someone speaking Russian. That was how he met Boris, a Russian émigré poet, just a year and a half out of the Soviet Union. They became Frisbee partners, meeting every afternoon for some free throws, and now this Boris was coming to New York for two weeks to write articles on New York City jazz for the

French review *Jazz Monde*. "So I gave him your phone number and he might call you," her brother wrote. "This is his first trip to the States. He knows no one and I told him you were a real cool and chic New Yorker." Fine, Kate thought.

The next morning she was vacuuming the living room when the phone rang. "Hello!" she exclaimed in that breathless, cheerful way of hers. None of this coy, inquiring "hello?" for Kate.

"I would like please to speak to Katia Odinokov," said a deeply accented voice.

"This is Kate," she said, trying to place this curious accent. French? Yugoslavian?

"Boris Zimoy is my name. Friend of brother's in Paris, and I here in Big Apple as zhournaleest to write about zhazz and I would like you come tomorrow and I cook lunch."

Kate held the phone away from her ear a moment. Was this for real? A man wanted to cook lunch for her? It was a little strange, but then, he was a Russian, not a Manhattan man. A Manhattan man would usually suggest meeting for a drink so he could make an easy getaway if things didn't turn out as he hoped, or dinner afterward if they did.

She forgot he was on the line when she said aloud, "I only got my brother's letter yesterday."

"Letter? Ehh. I no understand," the Russian said, jolting her back to their phone conversation.

She giggled. "No, I mean, that is very nice and I would like to very much," she said politely and slowly so he could understand every word. "But how can you cook in a hotel?" That's when he told her he was apartment sitting, right around the corner from where she lived. "Great, I'll see you tomorrow. At one?" she said. He grunted and they hung up.

Even though she had never seen him before in her life, Kate could tell Boris was very nervous the minute he opened the door to the fabulous Park Avenue duplex he was staying in, on this, his first trip ever to the United States of America.

Eugene the elevator man was nervous too. No, suspicious was more like it. He stood watching as Kate rang the doorbell and Boris answered the door. Kate looked uncertainly from Eugene watching her to Boris watching her. Boris, who seemed to be sucking in everything about her in one glance with his piercing Russian eyes, was definitely agitated. He saw a strikingly pretty American woman with a Russian face and he wondered what soul would she have, Russian or American?

Then Boris looked at Eugene looking at the two of them. Eugene shifted his weight and stood his ground. It reminded Boris of how he had been hounded not only by those nasty KGB men in Moscow but also by those people who called themselves his friends. He could just imagine what Eugene thought. Here was this stealthy Russian staying in Mr. Bunnell's apartment, while Mr. Bunnell wintered in the Dominican Republic, doing God knows what, opening the door to a young woman who obviously didn't know him. Of course Eugene didn't like the look of it.

Boris tried to understand Eugene's suspicion. Or was he just being—what was that American expression—nosey? He could agree that Mr. Bunnell didn't seem to be the type of guy to know any Russians. The use of the apartment had been arranged by friends in Paris. Boris was shocked when, upon his arrival, he presented Mr. Bunnell with a very expensive bottle of Bordeaux. Mr. Bunnell obviously had no idea how special it was, in fact barely glanced at it, said thanks and put it away with all his wine bottles. Then he disappeared back to Santo Domingo, leaving Boris alone to make his way in New York.

Eugene could deal with Mr. Bunnell's comings and goings and believed it to be his duty as a good elevator operator to be discreet and respectful, but of this Russian, well, he just didn't approve. He always acted so furtive—as if he were constantly being followed, looking over his shoulder, speaking in a low voice, shifting his feet, avoiding glances. No, he had to be doing something illegal, Eugene thought. What was going on here anyway? Probably some spy ring. He shook his head at the two of them, shrugged his shoulders and slammed the elevator grate.

"Come in," Boris said to Kate in a formal tone, secretly delighted that his English actually worked, deliriously happy to finally be in a place where English was spoken. When he had been studying it all those years in Moscow off those expensive, black-market Frank Sinatra records, he never really believed that what he was learning he would put to use, right here in Frankie's favorite town, New York, New York! He hoped in his excitement that he would not accidentally dish up phrases like "I did it my way" and "Luck be a lady tonight." He had seen American girls in Paris and was shocked how the French men looked down on them, but he didn't feel comfortable approaching them himself for fear they would be disappointed he was Russian and not French. But now, here was the real thing: a New York woman in New York!

Kate took a quick glance at the apartment and couldn't believe it. She had never been in a real New York duplex before; she had only heard about them. It was huge, like a house! And there really were stairs! There was a cozy fire burning in a fireplace. For some reason she got nervous. Her imagination took over and ran away. This guy has got to be KGB, she thought. Being an exiled Russian poet, that's a good cover. I better be very careful. Very. She handed her mink coat to Boris, who stood with his arms out, ready to take it. She looked to see if he was impressed, but no, he looked as if he were used to hanging up mink coats. It was a Russian "thing" to have a fur coat, a *shooba*. Russian women of a certain class just didn't feel right about winter if they didn't have a fur, and her grandmother felt Kate should have mink so men would think she was well off. It was one of those silly family things that blew around her, for Kate really didn't care about having a mink coat. Mink was too too. Too obvious. More for the Junior League set with their Hermes scarves wrapped around their ever-so-blond hair. No, she was just a good girl of Russian extraction, a first-generation American who grew up speaking Russian in New York City before she entered kindergarten, where she became totally American. In the end, she decided not to be the first woman in history to refuse a mink coat and so, when her grandmother offered her one, she took it.

Kate was so nervous she forgot or, more accurately, didn't notice how handsome Boris was. It wasn't until months later when she showed a picture of him to her friends that she understood he was not only handsome, but gorgeous, as her friends exclaimed. Looks never impressed Kate the way they did other women. To her, Boris looked just like an exiled Russian poet should, with a beard, of course, and most important, intelligent eyes. Deep, dark, searching and tortured eyes. His voice was soft and rich and he spoke delightful, halting English with an appealing, indefinable mingling of French and Russian accents. He was a compact man with the physique of a miniature Apollo. She was surprised that such a small man could be so masculine and so appealing.

He had that European toilette that American men simply could not duplicate. There was something profoundly sexy and trim about him, with a presentation as studied as a woman's. His hair was fashionably cut, his beard trimmed just so. He wore a silk shirt and wool slacks with great ease, Italian touches she was sure, and certainly not the casual blue jeans American men wore. Then there was that unusual cologne. She closed her eyes for a second to think about the scent. Oh my God, he smelled like Siberia! I am standing with a man who smells like Siberia. She had never been there, but she was sure it must smell like this. It was a wild, animal scent, exotic, deep, harsh and very lost. It reeked of the violence of wild boars, desperate and passionate Russian sex under furs in the middle of the night, with wolves howling outside the cabin, the crunch of ice crystals and, of course, immense danger.

"What a lovely apartment," she said, trying to be polite. She hoped her voice didn't give her away. She handed him a bottle of wine that she had chosen a few days earlier in the liquor store because it looked expensive but was in fact quite cheap. She realized she felt so distrustful and nervous because Boris looked so out of place in this Park Avenue apartment that was unfortunately decorated in what she called "early nouveau riche." Rooms like this distressed her. There was an attempt at good furniture, but the cheap, vulgar rugs and the poor assemblage of paintings and knickknacks showed the decorator's true sense. It was the lamps that really gave everything away. Lamps always told the real story, just like people's shoes. She quickly checked Boris's shoes. He was wearing chic Italian boots. Hanging just over the fireplace was what decorating magazines would call an *objet*, a three-dimensional plastic cloud that could be lit up by a remote-control squeegee on a table near the couch. How could such a poor-but-elegant Russian poet know such awful people? She began to redecorate the place in her own mind. She loved to redo other people's spaces and imagine them as her own.

As for Boris, well, he was just plain desperate. He was surprised to find that he had been all nerves from the moment he had arrived two days ago at JFK—what a hellhole of an airport! It was a lifelong fantasy come true, the object of all his dreaming in Moscow had finally been realized, and he still couldn't quite absorb the reality of his being in New York.

His desperation wasn't the pathetic, lonely kind. It was the desperation of sheer survival. He felt fine and calm in the Air France jet, surrounded by soft-spoken French people and happy Americans returning from their dreamy French vacations. But the moment the jet landed at JFK he was jolted. Suddenly he smelled Moscow. He snapped to at the familiar whiff of the violence of a certain kind of urban existence. There was the same aggressiveness, the same meanness, the same you're-on-your-own-here attitude among the people. In Paris, where he had been living since his escape from Moscow, the atmosphere was relaxed, the pace was slow. The French were more interested in gratifying their senses than in accomplishing things. They argued heatedly only about such issues as which was the best Camembert and what was the perfect wine to have with dinner. The French ambled when they walked, leaving a cloud of perfume in their wake. New Yorkers, like Muscovites, ran red lights and fought against the flow of traffic. He quickly saw they drank this nasty brown water for coffee. No, New York was one tough town. Unlike Paris, there were no cafés to set your ass down if you were tired on the street or too early for an appointment.

At the same time that he hated and was shocked by the nasty feelings he found here, he also felt at home because he knew well how to live in this battlefield. After all, he was a survivor. The minute he got off the 747 he noticed how the people changed. They started pushing each other and rushing. All of them seemed to know exactly where they were going. He was confused and frightened, not understanding the long halls with no signs. There were no baggage carts, just long corridors that led to drafty halls and people yelling. There was no one to tell him where to go or what to do next. He couldn't believe this mess was New York. Exhausted from the flight, he felt unequal to it all.

The immigration officer studied Boris's French traveling papers with great interest. He had no passport since he wasn't a citizen of any country anymore. He ripped up his Soviet passport the day he arrived in Paris on Aeroflot number 02, almost two years ago. With the metal stamp poised above the transit visa, ready to strike, the officer casually asked, "Soviet citizen?"

Boris's mouth dropped open. He was at once shocked and angry. Then he felt hurt. He shook his head vehemently. "No!" he said emphatically.

The officer hadn't expected this. "Well, what are you then?"

"Stateless person," he said defiantly.

The blue-eyed, pink-cheeked officer from Queens had never heard that one before and put the stamp down.

"Soviet émigré, then," he tried.

"No!" Boris said again. He thought quickly. An émigré is someone who has adopted a new home, and yes, while he lived in France, he had not yet adopted it as his new home, nor had he applied for French citizenship.

"Political refugee," he said, looking at the officer sternly.

The officer looked back at him and thought, Oh no, an emotional Russian nut.

"Exiled individual," Boris tried another one. He glanced around and swore at himself in Russian. People in the line behind him were staring at him with annoyed, impatient eyes. You fool, you've wanted to come to the U.S.A. all your life and now what have you done? They won't let you in if you keep this up!

They stared at each other for a half minute until the officer shook his head and said, "Soviet citizen," and stamped his papers. "Next!" he called out, pushing the visa back to Boris, not giving him any chance to disagree. And with that, Boris was in the United States of America, the seat of all Western decadence, land of his childhood dreams.

Next, he searched for his luggage in another huge, noisy room filled with people from many different flights, all yelling at each other and grabbing for their bags. Babies screamed in all the chaos. He picked out his luggage carefully, then stepped around a poor little girl who was throwing up, and after making his way through the customs' green "nothing to declare" zone, he found himself being pushed through JFK's famous frosted glass doors into a wall of waiting, searching faces. There he was struggling with his luggage, all by himself, being tossed right out into New York, just like that. He felt a bit sorry for himself. Now what? He felt self-conscious as he made his way down the narrow space with everyone jostling him, pushing him past them because he wasn't the relative they were waiting for. No one reached out to help. And then, as in a dream, suddenly he looked up to find Volodya's face staring at him and laughing. Boris gasped and collapsed into his arms. He hadn't seen Volodya and his wife since they left Moscow a year before he got out, and now here they all were in New York. They hugged and looked deeply and meaningfully into each other's eyes. Volodya and Kira expected him to stay with them in Queens, and when he heard Queens, he threw an emotional tantrum right then and there at JFK. But, they complained, he didn't even know this Mr. Bunnell, how could he stay with a stranger when they were his only friends here? No! He wanted to be in Manhattan, the real New York City. Finally, they saw how upset he was, and even though they were terribly hurt, they drove him to the city in Volodya's yellow taxicab. Boris felt a little sorry for them. While he was happy to see Volodya and Kira, he was embarrassed by them. They were his past, and this visit to New York was his future. When he left the Soviet Union, he became new and modern, a Western person, and they reminded him of his pitiful self back then, when his life was a constant struggle—a struggle to find Western things, plotting ways to get published, or just scrounging for things as banal as meat or toilet paper.

New York was so enervating! Everything people had said or written about it, everything he had ever fantasized about it was true. It was a wonderful but scary dream to live up to. He wanted to be sure to do everything right, here in the city of cities, Sinatra's town, the city of nightlife until dawn and Frisbees soaring high in Central Park. From the day he arrived, he coped with his constant agitation and fear by drinking scotch from morning till night. Scotch, his beloved scotch, which was so expensive in France, and in Moscow was black-market stuff, was here the national drink and best of all, affordable. He was in heaven. Every day, right after breakfast, before making his morning phone calls to all the people whose names he had been given, he poured himself a little bit of scotch. For courage, he told himself. And so on, through the day, in order to do any little thing, he always poured himself a little scotch. And afterward, to celebrate each achievement, he poured himself a little scotch. Just like Sinatra would have done, he was sure.

And now here he was with this Kate, the sister of his American Frisbee friend. Boris had no idea what to expect of her. He didn't have enough money to take her out for a meal, and besides, New York wasn't like Paris when it came to good, cheap restaurants by the dozen. So he resorted to his Moscow habit by inviting her over for a meal.

Now Boris was nervous about his cooking. He had gone around the corner to this American supermarket, D'Agostino's, whose decor was a joyous, orangey red. The food seemed to be smiling back at him from the shelves. There was music and everyone seemed to be dancing down the aisles with these huge, shiny metal and red plastic carts. He picked up chicken wrapped in plastic and tomatoes wrapped in plastic, even onions wrapped in plastic! The food even looked like plastic, but he loved it anyway, because this was New York and it was one hell of a town. All morning long he had carefully prepared his chicken dish, and now it was overcooked and dried out. He couldn't believe it! In his tiny Paris apartment he was a brilliant chef, improvising impressive dishes with no effort. He had learned from his mother in Moscow how to make inspired dishes out of nothing—he even joked that soup from an old leather boot had been his specialty. But here, he simply looked like a dumb man who couldn't cook. Boris was mortified. What would she think?

He took the bottle of wine she had brought and read the label, really studied it, and then pronounced, "Is a dessert wine."

Kate had never been with a man who, when he looked at a wine label, really knew what he was reading.

"Yes, of course," she said, although she was mortified that she hadn't known it was a dessert wine; she had thought it was just a regular white wine.

Boris assumed that she knew exactly what she had brought, too, but then when he looked at her, he wasn't so sure. "Is perfectly all right, we drink for dessert. Now I put in fridge." He laughed. He loved that word, it was so American. He came back from the kitchen. "Excuse me," he said, and abruptly dashed up the stairs.

Kate stood alone in the living room, a bit baffled. Why did he disappear like that? She got a little nervous. Here was a poor Russian poet who knew about wines and was staying in this fancy Park Avenue duplex. His English was too good to have been learned in a Soviet school, and besides, he spoke French, too. Could he be a KGB operative? But surely her brother wouldn't introduce her to a spy. She checked the door to see the number of locks she would have to open if she had to escape quickly. She had a flash of panic. He had gone upstairs to get a gun. She shook her head. Living with New York's daily violence had turned her into a wreck. Kate, you are a nut, you've been watching too many TV shows.

Poor Boris had gone upstairs to calm himself in front of the mirror and splash on more cologne. He wanted to have an American girlfriend very badly and didn't quite know how to go about it. It would make his stay here so much easier if he had someone to show him around. He hoped he was doing okay.

"Let me make you a dreenk. How about a kir?" he purred, coming back down the stairs.

Kate shrugged yes and followed him into the kitchen. It was a poignant scene: an ugly, yellow Formica kitchen, brightly lit with one overhead fluorescent light, where he had set a tiny kitchen table so neatly with plates and silverware and paper napkins folded just so. She looked at all the trouble he had gone to for her and she melted. It had been so long since a man had done anything nice—no, anything for her. He pulled open the fridge and took out an already-opened bottle of white wine. She loved the way he flipped the cork out, sniffed the top of the bottle and poured a little wine into a glass to taste it to see if it was still fresh. The way he swirled it first in the glass, then sniffed it again, then tasted it in his mouth, then nodded to himself, charmed her. Here was a very capable man, the kind she liked.

They went back into the living room with their drinks and he told her to sit on the couch. Then Boris ran upstairs again. Now what? What a curious lunch this was, all this up and down the stairs, back and forth to the kitchen. He came back down triumphantly waving a huge sheaf of papers in his hand.

"I have poems by the kilo," he said, pleased with his joke, and then handed them to her, she supposed, to prove he was a real Russian poet. Kate tried to be polite and shuffled through them, but this was no time to read lugubrious, intellectual and badly translated poems on dirty carbon copies that had served as Boris's *samizdat*. She looked up occasionally to find him staring at her with his intense eyes as she tried to read.

"I'd like to read them privately, when I can really do justice to them," she said as gently as possible. She put them down on the coffee table and pulled a copy of the *Voice* out of her purse.

"Here. This is the *Village Voice*. Look, it is filled with jazz clubs and tells you who is playing where. It will help you with the articles you must write." She spoke slowly and formed her words distinctly, watching him carefully to see if he understood her.

He nodded seriously and grunted as she turned the pages, sweeping the ads with her hand as if she was revealing the prizes behind the curtain on one of those TV game shows. He thought what a sweet girl she was to tell him about this. He remembered listening to the Voice of America and Radio Free Europe jazz broadcasts with his ear pressed to the radio he had strung together from spare parts, in the tiny Moscow apartment he had shared with his mother and brother, sixteen tiny square meters for the three of them. Anyway, now he was in New York and could see and hear it all *live*. He was quiet as he took in all the riches of the *Voice*.

He stood up. "Well. Okay. Let us now have some vodka," he said abruptly.

Once again she followed him into the kitchen, where she sat down at the tiny Formica table and watched as Boris arranged slices of thick black bread on a plate, then sliced some garlicky, half-sour pickles and laid sprigs of fresh dill over them. He picked up a piece of the bread and held it to his nose, inhaling deeply. "Oooh . . . Hmmm . . . Reminds me of Russia. In Paris all you get iz that white merde." Because of his wonderful accent, whatever he said came out in the most lovely and meaningful way.

Kate sighed. "Vodka makes me cry," she said.

At this Boris turned around from the freezer, where he was just about to pull out the bottle of Stolichnaya. His eyes narrowed. Ah-ha, she had said something important here, something very Russian. He was intrigued by her; she was at once so Russian and yet so American. She had dark Russian sloe eyes and a round face. To him, she looked somewhat Ukranian. Her baby-fine hair was shiny and cut in a crisp, swingy style, exposing an aristocratic Russian neck. Had she any idea how lovely she was? Boris saw in Kate the faces of many Russian women he had known; why, they could be sitting in a kitchen in Moscow right now. And yet she was undeniably an American tough cookie. He loved that expression.

"You are a Russian-American cocktail," he said gravely. He poured two glasses of vodka anyway and sat down, handing her one. "Well, to meeting you," he toasted.

"Welcome to New York," she said in a polite, small voice. They clinked glasses and he downed his vodka while she sipped tentatively at hers.

"What's this?" he asked in mock disapproval. "This is how you drink vodka." He bent his arm, "to the level of the third button on your shirt," he said, and showed her in one cantilevered movement the official Russian vodka-drinking movement. "Alley oop," and he swung his head back, pretending to drain his already-empty glass, reaching for some vodka drops with his tongue. She was charmed. He was so unself-conscious. Then he took a piece of black bread and sniffed it again, then wrapped it around a pickle and took a bite. With this, in him, Kate saw the gestures of her two grandfathers.

The luncheon took its proper, bizarre course. By now she had drunk a kir and a vodka and she found herself giggling inside. She was starting to be taken with him and was nervous. There was the wonderful way he served her, carefully arranging her plate with the tomatoey chicken concoction he had made. There was the way he broke off a piece of bread, then broke it in half, giving a piece to her saying, "Tiens," as if she was a French child. There was the way he rinsed out her vodka glass with

wine, swished it around, drank it, then poured fresh wine into the glass
for her. Then out came a plate of the beautiful French cheeses he had
brought from Paris. "Whew, did I smell on that plane." He revelled in
this mischievous memory. He put a chèvre to his nose and took a deep
breath, then put it under her nose so she could do the same. But it was
when he offered her the delicate French canister of butter in flowery
filigree paper that he enchanted her.

Afterward, she suggested they go to a new espresso bar in the neighborhood for coffee so he could see some American life. "Well, it's not
really American, it's more Upper East Side," she explained. She could
tell he was unnerved when he glanced at the menu board above the
coffee machine and saw that a cappuccino cost two dollars and fifty
cents. "This is my treat," she said. They sat uncomfortably on tiny
chrome stools for a while in a strained silence. She hoped he was enjoying himself. She glanced at her watch. It was 4:30 and winter dusk was
settling outside. She liked him because he was so different from any of
the American men she had known. But he made her a little nervous,
too. She looked at him glancing around the place, observing the people,
and felt a little sorry for him. He really was alone in life.

At lunch he told her a little about how he had been first censored,
then silenced, then jobless in the Soviet Union because of his writing
and how he escaped by marrying a Frenchwoman. She was visiting
Moscow with a group of activist Jews who had come to give support to
the dissident movement. She and Boris had met at a party and saw each
other a few times after that. She agreed to marry him to help get him
out, even though he wasn't Jewish. There was the five-minute govern-
ment ceremony, and for a joke, they went like all Soviet newlyweds to
Red Square and put her flowers on the Tomb of the Unknown Soldier.
There was nothing between them; it was a political act on her part. After
a year of filling out and submitting numerous forms and interminable
waiting and two horrible interviews with the KGB at Lubyanka to confirm his love of the motherland, he finally received permission to visit
his wife for one week in Paris. She met Boris at Charles de Gaulle, let
him sleep on a mattress on the floor of her apartment that first night and
filed for divorce the next day. He spoke no French; he knew no one. He
was on his own in the big bad Western world.

What next? Kate wondered. It was too early to go home and spend the
rest of Sunday evening alone. "Would you like to see another American
apartment? My apartment?" she asked.

Boris said he would like that very much, and when they arrived at her place he was very impressed, though he didn't say so. He just grunted. Even he knew it would be a cliché to say that in Moscow several families would have to live in this much space. Her apartment was like a cozy secret in this nasty, gray city. He approved of the piano and all those bookshelves filled with books. He was surprised to see a calico cat sitting in the living room as if she were a piece of sculpture. At lunch Kate had mentioned nothing about a cat. Boris got down on his hands and knees and began stalking Boo, mumbling seductive French baby talk. Boo glanced at her mistress with a look of total disbelief. No other male guest of Kate's had ever done this before. Boo tried to appear bored, but it was clear she loved it. She practiced a prance, staying just out of his reach when he tried to pet her, but came by when he wasn't looking and rubbed against his leg before skipping away.

Boris roamed around the living room like a caged lion, pacing up and down, trying to figure out if he should kiss her or anything. He had heard that American women were casual about sex, but with this Kate, he wasn't quite sure. He wanted to kiss her, but she wasn't giving him any signals. Or maybe she was, but he couldn't understand them? What to do? He changed seats from the couch to the overstuffed chair to the piano bench. He had a scotch, then another one. He looked at all the books on the bookshelves and then stared out the window at what she called her "Cole Porter view." Then she offered him a brandy. He sat very close to her on a chair and stared deeply into her eyes. Nothing. He was becoming impatient; it was getting late. He was not making any progress. Maybe he was losing his touch. Maybe he didn't understand something about American women. Maybe he should just go. He got up again and moved to the couch.

Kate was confused. Why didn't he at least try to kiss her? She thought she was being nice and friendly. It made her feel insecure about her appeal. Was there something wrong with her? Was she really that awful? Could he tell she hadn't been with anyone in so long? Or maybe it was him? Was he gay? But then she realized she had not made it very easy for him, had she? Wasn't this just like all men? She sighed.

Kate, she said to herself, what do you want? There was a war waging within her. As a rule she didn't like sex on the first date; it was so meaningless, and generally she had never been able to separate sex from her feelings about a person. She wondered, could she have a purely sexual encounter? Could that be enjoyable for her? Sometimes she envied her friends who seemed to find casual sex so easy and satisfying. In college she had tried "just having sex," but it didn't do anything for her. Maybe she was different now.

And why the hell not? She understood that this Boris presented her with an interesting opportunity. She was tired of complaining about loneliness and frustrated with having no sex life. Yes, she said defiantly to herself, why the hell not? Here was her chance. So, with great difficulty, she dragged herself up from the chair where she had been sitting and plunked herself down on the couch very close to him.

"I've never had a Russian kiss," she said. "May I have one?"

Boris smiled at her with a conquering glance. Finally he had broken through. He put his Russian hand on her Russian-American neck and gave her a kiss unlike any one she had ever had before.

Goodness, they certainly did kiss differently! "Another one?" she asked, at bit astonished, not quite understanding what exactly had been so wonderful about it and wanting to experience it again. Immediately.

He kissed her again. It was a kiss of quicksand, a whirlpool of a kiss. It was dark, and sucking, with a swirling followed by a gentle *whoosh* of air.

"No." He shook his head afterward. "That is not it."

She thought he meant he hadn't done his part right, but he was saying that she didn't kiss right. So he kissed her again and again and then said, "No, you don't have it."

Kate couldn't remember whose idea it was, but she thinks it was she who suggested that they take off their clothes and go to bed. If this was Russian kissing, she definitely wanted to try Russian sex. For some reason she didn't run through her usual list of worrying how fat her thighs were that day or how long she had gone without waxing her legs and all those concerns like, God what if I gross him out totally? As she undressed she thought for a few seconds and decided not to use her diaphragm. It was a safe time in the month for her. Besides, she was fed up with being such a good girl and being so damn responsible about everything. She wanted the chance to screw up and have a messy life just like everyone else.

He came out of the bathroom and she was delighted to see his colorful French bikini underpants. He climbed into her bed, surrounding her with the smell of Siberia. How wild! His body was the warmest she had ever touched. He seemed to radiate some sort of animal spirit as she stroked his furry chest. She thought, Russian men really are like bears.

Because she was nervous and had drunk too much wine so early in the day, her heart was beating fast. He sensed her discomfort and held his hands over her forehead and heart as if to heal her. "People drain my energy. I must be careful," he said in a mysterious tone of voice. Like magic, she felt some calming force from his hands draw the distress right from her. She lay still for a while as he caressed her, clearly enjoying her soft, fleshy curves.

Then he attacked her body and she understood they were two animals rolling in the mud together, snarling and growling playfully. He was taking bites and nuzzling her. Never had she made love like this before. And then, before she knew it, he buried his face into her and was lapping at her ever so beautifully, and even gratefully, like a thirsty puppy at a bowl of milk. His energy for her excited her. It was clear he relished her smell as he urged her on with his tongue. She started moaning. She loved it, but she felt too self-conscious to have an orgasm her first time with him, so she tugged him gently on the arms, her way of letting him know to stop. He climbed on top of her and thrust himself inside her, whispering, "Don't stop, don't stop," and he followed her body as he moved inside of her.

"Comme c'est fort, c'est fort," he groaned when he came. She thought he was saying it to be polite, but Boris meant it. Did he ever. He needed this badly. He treated sex as something very important and at the same time as something not important at all, something natural and necessary, like breathing. Here he was in New York having his first truly American sex and now he knew he would be able to make it through his two weeks here, that there would now be a woman to make it okay in that certain way, and that he could get on with other things.

Kate had been wondering what language they would make love in. English, French, Russian? And now she knew. Because he had cried out in French at the crucial, unconscious moment, he must have French mistresses. She didn't particularly like lovemaking that went so fast, but who was she to complain, and besides, the first time was always like that—like being famished and filling yourself up, not stopping to taste the food. The gourmet lovemaking would come later. She didn't dare tell him she hadn't had a lover in over two years. She thought he would think she was undesirable in some way.

They were lying there together, the calm after the storm, and Kate was just as surprised as he was when her eyes brimmed over and big teardrops rolled out of her eyes, down her face. "What's this?" Boris asked, trying to be lighthearted. He tried to comfort her, but she remained silent.

"But you must tell me what is the matter," he said.

She wouldn't tell him what was wrong, but she couldn't stop crying either. She felt so intensely sad.

"No? You won't tell me? Okay." He dropped it. He had tried to be nice, but he hated crying women and he wasn't going to baby her.

As for Kate, well, while she'd be the first to admit that she didn't know much about men, she did know she couldn't very well tell him the truth, that she wished it wasn't him, Boris, who was lying there beside her. How could she possibly tell him that she was crying because she wished it was her wonderful Dr. Manne who had just finished making love to her?

This isn't fair to Boris, she thought, and tried to compose herself. But with Boris's arms around her, she closed her eyes and tried to imagine it was Dr. Manne who held her. Dr. Manne with the inquiring, searching voice, those moist Italian eyes.

But it didn't work. When she opened her eyes, there was a Russian poet in her bed.

How Kate Met Frank

KATE FELT THAT Dr. Manne was the man every woman should have in her life. He was The Man Who Would Truly Listen. And since she had no man who would attend to her with all his heart, by God, she would pay one to listen.

On the whole, she felt that men were bad listeners and that was why there were so many hysterical women, both married and single, visiting shrinks in New York City. Whereas part of being a woman was knowing how to listen. Husbands, boyfriends, lovers and children thrived on it, insisted on it. It was her theory that housewives were addicted to the TV soaps because it was just another act of listening to someone else's problems. Even though making TV commercials was her business, she thought TV was bad because you just sat on your couch and watched while other people lived. You never saw the characters on "Dynasty" or "Dallas" watching television, now, did you?

It didn't seem fair to Kate that women often had to pay for services that men could usually get for free, provided by that girlfriend ever ready to listen to her man or that handy wifey back home, whose job it was to say, "How was your day, dear?" Kate belonged to the cult of women who had to pay other people to touch her, caress her, focus attention on her, soothe her, make her beautiful, but mostly listen to her, patch her up and then send her back out into the nasty world.

She had a Swiss facialist who scolded her for not coming in more often but told her she had excellent pores, and a Korean manicurist who always assured her that the shade of nail polish she chose was the most beautiful in the entire parlor. There was her smooth and fearless Japanese shiatsu man who could tell what she had eaten by the feel of her muscles, and Erna, her devoted Belgian leg-waxing lady, who told her, "You must suffer to be beautiful," at the moment when she ripped the hair out of her legs. She had a French hairstylist, who sprayed his hands with the latest gel and ran them seductively through her hair. She passed from one set of hands to the next.

Yes, a woman must have someone to listen, she sighed, to her deepest secrets and her most shocking fantasies, but mostly, to those nagging everyday indignities that added up and took their toll—from the butcher who shortchanged her on ribs to the bus driver who slammed the door in her face just as she ran up, having risked life and limb crossing the traffic. On top of all that, she reasoned, only a woman's analyst knows how she likes to come. Exactly how, in words. Just like a good garage mechanic or a top-notch lawyer, an analyst was definitely a plus in a woman's life. However, he also represented a most dangerous concept: he was the perfect man a woman could never have. And that's why Kate hated Dr. Manne. Well, she loved him and that's why she hated him. Because she couldn't have him, because he wouldn't love her back, she was going to make his life hell. Two could play at this game and she would make him pay. After all, wasn't it he who had turned her into one of life's more unpleasant notions, a woman whose love was unrequited. What else could he expect?

She had read enough books on therapy to know she was in for it. She would spend several years having this most intimate of relationships and then it would be, "Best of luck to you then," and a handshake, maybe. She would be cast out by the very man who had the key to her soul, who knew every inch of her beautiful and not so beautiful psyche. It seemed to her that New York was a city of all the wrong people walking around with all the right information. She thought of all the analysts who knew all their patients and how if only the patients could just get together and talk to each other. But it all came back to the same issue. People didn't know how to listen, and mostly, they just didn't want to know.

Why did the Psychoanalytic Institute have to assign her to such a handsome young doctor anyway? It simply wasn't fair. Kate felt a tremendous mistake had been made because she and Dr. Manne really were soul mates. They should have been lounging under the glass roof at the Temple of Dendur instead of sitting on chairs politely opposite each other and playing doctor and patient. Why, it had struck her the moment he came out to get her for their first appointment on a sweltering hot Friday evening last June. It had been his only available time that week and she thought sarcastically, Is this the best I can do on a Friday night, see a shrink?

She showed up at the institute in her sportif mode with an overnight bag and a tennis racquet. After her appointment she was going to hop on a train for Mantoloking, where she had been invited to spend the weekend at her boss's beach house. The waiting room was intellectually dingy. It shrieked of nervous and depressed people waiting to be called by their therapists. Kate could smell the building from blocks away. It was a hushed, sobbing, gray building that had absorbed so much misery, perverse details and fantasy that she could almost not bear to be there. She was thankful that their future appointments would take place in his private office after this "getting to know you" meeting tonight.

So who will my lucky doctor be? she wondered nervously as she sat on an ugly plastic chair, waiting to be summoned. Just then, a dark, young man—was he Italian?—with doe eyes appeared.

"Kate?" He looked at the other woman who was sitting in the waiting room with her. This gave Kate a few precious extra seconds to observe him.

"No, that's me," she said, and started to rise.

"Oh." Why did he look surprised? He smiled quickly as if to apologize for his error.

She got up and followed him into a tiny consultation room. I'm supposed to talk to *him?* Why, he's my age. We should be meeting in a bar or a class at the New School, certainly not here, not in this place. He closed the door behind him. She looked at the room, barely large enough for a couch and two chairs. She stood next to the analytic couch and looked at it, then put her bag and tennis racquet on it. "Oh, maybe I'm not supposed to do that," she said.

"Over here," he said, pointing to a chair.

She sat down and then immediately got up again to move an ashtray filled with cigarette butts from the coffee table next to her to a place as far away from her as she could with an exaggerated, distasteful air. It was obviously from the previous patients, for he didn't look like a smoker. She looked nervously at him as she sat down. Oh God, does he think I'm really compulsive or something?

Kate was quite dizzy in this small room, sitting so close to so handsome a man. She had to take deep breaths to calm her pounding heart. So what am I supposed to do, tell him stuff? She started talking about her career in advertising just to get going, but it all ended up at the same place: why wasn't she in love, why couldn't she find a man, what was wrong with her? "I bet you hear that from all your patients," she said.

"Yes," he admitted, "it seems to be on everyone's mind."

She noticed how evenly he spoke, but more important, how he listened. Never had anyone listened to her like that, sitting so quietly and attending to her with his whole being, soaking up her every word. Just who is this man and what does he think of me? she wondered, and kept on talking.

Near the end of their forty-five minutes, when she thought she had done rather well for her first therapy session ever, he asked, "Do you want to ask me any questions?" She shook her head no, but then decided to ask him how he would diagnose her.

"Histrionic," he said, without missing a beat.

Kate gasped. "That's awful!" she said, on the verge of tears.

"Oh, don't worry, it only means hysterical. It's a common diagnosis for the young women of today," he said calmly. He was thinking but didn't say it, "Especially unmarried women." He saw that he was making things worse, so he tried again. "It's really fine. It's sort of the 'in' diagnosis today."

"Well, what's the 'in' diagnosis for men these days?" she asked.

"It's a toss-up between obsessive-compulsive and narcissistic."

"Perfect," she said. Ah, yes, she thought, histrionic. I guess women have just gotten too messy for today's world. She sat there miserably, staring at the floor and weeping.

Her eyes wandered to him. "Where does all the sadness go? Into the air? Does it dissolve or float away or just stay there?" she asked. It was a dreamy question and his eyes looked far away. When he didn't answer, she said suddenly, "This is all a joke, right?"

"What's a joke?" he asked back.

"You and me. Here. Like this," she said.

He shook his head no.

She took a breath. "Well, what I'd really like to do," she said, groping for courage, "is to smoke some dope and go dancing with you." It was part command, part request.

He stood up. "I'm sorry but our time is up," he said gently, and opened the door to let her out.

And so, twice a week they met and talked. Or rather, she talked and he listened. They laughed together, but she cried alone.

Ah, Dr. Manne. Even his name was lyrical. He was the quintessential man, Mr. Perfect, with a face finely chiseled like a head on an ancient Roman coin. He had thick black hair and a wonderful sense of humor. When he laughed, the world was right, but when she asked him personal questions, he got mean. She asked him how old he was, and he replied, "Older than you." She understood that to mean he was her age. When she asked him where he lived, he said, "Near here." When she asked him if he was married he said that wasn't important, but what did she think? Kate thought, Of course some woman has snapped you up by now, are you kidding, but didn't say so. But then, she thought, maybe he wasn't married because he wore such drab, shapeless clothing. She could always tell when there was no woman dressing a man: he wore brown pants and brown socks, his raincoat was too short, his ties were too wide, and his inevitable navy blazer that he prided himself on was totally out of style.

Kate dressed him in her own mind. She took his job into consideration in order to come up with his look. He led a contemplative life, sitting long hours, thinking deep thoughts, wrestling with complex emotions. He needed both comfortable and comforting clothes. Comfortable for him and comforting for his patients. Cozy English tweeds would do it, high quality of course, with soft pastel knit ties. Sweater vests for winter, he was definitely a sweater vest man. Then he needed some nice new shoes, Oxfords would be perfect, and thick argyle socks in pale, acidic colors. She considered going to Bloomingdale's and choosing some ties to start him off and sending them to him anonymously, but then she figured he'd never wear them and that she'd never be able to keep her mouth shut. Besides, the ties wouldn't go with his current wardrobe anyway.

Kate always dressed for him. On Mondays and Fridays she thought, Today I am going to see Dr. Manne, and she would stare into her closet wondering what to wear. She inspected and reflected on the various combinations of outfits, trying on different things, wondering what he'd like, what she'd look best in, trying to vary her things so he'd always be surprised. She wanted to look lovely, no, more than lovely. Beautiful. Then she was shocked. "I'm acting as though I'm going to see my lover," she said, shaking her head. What an embarrassing thought! She tried to push it out of her mind, but once it had appeared, it wouldn't go away.

Maybe she really was a sicko. She decided she couldn't tell him about it because he, too, would find it weird and perverted.

Occasionally they would meet in the lobby of the building where his private office was located and wait for the elevator together. She tried to look at him as if he weren't her doctor, but just a normal guy, and wondered whether she would be at all interested in him if she met him at a party. He looked unexceptional, dowdy even, just like the waiting room of the institute that had assigned him to her. Once she saw him walking down the street ahead of her. Could that be her same doctor, the one who in that tiny room was so handsome? Why, he waddled like a duck.

As he stepped aside to let her enter the elevator first, politely, like a normal man was supposed to, they stood in silence while the elevator man worked the controls. She hoped they didn't look like doctor and patient, but man and woman, off to some assignation in the middle of the afternoon. She looked at him as the floors whizzed by and wondered, What woman holds his head in her arms, who is she who strokes his lovely hair? What woman sees him with his eyes closed, his breath released, tumbling out at last? Above all, what does he eat for breakfast? Kate always felt that was a clue to a person.

"I just wish we could be friends," she told him sadly one day.

He considered her words carefully as he always did before he spoke. "You get more from me—of me, as my patient, than you would if you were my friend," he said.

How could this be true?

For a few days afterward she thought about it and decided it was, in a way she couldn't quite understand yet, a very large thing to say.

Frank Loves His Job

FRANK MANNE WAS awakened at 6:00 A.M. as he was every weekday morning by his obnoxious alarm clock, a relic of the fifties that was given to him years ago by his father. He hated how his body jolted on schedule when the clock belched its loud, insistent buzz, but he couldn't bring himself to throw it out and buy a new one.

He moaned on cue and leaned over quickly to shut it off and then lay still, trying to calm his wildly beating heart after being blasted from his sleep. He thought about what he wanted most: a Mr. Coffee with an automatic timer so he could drift awake gently to the aroma of brewing coffee, and only when the machine beeped politely to indicate that the coffee was ready, would he get up. Yeah!

But he just couldn't bring himself to justify this purchase, which bordered just enough on the frivolous to make him a bit uncomfortable, not to mention the fact that he was always broke. It was annoying how most people thought analysts were rich, and good for nothing but gouging huge fees from their patients. He'd like to meet the person who had started that dumb rumor. His life was far from it. Being a garden-variety therapist hadn't been enough for him, so he had moved from Indiana a few years ago to tackle the big-time world of New York psychoanalysis. Now he was paying with his life. Virtually all his earnings and savings had to go into his own analysis, which was part of his training. Seventy dollars a session, professional discount, four times a week. Then he had to pay tuition to the institute where he was a candidate for psychoanalytic certification. On top of that, he had to carry two Manhattan rents, one on his apartment and another on the office where he saw his patients. None of his patients would believe it if he told them that he, a New York therapist, simply could not afford a Mr. Coffee. Besides, when would he have the time to buy one?

He savored the warmth of the sheets and didn't want to get up just yet. Just a few seconds more of this, he pleaded silently. He stretched his arms and his hands wound up on his cock. Old faithful, greeting him every day in a good mood, smiling, nicely erect, saying, "Hey, let's boogie!" What was it one of his patients had called masturbating the other day? Oh yeah, spanking the monkey. He thought he had heard everything: pounding the pickle, yanking the yodel, jerkin' the gherkin, pulling your pud, choking the chicken, waxing the carrot, beating the bishop, flogging the dolphin. He peered under the sheets. "Hello, you monkey. Do you want to be spanked?" He started laughing, then he groaned; it's too early to be laughing. He caressed himself. Even after all these years—"I'm thirty-five, for Christ sakes"—he was still amazed at how soft and delicate it was and how he loved the feel of it. He supposed a man never got over being fascinated by his penis. He considered whether he should masturbate here or in the shower. But he was too lazy to get out of bed. He viewed masturbating as he viewed having his morning orange juice, it was something you did after you woke up and before you had breakfast. It was like jogging or bike riding, you were just exercising a different muscle. For now, this utilitarian sex life would have to do.

He stretched and finally forced himself out of bed. He went to the window to peek through the venetian blinds for a glance at the weather. As he flicked open the slats at eye level he scolded himself again for not finding out the origin of venetian blinds. Did they use them in Venice or what? This morning during coffee hour at the hospital he would ask the nurses what they thought. It would be a good icebreaker.

Even though he had lived in this apartment for two years now, it was still a jolt to see the bars on the windows. What a way to live! Behind bars and venetian blinds. It was because he lived on the ground floor. This tiny studio was the only place he could find on the Upper West Side when he had arrived to start his new life in New York, so naturally he grabbed it, even at the ridiculous rent of $873.65, which the rental agent had assured him was a good deal. He felt like he was living in a bird cage right on the street. He hated how the outside seemed to barge right in, uninvited, the street fights, the honking of impatient taxicab drivers trying to maneuver around inexperienced suburban drivers who were parking on his street before heading for a stroll on trendy Columbus Avenue, the sloppy banter of yuppies, drunk on too many margaritas and taco chips. He of all people needed peace and quiet when he finally came home at night.

He flipped down the blind when he remembered he was standing there naked, even though no one could see him. Frank was a modest person, the kind of guy who checked at least three times to make sure his zipper was up before he entered a room. He was unsure about his looks, but thought he could be called handsome. In an Italian sort of way. He liked his thick black hair, his gleaming white teeth, his square, honest face. His patients all thought he was good-looking, but he couldn't tell from them because they might just be transferring, flirting or buttering him up for some reason he hadn't yet figured out.

On his way to the shower he glanced around his one room and wondered what his patients would think if they knew the reality of his life. It was furnished simply with a bed, a reading chair, a reading lamp and an old bookcase crammed with psychology textbooks and an old stack of journals and reviews from the American Psychoanalytic Society. Everything was either brown or beige, what his patient Kate had called bachelor colors. It embarrassed him that his apartment actually had that dingy smell of bachelorhood. Oh, he had a girlfriend, of sorts. They saw each other only on weekends, and then only at her place. During the week he was on his own. How he longed for the comfort of a woman's touch, her clutter of perfume bottles and makeup on the bureau, the odd, wilted flowers in a vase. He knew that with a woman in your life there was always an extra box of tissues in the linen closet, just waiting to be pulled out when the last tissue was used, or that spare roll of toilet paper always at your service, a surprise can of something delicious in the cupboard to save you on a rainy day. It was just the way women lived, the special way they thought about things.

Take Kate. She had painted a picture of his life that made him laugh when she finally stopped talking. "That doesn't sound like any life I'm acquainted with," he sniffed. She had described him living in a spacious, rambling Upper West Side apartment, the kind where you could yell in one room and not be heard in the rest of the place. He lived there with his adorable wife, who waited for him each night with a hot supper and sex. Was there a golden retriever? Yes, and a cat, maybe a baby, but Kate wasn't sure about that.

Last night he had fallen asleep in his chair with his books and papers scattered about him. He picked up a Chinese-food container with last night's chicken and snow peas that rested on top of the tiny black-and-white TV and threw it in the bathroom garbage can and turned on the shower. Woody Allen should stop using those incredible lofts for his characters and show the world how real people live in Manhattan, he thought, and he couldn't do any better than use my studio. He saw he was starting to feel sorry for himself. So he stopped himself from continuing this ridiculous, destructive train of thought. Right now, he just wanted to make it through his psychoanalytic training in New York. No, on second thought, change that to just getting through today.

He had his morning routine down so he didn't have to think too much about it. In and out of the shower, followed by a rigorous toweling down, which was often the only exercise he got. Then he wrapped the wet towel around his waist and started shaving quickly, only to nick himself. Damn! What was it his father always said? "You're never late when you're shaving." He slowed down and finished carefully.

He glanced at the time as he snapped on his watch. If he hurried, he could grab a cup of coffee and a Croissandwich at the Burger King on Broadway and stuff it down before his first patient arrived. Last night he had been so tired he let slip one of the cardinal rules he had set up for himself, to lay out his clothes the night before so he wouldn't have to think about it early in this morning. Oh well. Everything he owned was in brown and beige, so it all went together anyway. He threw on some brown wool slacks, a pale blue shirt, a brown and blue tie, a brownish beige herringbone jacket. As he tied his tie he thought what a stupid thing it was—just a piece of fabric hanging around your neck, or in a Freudian interpretation, a penis worn out in public. He shoved some patient files in his briefcase, slipped on his coat, and slammed the door, impatiently locking his three locks before beginning his walk up Columbus Avenue. He never wanted to be seen running by any of his patients, so he always walked briskly instead, even at the risk of being late.

His days were absurdly long, regimented to the second, and sometimes he didn't know if he were coming or going. He often longed for a normal life where he could fit in a session at the gym in the morning, or meet a friend for cocktails at six or spend an evening at the museum. But the life of a serious analyst is not his own, he kept reminding himself; it is a life given over to his patients, in this case, patients assigned to him by the analytic institute. He left every morning by 6:45 and walked to his office, fifteen blocks away, arriving by 7:15, just in time for his first patient. After his two morning patients he went to see his own analyst, who just happened to have an office in the same building, a few floors up. Dr. Janet, he called her. It was their joke. He wanted to call her Janet, but added the Dr. as a form of respect. Just as all his patients were in love with him, so he was in love with his own Dr. Janet. Then he dashed by subway to the hospital where he worked on staff as a consulting psychologist. He gulped down a cafeteria lunch and spent the rest of the lunch hour watching "All My Children" in the nurses' lounge. By three, he was back in his office, where he saw more private patients until he finished at 7:30. Then it was on to the institute for classes, lectures or supervision on his caseload of patients. Home by eleven.

On his two free weeknights he would go home straight from the office and collapse before calling Chirping Chicken for a delivery. What a ridiculous life for someone who already had a Ph.D. in psychology. He began having back problems. When he complained about this to his supervisor, she told him he was retaining his patients' pain in his lower back instead of letting it flow through him like a conduit. His life was a game of catch-up. When he wasn't working, he read psychology books and studied his patients' charts and notes, looking for those elusive themes in their lives and charting out their stages of development. When he had the time, he read some fiction. But what time? He had a subscription to the *New Yorker*, and the issues just kept piling up. How he ever managed to squeeze in friends, movies, museums, he never knew, but on occasion, he did. When did he shop, get haircuts, do the laundry? Somehow, it all got done.

He knew he wasn't supposed to have a favorite patient, but he did. Though she wasn't his favorite for the usual reasons. Rather, she was his most troublesome patient, and thus his favorite because he hated her so much. She really got his goat. What a pesky girl and so unpleasant! She was a bundle of raw feelings, unharnessed potential being spewed into the universe. He often wanted to take her by the shoulders and shake some sense into her.

He supposed he would consider her an attractive woman if he met her at a party. She was lively, talented and smart. But all she did was whine about her life. That, and hate him bitterly. The analysis had started out okay, but had degenerated into an exhausting, bitter feud. He had to admit he was a little afraid of her. She was an exasperating Russian princess, sweeping in and out of his office in all her different outfits. She had a silly job in an advertising agency and worked on ridiculous projects. What was it she bored him with last week? Oh yes, mints. She had been presented with research about why people ate mints, specifically chocolate-covered mints, so she could develop a campaign hitting hard at the right emotional buttons. She explained to him that mint eaters were different from chocolate mint eaters, who were different still from regular candy-bar eaters. And did he know why? He had no idea. And that within the chocolate mint category there were two kinds of people: the York Peppermint Patty person and the Junior Mint person. One preferred minty chocolate and the other preferred chocolately mint. Which one did he think was which? Then she asked Frank whether he preferred eating lots of small mints or one large mint? What texture did he like his mints to be, did he like them creamy and smooth, or soft and dry? Did he like to eat mints after a meal, or at the movies, or just as a snack food? She had actually used such terms as "snack food" and "tummy stuffer." His mouth started to water while he tried in vain to find some analytic interpretation for her discourse. She was blocking. Something was so painful to her she was evading talking about it. He would let her ramble a bit longer before calling her attention to it, hoping she'd get tired of it herself.

On his way home from work that evening he stopped at a newspaper kiosk and bought a York Peppermint Patty and a box of Junior Mints and ate both with alternating bites, trying to see what the hell she had been talking about.

As he turned off Columbus and onto Broadway Frank thought once again about feeling like an observer of life and not a participant. He often felt he didn't even have a life, so involved was he in the lives of his patients. While everyone else lived, Frank listened. He knew his patients' parents and their friends. He lived vicariously through all their vacations, he listened to the books they'd read and heard about the movies they'd seen. Kate always saw the newest movie before it was released and told him about the hottest novel before it was even published. She was his source for what was hip and hot and happening.

That was one nitpicky thing that really irked him about his job. Most every movie he wanted to see was hopelessly spoiled for him by some patient who was profoundly affected by it. The patient had to discuss it in detail with him, of course, and the plot would be shot to hell every time. It was an occupational hazard, he supposed, and whenever he went to a meeting of the New York Psychoanalytic Society, where he was allowed in as a provisional member, he would invariably raise this point during cocktail hour when he was groping for small talk, with the hope of appearing witty and urbane.

"Do you find yourself getting annoyed at your patients when they talk about movies?" he asked one comely blonde on a rainy Tuesday evening at a reception in the Frieda Fromm Reichmann Room.

"Huh?" she said.

"I mean the endings. They give away the endings." He gestured, he smiled, and the woman shrugged her shoulders and moved away from him.

He knew what his patients cooked and what presents they gave their secretaries. He knew where the sales were and which airlines had the best fares. He knew how they made love and what they said to their lovers when they came. He was a walking encyclopedia of la vie quotidienne—why, most days, he didn't even have to read the newspaper, for current events would parade right before him in his patients' ramblings. He was one plugged-in guy. It made him wonder, Where did these lives end and his begin? Did he indeed have his own life or was his life to be lived in the mirror of all these other lives?

For instance, two nights ago he stopped at a Korean vegetable stand to pick up something for dinner. He was in his usual state of weariness as he stood in the bustling shop filled with yuppies. He stared at the shelves with glazed eyes, harboring a recently acquired fear that one of his patients would happen upon him and catch him in the act of being himself. But instead of seeing what enticed him, he found himself automatically running down his list of patients and analyzing what they would choose. Tim would buy a six-pack and say to hell with it. Tony would make a salad from the salad bar, taking care to compose it with nothing red—no tomatoes, no radishes, no beets, no red cabbage, and no carrots either, since orange was too close to red. Cynthia would buy a bag of chocolate-chip cookies, eat them up, then throw up soon after. And Kate, hmm, she would buy a bunch of young, baby asparagus and a half-dozen fresh country eggs. She would make that peasanty Italian dish she had described to him once. He had to admit it sounded good.

Gently steamed asparagus with delicately fried eggs on top, covered with a sprinkling of only the freshest hand-grated Parmesan, mind you, then popped under the broiler for just a second. A glass of chilled white wine and a crusty loaf of bread. Jesus, he was beginning to talk like her. He stood in that private reverie, smiling like a fool, then shook himself. This is ridiculous! What do I want? He tapped his foot in irritation. He had no idea. Finally he decided on an avocado and some taco chips. Yes, he would make himself, one Frank Manne, some guacamole. That was easy enough. Maybe he'd even play hooky and watch some TV. It was hard being the steadying leader, the rallying point, the cheerleader, father confessor, the adoring parent, the stern but gentle friend, the phantom lover, the rival, the perfect person. It was hard, but oh, he loved it.

Damn! He didn't have time to pick up breakfast. He couldn't take the chance of meeting his patient with a Burger King bag in his hand and riding up in the elevator together like that; it would seem too low class. Besides, he wouldn't be able to eat it anyway and it would get cold. He turned the corner right past the beckoning Burger King and zoomed into the entrance of the apartment building where his office, his sunny confessional he liked to call it, awaited him. It irked him that his office was nicer than his apartment. He shared it with two other psychologists; it was the only way he could afford it.

Frank didn't say anything to the elevator man, who just looked at him and nodded, taking him up to the tenth floor automatically without his asking. He was relieved that his patient, Beau Appleman, was not waiting outside the locked office door as he often was. He searched for his keys and let himself in, picking up yesterday's mail, switching on the light and the white-noise machine in the reception room.

In his office, he threw down his briefcase and took off his coat, hanging it up in the closet, out of sight. He liked to appear calm and unmoved to all of his patients, as if he spent his life waiting for them in that room, sitting in his chair. He felt it would make a better blank canvas if they didn't see that he had to function just as they did. He opened the window a crack and pulled down the shade just a touch so that the morning sun didn't hit him in the eyes. He made sure his books were all lined up and emptied the wastebasket in the garbage chute down the hall, surveying the trash of his patients: a Zabar's croissant bag, loads of tear-filled tissues, an Almond Joy wrapper, the business section of the *Times*, a sales slip from the Athlete's Foot, a Chanel lipstick box. That last one was probably Kate's.

As he surveyed his office he thought of how she liked to dig into his decor, critiquing every new object he brought in. Nothing escaped her eye. He had a professional analytic couch, no regular couch would do for him, he wanted the real thing with an analytic wedge at the head. He had framed several posters and prints, one large folk nude by Zuniga, and a detail of a Matisse painting. The Zuniga Kate liked, the Matisse she called obvious. Maybe there she was right. He adjusted one of the frames and winced as he recalled the day Kate critiqued his framing. Maybe she had been right about that, too. On the floor was a Conran's rug in pastel green and plum on top of which rested two orthopedic chairs. He liked that touch of equality, that his chair wasn't any better than his patient's. The effect in the room was light, airy and minimal. Pleasant. There was a wall unit he had assembled himself and filled with psychology books. In certain empty spaces he placed seashells, a vase that his sister had given him and a little clock that could tell him the time from across the room.

Suddenly he noticed his answering-machine light blinking. Damn! He had walked out of here last night at eight, and now, less than twelve hours later, it was blinking. He played back the message. It was Beau Appleman canceling his appointment due to a bad cold. Shit. He never got to cancel his patients for a silly cold. He showed up rain or shine. This was really unfair.

He slumped down into the patient chair, feeling utterly defeated. And not even a coffee or a Croissandwich! He looked around and experienced the room from this different perspective. So this is what it felt like to sit there and look at him.

He had often thought about the role of the analyst in contemporary life. Why, an analyst was just a modern-day philosopher, showing people their options for living. Society was extremely disassociated, he felt. People were not connected with their own souls. "We don't know ourselves, so how can we know others?" he wrote on his application to the institute. "It is only by knowing ourselves that we can hope to find the universal meaning of life. The cosmos is within us, we must only be brave enough to look. And once we experience the divine self within, then we will see that same divine self in others." He bemoaned the lack of spirituality in modern life, finding most people to be dry and suffering from an absence of magic and mystery. Kate was a perfect example. An intelligent woman, floundering around in her own life, so unconnected was she with her inner core.

What could be more exciting than a life of the mind, of delving into the innermost parts of human beings, into their darkest corners, flinging open the doors and letting the light stream in? He wondered why the whole world didn't want to be analysts. Being an analyst allowed him to play a bigger game in life, giving him a safe perch from which to observe the blood and guts of living, sort of like playing with fire and not getting burned.

The office was quiet. Unusual, for he usually experienced it as a place of human voices. Frank relished these moments of peace and the sound of solitude. He took a deep breath and sighed, and within minutes, he was fast asleep.

Boris Loves New York

FOR BORIS, the precious days were passing by too quickly in a frosty blur. "New York in January," he crooned to the tune of "April in Paris" as he pushed off on his rental skates at Rockefeller Center and looked up at the massive buildings soaring defiantly into the stern, gray sky. Being Russian, he easily became morbid at the thought of having to leave, of how in a very short time he'd be back in Paris. He could just imagine lying on the mattress on the floor of his studio, listening to stupid French radio and how he would look up at the spires of St. Sulpice just outside his window with its stained-glass windows glittering in the moonlight and wonder, Was I really there? In New York? In winter? It made him skate even harder, trying to embrace the reality of it now for the dream it would become.

He lived twenty-four hours a day, his whirlwind, daytime ramblings followed by a succession of smoky nights in Greenwich Village jazz clubs. He'd cap off the night with the dare of riding the subway back to the Park Avenue apartment at 3:30 in the morning, just him and the stoned hoodlums on their way to home. In the mornings he would replay the cassette tapes of the interviews he conducted for the magazine articles he was going to write, listening to himself speaking English. He worked his way through several bottles of Scotch, but mostly, he drank New York. He was positively giddy on the riot that was this crazy city, roaming the streets, soaking up the grittiness that made the place electric.

How he loved American money. Silly, floppy green dollars, the vulgar, brash paper that ruled the universe, the American dollar with its unimpressive, naive bits of change. American money looked ridiculous after carrying around serious, historical Russian rubles and those haughty, elegant French francs, but having it finally in his wallet after all these years was what mattered.

He preferred the motley parts of the city, for they expressed the true flavor of New York, the old New York. Besides, he had enough elegance living in Paris. Park, Madison and Fifth were nothing compared to rue de Rivoli, Avénue Foch, and the Faubourg St. Honoré. Rockefeller Center was kitsch compared to the Place Vendôme. Staten Island vs. the Ile de la Cité? St. Patrick's was a thug compared to Sainte Chapelle. So he stuck to the fringes.

He patrolled his favorite honky-tonk Canal Street like a land baron, looking for all sorts of treasure in the junk bins. What a carnival, a wild black-market bazaar! He was at home here; it brought out the scavenger the Soviet system had made out of him. He found extraordinary electrical gadgets that never would have existed in Moscow, would have cost a fortune in Paris, but for which he paid only a dollar here! The best part was that no one yelled at him for pawing through the bins; in fact they loved it when he did. He found odd transistor pieces, lightbulb sockets, hubcaps, monster sponges, rubber gloves, rope, plastic cubes and things he didn't know what to do with. Oh, America, the beautiful!

His prize purchase was a "hot" toaster oven that some dudes were hawking on Fourteenth street. Now this was really fantastic, he thought, just like a movie, as he saw a truck screech to a halt, the back doors slam open and two guys jump down and start to sell what he was sure was stolen merchandise. In Moscow he had, of course, purchased things on the black market, but it was secretive and you had to know people. Here, it happened right in broad daylight! And with such capitalistic joy! He stood back to admire the furtive eyes of the hucksters, looking out for the cops, and enjoyed their singsong banter. "Check it out! Check it out! One for twenty-five, two for forty! Check it out!" Who would want two toaster ovens? He couldn't keep the stupid grin off his face as he walked down the street with his first General Electric appliance under his arm. He felt proud of the GE logo and the color pictures of toasted sandwiches with melted cheese spilling out the sides, grilled bacon, baked potatoes and chocolate cupcakes. If only his mother could see him now!

He tried to imagine how fine it would look sitting so shiny, so American, on his kitchen table in Paris.

He made Katia—that's what he called Kate—take him to Bloomingdale's, where he bought colorful bikini underpants with Bloomies written on the seat. He felt sure the Parisian girls would get a kick out of them, even though he didn't tell her that. After work, she took him on different walking tours, one night to Chinatown, where they ate incredible food that put him in a spin, and afterward on to Little Italy, where they sat at a tiny table in a tacky café. He let her order since he had no idea and that was how he ate his first cannoli, washing it down (what a vulgar expression she used) with cappuccino. He was in heaven because Frank Sinatra was singing on the radio, and here he was, in Mafia town, watching the street gangs play outside the window. It was a little rough, but Katia didn't seem to be uncomfortable, so he guessed it must be okay.

God, she was a tough New Yorker. He was both impressed and appalled. The way she stepped over bums sleeping in the subway without missing a beat. "Don't breathe," she said through her nose, "they usually smell awful." She had eagle eyes and steered him casually across the street away from bums pissing in alleys or shooting crack on brownstone steps. She was fearless when she was panhandled. She knew who was hustling and who was really in need. When hustlers asked her if she had any spare change, she would look them back squarely in the eye and say, "Brother, I ask you, what is 'spare' change? I work very hard at my job and no change is 'spare.'" Instead of ignoring the homeless, she "adopted" a certain few of them and picked up a cup of coffee and a bagel when she knew she'd be passing by their sidewalk stake. She knew how to elbow her way into a crowded subway car and the best place to stand during rush hour. Her jaywalking was like a ballet and he was intrigued at how she could capture the one empty taxicab on a crowded street on a rainy day. The day they went to the Met to see the costume exhibit, the line was so long he took one look at it and said, "No way, I spent my whole life standing on lines and I'm not going to do it here." He tugged at her hand to leave.

"Don't be silly," she said, and took him to the head of the line. He had to keep his mouth from dropping open when she urgently told the guard that they had just come out of the show, but that she had left her hat back in there and could she pleeease go in and find it? In they went.

She put up with the daily indignities of Manhattan life in such a casual way that it often seemed to Boris that she didn't notice the insult of it all. But he knew her subtle eyes were always on the lookout for that one dangerous misstep that could result in disaster. She was equally alert to the serendipity of opportunity that made living in Manhattan such a pleasure. Salmon specials at Zabar's, private sale days at Saks, she zoomed in on it all.

It wasn't so much seeing things in New York that impressed him, it was the sheer joy of being there, of being a part of it, being jolted uptown and downtown in the subway, having access to a telephone book filled with all the Russian names of his youth, using the street phones that he had seen in so many movies, making his wrist sore from flipping channels constantly on the cable TV. He couldn't get enough. "Fantastic," he kept uttering under his breath in his thick accent. Beautiful women with red lips. Businessmen in suits. Rich people in limousines. Waiters who were actors. New York City policemen in blue uniforms swinging sticks. And everyone rushing around like mad, trying to accomplish, to succeed, to get rich.

"Katia, please," he would say, handing her his camera. He had to have his picture taken all the time in the silliest places, in front of a parking meter, a yellow taxicab, Macy's, sitting on the Fifth Avenue bus. "I'll send to my mother," he said as he posed, and she looked at him not quite understanding how her brooding Russian poet could be so silly. Boris didn't care, he just prattled on happily while she snapped. "So she will see I finally made it to *my* town."

As they strolled he told her how when he was twelve he had to give an oral report in school, on any topic of his choosing. "I spoke to my class for two hours about New York. The Empire State Building, Broadway, Greenwich Village. And you know, it wasn't like I could go to a library and just look up New York City. New York did not exist in any book in the Soviet Union!" As he remembered this he became very proud of the young Boris who had somehow gotten all this information.

People in the West just didn't understand what they had, he railed. For instance, had she any idea that there was no such thing as a telephone book in the Soviet Union? If you didn't know a person's phone number, well then, you weren't supposed to know it. There was no such thing as a map of the city. If you didn't know where you were going, well then, you weren't supposed to be going there. The stores didn't have names, they were government-owned and you shopped at Bread Store number 307 and Meat Store number 636. Did she know Moscow was pitch black at night? There were no street lamps to light your way, not even signs illuminating the stores, just bare, low-watt light bulbs casting sad shadows on pitiful leftovers if you had the misfortune of having to shop on your way home from work. The city was forbidding and uninviting, the warmth to be found only in the arms of a lover or in the curtained rooms of only your closest friends as you lifted your glasses of industrial-strength vodka.

He recalled with some embarrassment how he would carry a light bulb into the communal kitchen when his mother asked him to heat up some water. This Katia couldn't believe.

"Yes, dear," he said impatiently. "You carry the light bulb into the kitchen when you want to cook. You screw it in, you cook, then you unscrew it and take it back with you when you leave. Every family did this."

He wasn't finished. "Every American youth, upon reaching the age of eighteen, should be sent not to the army, but to the Soviet Union for a month," he said emphatically. He felt sure that would put an end to this Western unhappiness he found pervasive in the culture. Such a neurotic people. He was shocked at the emptiness he saw in the eyes of Americans and the way they just consumed life like it was junk food. Lots of money but no soul. Life seemed to be about buying things, and when they did, they couldn't understand why they still weren't happy. All this endless, empty conversation about wanting that new car instead of the one they drove, or being pissed off when the waiter told them the kitchen had run out of shrimp.

One day he went by himself to Brighton Beach in Brooklyn, to see how the recent Soviet Jewish émigrés lived. He walked on the streets they had transformed into what was now called Little Odessa, and it disgusted and depressed him. It was a sick Soviet idea of how to live in New York. Why leave Russia to live in this pathetic, filthy, bad copy of Soviet life? It saddened him to see how vulgar these émigrés had become, and so mean and capitalistic! They had traded their lives, and for what? They lost their souls, their grace, their Slavic nobility of bearing. Now they would live out their days in their own brand of Soviet–U.S. hell.

He did, however, enjoy all the Russian food shops and he brought back delicacies that he fed to Katia with delight. One of the things he missed most was Russian pickles. He ate so many pickles during his stay—half sours, Katia told him they were called, that she started calling him "my little pickle" in Russian. It was when he bought some pilmeni, a Russian form of ravioli, that he knew Katia had a Russian soul. It was all in the look of reverence on her face when she bit into one. He made her sit like an obedient child at the table while he cooked them carefully in chicken broth, then brought a plate of them, steaming, to the table. He sat down next to her and garnished the pilmeni with sour cream and a sprinkling of freshly clipped dill. The two of them sat there with very serious looks on their faces as they devoured them, licking sour cream off each other's mouth with their kisses.

Ah yes, there was Kate, his Katia, he liked to call her. He whispered her name, in baby talk, in singsong, Katia, Katinka, Katusha, Katerina, but not Kate. So warm and beckoning, she was his treasure, an extraordinary combination of Russian sweetness and American spirit. Such a playmate, such a support. She had made New York cozy for him, providing the personal touch he needed so much. She was the link to the city of his dreams. He liked her life, her silly but glamorous job in advertising, her apartment, her calico cat. "Send Boo to me in Paris," he crooned, "and I'll feed her pâté."

He spoke only French to Boo. "My grandmother always told me that I must speak French to cats, German to dogs, and English to people," he told Katia, who giggled with delight. He listened seriously when she told him that Boo was the perfect Upper East Side cat, that she loved barbecued chicken from the deli (especially when it was still warm), she loved manicures (having her nails clipped by Katia), and she loved having her hair done (brushed by Katia).

He found Katia's American gaucheness touching; she was a fresh change from the Frenchwomen he despised. She had none of that moaning bitchiness or queenly complex. But Katia was not woman to him. Woman had to be something unreachable, mysterious, unexplainable. And Katia was too open, too willing, too warm. The way she flopped down next to him on the couch like a puppy. He knew it was his problem, but for him, a woman had to remain difficult, a bit out of reach so he could strive for her. But he was unwilling to investigate the cause of his feelings and uninterested in changing his ideas, preferring instead to remain unconnected. He didn't want anything permanent with Katia. Or with any woman, for that matter. He had too many poems to write and novels to think about. He wanted to get published and make up for lost time. Besides, in a few days, he would be returning to Paris.

Kate Loves Frank

THE DAY AFTER she lay in bed with Boris for the first time Kate told Dr. Manne what he had been waiting eight months to hear. Instead of telling him about meeting Boris and about finally having gone to bed with a man after two years, she told him what countless other confused women have told countless other confused analysts. She told him that she loved him, that she wanted to have him as her lover, that she fantasized about him making love to her.

It wasn't that she didn't like Boris; she liked him. A lot. He was exotic and fun and she planned to have a great time with him. Certainly she was relieved—no, ecstatic—to finally feel sexy again and have a lover to keep her warm on these blustery freezing nights. But he lived in Paris and would be leaving in a few weeks. How attached could she get? Her obsession with Dr. Manne had grown slowly over the months. She was deep and thick into it.

As she told him she loved him Kate was furious. She felt like she was reading a part in a play, carefully reciting the laborious, cliché-ridden dialogue of a woman in traditional Freudian analysis. Just before she had started seeing Dr. Manne, she had read several books by Freud and learned, much to her amazement and horror, that she would develop this bizarre attachment to the doctor, but that it wouldn't be real—well, it was real, but not really—and that somehow, it was through this peculiar love affair called transference, that healing would begin. As she read she vowed to herself that she would never succumb to this foolishness, and so on this day, she couldn't quite believe she was actually saying these words to him. It was humiliating, but worse than that, it was common. Kate hated to be common.

But how was she going to convince him that this wasn't transference, it was love! That the two of them had the real thing! This therapy was a rude cosmic joke; a mistake had been made in matching them up as patient and doctor.

Kate envisioned doctors all over town sitting there and trying to keep the smiles off their faces, how they would affect compassion and concern, and with great delicacy, lean forward and say, "Tell me all about it. Just what, exactly, would you like to do with me?" And she heard the voices of women shouting desperately all over Manhattan, "No! You don't understand! This is real! I'm not just another case, this is really it. I'm different!" Oh, the shrieking.

There Kate sat. Dr. Manne certainly didn't look surprised. He sat quietly in his chair, facing her with all his attention, his concerned brown eyes very tender at this moment, his legs crossed, hands folded in his lap, waiting for more.

Kate pulled a tissue out of the box that rested on the bookshelf beside her. The tears were spilling over. Humiliated tears, tears of fear and anger, of confusion and of love. So many tears! It was the last tissue.

"Will you please get me some more Kleenex?" she asked, sniveling and embarrassed, annoyed, too, at having to deal with such a mundane subject as tissues after her proclamation of love.

Dr. Manne stirred out of his analytic reverie. Damn! A break in the confession all because the Kleenex had run out. He panicked. The charged moment was gone. Inside he was furious, but he hoped he merely looked the tiniest bit confused. In a moment of inspiration he took a handkerchief out of his back pocket and offered it to her.

"Here, use this." He did not want to leave the room to find more tissues and give her time to compose herself.

Kate was shocked by this gesture, but held her hand out mechanically to accept it. Part of her was extremely touched, but mostly, she didn't want his damn handkerchief, she wanted something he would probably never give her. Besides, how could she wipe her mascara and blow her nose into his lovely handkerchief? It seemed too intimate. And then what? Would she have to take it home and wash it and give it back? She'd never give it back, she'd wash it and keep it forever. And what a masculine notion, a man giving a woman his handkerchief to cry in.

She didn't think men in New York carried handkerchiefs anymore; they carried little plastic packets of Kleenex instead, in their briefcases. How romantic that Dr. Manne still carried a real handkerchief. She remembered reading in Amy Vanderbilt when she was a little girl that a gentleman was always supposed to have two handkerchiefs, one for himself and a clean one to offer a lady in distress. It was a sign of good breeding.

"I always carry a clean handkerchief," Kate's father used to say to her every morning after breakfast when she came in to watch him tie his bow tie. He always reached into the drawer and pulled out a handkerchief. Then he'd turn away from her and unbutton his pants and dip, bending his knees, and tuck in his shirt, then zip up his pants, turning around to face her, finally buckling his belt. It was Kate's job to iron the handkerchiefs and the pillowcases. She remembered standing for hours in the damp basement with the ugly cement floor, believing herself to be Cinderella as she patiently ironed handkerchiefs, one by one, for Daddy. He loved it when she ironed his handkerchiefs. "What nicely ironed handkerchiefs," he said whenever he discovered a fresh pile, neatly folded, in his top drawer.

"I don't know how clean it is," Dr. Manne said tentatively, then sat back down uneasily.

"That's all right. I'm not squeamish about these things," Kate said. There was a tremendous silence as she unfolded it. They sat there. The scene was rolling out in slow motion.

"No! I mean, when I said it wasn't clean, I didn't mean it was used. I just meant that it has been in my pocket for a while." He spoke slowly and chose his words carefully.

"That's all right," she said again. She held the handkerchief politely in her hands, dabbing her eyes with it occasionally.

She talked and cried and he sat there and listened. She told him of her love, how he was the only man who understood her and her pain and what made her happy and that he was the man she had been looking for all her life. He didn't say much of anything at all, and when the forty-five minutes were up and he told her it was time to go, Kate didn't know what to do. She held the crumpled handkerchief up and asked, "Should I wash it and then return it to you?"

"No, I'll take it," he said, and held his hand out. She thought this was great. Dr. Manne holding his hand out to take back the soiled handkerchief, as if he were taking her sadness away from her, holding her very own tears in his hand.

Kate Tries Loving Other Men

FRANK GOT HIMSELF a glass of water and pulled a package of puffed rice cakes from his L. L. Bean bookbag. He had a free hour, so he sat back down in his chair to eat his Spartan snack and think about Kate.

She was perfect, he mused, a classic example of the symptoms of our time, a 1980s style, bright young woman who excelled in her career, but whose personal life was a disaster. The scales had certainly tipped for women. Once they had been masters of the home and hearth, ruling over the kingdom of personal relationships. But now, New York City was filled with intelligent women like Kate, women whose intelligence positively shone at work, in addition to being beautifully dressed, immaculately coiffed, skillfully made up. These women put the average, wrinkled man to shame because a man didn't have to worry about the externals to succeed. These legions of women in their jogging shoes returned defeated at night to empty apartments and cartons of Haägen Daz. Oh well, he thought, each generation pays for something, and this struggle, this disassociation, was this one's particular hell.

He was fascinated by how women seemed to identify themselves with what they didn't have in their lives, whereas men defined themselves by what they did have. Instead of thinking, I am a top New York copywriter with a fabulous apartment, a busy, glamorous life, attractive and with an expensive wardrobe, Kate viewed herself as an unappealing woman and a failure because she wasn't married. A man in the same position would identify with everything that was swell in his life; he would receive ego satisfaction from it. The lack of a woman would be just a minor obstacle to be overcome, but it wouldn't affect his entire self-image.

Good Lord! God knows how hard she had tried to meet men in this damnable city! But what could he do? Nothing. He had heard every story, every ruse, every escapade of participating in things she liked with the hope of meeting a like-minded soul. But to no avail. For instance, she was an avid reader, so she signed up for the poetry-reading series at the 92nd Street Y. What could be more perfect? But after a few sessions she reported that the audience was filled with adoring women listening to the mostly male authors. Where are all the men readers, she asked Frank, is it only women who read? Undaunted, she made up the strategy of coming in late and, just before the lights dimmed, walking down the aisle slowly, looking at all the empty single seats and choosing the one next to the most handsome or most interesting-looking man she could find. But inevitably it turned out that the seat on the other side of the interesting man was filled by a possessive woman who had dragged him to the reading.

She pushed this philosophy into other parts of her life. For instance, Kate told him, she had observed how women chose seats on a train or bus. They would enter tentatively and head for the "safest" seat they could find, which was a seat alone, or next best, a seat next to a respectable-looking woman. Her strategy would be different from then on, she told him. She would stand in the front of the car or bus and choose the most interesting-looking man and then go directly for the empty seat next to him. She loved doing it; in fact, she didn't find it at all hard to do, but found that her action generally scared the man. She complained to Frank that she couldn't win. It was clear from the way their eyes lit up when she entered the bus that they wanted her to sit next to them, but when she did, they burrowed further into their reading, so uncomfortable were they for having been singled out when there were all those other empty seats to choose from.

She had signed up for Sierra Club hikes because she loved to hike and everyone had always told her, "Sign up for Sierra Club, you meet the sexiest men there." Sierra Club did sound like he-man, outdoorsy types in flannel shirts with the wind in their hair. Instead she met what she called losers, ninety-pound weaklings or shy, sensitive types who were hopeless in the wild and had to depend on a club to get them out of the city. The men Kate wanted to meet were the rock climbers who planned their own trips with geological survey maps. They would be men with cars, men who carried flasks of whiskey and pitons strapped onto their belts. "You know," she said to Frank, "men who wouldn't be averse to making love on the side of a cliff." Frank said he understood.

One winter she joined a folk-dancing circle. Well, there at least she got touched by men, because the athletic style of dancing called for lots of physical contact, being swung by your partner high and low, then shifting down the line and having another man take you in his arms. Why, during the course of a dance, she told Frank, one could be touched by as many as eight different men! Folk-dancing nights were hot stuff, she said sarcastically. It was the only place in Manhattan she had found where men outnumbered women five to one, and women were so much in demand that men would reserve you several dances ahead of time to be assured a partner. "So," Frank asked, "what was wrong?" Well, she supposed it would be fine if she wanted unconventional men with long, greasy hair, who liked to do Olde English contra dances, or nerdy university types. There were lots of foreigners, especially Indians. She supposed they were there because folk dancing afforded them the exciting but entirely safe and proper opportunity to put their hands on an American woman. She told Frank of one Indian, a roly-poly dancer who yelled delightedly at her every time the music came around, "And now we swing!" thrashing her around the floor with such force that she was dizzy and had to sit down.

On weekends she took long walks in the rain and had breakfasts at coffee-shop counters. She wandered through museums on Sunday afternoons and SoHo galleries midweek during her lunch hour. She rode her bicycle through Central Park on those interminable, hot Saturday afternoons when all the city was away for the weekend, hoping to bump into a male counterpart who also had nowhere to go. Her theory was that if she was there, there must be others like her there. But she always returned to her apartment alone. She joined a health club and tried to start conversations with men in the sauna but found they were too embarrassed. Men are more scared than women, she told Frank. He agreed with her. She continued, "If women only *knew* how insecure men are! And it all stems from the size of their penis! I can't believe it! All a woman has to know, is *that*. That it all begins there and ends there. Every woman should be required to learn how to say, 'You have the biggest and the best and you really know how to use it.'" Frank didn't like hearing her say this, but he had to admit to himself that what she said was true. The old goddamn performance anxiety was the key to many a man's psyche. Men had to get it up all the time in every aspect of their lives. Sometimes being a man was just too awful to think about.

One summer she decided to try the Fire Island scene and joined a group house in Fair Harbor. She commuted every Friday on the Long Island Railroad, the "Oklahoma Land Rush" she called it, fighting her way onto the train, swilling beer with the best of them, and still, nothing. She learned that summer that she hated women who wore makeup on the beach. She explained the "sixish" to him, a BYOB cocktail-hour ritual on the dock in Fair Harbor where all the singles gathered with drinks in hand, supposedly to watch the sunset. But really, it was an opportunity for women to look at men and be seen by men. Kate had said it reminded her of Jerome's paintings of the Abyssinian slave markets. She was shocked by this disgusting display, finding herself in the midst of hundreds of heavily made-up, overly tanned, aggressive, nouveau riche, vulture women who were looking for an owner. He burst out laughing at this point. Kate described how they all had that hungry look in their eyes, a look that said, I will kill for a man if I have to. Frank said, "Aren't you getting a bit carried away?" "Oh, be quiet," she said, and continued her tirade. How she pitied the unassuming, unattached male who happened to walk by. But, she countered gleefully, since the dock was packed with women in the ratio of ten women to one man, the women spent most of their time looking at each other. And the way the women looked at each other! That was even better, Kate said. They assessed their competition, guessing age and weight, comparing sexiness, clothing and style, and finally gauging the other's general desperation level. Hardened and bitter women; ooh, it was an ugly scene. Women parading in front of other women sitting on the railings, passing judgment. Frank shivered, thinking of Kate in their midst. Men sure had it easy, Kate told him, they were valuable by the sheer fact of being born. The women on the dock had fallen to the point where they had no special requirements for a man—like brains, charm, personality, education or even money. It was so bad it got down to that if he had a penis, he would do.

She took a juggling class at the New School. "Beginning Juggling," it was called, and the class was filled with weirdos, but nice ones. She was sure she'd be the first person in the history of time never to learn to juggle, but she did learn, and quite well, too. He used to find her juggling in the waiting room when he came out to get her for her appointment, and she'd come into his office laughing and flushed. Juggling did look like fun, he had to admit.

Finally, there was her writing class. This he remembered in fine detail because she had taken the course only this past summer and filled him in on the goings-on each week. Didn't he think summer was the perfect time for a writing class, she asked, what with wistful evenings in Greenwich Village, lost hours that beckoned with breezes, flirtation and possibility? At least a glass of wine after class, no? So she decided to try her hand at writing short stories, poems, anything.

On the first evening of class, she obediently appeared on time, ever the good student. She loved the familiar smell of classroom hallways, chalk, perfume, sweat. She searched for the room number written on her admittance slip, glancing at the tentative looks on the faces of equally confused students as they walked by, all asking her as if she would know any better, whether this was the room for "Finding Your Voice: An Introduction to Fiction Writing." Everyone had shiny new notebooks, ready to take volumes of notes during the lecture. Kate was the first person in the room and sat confidently in her chair in the back room, the better to survey the men as they wandered in. Here she was rewarded; there were lots of men in the class.

Then the teacher came in, and, as Kate reported to Frank, "I knew then it was all over." Suddenly she felt electric. My God, this is ridiculous, all these men in the class and you go for the teacher, she admonished herself. Jerome Rosen was his name. He was dynamic, intellectual, funny, profound, but more than all of this he was touchingly human and very insecure. And old enough to be her father. Ah well. He was boyish in his wonderfully wrinkled khaki suit with a silly bow tie, his long hair combed to cover thinning areas. Why, he was nothing more than an overgrown Jewish preppy. She knew immediately he would be a good kisser.

Jerome surveyed the room, looking at the women first, then looking at the men. It was a critical gaze, discerning but with a hint of humor; he had taught this course for years. "This is 'Finding Your Voice,' course number 231-E," he said officially. He put on his glasses and smiled. Peering over them, he said, "Now I know all of you are really here to pick up somebody." The class laughed and was charmed. "There, now that I've got that out of the way . . . we can proceed with learning how to write brilliant and compelling short stories. And I hope," he said coyly, "that you find your soul mate in this very room."

He gave them all little index cards to fill out with their names, educational background, current occupation and favorite author. After several moments of furious scribbling and the usual stupid questions, "Do you want us to write on the top line?" one girl squeaked, and "What if I have two favorite authors?" a tall guy yelled from the back, they all passed their cards to the center of the room, where they were neatly gathered and passed up to Jerome. He held the cards, and when your name was called, you had to tell the class about yourself and why you wanted to write.

According to Kate, she felt Jerome had noticed her immediately and liked what he saw sitting in the chair, so still and alert. He wondered who she might be and what her story was. Please God, don't let her be a dope, Kate imagined Jerome saying to himself. When he called out the name Kate Odinokov, he was delighted with the way she raised her hand and that hers was such an interesting name. He smiled at her. "Kate?"

"Well, uh, I have a lot of free time, and I've always kept a journal and . . . and now I want to get serious about my writing," she said, and shrugged her shoulders. She felt his piercing eyes and was embarrassed. Was it just me, she wondered to Frank, or was Jerome feeling the same way?

The class took its leisurely time through the teasing summer, meeting twice a week for ten weeks. Every time Jerome walked in, he would look for Kate, she just knew it. She was proving to be as interesting as he had hoped. It was a sociology of classroom behavior that Kate had noted over the years, that most students sat in the same seats they sat in on their very first night of class. But not Kate. She worked the room. Every class she switched, sitting in a different seat, next to a different man. She reported that Jerome noticed and seemed amused and fascinated, looking for her when he entered the class. But she didn't seem to find a man she liked and never sat next to one more than once. Finally, after she had been through the entire room, she sat by herself on the aisle.

Jerome was intrigued by her writing. She could tell because when he gave in-class writing exercises, he would always wait a few people out before calling on her to have her read aloud what she had just written. And he seemed a bit charmed after she finished and she thought he was always on the verge of talking at length about her style and subject matter, but instead he just said, "Okay," and pointed abruptly to the next student.

As the weeks progressed Kate felt herself slipping into some sort of dread. The class was so inspiring about literature and good writing that it silenced her. She remained wordless. In the end, she never turned in a short story. She tried to write, in fact, she wrote volumes in her notebook, but she felt it was mush, unfocused drivel. She had no plot, no urgency, no story to tell. Nothing compelled her. How awful to have the desire to write and have nothing to say!

After every session, on her way out of class, she saw Jerome go through all the papers that had been heaped on his desk by eager-looking students who hoped he would discover in them the next Norman Mailer or whoever it was they admired. She knew he was looking for a story by Kate, but it never came to pass. She hoped he found her silence eloquent in the light of all the other students, who, without embarrassment, handed in reams of junk for him to read.

Finally, the last day of class arrived. Kate was feeling bad about not having turned in a short story. Jerome must think I'm dumb, she thought. Oh well. She decided to make at least a poetic gesture, to thank him for the profound state of silence he had put her in these last few weeks. She baked him some madeleines. "Don't you think that's an appropriate gift for a writing teacher from a student who lost her voice?" she asked Frank. Perhaps when he dipped them into his tea, a flood of memories would descend upon him, helping him, at least, to write.

Kate marched into the last class and sat nervously in her chair, waiting for Jerome to come in. Several students were milling around, talking in animated tones. By now everyone was friendly, after having exposed innermost feelings to each other during the class critiques. Her heart was beating fast. In walked Jerome, cozy, slouchy Jerome, so passionate about good writing, such a stern and gentle and crazy teacher. She saw him glance at her and look away. Then she stood up and walked quickly to his desk with her basket of madeleines. He looked up.

"I didn't write anything—" she began.

"I know," he interrupted.

"But I did bake you some madeleines." Then she faltered. It suddenly seemed so silly. After all, this wasn't the second grade, where you brought the teacher an apple. And what made her think that madeleines were a fair price for a short story?

He took the basket from her and put it quickly in his shopping bag so that the other students wouldn't see it. By now, the madeleines were crumbly and pathetic looking because she had been carrying them around with her all day.

"What's your phone number?" he asked with his pencil posed. Kate was too stunned to think and she blurted it out automatically. The students began hovering around them since it looked like he was holding an impromptu court. There was no time to say why, or why didn't you write, or I've wanted to talk to you.

She walked back to her seat and was unhappy for the rest of the class. Jerome gave his final farewell speech, the "go forth and write, be brilliant, surprise me someday" speech. It was an impassioned plea for good writing, inspiring all to believe in themselves and create literature. He then begged the students not to send him things to read, thank you very much, now that the class was over. They had had their chance with him and he had plenty to read on his own. And he would be pleased not to see any of them in this class again, they must press on, he had given them all he could. He bowed and said a final thank you. The course was over. Everyone clapped and surged toward his desk. Kate got up slowly and left the room quietly. Of all the men in this class she had come to meet, she had gotten what she least expected: the teacher. Jerome had watched her all semester working the room, and in the end, she finally made it up to his desk.

Jerome never called her. Frank wondered about this for several weeks along with Kate. Privately he was relieved; that was all she needed now, an affair with a married man.

And then something happened that Frank about which was a little bit embarrassed. Well, he wasn't embarrassed per se, for he was an analyst and nothing was supposed to embarrass him. Actually, it was his own behavior that he was ashamed of. One day when she walked out in a huff, Kate left her satchel in Frank's office. She phoned him when she arrived at the agency and asked him to put it in a safe place, that she would stop by after work and pick it up.

"And don't look through it!" she yelled at him.

"I have no intention of looking through your things," he assured her. Then he added, "Do you trust me?"

She was silent. "Yes. I do. Against all better judgment, I trust you," she replied.

Well, the first thing he did was look through it. After all, I am her analyst, he reasoned, there can be no secrets from me. Besides, what could she possibly have in there that she wouldn't want me to see? Then he thought how Freudian it was that he was looking through a woman's bag. Worse, and more titillating yet, this was a forbidden bag, one that he was expressly told not to look through. He found a pair of swimming goggles and a towel, a real (not plastic) tortoiseshell comb, a Rickie Lee Jones cassette, the *New Yorker*, a tube of Chanel hand cream, a corkscrew (she told him she was never without one), an apple and a notebook that said, "Finding Your Voice." He slipped the Rickie Lee Jones cassette into his Toshiba (he wanted to hear what kind of music she listened to) and began flipping through the notebook. It was filled entirely with her handwriting. He stopped at a random page and read:

> All I could think of all day was getting home so I could rub my breasts. All day long I could feel them pulsing, swollen, hot and cold at the same time. And ticklish and hurting. Every month this happens to me and indeed it is a torture. It announces the week before my period and suddenly I feel like a walking WOMAN with breasts about to explode.
>
> The men I see do not know the exquisite pain I am in. Could they ever imagine this state of sexual arousal that a woman wanders around in when her body takes control of her? It is my silent, private hell, this constant reminder of my sexuality, so unused, untasted, unexplored.

Jesus, he gasped. Thank God she hadn't turned this in to Jerome. He was at once embarrassed for her and aroused by this honest exposure of her own sexuality. He had no idea she felt this way. What extraordinary expression, what thoughts. Then he felt hurt because she had confided these thoughts to her writing and not to him. Being human was the highest achievement in life and suddenly he found himself in admiration of her frailty. He turned the page.

> Lordy, I was in some sexual heat today. Just a body of desire, melting. I never imagined such desire could be possible. A quivering body, dying at the thought of being touched, yet knowing I would not be. Having nowhere to turn, condemned to living with this insatiable urge.
>
> There I was, this woman dressed for work, going through all the motions of my day, riding the subway, ordering a coffee light at the deli, saying hello to my secretary, but all the while whimpering to be kissed, held, touched, caressed. A woman who just wanted to be groaning, grunting, moving, wet. My body ached, my heart ached.

Frank slammed the book shut. He couldn't read any more. Such a poignant voice was crying out in those pages, such loneliness. And she was just one of millions of people in this city, no, in the world, who was just trying to make her way, live as best as she could, trying to make sense of this thing called life and all the unfairness therein. He felt dirty and ugly just then, no better than a petty voyeur. But mostly, he was disgusted with himself because she had asked him and then trusted him not to look through her satchel. What was happening to him?

Frank Loves Jo Anne

THANK GOD for Jo Anne. Thank God he had Jo Anne. These words repeated like a refrain in Frank's mind as he carried himself through his days. He was surprised at how true it was, that it really did all boil down to having one person of consequence in your life. Even though the majority of his time was spent away from her, in the company of other people, doing his life's work and receiving tremendous satisfaction from it, it was the knowledge of her being, the sheer existence of Jo Anne, that made his life okay. Because they both led demanding lives, she insisted they see each other only on weekends. It didn't matter that during the week all they did was chat sleepily on the phone from their beds in their separate apartments before caving in to sleep, the "us" factor was at work.

What a drug it was, this connection! Being received, being made to feel your life mattered. There were days when he railed against the very idea of what it took to make him feel good about his life. *Why* did it all boil down to connection with a person? He felt like a hypocrite with his patients, when one after another they cried, "If only I had someone, then my life would be okay!" He impassively urged them to look elsewhere for the true source of their happiness. No matter what their age or whether they were gay or straight, virgins, divorcées, even unhappily married, they all craved the same thing.

"I'm not running a dating service," he said to Kate, so exasperated was he with her harping about men. It became his cri de coeur with all his

76

patients as he tried to redirect their thinking, stressing that a relationship wasn't a solution, rather it was the start of a whole new set of problems. He urged them to seek satisfaction in their work, their hobbies, their friendships, their parents and family. He stressed personal daily pleasures like reading, cooking, television. "Happiness does not come from relationship," he actually heard himself say to Kate, when he knew it was the very thought of Jo Anne that got him through the day.

When they pressed him, he told his patients to be themselves, just to concentrate on developing themselves as people, and love would find them. "Why, you might be standing in the subway during rush hour looking for a token. . . ." He was in the middle of what he considered an eloquent speech when Kate jumped up from her chair and launched into the theme song from "Candid Camera." "When you least expect it, you're elected, it's your lucky day! *Smile!* You're going to fall in love!" she sang. She held her pose and then sat back down. "Give me a break, Dr. Manne." She was totally disgusted with him. "This, my mother can tell me."

Wasn't he proof of his own advice? Sometimes, though, in his sadder moments, he scolded himself for telling patients that if they really, but he meant really, wanted to meet someone, they would. Come on, Frank, how can you honestly say that? Life isn't always fair; you don't necessarily get what you want; there were plenty of nice people walking around lonely.

He thought about how he had met Jo Anne. He remembers the first thing that struck him about her was her austerity. Yes, austerity. In the midst of this sloppy world, in the midst of excess, impreciseness, emotional overload, there was Jo Anne. On this day, Frank felt a miracle had been delivered to him. She was a superb minimalist and unemotional to the point of his sometimes wondering how she could be an analyst dealing in the realm of emotions. But Jo Anne was a brilliant analyst with a razor-sharp mind that could reduce complex human acts into the most logical and simplistic terms. She straightened out the lives of countless women who trooped in and out of her office and even had a waiting list of patients. Of that, Frank was more than impressed, he was jealous, "but in a nice way," he told her.

He could think of no better person with whom to spend his time. His days were spent sorting out his patients' lives and now he had Jo Anne to help him with his. She was as clear as a bell. She spoke lucidly, saying exactly what she thought, and even had the rare ability to analyze herself. Having her gave him something to look forward to. After all, he needed someone to love, too! It was hard loving, yet not really loving, his patients. He had some trouble with that one. Jo Anne tried to explain to him that he seemed too withholding with his patients, so scared was he of loving them in the wrong way. She thought his uncertainty was causing chaos in their minds. Jo Anne, understood everything.

Now that he knew her, he was surprised she had even gone to the cocktail party last September where they met. He remembers how happy he had been to return from vacation and find the invitation to the party at the home of the eminent psychoanalyst, Dr. Allen Geer Olderman. Dr. Allen Geer Olderman (he always used all three names) was chairman of the institute's analytic training program, and every autumn he hosted a welcome-back party for all the Ph.D.'s when they returned, supposedly refreshed from the traditional August break.

Frank had just come back from Maine where he had spent four glorious weeks driving through the cool, deep green pine forests. He chose Maine for that year's vacation because it represented a primeval place for him, evoking a certain majesty that he felt was crucial for cleansing and rest. He remembers how on the second of August he had gotten up early to pack so he would be able to walk right out of his office with suitcase in hand after his last patient at noon. Yessiree, he headed straight to the Budget rental car office on Broadway, signed the papers and drove off without a care, leaving the vicious New York afternoon to fend for itself. Oooh, the city had gotten so mean that summer.

From past experience he knew the first week of vacation was usually a difficult transition period. He spent his first few days in a daze, on overdrive from a year's work, finding it hard to extricate himself from his patients' problems. His mind raced, silly thoughts jazzed up his head, he couldn't settle down. But slowly, as the days passed, his mind emptied and he was able to breathe more lightly and relax. He could hear his own heart beat and live without any obligations except his own pleasure.

Maine did the trick. He stayed in a log-cabin motel, swam in icy lakes, caught up on his reading, walked on rocky beaches and hiked through the forests, enjoying the feel of spongy pine needles under his feet. He cracked lobsters with hammers at the lobster shanties and drank countless paper cups of cold beer. He began to feel like a normal person.

He made sure to visit L. L. Bean in the middle of the night because several of his patients had mentioned that it was the only way to go. What fun would it be to go in the middle of the day, they said, when the whole point was that it was open twenty-four hours? So he set his alarm for 2:30 A.M. and dragged himself out of bed and drove an hour to Freeport. To his surprise, the place was jumping; it was a party! He got caught up in the romance of the hunting equipment, but he thought of hunting souls instead of grouse. He fingered the hunting knives, good for cutting apart a person's past; he played with the compasses, wishing that they could point to a person's happiness. He sat in the canoes, good for a float down the river of the unconscious. He crawled into the tent displays and lay down in the sleeping bags. In the end he bought a sweater and a pair of beaded deerskin moccasins, hoping that they would remind him of Maine on those cold, wintery New York nights when he sat up late studying patients' charts.

During his trip he kept telling himself, things must be different this year, things must change for me. He looked for answers in the expansiveness of the rugged pine-tree mountains, he scoured the rocky coast, and by September he felt he had indeed reached a new level of understanding about himself as he headed back eagerly to start his next year in the city.

And then he met Jo Anne, surprising since she never went out. He knew she dreaded leaving her apartment; although she said she just didn't see any reason for going outside. He once supposed she could be diagnosed as phobic, but now that he knew her, he accepted her claim that it was a matter of choice. By meeting her, he saw that in Manhattan one could live without even stepping outside of one's own four walls. In Jo Anne's case her patients came to her, so that took care of work. She ordered all her food from the takeout deli. The deli even brought her hot coffee in the morning. She loved coffee more than anything else. On weekends when he stayed over he made coffee for her. He woke her in her most favorite way, by holding a steaming cup of coffee under her nose until she opened her eyes. Then, like a baby reaching automatically for a nipple, she sucked up some coffee, and then released the cup with a big smile.

She phoned her grocery order to Gristede's twice a week and they delivered. Anything she needed, from sheets to sourdough bread, could be ordered from one of the many catalogs she got, and there was always B. Altman's, where her old college roommate was a merchandise manager. She would arrange to have things sent by messenger. Books came by mail. She did have to go out to the post office occasionally, although she had tried to get her mailman to buy the stamps for her and deliver them. She never had to set foot into a bank. Transactions were handled by mail and phone.

They met over the hors d'oeuvres table at Dr. Allen Geer Olderman's party while his wife, Doria, an amateur cellist, was playing for the guests. Frank was in a great mood; this party was just what he needed to get into the fall social swing of Manhattan. He strolled around and overheard conversations that all sounded the same. "And what did you do for August? How did your patients do while you were gone?" Jo Anne caught his eye because she was one of the few people not jabbering away; she was instead standing at the table looking at a plate of food. She was wearing loden green corduroy pants and a mustard-colored sweater. Her hair was mousy brown and waved about her shoulders. She wore tortoiseshell glasses and no makeup. Clearly she was a woman who felt appearance was inconsequential in this world of so many other things to be concerned about. Yet she was attractive because she was totally herself, right there, out front. She looked intelligent and direct. Her mouth was curled in a snarl. "What's that?" she asked nobody in particular. He looked at the plate she was staring at.

He gave her a big smile. "I'm Italian," he said. At the time it seemed like it would explain everything. But the second it was out of his mouth he regretted it. How could he be so stupid?

But the amazing thing about Jo Anne was that she got it. Here he was being totally inept, answering a very simple question with an obtuse answer, and she got it.

She looked him up and down and then laughed. That made him feel better. "Oh," she said calmly. "That means you know what this is because it is an Italian dish. And I suppose, if it is Italian, then it goes without saying that it must be delicious."

Frank nodded. "It's mozzarella. Looks like smoked mozzarella and sun-dried tomatoes. With olive oil drizzled on top. Basil too. You see they put them in the sun to dry. Like prunes. And it is delicious. According to my patients, this is the 'in' hors d'oeuvre this year." He held the plate up for her to take one.

"Like this?" she asked, and gingerly dipped her fingers into the oil to pick one up. She took a bite.

"My name's Frank Manne."

She waited until she finished chewing. "I'm Jo Anne."

"Hi. Jo Anne what?"

"Just Jo Anne. Gallagher is my last name but no one ever uses it, and that's fine with me. People seem to find Jo Anne to be quite enough name for me."

"That's great!" Oh God, was he being too agreeable?

She took another sun-dried tomato, chewing and surveying him critically. "Man is a pretty funny last name for a man to have," she said.

"M-a-n-n-e," he spelled.

And so they stood, balancing their plates and cocktails, and talked. They found out where they had gone to school and what their specialties were, about whom they knew and whom they didn't know, who their favorite analysts were and after whom they tried to model themselves. Frank was delighted to find such a smart female colleague. By the end of the evening he was ecstatic, he'd actually found a woman who understood, to whom he could talk on an analytical level—socially. She was one of "them," or rather, "us." At one point, when dessert was served, oversized cream puffs and all the strawberries you could eat, Frank plunged his fork down to take a bite and his plate turned over and splashed whipped cream on everything. He felt like such a jerk, but she was very cool about not making a big fuss and helping him to clean it up. He appreciated that.

It seems she had come to the party because she was trying to change, trying to get over her supposed phobia about going out.

"But frankly, Frank," (she found this hysterically funny and couldn't stop laughing) "I really don't care about it. We're speaking confidentially, right? It doesn't bother me that I don't go out. It only bothers my analyst, who thinks there's something terribly wrong with it."

Confidentially. That became "their word," like other people had "their song." They often started each phrase with "confidentially," or "I'm going to confide in you," or "We can be confidential about this, right?" They felt it put their friendship on a plane above ordinary human interaction, which wasn't conducted on a particularly confidential plane at all.

One of the things Frank liked about Jo Anne was that he could confide in her his feelings of nervousness. He knew she could deal with them analytically. For instance, when the party ended, they were able to have a lengthy discussion about leaving. He said, "I guess I'm going to go, and since you live in the same general direction, and I'd like to, how about if I walk you home? It doesn't have to 'mean' anything, if you know what I mean, but I would like to spend this extra time with you because I've enjoyed meeting you, you're very nice, at least the little that I know of you is nice and—"

"Fine," she interrupted him.

It was months later that she told him, "You know, Frank, one of the things I like about you is that I can handle you. You are transparent to me—no, easy is more like it. You are very sweet and aren't too much trouble. I like that in a man." He remembers not knowing quite what to think. Was that a compliment? He didn't tell her this, but he felt men were an enigma to her. In spite of the fact that she counseled her female patients that "men were people, too," she basically had no use for, or real understanding of, men. She was Zen; content just the way she was. Even so, Frank decided he was good for her; he would add an element of the safe unknown into her life. Besides, as a woman and a therapist, she should have a man in her life, especially if she was going to counsel her patients about men.

And so, within a month, it became Jo Anne and Frank Manne. "It rhymes," he said. He also pointed out that their names each had two syllables and were the same except for one letter. "M is for masculine," he said. "It must mean something that our last names are so close, don't you think?"

"I don't know about that, but I do know that I'm delighted to see that a man can be sillier than a woman," she said.

Frank had found a haven. But only on weekends. During the week he was on his own. She insisted on it, so as not to get in the way of the work. Their relationship was something apart from the regular life. Time stood still in her apartment, so divorced was it from the energy of the city. On Friday nights when he went to her place, just six blocks north of his studio, he felt safe from the world. They liked to lie on her two couches, on their backs, staring at the ceiling, talking to each other through the air, their words bouncing around the room. This freedom made him feel giddy and reckless; it was a turn-on. In the evenings, they often watched television because Jo Anne adored television. It wasn't enough that she watched the lives of her patients through their ramblings. No, she wanted more. She especially loved the weekly shows, where the faces became familiar and she could become entangled in the characters' lives. She liked seeing how emotionally correct the shows were, whether they really dealt with the issues. She read the newspaper avidly, scanning the reviews of new shows. She considered watching pilot programs an honor and an art because it was a chance to get a peek at the workings of the Hollywood creative process and judge for herself whether a show had any merit before the media pounced all over it.

Frank viewed it as a sign of his own maturity that he could accept Jo Anne as she truly was and not make her change. It was something about which he always counseled his patients, to "celebrate a person's otherness." Wasn't it he who told his patients that having a relationship was not about trying to make someone else more like yourself? It was about *how* two individuals *interacted*.

That Jo Anne didn't go out, he found eccentric; that she didn't like sex, he realized, would take some adjusting to. After some soul-searching on his part, he decided it was just that she hadn't developed a taste for it yet, and that it was his job to be an attentive lover and turn her on, sort of like a junkie hooking a potential addict. They talked about it, this little problem, for she had no aversion to discussing anything. In fact, her indifference made him all the more passionate. It gave him a challenge and he liked challenges. Wasn't that what his work was about anyway—the challenge of helping people find happiness in spite of themselves?

Lately Frank had been thinking about movie sex. What annoyed him was how the sex was always so marvelous; you watched two gorgeous movie stars with perfect bodies gobble each other up, always reaching climax, and usually simultaneously. And the first time the characters became lovers, they made love magically knowing all the right things to do. It was always fabulous! Incredible! A spiritual experience! Well, what about real sex? What about embarrassment or hesitation, shyness and fumbling around? What about, oh God, is my body gross, or what if I can't get it up, or I don't like what he's doing but I don't want to hurt his feelings, or I just don't think I can come tonight, I'm a bit nervous, you go ahead. From his patients he knew there was a lot more bad sex being had than good sex, more clumsiness than finesse, more confusion than communication. He felt the movies gave sex false press, making regular people think they were inadequate. When he discussed this with Jo Anne, she just shrugged her shoulders.

"Frank, reality isn't interesting to people because they have that every day. You of all people should know that. People don't want to see themselves on the screen, they want to see some ideal of the way life might be. Who wants to go to the movies and see bad sex when you already have that in your life?"

That sounded like a learned comment from a woman who didn't seem to want to contribute to the improvement of what Frank considered to be their sad sex life. "But it adds to people's unhappiness because they can't measure up," he countered.

"What can I say? Don't you have any patients who are in advertising? They'll be the first to tell you that in commercial land, reality isn't acceptable. That's why when they "do reality," it's always some heightened version of it. You know, happy families, handsome, slim people, puppies, kittens, nice kitchens, big bathrooms. You know, the whole shtick."

He thought about Kate and the various advertising stories she told him that drove him up the wall. There were times when he could barely stop himself from telling her that he thought what she did was ridiculous. Then he remembered a lofty thought from Pirandello that she had thrown at him just last week when she sensed he was outraged. It went something like, "Pretending is a virtue. Because if you don't pretend, you can't be a king."

This still didn't resolve their sex life. The major problem was that Jo Anne didn't perceive it as a problem. What could he do? She just didn't like sex; it wasn't important for her. He had tried to understand; at one point he tried to adopt her attitude and concentrate on appreciating the rest of their relationship. But instead, he walked around feeling like a bad boy all the time for having his desires.

They had been seeing each other for six months (could you call it dating if you never went out?) when Frank did a weird thing. Since they were both analysts, neither answered the phone directly. Their machines did the screening. It outraged Frank that he and Jo Anne never had a normal telephone exchange where one called and the other answered. It boiled down to their machines talking to each other. At first this intrigued him, but then it became frustrating. He started leaving long messages on her machine, talking to it as if he was talking directly to her. In the midst of messages from her depressed patients, there would be a long chat from Frank. Frank found out only after Jo Anne confessed, that sometimes, even when she was free, she would listen in on his call while he made it. She admitted that it gave her a sense of power.

So one day Frank left a sexy message on her machine. It was a way of flirting, wasn't it? He did it for himself, but he was also doing it for her. With the message on tape, she could take it at her own speed. She told him the whole story. Her last patient had just exited tearfully, a forty-two-year-old woman who had just started her own business and whose partner turned out to be sleeping with her boyfriend. Jo Anne had just come back from the kitchen, where she had made herself an iced tea, then settled back into her chair, flipping the machine on.

"Hello? It's Jeanette Gould. Can we reschedule my Wednesday appointment for another day? I've got a business trip to Akron, can you believe it? Akron! Yuck! Have you ever been to Akron? Please leave a message with my secretary. Thanks. Bye."

The next message was from a colleague. "Hi, Jo Anne, Merry Swift here. I've got a patient for you if you've got the time. Give me a call. Say, did you see that article of Puckett's in last month's journal? What, is he kidding? Take care."

A hang-up. Another hang-up. Patients just calling to hear her voice.

"Hello. Guess who? Your most depressed patient, I'm sure. Oh well. Just wanted to hear your voice. Bye."

Then came Frank. His message started with a big sigh. "Oh, Jo Anne. What I really want to do is come over to where you're sitting—I suppose you are in the blue chair right now—and put my head in your lap. I think that would be a comforting thing to do and I need comforting. Maybe you would stroke my hair. My patients just drain me and I just want to be held."

There was a long silence but he remained on the line. Then he said, "I would then like to unzip your pants." At this point Jo Anne sat up. Frank's voice admitted that even he was amazed at what he had just said.

"And you'd be telling me, I can just hear your voice, 'Frank, what are you doing? Cut it out. No.'" He mimicked her voice perfectly. "But I would do it anyway. Zip, zip, zip. No, make that unzip, unzip, unzip. Then I would bury my face into your cunt. You know something? I really do like that word. That's where I'd really like to be right now, smelling you, sucking you, kissing you, playing with my tongue, right there in the chair where you face your patients, that's what would make it really good, you know. So that when you see your patients, you would know what you had done in that very same chair."

Once again there was silence as if he was thinking. "Then I would sit on you—not rape you, but force myself on you. I'm a man and I need it, Jo Anne. And I know you want it but you are too ashamed to ask. I would unzip my pants and take them off and sit on you in your analyst's chair and fuck you. Oh God. I'm horny just thinking about it. I'm even touching myself right now. Oh God. I'm going to play with myself now, on this tape. Yes. I want you to have a tape of my coming. It's important that you see me like this, a man who is just like any other man. I have needs, too, Jo Anne." There were lots of *oh*'s and deep breaths, and finally a long sigh of expelled air and tension. There was a click.

Jo Anne was stunned. She turned off the machine. She didn't know what to think. Was he a pervert? He couldn't be. It was Frank. "Jesus," she kept saying to herself, over and over. Her patients discussed this kind of stuff with her all the time and she had never thought anything of it. In fact, she encouraged them not only to share their fantasies with her, but to share their fantasies with their partners. But was *this* what it was really like?

So why did she expect different behavior from Frank? Surely he was a normal male and this was just another form of sexual expression. She lit a cigarette from the pack she kept in a drawer—she didn't smoke, but it was there for occasions just like this one. She was totally unsure of how she felt and she didn't like that one bit. She watched the smoke curl from the cigarette in a hypnotic state. She rewound the tape and played it back. Does this arouse me? She had to consider this, too, instead of just passing it by. She rebuked herself. No, what aroused her was his unembarrassed need, his humanness, his not being ashamed to do this, his willingness to take a risk. Yes, this is what endeared him to her. No other man had confided his need for her like this. But does needing mean loving—if someone needs you, does that mean he loves you?

She decided to play the tape again and see if she could masturbate to it. She smirked—this is some relationship we have, two analysts masturbating to the sound of each other's voices on their answering machines. She unzipped her pants, flicked on the tape and started stroking herself. But then she stopped, the tape had rewound too far back and she had to listen to her other messages again, and by the time Frank came on, it was hopeless. She decided she was being too self-conscious because she was trying it in such an experimental mode. She became impatient and said, "This is ridiculous, I don't have time for this," and quickly zipped up her pants as if someone had seen her and she was embarrassed. All this is what she had told Frank.

Jo Anne wore only one thing. A pair of wide-wale corduroy pants in a dusty green color. Day in and day out she wore them, and once a week she put them in her miniwasher in the bathroom, then transferred them to the minidryer. During this short time she wore a different pair of pants, royal blue corduroy, but put the green ones back on the minute they were done. She couldn't be bothered with clothes; they just didn't interest her. Frank had never seen her in a dress or in any other outfit, for that matter. They both agreed she was a real nut case and laughed about it. But Frank told her he loved her that way.

Because she couldn't come? The analyst's rescue fantasy came into play. He wanted to be the man who would unleash her, who would open the doors to the magic kingdom of her sensuality. But more, he wanted the power he was sure would come from turning her into his sexual slave. He fantasized that once she had come, she would drag after him, begging him to fuck her all the time. He tried to imagine her when she at last did come, but it was beyond his grasp; the look on her face was blurry to him when he tried to see it.

So their sexual relationship was a primitive one. That's how he described it to Dr. Janet, anyway. Jo Anne seemed to let him use her; in fact, she got a teensy bit turned on if she felt she was being humiliated. She let him do what he wanted with her, feigning surprise when in the middle of the night he would roll her over onto her stomach and mount her from behind. "What are you doing?" she would ask. Of course, she knew exactly what he was doing.

Frank reassured her. He told her he loved her in spite of all this because she was such an extraordinary psychologist. She suspended judgment beautifully and her patients flourished because of it.

"Jo Anne, you're a fine person. You answer to a higher calling, helping other people actualize so they can be happy. So what if you're a little crazy? We all are," he said as they lay on her two couches, staring at the ceiling. It came naturally to him to take care of someone. But now he could really enter into her care; no professional ethics were operating here. This was his own life.

Jo Anne was disgusted. "You sound like a yuppie, Frank. Don't you see what you're doing?"

"No," he replied. "What?"

"Yuppie dating."

He looked at her.

She continued staring at the ceiling. "Yuppie dating is intellectual dating instead of gonad dating. It's like a lawyer dating a lawyer because each thinks they should be dating a lawyer, not because they crave each other. You like the *idea* of me, you don't like *me*. That's why young people are so confused today. It's time we got back to the real reason why people should hook up with each other. Actually, I'm even considering writing a paper about this."

"That's the most ridiculous thing I've ever heard." Now it was his turn to be disgusted. Then, in the angry silence that followed, he tried to consider what she had said. Could she be right? No. He would rather be with Jo Anne with her corduroy pants than, than who? Than Kate with all her many outfits. Kate, who was so busy with the business of living, worrying about the perfect nail polish for toes this spring. Kate, who was always telling him what to do with his hair and where to eat dinner in Little Italy or SoHo or wherever it was that she had just been. Poor, sex-starved Kate who . . .

Kate. Damn her! Why did she have to pop up all the time? She was a curse. He didn't dare mention her name in front of Jo Anne. It was a sore spot for him. A little while ago he had told Jo Anne all about Kate, hoping to get some professional advice about handling her. What had started out as a calm discussion had turned into the nastiest fight they had had so far.

He remembers telling her, "She hates me so much. She absolutely exhausts me. I must be the wrong doctor for her."

"No," Jo Anne said. "It's obvious. She adores you."

"Oh, Jo Anne, how can you said that? She's totally nasty at every opportunity."

"No, Frank, the problem is deeper than that. The problem is you. *You* like her and *she* knows it. *That's* what makes your sessions with her so uncomfortable."

He blew up. "It's not true! How dare you say that? You are really something." He jumped up from the couch and started pacing the room, yelling at her. "I'm sick and tired of all this analysis we do! I do it all day and I have my own analyst, thank you. Let's do something else. Let's go for a walk in Cental Park. Like normal people."

She looked at him and received the barb directed at her as proof that what she had just said was true.

Frank stared back at her, realizing that Jo Anne had pushed one of his buttons. He had fallen for a patient, and what's worse, he hadn't realized it until she'd pointed it out.

Kate Loves Boris

KATE LOOKED ON Boris's visit to New York like a Russian fairy tale read late into the night. He swooped into her life and took her totally by surprise. She had met her Russian prince and she had become a Russian czarina. It was the last thing she thought would happen, seeing as she was in love with Dr. Manne.

It was as if the minute she told Dr. Manne she loved him—she fell in love with Boris instead. Poor Dr. Manne, he would really be in for it now. Not only was she angry because he had spurned her love, but now she would wave her exotic Russian lover in his face.

Ah, to have fallen in love during the nastiest two weeks of the year, when the days were mean and short. No one falls in love in January; why, how—how absolutely Russian! And never had she thought she'd be attracted to a Russian man, for after growing up around them, she thought she was allergic to them. And with a suffering dissident poet, no less! How romantic! Not only had she found a man, but a cause, too. When Boris left, she promised herself she would look into joining the American chapter of PEN. She could just see herself marching in protest against imprisoned writers in the Soviet Union, wearing a kerchief on her head.

She thought with great pleasure of the nights she spent in bed making love with this wild, secretive Russian, and just couldn't decide, was he or was he not a KGB agent? He certainly was mysterious and complicated enough. She had to admit the mere possibility of his being an agent turned her on even more. Would she someday write her memoirs? *My KGB Lover* by Kate Odinokov. This flirtation with the unknown made her more nervous and tentative around him than she would have liked. But mostly she marveled at his manliness and loved how he cooked for her almost every night with great ruffles and flourishes, dropping the pasta into the boiling water with a twirl so it fell expertly in a perfect spiral, or whisking a vinaigrette just so with his wrist, and then dipping his pinky in for a taste.

One thing that made her think he was a spy was how he left her at night. She couldn't understand it. It hurt her terribly the way he would cook dinner and they would go to bed, make love and watch TV, but at midnight, when she was just starting to fall asleep, he would slip out of bed, get dressed and go back to the Park Avenue apartment. Or so he said.

"Boris, why? It hurts me so when you leave. I hate to sleep alone. I hate, hate, hate it," she said, pouting.

"Baby, I have to. I cannot stay with a woman. I never stay with a woman. I must have my own bed. It is why I don't have women to my studio in Paris at night, for I cannot ask them to leave."

"Don't you like me?" she asked.

He ignored her question. "I like going back with smell of you on my beard and elevator man can sniff you on me. Yes, is true. He knows what I've been doing. I love it. He is jaloux, and I get out and go into my apartment, smiling." He had a gleeful expression on his face when he told her this; it was clear he liked being an impish, bad boy.

Kate looked at him with a thoroughly uncomprehending look. How could a man not want to spend the night with me? How could he drag himself out of my warm, cozy bed, withdraw his arms from my silky body and not want to sleep nuzzled together and wake up from time to time and make love again, half-awake? She tried repeating it to herself; maybe then she would understand. To get dressed and go outside into the freezing January night, then face your elevator man with the smell of sex on your face, then get undressed and go to bed again? Alone? It made her doubt herself, and then she wondered if she was unappealing in some way. But it was useless. No matter how much she begged him to stay, he wouldn't.

Was he meeting agents somewhere in these jazz clubs he went to? Were all these interviews just a cover for some Soviet activity? And now, would her phone be tapped, would her mail be monitored? Would she be followed on the street? Was she a woman Boris had innocently met, or had he incorporated her from the very beginning into his cover so he could operate in full view? Then she asked herself the big question: could she still love if him he was KGB?

She believed it was the night she took Boris to Carnegie Hall that she fell in love with him. Her boss stopped by her office at the end of the day and offered her two tickets to a concert because she couldn't go. "Carnegie Hall, that's pretty New Yorky, don't you think?" she said to Boris over the phone. "I'm leaving the office now. Meet me at my place for cocktails and canapes while I change." She loved the word *canapes*, it was so thirties, or was it fifties?

They were sitting around sipping wine when she pulled out of her purse a catnip mouse that she bought that day for Boo.

"Have you ever seen one of these?"

He hated to say no, but he didn't know what it was.

"It's catnip. Marijuana for cats," she said, and handed it to him so he could inspect it before he gave it to Boo.

"We do not have this sort of thing," he said, meaning we in Russia, as he watched Boo. How she danced for them! A catnip ballet, filled with leaps and flying jetés, acrobatics too, somersaults and triple rolls. And then, after the fury, silence. Boo was drunk and lolled on the floor, staring at the two of them with a foolish grin.

"I better change," Kate said, glancing at her watch. She dashed into the bedroom and threw on her black velvet pants and a black V-neck sweater that she liked to wear with the V going down her back. She liked her back and thought backs were sexy. Then she painted a streak of taxicab yellow under her fashionable eyebrows, which she considered her best feature, and painted a red, red mouth. She surveyed the effect in the mirror and felt very neo-Japanese to complement his haute nouvelle look that was all the rage of Paris. He was wearing an itsy-bitsy, teeny tiny red bow tie with a gray print Kansai Yamamoto shirt and charcoal black trousers.

"I'm ready," she said, presenting herself to him a mere five minutes later. She liked being a woman who could look gorgeous in no time flat. They walked to Park Avenue and he was appalled at how she stepped out into the middle of the street and stole a taxi by simply barging ahead of another couple who had hailed it.

"But this is how you do it in New York, baby," she said to him as he took her firmly by the arm and steered her away, letting the couple have their cab. She was miffed. He had made her feel like a bad girl. They rode silently in another cab until he turned to her and said solemnly, "We must start a traffic in catnip." He sounded very official. "The Franco-American drug connection of nip for cats."

She loved his sense of drama and how he put things.

"Do you think Parisian cats would react the same way to American catnip?" he asked.

"I'll buy you some to take back and you'll just have to try it out."

Kate could see that Boris really enjoyed his first visit to Carnegie Hall. He told her that it made him nostalgic for Moscow, and even nostalgic for New York, because he had heard about Carnegie Hall his whole life. He laughed at his own sentimentality. He was surprised by the simplicity of the hall, its clean, pleasing lines. It wasn't at all as grand as he had imagined. He liked the way people just thronged into the open doors as if joining some great party.

"You're in luck, we've got box seats," she said, waving him in. As he hung up his coat in their private vestibule and smoothed his hair in the mirror she explained that they would be listening to the American Composers Orchestra, a group dedicated to playing the music of contemporary American composers. After the first piece, a rousing bit of modernism by Elliot Carter, Kate studied how Boris clapped with such noblesse oblige. How dapper he looked as he surveyed the audience below them. When the composer stood from his seat in the audience to take a bow, Boris politely nodded in his direction and lifted his hands ever so slightly in homage to his achievement, and Kate thought how very lucky she was to be with such a charming man.

After the concert she wanted to take a cab back because it was cold and late, but he insisted they take an invigorating hike up Madison Avenue. The gusts pierced through her coat and made her face burn with tears, but Boris thought nothing of it; he loved cold. They marched up the empty street lit brightly by the opulent store windows. She wanted to educate him, so she tried to pause in front of almost every shop window, saying, "Look, Boris, look." But he pulled her along, bored with it all, not wanting to stop. He said, "Baby, we have all this in Paris. Come to Paris, it's better in Paris. This is nothing."

When they finally made it to her apartment after stopping to pick up some chocolate pastries at a fancy all-night deli, Boo was still languorous from the catnip. Kate noticed how her cat had become a coquette with Boris, lying on her side and staring at him with great adoration.

"Are you a Balanchine ballerina?" he crooned in French. "Would you like some champagne?" He drew the word out, cham-p-a-g-n-e. Boo slid onto her back with front paws outstretched and looked at him from upside down. Kate came out holding a tray with a pot of tea and the pastries and watched her cat flirt with her man.

So here we are, she thought, two Charlotte Ramplings, adrift in Manhattan, sharing an apartment, doing the best we can, making up life as we go along, both charmed by the same man. She had no idea how Boris felt about her. He was curiously warm and distant, sweet and cool. But she didn't care. At that moment she felt something click. Could it be that she had segued from being a single person into being one half of a couple? Whatever it was, she liked it.

The next day, Saturday, was Boris's thirty-ninth birthday, and Kate planned a surprise. He had mentioned his birthday once a few days earlier and seemed diffident about it. When she asked him what he'd like to do for his special day, he got uncomfortable and dropped the subject immediately. She decided that he was probably unused to sweetness in his life and always prepared for disappointment. That's when she decided to surprise him. A few days earlier he had given her a manuscript of one of his new short stories. It was in English, terribly typed and filled with his penciled corrections. He asked her if she could find someone, maybe a secretary at her office, to type him a fresh copy.

"Please, can you do that? For me?" he said dramatically, holding his hand over his heart.

"I'll try to find someone," Kate said.

But the time had run out and she couldn't find anyone to type it, so she decided to give him the gift of her time and type it herself. She was sure she could do a better job, and while she typed, she edited the story and cleaned up the bad translation. As she worked, Boo sat on the desk and read every word, while munching on rubber bands, batting pencils around and enjoying the hypnotic *tap tap tap* of the typewriter, jumping with delight every time Kate used the carriage return.

It was a bizarre tale about a Russian émigré living in Paris and how he gave drugs to a very pretty Spanish girl, Alma, and one spring they went to Venice together and he saw her jump off the Bridge of Sighs and drown while he floated in a gondola off in the distance. Kate started feeling woozy from this eerie story. As she typed she felt like she was stepping inside the story, becoming part of it.

When she finished, it was four o'clock on Boris's birthday. She jumped up from the desk and dashed to the Kopy Kat Boutique and waited on line patiently until it was her turn and asked for five copies. Then she stopped off at her local stationery store and bought a pen that flowed with gold ink. Boris had used her gold pen the other day and pronounced it "fan-tas-teek," so she decided he must have one. Back at the apartment, she wrapped the manuscripts in some royal blue tissue she had saved from a gift someone had given her and tied it up with a silvery tinsel ribbon she found in her box of Christmas-tree trimmings. She riffled through the box of birthday cards she collected whenever she came upon a good one and found an avant-garde black-and-white Duane Michaels photo she had picked up just days earlier in a SoHo card shop and wrote in gold, "Happy Birthday to my Russian poet prince. Love Kate." By then, it was almost time for Boris to show up.

She was changing when the lobby buzzer sounded. She dashed into the kitchen to buzz him in, then rushed into the living room to hide the presents under the couch. She tried to look calm and casual when she opened the door. He held a bottle of champagne and looked glum. "I thought we could drink to old man time," he said morosely.

"Come in, come in." She laughed and put her arms around him. He was acting like one big baby.

"Oh, bad news, baby," she said, picking up his morbid tone of voice, kissing him once on each cheek, French style. "I couldn't find a typist for your story." She held up his worn original copy for him to take back. His face fell and he waved it away. She put it on the entrance-hall table.

"Go sit," he said, pointing to the couch, and walked directly into the kitchen. She heard him banging around the cupboards. "Where are your wineglasses? Oh, I found them." He came out with the champagne and two goblets.

"No, wait," she said, and jumped up. She went to the living-room cabinet and pulled out two antique, etched, champagne flutes. "From Yugoslavia," she said, displaying the flowery, tall and delicate crystal for him.

"Ah, now this is fan-tas-teek," he said, taking one from her and twirling it around in his fingers. This was exactly the sort of thing he liked. He sat down next to her on the couch and popped the champagne and poured it. She held up her glass to him and sang "Happy Birthday." He listened very solemnly.

"My God, is this what they sing here?" he asked in mock disgust.

"Yes, baby."

"Hmm. Not so nice."

"Well, what do you sing?"

He leaned back, closed his eyes and sang a dramatic Russian birthday song called, "Novoe Leto," New Summer. "Hmm," she agreed. "Happy Birthday to You" was a paltry ditty indeed.

"It's okay," he sighed, "forget it." They leaned back on the couch, sipping the champagne in silence. He was a million miles away, lost in Russian birthday memories.

"It's excellent champagne, baby," she said.

"It's not excellent, it's okay," he corrected, trying to educate her, "just okay."

She couldn't stand it anymore. "And here is a little cadeau for Boris!" she whooped, pulling the crinkly, gay package out from under the couch.

His face lit up. What a surprise! He hugged her, rocking her back and forth. With great drama and glee he unwrapped the present, wondering what it could possibly be. When he realized it was his story, and so perfectly, beautifully typed, and such clean white paper, he held it to his heart and sighed, looking at her with great affection.

"I did it myself," she said, bouncing up and down on the couch, happy with her little ruse. "It took me all day long."

He took her face between his hands and gave her Russian kisses, strong ones and delicate ones. He thanked her for her picture (she had thrown that in at the last moment) and with the gold pen that he was thrilled to receive, he wrote on a piece of paper: "You are sweetest girl in U.S.A. Boris Zimoy."

They snuggled together, sipping champagne, Boris happy with the fuss that had been made over him and Kate delighted that she had pleased him.

"Now, if only we could hear some Schubert, that would make it really something," he said wistfully.

"Really?" Kate said. "That would make it something?" She got up and put on the Guarneri playing a Schubert quartet in D. She sat back down with a big smile and kissed him on the cheek. "Happy Birthday, Boris," she said. And they closed their eyes, sipped champagne and listened to Schubert. How perfect could life be? She had never known such contentment. This was all she had ever wanted. It had always seemed so elusive and here it was.

They took the bottle of champagne to the bedroom with them and he gave her a multitude of champagne kisses as they watched American TV in bed. He couldn't get enough of American TV, but he thought the commercials were terrible. But that evening, Kate didn't want his attention on the TV, she wanted to be ravished, so she shut it off. Boris sat up and did impressions of Khrushchev, Brezhnev, Andropov, followed by impressions of bitchy Frenchwomen and gay Frenchmen. Kate giggled and giggled.

"What can I do for you?" she wondered out loud. "Oh, I know," she said, and sat up straight and assumed a patriotic look on her face. "I learned this at summer camp." In a sweet, pure voice she sang,

> "I like the United States of America
> I like the way we all live without fear
> I like to vote for my choice
> Speak my mind, raise my voice
> Yes, I like it here.

> "I am so lucky to be in America
> And I am thankful each day of the year
> For I can do as I please
> 'Cause I'm free as the breeze
> Yes, I like it here.

> "I'd like to climb to the top
> Of a mountain so high
> And lift my head to the sky
> And say how grateful am I
> For the way that I'm living
> I'm working and giving
> And helping the land I hold dear
> Yes, I like it
> I like it
> I like it here!"

Boris roared. Now it was his turn to be delighted. He kissed her on her bare shoulder and called her "my little trooper."

As she lay back in his arms and felt him doze off she wondered what would happen to the two of them. He would be leaving in a few days! Would she move to Paris and become French? Would he move to New York and become American? Would they live happily ever after?

She moved out from under his arm and lifted herself up, gazing at him lightly sleeping, adoring him with her eyes. She caressed his chest with her cheeks, brushing her lips against the soft black fur of this body. She ran her face along the length of his arms, trying to memorize him, licking the delicate inside of his elbow, breathing deep the smell of his armpits to hold it forever inside of her. Like a Rosary, she summoned up a litany of all the things he was, reciting them in her mind as she explored his body with her mouth. This is the body of a man who is all alone in the world, a man who was born at age thirty-four when an Air France jet set him down on Western soil. A man who can never see his home again. How nervous he must have been when the plane at Shere-metyevo started boarding for Paris. Did his whole body scream with what he was about to do? This is the body of the man who at eighteen had to serve in the Soviet army and almost died during his two years in Siberia. This is the body of the boy who spent happy summers as a child in the Crimea. It is the body of a man who has lived the infamous double life of an average Soviet citizen, and the constant danger of an underground rebel; the body of a man who lives in constant despair over his raped life, who loves his country so much that every day in the West is both a blessing and a torture. This man is the link to my heritage. When I kiss him, I kiss Russia, I kiss my soul. He is the key—to me.

She thought back to her college days when she had been taken over by all things Slavic. They had been a Russian troika, Kate, Donna and Shelley, three nineteen-year-old girls, seduced by the Slavic department of George Washington University. Like lovesick adolescents, they were hooked on the drug of Russian literature, bingeing on Dostoyevski, Lermontov, Chekhov, Tolstoy, Gogol, Pushkin. They craved the intensity of this appealing and lush picture of Russian life, so rich in thoughts, feelings and emotions that overwhelmed. It catered to the intense senti-mentalism of their lives just then. They longed to be Masha in despair at the Black Sea, beautifully at a loss for words on a hot afternoon, sitting at a tea table and staring forlornly at her married cossack lover while fingering a bowl of sweating cherries from Azerbaijan.

At the beginning of each semester they would come out of the book-store, struggling under the weight of novels piled high, twelve books for the Russian Novel, fourteen for Philosophy and Literature and only six for Soviet Literature from World War II to the Present—Solzhenitsyn didn't write lots, he just wrote long. Kate held memories of them sprawled with blue-jeaned limbs on the beds of their infamous dorm room, number 636, Shelley on the top bunk, Donna on the bottom and Kate on the single bed across the tiny room, their long hair falling over their shoulders, reading late into the night, marathons of one fat volume after another, the room in darkness except for the tiny pools of light from the reading lamps above their heads. One by one, they would drop out, Shelley, usually the first to turn off her lamp, Kate not far behind. It was Donna who took diet pills to stay up late and read and smoke cigarettes.

But that wasn't enough for Kate. She took intensive Russian, which met five days a week at 7:35 A.M., true concentration-camp hours. It was taught by "professors" who she was sure were CIA/KGB operatives. What better cover than teaching Russian in a college in Washington, D.C.?

Goodness, she hadn't thought about those days in a long time! By now her lips had traveled down Boris's body and she was nibbling on his toes. He was breathing deep with pleasure. In her arms, in her mouth, she held her own little bit of Russian literature, a real Russian poet, a dissident, an émigré, a man whose suffering and pain made her feel alive. As she straddled him with her body and stared at his face while she moved on top of him, she silently vowed her life to him. This wasn't love; this was something bigger, something much more important. She would make his life sweet, she would try to give him everything that had been taken away from him. Maybe he didn't love her now, yet, but she didn't care. She would be so good to him, he would find himself needing her, wanting her and, finally, loving her. She watched him as she came deeply and noticed a look of despair on his face. She lowered herself down next to him and kissed him on the cheek. She fell asleep in his arms, and when she woke up the next morning, he was gone.

Boris Loves No One

AFTER DRESSING QUIETLY so as not to disturb her, Boris stood in the doorway of Kate's room to observe the sleeping woman he had just left alone in the bed. How he envied her this sleep, so effortless. His eye admired the picture she made and he remembered his camera was still on her bureau. He liked the way the down duvet exposed the graceful curves of her back, how her chestnut hair scattered lightly upon her neck, those swimming shoulders, and her arms weaving in and out of the tumble of pillows. He would call it *Woman Asleep with Manhattan Outside Her Window.* The cat was curled tightly in a ball, asleep in the nook between her legs. He smiled. That cat was no dummy; she knew the best place to be. He snapped the picture and Boo looked up.

He sat down on the love seat in her bedroom, not yet ready to leave her feminine lair. Ahh, his damned insomnia! It not only ruined his nights but tortured his days with a merciless exhaustion. How the haunting thoughts of his past came tripping in the window of his atelier while all of Paris slept, dreaming only of their café au lait and fresh croissants. What provincial salopes those Parisians were! Night was a dangerous time to be wandering through the murky places of his soul, for he knew the rules of life were suspended in those few hours between pitch dark and dawn. He would make himself get dressed and walk down to the Marais. He needed to be around people to feel safe. At least the whores on the street were friendly. They knew from his gait that he wasn't a customer, but a kindred, restless spirit out on the street for a stroll. He often ended up in one of the quartier's picturesque, seedy all-night cafés, where the fishermen hung out in the early hours of the morning. He liked to stand at the bar and treat himself to a steaming bowl of fresh fish potage while he listened to colloquial French banter around him. A few cognacs later, he would stop at his boulangerie, where the baker knew him, and pick up a hot ficelle from the first round of the night's baking and head home to wrestle with a few hours of unhappy sleep.

At these times he was often plagued by memories of his whining brother, a victim of the Soviet dream. He wondered about cherished friends he left behind and to whom he had never said a real good-bye before leaving on his unsuspecting, one-week trip to see his French wife in Paris. "Of course I'll be back," he reassured them. "My whole life is here." No one could be told; sometimes he was too frightened to admit it even to himself. Just before he left he was fretful and restless, taking long walks through his beloved Moscow at night, crying as he tried to memorize places in his mind, making soul imprints that would be the only souvenirs of his life. He mourned his friends as he thought of the price they would have to pay for his vanishing. Visits from KGB, invitations for interviews "downtown." Promotions and raises denied. They would never get his letters. He would be dead.

He worried constantly about the frail health of his mother, and the fact that he would never see her again made him weep. They would never let her out for a visit, and even if they did, he was not so sure he would want her to come. To arrive in Paris and see the aesthetic abundance, no, excess, the decadent beauty of marzipan fruits piled high in a store devoted entirely to the art of marzipan. The épiceries, papeleries, parfumeries, all bursting with pleasures—it would all be too much for her. To realize at her late age that she had spent her entire life in hell, and for what? Oh, the nonsense that had been his life in Russia. The hours he spent on lines to buy food must have amounted to five years at least. The stupid games he had to play with people's psyches to get what he needed made him feel like a prostitute. No, it would be better if she stayed there.

People had no idea what it was like to walk out of your life—leaving *everything*—your unmade bed, the milk frozen in the ice on the windowsill, your beloved cat after a pat on the head, your cherished books, your photographs, your *life*, leaving it all to turn into a ghost town in your mind.

Now he was paying for his freedom with mutilated letters from home, having his atelier roughed up by vulgar KGB thugs and being followed —not all the time, but on occasion, just enough to remind him and make him uneasy, their way of saying, We don't like people who don't play by the rules. So stupid how their Soviet-made suits gave them away. But it's what they wanted, to instill that perfect little bit of uncertainty. Oh, they were so good at that! He got the message. He was also paying for his freedom with his health, suffering now for the nonexistent medical treatment he had been forced to endure. He could thank the Soviet Union for his weak heart and his bad lungs.

Poor Katia, he couldn't blame her. He tried to explain, but she just didn't know, like most Americans didn't know. She had asked him the stupidest questions, like "Well, what sort of things did you cook?" He remembers the fury he felt, and then, a new emotion, intense embarrassment at having been forced to live a life of humiliation.

In a sarcastic tone he told her, "Whatever you could find, dear, with the rubles in your pocket. Then you took it home and put it in a pot with an old shoe and cooked it."

"Your country is a bad joke, baby," she said sadly.

"A bad joke with very big bombs," he said icily.

"But if they can't build a building... you know I read in *Time* how they forget to put sand in the cement, so before it's finished, it's falling apart, and if they can't make elevators work... how is it that they can actually build bombs?"

"Ah, now that is a scary question," he said, laughing.

He could never let go of these thoughts, of the rape of his life and his beloved country by the Soviets. And for what? A country that treated its people like children, all the time depriving them of their right to happiness? A country where you had to learn to operate outside the entire system in order to feed, dress and take care of yourself? A place where a simple thing like putting a letter in a mailbox was akin to posting it in a garbage can?

Now he was fighting a new battle, struggling against the stupidity of time to write, write, write. All he wanted was solitude and sunlight, the space and freedom to write. Even so, in his darkest hours he longed to return to Russia. He missed the sharp bite of life and the intensity of personal relationships. He found himself pining for the strangest things, like the wide Moscow boulevards teeming with people muffled under fur and scarves, their eyes peering out in a dull glaze, revealing nothing. He missed the squeak of hard-packed snow, the sting of a glass of hot tea in his hand, the sweetness of pressing his body against his Russian girl-friends as they rode down the surreal, ten-minute-long metro escalators into the underground. Westerners could never understand how he could even dream of going back. How could they? They had no idea what he was talking about when he tried to explain to them these things. So he stopped.

There was a price to pay for everything. In the U.S.S.R., he could get by on very little money, but in Paris, he was forced to worry about money all the time. How to earn money? How to live? What he consid-ered necessities had quickly become poisoned by the seductions of Pari-sian life. In Paris, a leather jacket by Issey Miyake became a necessity; a Kenzo sweater, something he just couldn't live without. He was ashamed of this horrible new sickness that descended on him. France was not like America when it came to getting part-time jobs. No such thing as waiting on tables while writing the great Russian novel existed in France. Being a waiter was a full-time career, an honored profession; men supported whole families on their earnings. Besides, he sniffed, it was beneath him, he had already wasted enough time in Russia with his life. He wasn't going to give in to the bourgeois game of earning a living and trying to write on the side. No, he was going to do it on his terms, make life bend to his will. No more compromises, no more games, he was going to be a tough bastard.

The intensity of his thoughts woke Boo up. She noticed him sitting on the love seat, jumped off the bed and came up to him with a plain-tive look. She meowed loudly in a show of sympathy. "Tais-toi," he said, bending down to pet her. He glanced at Katia to see if she, too, had been awakened by the rampage of his mind.

Why couldn't he just love her and be normal? He had made it a rule never to waste his time thinking about other people's problems, but he did feel sorry for her. She was so caught up in her bourgeois dreams. It wasn't her fault, he reasoned, she was just living her American life to the best of her ability, confused in the mess of her silly American prob-lems. She had the capacity for a deep, rich life, but instead she was tangled up with her stupid shrink and asking all the wrong questions. Should she get a new job? Should she have her teeth capped? Why couldn't she lose weight? Why was she so lonely? Why couldn't she meet men? Should she stay in New York City? Should she join a new health club? What course should she take at the New School? She was so much better than all of this, but she was undiscovered to herself. What she needed was very simple.

"Love yourself!" he admonished her one day when she had gotten tangled up in her absurdities. He said something so painful, it seemed, that she looked alarmed. He stroked her hair gently. "Love yourself, baby," he said softly, "it's the hardest thing to do."

For about two seconds he tried to imagine why he didn't want to create a new life for himself with a woman, start a family and surround himself with softness and support. A future circle.

He just couldn't! It meant compromise, it meant stupid things like who buys the groceries, you never make the bed, should we have a femme de ménage, you forgot the bread, what should we have for dinner, no, we had that last night. Such bullshit! It degenerated from lust and love into a battle in a prison. Too much of his precious time would be taken up with the business of living. No, he wanted acres and acres of solitude. He wanted to speak to no one before noon every day. He didn't want to have to yell out, "Good-bye! I'm leaving for tennis. I'll be back at five!" The way he lived now, he kept his life all to himself. His writing friends knew nothing about his tennis friends, his neighbors knew nothing about his work, his girlfriends knew nothing about his tennis friends. No, everything must be kept separate and private.

This was both his heaven and his hell. The solitude of his life tortured him, and yet it was what he most craved. Ironic, how on Christmas Day in Paris he longed for nothing more than to be invited into a large family, to drink champagne with relatives caught up in the struggles among themselves. The idea of grandchildren, children, husbands, wives, lovers, brothers, sisters, cousins, nieces, nephews, aunts, uncles and parents. He loved the complexity and the messiness of it, the misconnections, the laughing, the hurt feelings and tears and petty misunderstandings, the belonging, the timelessness of family life, the grand drama on such an intimate scale. He smiled. What a sentimental bastard you are, Boris! But in private only. Sentimentality and family life was fine for other people, but not for himself.

He caressed Boo once more and left Katia's room, letting himself out of her apartment, closing the door carefully behind him. He rode down in the elevator silently. On the street, he left his coat open and breathed deep the icy January air; ah, he loved it! Paris was never cold enough for him. He decided to take a stroll and savor one of his last nights in New York City. Besides, he couldn't sleep anyway. He realized he was nervous about going back to France. Paris now seemed too precious, too finicky. How could he bear the nasty, constipated, scheming French after this dazzling fling with the Big Apple? Americans were so open about their desires and motives. They just named what they wanted and then figured out a way to get it. A perfect vulgarity. Here, there was an intoxicating sense of possibility. Everyone was in their own world, doing exactly what they wanted to do, and if they weren't, well then, they were tortured with the knowledge that they *could* be doing it. This divine energy had crept into his system. He believed that here in New York he could make things happen for himself.

It was a weeknight, so the upper East Side was relatively quiet, but still jumping by Parisian standards. The singles bars were doing good business; he noticed the yuppies on the street, rushing home in their business suits from their late suppers. The delis were lit up with neon, their windows an ugly jumble of beer bottles, magazines and muffins. No gorgeous window displays like in Paris. Oh well, that was one thing the New Yorkers could learn from the Parisians. The life of an urban Parisian had its points, he had to admit. Paris in one way was a most pleasant place to be a poor writer, for he still had his great wines and excellent fromages, tennis afternoons at the Luxembourg. . . . The visual treats were free, vistas that let his spirit soar, café society, places to put his ass down and daydream.

Ah, but the French were so nasty to foreigners. How delightful to find the New Yorkers loved his accent. He was welcomed instead of spat upon. He was considered to be someone special, mysterious and alluring. And the way American women flirted with him, my God! Outrageous! He started laughing. They must be so starved! The ludicrous American men were about as flirtatious and sexual as balls of wet dough. How they ignored these beautiful women on the street! No wonder American women adored foreign men on their trips abroad. They loved the attention there, and for good reason! Now he had come to a sore spot within himself. For French women, he did not exist. They looked right through him as if he wasn't there because he was not French.

He could probably live very comfortably here in New York, earning his living as a writer or in a variety of odd jobs, and getting by for just being a Russian émigré. He had seen it happen to other Russians. Maybe he could get grants for his writing. Katia had given him a whole book filled with grants just waiting to be asked for. Incredible. He could teach. Certainly, he would have no problem finding women to take care of him, if that's what he wanted. But the crux of the matter was he didn't want to start all over again in a new city. It would be too painful to build his life from zero once again. No, Paris it would have to be. A gentler life would be the price he would pay. New York would be like going back to war, and he would need to learn a whole new set of combat skills. He would maintain his friendship with Katia. She could be very helpful to him here in New York while he stayed in Paris.

Boris made his way back to the apartment on Park Avenue, where the shift had changed and there was a different elevator man, one who didn't care when he came and went. He stayed up all night, switching channels on the cable television and eating Haägen Daz ice cream right from the container with a spoon. It reminded him of Russian ice cream and it made him very happy.

Kate Hates Frank

ONE THING KATE never told Dr. Manne was how she liked to dance alone in the living room, late at night, in the dark.

Dancing alone, or rather, dancing with herself, she called it, was something she had started when she was about twelve, living at home in the suburbs. Her parents had finally bought a cheap stereo, and when they went out for the evening, or when her mother pulled the car out of the driveway to go grocery shopping on a Saturday afternoon, Kate would watch from her upstairs bedroom window, run down to the living room and put on some music very loud and prance among the coffee tables.

Sometimes she would dash into the kitchen, fling open the fridge and rummage through the vegetable drawer until she found the perfect carrot, cucumber or zucchini. Then she'd slink back into the living room, and holding the carrot as a microphone, she would pretend she was a singer in a rock-and-roll band, singing her heart out, gyrating her hips, flailing her arms about in a precise, choreographed routine, driving the young men in the audience wild with their fantasies about her, the queen of rock and roll, the high priestess of jazz, the angel of folk. "Pissing and moaning music," her father called it. The music changed as the times changed. First, there was Dionne Warwick and Lesley Gore, then the Beatles blasted into her life and she became a Beatle-maniac. She joined the official Beatles fan club, she wore a leather Beatles cap to school and made Beatle necklaces from Beatle bubblegum photo cards. She wallpapered one entire wall of her bedroom with photos from Beatle magazines and even sent away for a two-inch-square piece of Paul McCartney's sheet. She would strut about to *Sergeant Pepper's Lonely Hearts Club Band*—a real razzmatazz show she put on for that one, playing all four parts and sometimes even assuming the role of the mysterious "fifth" Beatle, the woman they all loved. Later on, she grew into Bonnie Raitt's raunchy blues. "I don't have to beg you to love me, 'cause somebody else will," she'd wail. And when her mother walked back in the front door, she would be sitting quietly on the sofa, reading a book, a little bit out of breath.

Now she was an adult woman, thirty-three years old. True, it was her own living room in her own New York apartment and now she only danced in the dark, but still, Kate was worried. Was dancing with yourself the same as playing with yourself? Was she a pervert or psychologically retarded in some way? Surely her fantasy life should have escalated into some new X-rated territory by now. She thought of her friends who had gone on to new forms of gratification, past marriage and childbirth into stenciling folk-art designs onto wooden floors and making Shaker chairs from kits, while she was still stuck in adolescence, dancing in the dark. She wondered, Did everyone have their own secret fantasy flare-ups? Maybe they did, but didn't act on them? The more she thought about it, the more confused she became. No, she finally decided, there was something deficient here; it was time to have her fantasies met in some real-life manner.

She refused even to discuss this with Dr. Manne because it was too humiliating and that made her resent him even more. What good was an analyst if you couldn't tell him your fantasies or things that worried you? She was sure this represented some flaw in him because she didn't feel safe enough to reveal these shameful things. Why, dancing in the dark was just the tip of the iceberg when it came to her fantasy life. At the office, the art director she worked with had gone so far as to present her with a blown-up, life-size photograph of Ricardo Montalban, so well known was her propensity to live on "Fantasy Island." Whenever she went off on a tangent, he would just shake his head and point at the picture of Ricardo.

Oh well, she thought, other people have sex, the least I can do is dance. And suddenly she was an alluring woman in a bar where there was no dance floor. That was very important, that added to the coolness of it all, the you-people-don't-have-any-imagination attitude she liked to think she had. Seized by an ambiguous look across a crowded room, she and this man—why, wait, it was Mikhail Baryshnikov—started a sophisticated flirtation, a come-hither sort of opening, and then found themselves in each other's arms in a dance of tremendous style and verve. The patrons in the bar were captivated by them, these two strangers in the night dancing so sublimely and with such abandon.

For Kate, what mattered was the magic of these two souls, never having danced together before, suddenly transported by their individual passion into the perfect, synchronized dancing couple, each magically knowing the other's moves and flowing as one. That's where the mystery lay. Oh, if only life was like a musical where people could burst into song and dance over a glance.

On this particular night she put on Rod Stewart's sexy rendition of "Tonight's the Night" and started with slow, sultry moves, building slickly to a rite of sexy bird and catcalls. Kate watched her shadow on the walls as she danced so smoothly, so splendidly, if she did say so herself. Then, breathless, she stopped. She sensed something eerie. With heart pounding, she ran to the window, hid behind the drapes and peered out from behind them, wondering if what she suspected was true. Was the janitor across the street watching her? The moonlight had given him away. No, the moonlight had given her away. All right, the moonlight gave them both away.

As she stood behind the drapes poking her head out she saw him gazing in the direction of her window with glistening eyes that seemed to beg for more. Oh God, did he go home to his wife and say, "Sweetie, you'll never believe these poor, horny, Upper East Side ladies!" Was she going to start getting weird phone calls with heavy breathing? Was he going to hide in the shadows and attack her some night when she left the apartment?

But the fantasy went on. While she danced with Baryshnikov, there was always one man sitting alone in the crowd gazing at her. He represented the man who wanted her but could never have her. This she couldn't figure out. *Why* couldn't he have her? To make matters worse, this man always turned out to be Dr. Manne.

Was it because she was so angry with him for not loving her? She felt so rejected by him that she wanted to reject him first. So she made up the idea that it was he who wanted her so she could slap him in the face with his desire. This is what love drives people to do? How awful. This was getting sick, really sick. She knew that professional etiquette and duty demanded no personal relations between the two of them. So he played doctor and she played patient as they slugged it out in the motions of psychotherapy. Still, she wanted nothing more than to make him pay for all the suffering he caused her.

Even though she had decided that she was in love with Boris, she couldn't stop thinking about Dr. Manne. She thought about him all the time; it was awful. She cooked her meals in his name, as if for him. Now what would he like for dinner? she would ask herself when she was strolling down the aisles of the market. When she tried clothes on at Bergdorf's, she studied herself carefully in the mirror, trying to gauge whether this outfit or that would please him more. All the while she wondered, was he equally obsessed with her? She tried to read his behavior in their sessions. For the most part he remained a cool enigma, but occasionally she saw the tiniest glint in his eye that gave her hope.

But instead of trying to charm him into loving her, winning him over seductively, she went to her sessions seething, caustic, sneering and putting him down every chance she got. They were engaged in a sophisticated chess match of wills. She watched as he tried to retain hs analytic manner, but once she smelled that he was afraid of her, it was all over. She was able to manipulate him and both of them knew it.

"Say, Frank," she said just this week, "where'd you get that watch?"

It was the first time she used his first name and she thought she saw him cringe. He always called himself Dr. Manne when he had to call her to reschedule an appointment. "I'd like to speak to Kate Odinokov," he'd say politely when she answered her office phone. "It's me, it's me," she'd say, knowing it was him immediately. "This is Dr. Manne," he would say formally.

"What about my watch?" he asked in a noncommittal voice.

She lit into him with the gusto of a vampire having tasted blood. She was delighted because he was the analyst and he had to take it, those were the rules. She could "act out" and he had to be the mature one and figure it all out. She didn't care what it all meant, she just wanted to let him have it.

"No one wears digital anymore, or haven't you heard? Well, I guess it's a watch you were given by someone, because no one would choose such a kitschy thing for himself. You know, it looks like the kind of watch someone from Indiana would buy. But you should be careful."

"Why is that?" he said evenly.

"Because a watch really tells a lot about a person." A pause. "Just like shoes do."

They both looked down at his shoes and he couldn't keep himself from laughing. She tried to keep very still, with a severe look on her face, hoping her tone would make him nervous about his tasseled loafers. She watched closely as he tried to keep the wildness out of his eyes. She knew that he knew that she was baiting him. But she also wanted him to see the truth in what she said. She wanted to make sure he understood her tremendous good taste and admired her for it. Didn't he see that even if she wore just a simple black skirt and sweater, it looked different and, well, special on her?

"Why are you doing this?" he asked.

"Doing what?"

"Talking about my watch and shoes."

"I'm trying to help you, your coming from the Midwest and all, I just think you could benefit from my style." She shrugged her shoulders as if he had some problem.

"Is this how you want to spend your sessions? Talking about my watch and shoes? What are you really feeling right now? You hate me very much, don't you?"

She became very quiet. No! She loved him. No! She hated him. Inside she was churning with fears and uncertainty; her feelings overwhelmed her. She was desperately unhappy and couldn't find her way out of her confusion.

Just when he thought things had calmed down, she started in on him again. "But you know, Frank, it's not really the watch, it's your ties that drive me crazy. What are they, polyester? So short, so wide, so beige." On and on, one by one, she picked his wardrobe apart.

Another day she lit into his office, starting with how badly the paintings were framed. "Whoa, let's back up, forget the framing, let's talk about the paintings themselves," she said. *Reproductions* of oils? Was he serious? And then she moved on to how terribly they were hung. She launched into an explanation about the proportions of paintings to wall space and the famous theory of eye level and the alignment of lines.

There was the day she lifted up the rug. "Don't you know about rug pads? You really should treat yourself to one; after all, you spent some change on this imitation dhurrie rug. My mother always said, 'Rugs love rug pads.' A pad puffs out the rug and makes it last longer."

Despite her tone, she really *was* trying to help him, to shape him up, as it were. There were times when he even agreed with her yet wouldn't budge and damn, how she hated that! Like the time she told him his huge areia palms would love to spend the summer out on the terrace outside his office, and he agreed, but did he put them out? Of course not. He would never do anything she said.

One day after such an attack he asked her, "Is this how you flirt?"

No answer.

"Is this how you treat the men you love?"

No answer. She thought about Boris. She treated Boris ever so sweetly. More silence.

"Why are you so angry at me?" he asked softly.

All this worked Kate into a frenzy. Her mind raced: Why am I such a monster? She was in a panic. Every time she sat in his waiting room with the nervous anticipation of laying her eyes on her loved one, she begged herself to be nice him, for that was what she really wanted. With each session came the sense of a fresh start, a new chance to behave properly, and that made her love him even more. There was that conspiratorial glance when he came out to get her, the way he signaled her silently with his eyes; it's time, come in, talk to me. She would get up and follow him into the room like a zombie, delighted to be with him and yet dreading to find herself there under the delicate tenderness of his gaze. He sat in his chair with that receiving look on his face, waiting for her to begin speaking. Sometimes she caught a look in his eyes that she thought said, "And how are you going to beat me today?" And sure enough, she would start in on him again, much to her own dismay.

Frank Hates Kate

IN HIS SESSIONS with Dr. Janet, Frank railed against Kate. How could a patient affect him so much? He tried to be nice to her, and the nicer he was, the more she unleashed her wrath. Maybe he shouldn't have her as a patient if he had this effect on her and she had this effect on him and what was going on here anyway? He was trying to hold on to himself through the whirlwind of her emotions, but his grip was weakening. Then he got angry at Dr. Janet because she wouldn't tell him what to do.

Finally, one day, he lost it. There was "the episode," as it came to be called by everyone—Kate, Frank, even Dr. Janet called it that. If only the mind could be like a video cassette where you could erase a bad memory. But no, the episode would forever be his souvenir of Kate.

He had finally succeeded in getting her to move from sitting up in the chair to lying down on the couch. He loved it when his patients agreed to lie down on the couch; it made him feel more like an analyst. It deepened the way in which he was able to listen to a patient and it was easier to slip into an analytic reverie when he wasn't being watched.

He recalled everything about that day; the details were etched painfully into his mind. When Kate walked in the door of his office, he never knew what to expect, the lady or the tiger. He both dreaded and looked forward to her sessions, remaining wary until she had spoken her first few words so he could see which it would be.

It always took her ages to get started and this day was no different. He watched her preparations with amusement and annoyance as she settled herself on the couch, adjusted her skirt, crossed her legs, brushed a piece of lint off her shoe, pushed up her sleeves, inspected her manicure, ran her hands through her hair, cast a lingering glance over the titles of the psychology books on his wall unit, took a deep breath and finally started talking. She reminded him of Ed Norton in "The Honeymooners," who was famous for all that preparatory posturing before settling down to eat or face his opponents in a game of pool. Today, he couldn't contain himself. "Have you ever seen 'The Honeymooners?'" he asked her.

"No, I've never seen 'The Honeymooners,'" she mimicked. She didn't bother to ask him what his comment meant, because she was consumed of late with Boris. He was glad she had fallen in love with this curious Russian because he thought it might give him a reprieve. Little did he know.

She sighed, groping around for a topic of interest in her mind. "Hmmm. I'm angry at you today," she whispered in a timid voice.

"I'm listening," he said quietly to acknowledge her and give her permission to continue. This was a common opening for therapy patients but a first for Kate. She was starting to be able to name and express her feelings. Good, he thought, maybe we'll get into something interesting right away.

"Well, I don't know. I had a fantasy. But I'm afraid to tell you." She looked at him to see if it was okay to keep talking.

"Go on." He nodded, steady.

"It's not a fantasy really because fantasies are happy, aren't they? I'm thinking more of a negative fantasy. Something . . . um . . . not nice." She lay quietly for a while. There was no particular urgency or anger in her voice.

When he didn't answer, she continued. "Well, what I want to do is to go up to your bookshelves and throw all your psychology books—no, fling them on the floor. I want to have a tantrum." She lay there calmly as she spoke, staring at the ceiling.

Suddenly he found himself yelling at her at the top of his lungs. It was he who had the tantrum. "I'm sick and tired of this! All you want is my penis! When will you realize you can't have my penis?

"Don't you see," he continued in a seething rage, "that you can't have my penis, so you want to ruin my books? Yes, I have a penis! Yes, I enjoy using my penis! And no, I will never use my penis on you!" He kept saying the word *penis* over and over again as if it was liberating for him to say it.

He stood up and marched over to the door and flung it open. "This session is over," he announced.

Through his own confusion he could see Kate was stunned. During his extraordinary outburst she had been absolutely quiet, gripping the sides of the couch with her fingertips. She turned her head to the door, where he stood fuming, and stared at him. When she saw his fury, she got up quickly and scooted past him with a frightened look on her face, as if she had been a naughty little girl.

Frank shut the door behind her and immediately went into a panic. Oh my God! He started shaking. He paced the room, wringing his hands. No, no no! This didn't just happen! He went to the phone and dialed Dr. Janet. She wasn't in, so he told her answering machine the whole story. "What should I do, what should I do?" He despaired. "I don't know what got into me." He was frantic for his lack of professional behavior. The rest of his day was hell. He couldn't get over what he had done. He thought about the rest of his female patients and nothing like this had ever happened. Their falling in love with him didn't affect him at all. What was it about Kate that pushed so many buttons in him? Okay, so Jo Anne had pointed out that he liked Kate, but why did he find it so threatening, and how could he be attracted to a woman who treated him so awfully? He was just having countertransference on her transference, wasn't he? After all, since she didn't really love him, he didn't really like her either, right?

When Dr. Janet finally reached him later, she counseled him to do nothing, to wait and see how Kate responded to it all first. Damn! This was the part about being an analyst that he hated, how he had to play analyst when he would rather play person and just phone her, apologize and ask her how she was feeling.

He was so relieved when Kate called him that evening at home. He had been hoping she would. He tried to keep an even keel on his voice.

"This is Kate and I'm very upset," she said, her voice shaking. Then she started crying so hard she could barely talk. "I'm so angry at you!"

"I'm very—"

She interrupted. "I'm upset because you're always asking to hear my fantasies and here I told you one, a rather tame one at that, and you freak out."

"I'm sorry. And you're right. I'd like to hear, right now, everything you have to say," he said.

"Well"—she sniffed—"why did you yell at me like that?"

"I don't know." He sighed loudly into the phone. He wanted to communicate his distress to her. It felt like the first time he felt he was speaking naturally to her. "You keep pushing me and pushing me for a reaction, and well, you finally got it."

"It was awful," she said.

"Yes. And when you finally got a rise out of me, you didn't like it. It makes me wonder, Kate . . ." He drifted off into thought.

"Wonder what?" she asked softly.

"Is this what you do to men, push them away from you?"

She didn't answer. They had a few moments of silence over the phone. Then she said, "You know, today I was so upset, I told all of this, what happened in your office, to a friend of mine. And he told me that this was not about my wanting your penis; rather, it was about *you*. It is about *you* being afraid of *me*."

He took a deep breath. Here goes, he thought. "There is some truth to this," he said.

"So," she mused, "you like me."

He could almost hear a smile dawn on her face over the phone. He stayed on with her until she had finished her say and felt better. He told her that he had been wrong to end the session like that and that he apologized. She was silent. Finally he said, "Is there anything else you'd like to tell me?"

"No," she said. They hung up.

When Kate came in for her next appointment, she stood in the door of his office. "It seems that there are some things that are too personal to discuss with you," she said in a condescending but gentle tone. "They upset you too much." He watched for a long moment as she looked at the couch and then at the chair and then back at the couch. Finally, when she chose to sit down in the chair, he knew she would never lie down on the couch again and he heard the window shut on the secrets of her soul.

Boris Leaves Kate

ON THE MORNING of his last day in New York, Kate played hooky from work and picked Boris up at his apartment for one last walk together in the city. With arms linked, they ambled slowly through the wintry gray of Central Park. They didn't speak. The forlorn and desolate park heightened her feelings of sadness and confusion at losing Boris. How can this be, she thought, he drops into my life and now he must leave? Just like that? Everything made her sigh. The charcoal-colored bare tree branches etched sharply against the low, puffy sky, the empty park benches that on hot summer days were filled with lovers and their ice-cream cones. She stopped at one of her favorite vistas, the overlook at Bethesda Fountain, and pointed to an arbor of trees and benches in the distance.

"Doesn't it look just like Paris?" she sighed.

"No baby, not at all."

"Yes it does. It does too," she said, pouting.

He shrugged his shoulders and they continued walking. She knew he didn't like her romantic ideas about Paris, where she had studied for a year during college. Yes, Paris was beau-ti-ful, he said, but she—he always called Paris she—was also an impossible bitch of a woman. It was easy to live in Paris and have sentimental thoughts, the city seduced you so. Maybe that was why nothing got done in Paris like it did in New York—the Parisians spent their time being charmed with the *idea* of their lives. Perfect for Kate. Boris tried to convince her that she was at odds with her New York life, because he felt she was a European woman. He gently suggested that perhaps she might be happier living in France or Italy, and he always ended discussions such as this by yelling at her. "And baby, get rid of your bloody shrink. Live! Just live!"

They strolled up Columbus Avenue, then walked back through a different part of the park to her place, where he planned to cook her a final meal. Halfway home, in the middle of the park, she suddenly felt very sick to her stomach. By the time they were in her neighborhood, she told him she had to pee desperately. He tried to make little jokes about it, to put her mind off it so she could make it home, but he saw that she was in tremendous pain. When they finally reached her apartment, she fumbled with the keys, threw open the door and ran screaming into the bathroom. He went into the kitchen to start their lunch.

"Damn!" She emerged from the bathroom close to tears.

"What?"

"There was blood in my urine. That can only mean one thing: urinary infection. Oooh, I hate it! It's awful! Why does this happen to me?" she moaned.

Boris panicked. He hadn't understood a word she said. He rummaged through the black leather bag he always carried with him and pulled out his Russian-English dictionary. "Find it," he said, handing it to her. Having no idea what she was going to come up with, she flipped through the pages while he stood there impatiently. She handed him the dictionary with her finger on the entry *cystitis* in English, followed by a definition in the Cyrillic characters of Russian.

"Ah, cystite," he said knowingly and with great sympathy in French.

The pain took over her whole body suddenly and violently. She felt chilled and weak. What a banal way to end her love affair. Now they wouldn't be able to make love after lunch as she had planned. She took a pill that she had saved from her last attack and phoned her doctor for a prescription. He questioned her over the phone. When was the last time she had an infection? Two years ago, she said, and realized it was the last time she was with a man. Just her luck, or was it punishment? With Boris cooking in the kitchen, she had to listen to her doctor lecture her once again about how the penis rubs inside the vagina and that she must get up and pee after intercourse, otherwise it would happen again. Then he took the name and phone number of her pharmacy and told her she could pick up her prescription later this afternoon. She went to her bedroom and changed into the clothes she liked to wear when she wasn't feeling well: pale blue sweat pants and a baby pink, lamb's-wool sweater. On her feet she wore thick white socks.

Boris prepared their last lunch of pilmeni in sour cream and dill and they ate without saying much. This surprise ending subdued both of them. After they finished eating, they moved to the couch, where she lay in Boris's arms, both of them lost in their own thoughts. This is what she craved most, the gift of sharing silence with someone. Time seemed to be very ugly just then, each moment passing in slow motion, drawing out the torture of his leaving, but at the same time passing too quickly. The final moments were heavy. Kate's heart was sad and Boris was nervous about going back to Paris.

Then, suddenly, it was time for him to go back to his apartment and wait for Volodya to pick him up in his big yellow taxi and take him to JFK. His time in New York was up! Kate accompanied him down to the lobby of her building so she could pick up her mail. She pretended it wasn't a big deal, his leaving. She tilted her head. "Bye," she said casually, and waved him off with a limp hand.

He kissed her firmly on each cheek and then gently on her mouth. "Ciao, baby," he said. He stopped at the door, paused and stared at her intensely for a final moment. She smiled a half smile, shrugged her shoulders and turned to go to her mailbox. When she looked back, he was gone.

Later, she went out to the pharmacy on the corner to pick up her prescription and spent the rest of the afternoon in bed sipping camomile tea, lost in the haze of pain from her body and sadness from her soul. She felt defeated and terribly sorry for herself. This is the price my body is paying for its pleasure? Being left alone, is this the souvenir of love? Why, she railed, was it her luck—or misfortune—to meet such an unusual, wonderful man and then have him whisked away from her? It simply was not fair. There must be a conspiracy against her. She shook her head. Don't think now, she admonished herself, you're in no condition to think anything. Just get better.

As afternoon drifted into dusk and into night she didn't bother to turn on any lights. She fed Boo, put on the Schubert that Boris loved and lay back down in the darkness, cradling herself with her arms. She tried to imagine his journey. Now he is in the plane sipping a vodka. Now he is taking the plastic wrap off the cold silverware and peering under the silver foil of his modular airline dinner. Now he is watching the movie, now he is trying to sleep and so must she. Good night, Boris. At three in the morning she awoke. She felt better and went into the kitchen to fix herself something to eat. Boo tried to lobby for breakfast and she threw a few crunchies in the bowl for her. She heated up a can of escarole soup and sat on her bed eating it, not caring that the crumbs from the Saltine crackers were filtering onto the sheets. Now he is arriving in Paris, it is morning there, a sharply bright crisp winter day. He is speaking French again, he is on the metro, he is lugging his suitcase up the three flights of stairs to his atelier. He is home. He is taking a shower. He is making himself a cup of his beloved thick coffee. He is unpacking. He is plugging in his toaster oven. He has forgotten about me?

Paris

Kate Loves Boris and Paris

KATE JUMPED at the opportunity to work on the Rémy Martin cognac account when it came into the agency that spring. She lobbied for the assignment with great energy, reminding everyone that her ideas for wine coolers had won that account, so she would be a natural on cognac. Besides that, her French was very good. There were two crucial weeks when she spoke a lot of French on the phone to the dial tone whenever she saw her creative director coming down the hall so he would truly understand what an asset she would be on that piece of business. In heart-to-heart chats she told him she felt an extraordinary affinity for cognac and it would mean seeing her ads in the best magazines, like *Vogue* and the Sunday *Times* magazine. She didn't mention that she knew it would mean trips to France to present campaign ideas to Rémy's management, based in the town of Cognac in the département of Charente.

When the time came for the first research trip to Cognac, only two out of the four people on the account could go. In the interest of fairness, the creative director made his decision by tossing a coin. There was that one awful moment when Kate's fate spun in the air. Heads, she stayed in New York, and tails, she won a trip to France. And Boris.

Boris met Kate's plane at Orly. She impatiently endured the hour-long flight from Bordeaux to Paris because she knew that at that very same time he was on his way to the airport to meet her. She searched anxiously for him when she entered the terminal and thought he hadn't come, but then saw his face peering down at her through the glass windows on the balcony. He didn't look particularly happy. Oh well, she decided, maybe he was a bit concerned about how they would be after six months; that was only natural.

She had just concluded her fairy-tale trip ("It's a job, and someone has to do it," she joked with all her left-behind colleagues) to the très sympathique town of Cognac, where she learned all about the ins and outs of cognac and fine wines. Goodness, she had been wined and dined up to here, with morning wine tastings in airy white rooms (so you could appreciate the color of the wine better), with little metal sinks by each place (to spit the wine out) and platters of French bread cubes (to clean your palate). These were followed by luncheons of five courses and five wineglasses set out in front of her. Then came the dinners. One dinner was held in a charming country farmhouse by the Charente River, another in a grotto restaurant set into the cliffs overlooking the Atlantic. Platters of langoustines and prawns piled high were brought to the table, and that was just the appetizer! At the end of the meal, hundred-year-old cognac was served! As she looked back on the trip she realized that she had been in a constant state of hangover but that she never got drunk because she kept eating the entire time.

Her bright red high heels slipped into the dry dirt clods as she walked the revered acres of the world's most famous vineyards, her fingers caressing the ripening grapes of the world's most ancient and revered grapevines. No one informed her that morning that they would be hiking through the vineyards, so she hadn't dressed correctly. No matter. Bravely, like a trooper, like the tough New York cookie that she was, she said to hell with it and marched on in her red heels. She learned the ABC's of grapes, fermenting, distilling, aging and bottling. In the redolent caves, she tasted aging cognac drawn from an ancient oak cask by a serious, young French oenologist in a white coat. She hoped she didn't look like a dumb American and was only too aware how he was watching her critically as she brought the wooden dipper to her mouth. It was so strong, the overpowering scent nearly knocked her over, and when she took a mouthful, she was on fire. One thing she would never forget was the sight of the bare-chested Portuguese men making the oak casks over fires on the ground. She was so taken by their masculinity, their sweating, heaving bodies, their strong arms shaping and bending the wood slats, that at one point she felt shy and had to look away.

The French public relations woman, a woman about Kate's own age, looked her over and Kate didn't let a thing about the Frenchwoman pass by unnoticed either. They were both searching for tips and clues as to the other's style. When Kate pulled out her red sunglasses, the ones she had bought off a jiving vendor on the corner of Sixth Avenue and Forty-seventh Street, Nicole admired them, but then Kate just loved Nicole's yellow Yves St. Laurent sunglasses. Yellow, that color would never have occurred to her; she would definitely look into it back home. She noticed Nicole stealing glances at her high-tech, black plastic Timex, while Kate coveted Nicole's elegant Cartier watch. Kate loved the stylish way Nicole lit her French cigarettes, and hoped that Nicole envied her crisp, American health style.

She enjoyed her trip to Cognac, but she couldn't wait to see Boris. Everything had worked out perfectly. It turns out Boris was apartment sitting in the eighth arrondissement, in a bourgeois, modern penthouse owned by a couple who had gone to the States for the month of July and knew that Boris needed a respite from his stuffy, dark studio. He was delighted to have their place, an aerie, white and bright, with steps leading to a private rooftop garden complete with picnic table and umbrella. The apartment was a saving grace for him, a bit of luxury in his penniless writer's life. It made July bearable.

"I detest this quartier," he said as they ascended at the metro stop, Étoile. "It is so sterile, like your Upper East Side." He struggled under the weight of her suitcase. Kate tried to take it from him, but he insisted on dragging it himself. Kate figured it was hot and he was grouchy, so she let his complaining pass. She couldn't believe she was actually here, in Paris! With Boris! So last January hadn't been a dream; she and Boris were real. It was only appropriate that she had a Russian lover in Paris; after all, she was that kind of woman, she told Frank just before she left.

"But does he want to see you?" Frank asked. "And what if he has a girlfriend?"

Kate brushed aside his questions impatiently. She assumed Boris would be just as happy to see her as she would him. "Look," she said. "I can't be responsible for how he feels. I only know that I want to see him and I have to be in France anyway, on business right? So why not? As for girlfriends..." She hadn't thought about that possibility. "He's an adult, I'm an adult. Six months is a long time. It would be naive for me to assume he'd spend all this time alone, but..." She hoped she

sounded strong. Then she said, "Something inside me tells me he
doesn't have anyone. Anyway, that's something I'll have to deal with
when I get there."

"It's wonderful!" she said about the apartment, which looked like a set
from an Eric Rohmer film. It was all white and decorated with modern
French furniture that looked expensive, but was crummily made, as she
knew most French furniture was, unless you bought the super expensive
stuff. Finally, alone with Boris in this strange apartment, after six
months of longing, she felt shy. Oh well, that's what happens when you
live on daydreams and fantasies, she sighed. Of course they had written
letters and phoned each other occasionally... but still, she was overwhelmed by his handsome, almost untouchable face and body. He was
so precise and delicate in his movements. He wore a black fishnet T-
shirt that an American man could never have worn without looking
low-class, and a pair of white pants. He came up to Kate from behind
and put his arms around her, exploring her body, and when his hands
reached her stomach he laughed.

"Too much foie gras," he said, feeling her rounded tummy.

"Yes." She was embarrassed and tried to get away from him, but he
held tight.

"You were in Bordeaux. It has the best food and wine in the world.
You're supposed to eat there. You did the right thing," he said, and let
her go.

He mixed two vodkas with grapefruit juice and they went up to the
roof and sat at the picnic table. Paris was blazing and Kate kept her
sunglasses on. After a few moments Boris reached out and took them
off. He looked at her in such a searching way that she became shy. What
was he looking for, what did he want to know? "No," she murmured,
and gently put her hand on his face to turn it away from her. But this is
what she had wanted, to be with him again. Why did she feel so self-
conscious?

"You must not cover your beautiful eyes," he said. "From me, or from
the world." Kate couldn't take his piercing eyes studying her and looked
away. They sat for a while in silence until he said, "Well, it is time for a
siesta."

"Now?" she asked nervously.

"Yes dear, now," he said, and took her hand.

That meant he wanted to make love. Even though she knew that making love would probably erase the awkwardness between them, she was hesitant. But it was the easiest way to quickly strip away all shyness and polite conversation so they could get down to themselves.

For Kate it was a dream to touch his body once again, the body she had fantasized about for months. Of course she hadn't made love with anybody else, so for her this lovemaking, his touching, the feeling of him, was a deliverance. She felt chubby and unappealingly desperate next to his well-cared-for, sinewy body. While he was inside her, she started crying. It startled him at first, but then he seemed to like it.

"Cry, cry," he said, caressing her. "For me, a woman is something wet," he explained gently. "Here"—he touched her eyes. "Here"—he touched her mouth. "And here"—he touched her cunt. He was being playful, but she didn't find it funny, so she cried even harder. These were primal tears that came from somewhere inside, somewhere very deep.

The next morning Kate slept while the Mirage jets roared across the blue French sky. It was July 14, Bastille Day, and Boris got up early to take up his post on the roof and watch the parade march down the Avenue Wagram. He saluted the jets flying overhead, with blue, white and red smoke spewing gaily from their exhausts as they zipped in formation over the Champs Élysées before circling the Eiffel Tower. Bastille Day marked the anniversary of his arrival in Paris from Moscow. He considered July 14 his true birthday, and today, he was five years old.

When Kate woke up and realized he wasn't in the apartment, she went up to the roof to look for him. The sun was already high, beating down with a vengeance. The view was magnificent, the rooftops of Paris, the Eiffel Tower, the Arc de Triomphe, all glowing and shimmering in the heat.

"My God, how you sleep like a baby," Boris said jealously. He was sunbathing nude but with a hat on. He looked so comical. "You know, I have not slept with a woman all night in many years." He was listening to the BBC news broadcast, swearing under his breath the entire time, commenting to himself about the world events. From time to time he got up from his ratty Heineken beer towel and turned on the faucet, dousing himself with the hose. He took off his hat and held the hose above his head, reveling in the icy water, giggling as it cascaded down his sun-ripened body. When Kate leaned down to kiss his stomach, it was scorched and sweet.

* * *

Her four precious days in Paris passed like a fever dream. Day in, day out of sweltering, impossible, erotic heat. It was so hot she couldn't think straight. She wandered the streets in a slight daze. Her breath was delicate and pale. Beads of sweat formed on her brow and on the back of her neck. Bees buzzed around éclairs, the red tulips in the Jardin du Luxembourg stared brazenly up at the sun. She wondered, How could they do it? It was all she could do to smile wanly and nod yes. She agreed with everything because saying no took too much. What she wanted was to sit in a café in the shade, so limp, and order citron pressé after citron pressé or maybe, round after round of bière panaché, icy cold beer mixed with icy cold limonade.

She decided the French weren't very good in hot weather. They considered it a personal insult. Heat was simply not part of the delicate Parisian mentality. It was vulgar and rude. But the weather was having the last laugh this summer and put them in their place.

Kate was very good at devastating heat. She blossomed in it. She told Boris, "New York gets very hot and very desperate in the summer. They say you can almost fry an egg on the street, it gets so hot in the city. It's true. And New York gets dangerous and nasty in the summer. Fights break out, people get killed. Life gets very basic all of a sudden. And raw. A sexual desperation lingers in the air." Every summer she moved about smoothly in a state of almost constant desire. Her motto was, "It can't ever get too hot, baby."

Whereas Boris lost all hope in a heat wave. He missed the Moscow weather, the most brittle, nasty ice cold in the world. Damp, dank, fuck-you weather. And months of it on end. He loved nothing more than to walk down a street in the subzero cold with high winds, his coat wide open and no hat. When Kate had seen him do this on freezing days in New York, she asked, "How can you do it, baby?" He just shrugged. "This is nothing," he said. "It's because my body temperature is so high," he added by way of explanation.

He coped in heat like this by showering about five or six times a day, then dusting his body in a shimmery talc, apricot scent or forest fern. She loved how these light, fruity fragrances mingled with his Russian scent. Then, every day, starting about noon, he made drinks, lots of vodkas with grapefruit juice. He wandered the apartment with a glass full of clinking ice. He took a drink into the shower, then he was really in heaven. Or he took a drink and lay in the sun. The sun part of hot weather he liked. He felt it healed him, that it went straight to his heart and made him strong. He liked to buy Tahitian Ylang Ylang oil and rub it all over his body. Because he was such a swarthy Russian, he turned almost black in the summer.

Ah, to be in love and in Paris, what more could anyone ask for? Kate loved the sensual life they led, suspended between waves of heat and silence, lost to the world in their own private existence. Breakfasts on the roof, catered by Boris, faded into stargazing under the moon, when they sought relief from the day's heat, sipping the cognac she had brought back from Cognac before they went to bed.

Boris wrote in the morning and she left him in peace, strolling the streets, shopping, daydreaming. She had no desire to go into museums or be touristique. No, this trip was not about that. Paris this time around was simply a backdrop for the man she loved. She was finally leading the international life she craved. By the time she returned to the apartment, he was in the tiny kitchen wearing nothing but a towel wrapped around his waist, merrily preparing lunch—usually a salad, bread, cheese, sausages and wine, which they carried up to the roof and ate, naked, under the umbrella. Lunch was followed by a siesta. Boris told her he loved the stillness and Mediterranean quality of love in the afternoon. While the ordinary day blazed in the afternoon's merciless white heat outside, the bedroom was dark and cooled by a fan. It served perfectly as the theatrical set for an otherworldy kind of touching. Kate dipped her toes gingerly into this new level of eros, for this lovemaking wasn't tied in with the usual romance of a candlelight dinner, it wasn't a culmination of anything. Rather, it was two people taking time out from the middle of their day and entering into an mutual exploratory pact, suspended somewhere between grace and hell. With Boris she felt more animal like and womanly. Sometimes, she even embarrassed herself.

After they woke up, they took showers and he would take her walking. He walked her all over the city, showing her his Paris, his discoveries, his favorite places, holding her hand the entire time or slipping his fingers into the belt loops of her denim skirt. "Now baby, *this* is the real Paris," he'd croon, emphatically presenting with a sweep of his hand the mansard roof of an old hotel in the Marais or a traditional working-class wine bar where they would pop in for a glass.

"Close your eyes," Boris once said as they walked down a certain street, taking her by the hand to lead her.

"Why?" she asked, eyes closed, with a smile slowly creeping onto her face.

"Because this is not an especially beautiful street." He pouted coyly, enjoying his own French affectation.

She had to admit, he did know his Paris. Never before had she been with someone who truly saw the city, who could so appreciate its splendors. They stopped every so often for courage in a café, usually a refreshingly tart citron pressé. On their way back to the apartment one afternoon they passed by the petit Arc de Triomphe du Carousel inside the courtyard of the Louvre. Boris set down his black leather bag and pulled out a Frisbee. He opened his arms wide and spun around. "Have you ever played Frisbee in such a beautiful place?" He laughed. *"Imagine!"* He never let Paris stop giving him pleasure. In fact, one of the things he found lacking in the Parisians was that they didn't enjoy Paris anymore. In the evenings Boris and Kate went to sit in the icy air-conditioned movies where they would eat Grand Marnier ice-cream bars and snuggle. *"J'adore le cinéma,"* he whispered in her ear every time the lights went down.

Kate especially loved to watch Boris do the marketing. He was at once so graceful and shrewd, so exacting and so free. He would buy impulsively if there was something really special or if it was a good buy. He knew good tomatoes from bad ones, he knew when raspberries just looked pretty but didn't have any taste, he could tell when potatoes were old. He chose fresh herbs as if they were junk food, tossing them into his basket with a "pouf." He loved walking into a fine charcuterie and seeing if there was anything worth his precious while, acting blasé and serious in front of Kate, who was openly delighted by the glistening pâtés, saucissons and hors d'oeuvres variés. He was intent on inspecting everything very critically, looking for the just right morsel for her. And when she asked him what he had just bought, he would wave her off with his hand and say, "Later baby, I'll explain you later."

On her third morning they were both in the bathroom together when Kate noticed Boris's bottle of Yatagan, his Siberian cologne, was almost empty. "Look," she said, holding up the bottle.

"Yes, dear," he said in an exaggerated Russian accent, annoyed with her because, of course, he knew darn well it was almost empty, and that would be the end of it until some windfall came in. Kate realized her mistake immediately. They finished dressing and went out to shop for the souvenirs Kate had promised to bring back to her colleagues at the agency. After all, she had been the fortunate one, getting this plum of a trip. She felt a touch guilty and a lot lucky.

By afternoon she was in a funk. Paris had gotten even hotter and became insufferable with its plague of tourists. The streets were totally congested and they were still trudging around with the list of things she had to buy. Kate descended into a gloom. She knew her trip was ending fast; tomorrow would be her last day. Four lovely days after six lousy months of being alone. What kind of love life was this? After waiting for an hour on line at a Crédit Lyonnais to change money, Boris was beside himself. This was the Paris he hated. He decided to cheer her up, to snap her out of her funk by taking her to one of his favorite places. He dragged her to Samaritaine, Paris's largest and most bourgeois department store. She complained the whole way. "Baby, I told you, I don't want to shop in department stores, we have those in New York."

He just grunted, took her hand and dragged her in and out of different sets of stuffy elevators, pulling her through crowded floors jammed with people and merchandise, then up odd sets of circular stairs that grew smaller and darker the higher they climbed. "What are we doing this for?" she asked like a petulant child, annoyed with this wild-goose chase. But Boris seemed to know exactly where he was going.

As he pulled open the final door the light blasted her. They stepped into an oasis, a silent rooftop garden occupied by only a handful of French enjoying a most extraordinary three-hundred-and-sixty degree view of Paris. Very few tourists knew about it; for some reason, they skipped over it in their Guide Michelin. Boris explained to Kate how this place had been a saving grace for him when he first arrived from Moscow. An old Russian countess who had been living in Paris for the last thirty years told him about it one afternoon when they were having tea in her bourgeois manqué apartment. He arrived at her place with a tin of caviar he had brought out of Moscow. It was the last thing of value he had; he was flat broke. He decided to present it to the poor, aging countess because she would truly enjoy it and endow it with the most value. She would make him feel like a millionaire. This is how he acted when he was poor. Instead of holding on to everything all the tighter, he let go completely. In this way, he freed himself from his own poverty.

So, he would go often up to his million-dollar view on top of Samaritaine and sit with his papers and books and work on his decrepit portable Russian typewriter, writing his first novel in the West while drinking in the priceless picture of Paris. There was no charge; it was entrée libre, but he knew he had paid dearly for the privilege of this view. His mother and all the friends and family he left behind were also paying for this view; only they weren't there to enjoy it. It was a stolen pleasure, one he could never get enough of. And now with great delight, Boris presented Katia with the view: smoky, smoldering Paris, all of it laid out like a jewel at her feet.

Kate stood there. "What?" she said. She saw nothing. When Boris swept his hand for her, she said, "Hmm," and tried to spin around and look. She realized she should be appreciative, but about what exactly? She couldn't take it in; her eyes were glazed over with her own unhappiness.

Just then she was overcome with the hopelessness of them, of the two of them, together. For the first time, she saw that Boris was a bit sauvage. He was truly alone and would never belong to her or to anyone. She did not know why she understood this then or why these thoughts chose to descend on her at that moment, only that she felt like a victim. Of him. Of herself.

Why couldn't she enjoy the moment? Love him, love them together, right then and there, on the roof? Why couldn't she throw her head back, like she was in a movie and spin around and around, laughing, hugging and kissing him? Why couldn't she push her hunger away and accept him as he was, that he lived in Paris and she lived in New York and he didn't want to change any of it. No! He was her soul mate and she wanted him! She would find a way to make him understand how important she really was to him. She could help him, she could make him love her.

Boris saw that she was caught up in her own misery and didn't see anything. He was disgusted with her. He had tried, but he could do nothing. Without saying another word, he took he hand and they went back down the stairs and all the elevators.

Back on the main floor they passed the perfume counter, and Kate said, "Wait, I want to buy you some Yatagan." He tightened his grip on her hand and kept walking. "But yours is almost out and you must have your cologne," she protested. She felt it was important that he have his signs of civilization, and besides, she saw that it was how he lived: he couldn't buy postage stamps, but he would drink expensive, single-malt whiskey. He preferred being poor in this way. He reasoned that if he spent his money on the necessities, there would never be enough left over for the truly nice things of life.

"No!" he said, and dragged her away from the Caron counter. They had a skirmish right there on the floor of Samaritaine. She started crying in total confusion as he kept yelling, "I do not want you to buy me anything! Not a thing!" He grabbed her by the hand and pulled her into the metro, punching her ticket for her. They rode home silently in the stifling heat. From the look on his face she was sure he thought she was impossible, but she didn't care. All she thought was, He is mean.

When they got back to the apartment, Boris took off his clothes and went up to the roof with his prized first edition of Henry Miller's "Tropic of Cancer" and lay down in the late afternoon sun to read. Kate slunk off to the library, where she flicked on the television. She liked to watch French TV to improve her French. She sulked as she watched her favorite show, "Ni Oui, Ni Non." It was an absurd quiz show, produced as childlishly and primitively as only the French could. Kate wondered if the fancy French TV execs knew how embarrassing this show really was? It made a mockery of the French national personality. The contestant, some poor schmuck from a provincial town like Nantes or Toulouse, was asked a barrage of questions in rapid fire and he had to answer them without saying oui or non. He had to answer with responses like, peut-être, or de temps en temp, or je l'aime. But then the questions started coming so thick and fast that the silly frogs always got caught in their underwear when the emcee tossed in a subtle question like, "Have you ever been unfaithful to your wife?" How skillfully he would lather them up, get their confidence roaring and then slip it to them. After a half hour of this nonsense, she went up to the roof.

There was a soft breeze as the Parisian dusk was finally starting to cool off the day. But just barely. Boris lay in his usual spot with a towel around his waist, reading calmly and listening to the BBC broadcast of classical music. He looked at her and put the book down. Kate came over to him and got down on her knees and put her head on his chest, feeling the warmth of the sun. She kissed each shoulder and then sat up.

"You must know yourself," he said strictly. "You must know what happened in Samaritaine. Self-analysis." He shook his finger at her. "That is all there is."

She looked at him sadly. They sat there in silence. She didn't know what to say, she felt so lost. Then he became gentle. "Love yourself, baby. It's the hardest thing to do. Believe me. Love yourself and the world will be yours."

The next morning she told Boris she had more errands to do and it would be easier if she went on by herself. Like a woman with a mission she sat on the metro, determined and calm. She knew what had to be done; it was a womanly act. She marched back into Samaritaine and went up to the Caron counter and asked for a flacon of Yatagan.

The bitch behind the counter pretended not to understand her. Kate knew from experience that this was a punishment for her foreign French accent. The woman looked at her blankly, then turned around to the other girls behind the counter with a shrug and a look that said, "These américaines are so gauche" and continued her conversation.

By now Kate had had enough of the constipated French. She put her hands on her hips and said to the counter girl in her perfect schoolgirl French, "Pardon, mademoiselle, est-ce que vous êtes américaine?" There was a ripple of laughter from the counter girls. The woman to whom her question was directed looked insulted.

"Non!" she replied arrogantly. "Et pourquoi vous m'en demandez?"

"Ah," Kate said sweetly. "Je croyais si, parce que vous parlez français avec un accent américain!" At which point she smiled her most jejune smile.

Boom. That did it. Two could play this game. That was hitting the French right where it hurt most: their precious, stupid French accent. In any other country of the world Kate had found that people warmed to you if you tried to speak their language, in fact they bent over backward, delighted at your efforts. But the French made it so hard to let you love them. You tried to, but they pissed on you all the way. After some thought Kate had developed the toilet-paper theory, concluding that the crisis in the French national personality hinged on this minor but very important product. It was obvious that the scratchy, waxy toilet paper they used in France didn't do a good job, so the whole nation was walking around with scratchy, dirty behinds. No wonder they were so grouchy! How was it possible that the French could live so close to the Italians and the Spanish and not pick up on their joyous way of life, their ebullient personalities and warmth?

When Kate saw that the French girl was sufficiently subdued after their little contretemps, she tried again. "Yatagan, c'est un parfum de Caron, pour les hommes."

"Ah oui, bien sûr, Yatagan," the girl said amicably as if *now* she understood, whereas before Kate must have been speaking in another tongue.

* * *

That night, her last in Paris, Boris made a simple farewell dinner of sausages, potatoes, onions and fennel, which they ate quietly on the roof by candlelight accompanied by a frosty bottle of Brouilly. Kate was wondering why this same French bistro dish that she had prepared on numerous occasions in New York seemed to taste better here in Paris. Both she and Boris were subdued and didn't say much. It was the exhaustion after four days of total togetherness. Kate wondered if he was sad because she was leaving. He seemed to have enjoyed her company. She was lost in her own thoughts, trying to understand this intense weeklong journey she had taken outside her life and what it all meant. She sighed as she ate, glancing up occasionally at the stars. It was comforting to realize that when she looked up at the stars in New York, he would see the same stars in Paris. They would be her cosmic link to him when she felt lonely. When they finished eating and were sitting with their wine, she took his hand and squeezed it and was happy when he squeezed back. Oh good, she thought, he's going to miss me. They washed the dishes and she went to bed. Through the slats of the bedroom door she could see him sitting in the living room. He was listening to jazz, sipping cognac and smoking a Cuban cigar a friend had given him.

She was up early the next morning. While he slept, she showered and got her bags ready for the flight. When he finally did get up, she called to him, "Don't worry, I'll make the bed." He gave her his "ça m'est éçal" look and headed for the shower. Kate took the keys and dashed out to the boulangerie to buy some warm croissants for breakfast and stopped at the supermarché to select some French saucisson to take back to New York. They were so cheap here and so expensive in the States. As she strolled back to the apartment she felt nostalgic. How she hated leaving all this behind! She was so good at the charm of French life, it suited her so well, why, she could really be at home here. She buzzed the entrance button of the apartment building and sadly pushed open the heavy door.

Before she knew it, it was eleven o'clock and time to leave for the airport. Boris was putting change in his pocket and looking for the keys while Kate stood nervously at the door. Just at the moment when they were about to walk out the door, he took a deep breath and said in a husky voice, "Well, okay then. Let us sit down."

Kate gulped. It was an old Russian religious custom that when someone was about to leave on a long trip, someone called out for a sit-down. It was a final gathering, to sit together in silence. On the surface it was to wish them Godspeed, but in reality, it was to make a final memory of being together. Just in case.

Kate was charmed and saddened by this strange custom that she had experienced as a child, but never in her adult life. She associated it with her grandparents, not with people her own age. Oh, those Russians were something. They escalated all emotions, and if a good-bye was sad, they turned it into a memorial service for the potential death of the person sitting right there in front of them. How Russian to stare the possibility of finality right in the face, to take it head-on so that you would never have that petty wish, "I wish I had said good-bye."

Boris sat down in the living room and Kate nervously took a seat opposite him. It took only about ten seconds before she started shaking and crying. She jumped up and came over to him, settling herself into his lap. He stroked her arms and looked at her, tilting his head, staring deep into her eyes. He smiled at her unconventional interpretation of the Russian custom, charmed by her sentimentality but wary of the responsibility of what her sadness meant. And so they sat in silence, she, muffling the sounds of her teary sighs until she could stand it no longer and he said, "Okay, it's okay," and stood up to leave.

At Charles de Gaulle she went into hyperspace, nervous about her flight and desperate to elicit some feelings from him about her leaving, about their future together. She looked at her fashionable Russian émigré riding the haut moderne tubular escalators and wondered why he seemed so forbidding. He held her hand, he kissed her cheek, he made little jokes and pretended to wave to people he did not know. She wanted to ask, So when will we see each other again? She wanted to tell him, I love you, I want to live with you. But she couldn't. He had put up a silent wall, drawn a line around himself that she didn't dare cross. Or was it just that he found her leaving so painful that he sought refuge in being all business, preoccupied with checking her bags, finding her gate, making sure she had enough time in Duty Free. The precious seconds were slipping by. She felt like she was in one of those forties movies where the hero and heroine secretly loved each other but didn't dare say it. Kate would sit in the dark of her bedroom, watching the screen, yelling, "Tell her you love her! Just say it!"

When it came time to say good-bye at the immigration checkpoint, she bullied herself, Don't you dare cry, Kate. Boris wouldn't want to say good-bye to a sad sack. She wanted to leave him with the memory of a lovely Kate and so she smiled bravely and turned away quickly, rummaging for her passport so he wouldn't see her burning face. She shopped at Duty Free, picking up Campari, vodka and perfumes with tears rolling down her face. Leaving Paris meant going back to her life of working twelve-hour days and being condemned, once again, to single-dom in New York.

When Kate arrived at JFK, she got nervous all of a sudden about try-ing to sneak her French saucissons into the country. Normally she was a no-holds-barred, who's-afraid-of-a-little-government-clerk, I-don't-follow-the-rules kind of gal. But for some reason on the plane she be-came frightened after reading the customs declaration form, which strictly stated, NO MEAT OF ANY KIND MAY BE BROUGHT INTO THE UNITED STATES. FAILURE TO COMPLY WITH THESE REGULATIONS MAY MEAN CON-FISCATION, IMPRISONMENT, FINES, OR EXPULSION." She saw herself sit-ting in jail because of French saucissons, so she declared them.

The custom man's eyes lit up when he saw what she had written on her yellow declaration card. "Garlicky but subtle, perfect for cocktail time with crusty French bread and cornichons, pure pork French sau-cissons."

"Let's see the meat," he said gruffly. It sounded so vulgar. When Kate pulled out her precious sausages, redolent with the wonderful aroma of garlic and peppercorns, his eyes got even bigger. "I'll have to take those," he said too quickly, trying to control his eyes and quivering mouth as he scooped them up.

Kate was furious. She stomped her foot. So that's where being a "good girl" got you! She should have just walked through like she always did. "Those will really taste good tonight, huh, officer?" she drawled sarcasti-cally.

The customs agent looked at her with a vexed look. He wanted to shoo her away. "Ma'am, these are against the law! Move along now," he growled.

How appropriate she thought as she zipped up her bag and slung it over her shoulder, moving away from the counter and out into the inter-national arrivals hall. Wait until I tell Frank about this! How perfectly Freudian! I have this wonderful, sexy time in France, and when I come back to New York, my sausages are taken away from me.

As she settled into her bed that night she thought of how Boris would already have gotten into the bed they had shared for five nights. Would he miss her a little? Or would he be pleased to be alone again? She had tried to sleep smartly and quietly, knowing not to disturb him. Just that morning he told her that her deep sleep must have rubbed off on him because while she had been in his bed he slept deeply, too.

She imagined him relishing his privacy and spreading his arm out to what had been her side of the bed. What? A crinkling noise. What's this? His hand would grope under the blanket and he would pull out a plastic bag with a box inside. A bottle of Yatagan. Un petit souvenir. He would smile. It was the perfect way to give him a gift actually, something he could find alone so he wouldn't have to thank her.

New York

Frank on Kate

EVEN THOUGH she had been gone only ten days, Frank was looking forward to Kate's return from France. Occasionally he would add six hours to the time trying to think what she would be doing now. I'm just sitting down to dinner and she's been asleep for hours, or I'm just going to bed and she's having breakfast. One day he caught himself scanning the weather page of *The New York Times* to check the forecast for Paris. "This is ridiculous," he said, and flung the paper away. When news of a plane crash at JFK came blaring over the doctors' lounge radio at the hospital, he became pale until he heard it wasn't any flight from Paris. But mostly he had been worried about her with this Boris character. Although he couldn't tell her, he didn't like a single thing she told him about their "relationship." He adamantly assured himself and Dr. Janet that he was worried from the point of view of a doctor who didn't like to see his patients get hurt. It was plain to see, this Russian poet was no good. She had illusions about him and didn't see that Boris couldn't care less about her.

So he was greatly relieved when she walked in the door on time for her appointment and flashed him a big smile. She sat down and immediately began rummaging through a black leather satchel, one that she must have bought in Paris because he had never seen it before. He waited patiently.

"It reminded me of you," she said, and handed him a bottle of cologne she had bought in Duty Free. "I know I'm not supposed to give

141

you presents, but I bought it because I missed you and I thought it would make me feel closer to you and so I brought it with me today anyway because this is how I *feel* and you are always telling me to tell you exactly how I *feel*, to hold nothing back." She took a breath and continued, "I could have left it at home, but I didn't, and you don't have to take it if you don't want to." She sat back in the chair defensively, sighing after her monologue. She made an offering and prepared herself for the rejection in one swoop.

Frank stared down at the box he held in his hands, turning it around slowly, weighing the idea in his mind. Well, it was inappropriate, but it was a nice gesture. Shrinks always had to deal with patients' presents. Goodness, it was a whole subject to be gone into; I mean, you wouldn't bring your dentist or podiatrist a bottle of cologne, now, would you? That's the example he used to get his patients to understand and explore what they were doing. Yatagan. Caron. Paris. Cologne pour homme. His fingers caressed the cellophane that sealed the box. Yatagan, what a bizarre name for a cologne. It sounded scary somehow, maybe even dangerous. No, it sounded like a country on the Risk game board, like Irkutsk or Turkestan. He preferred tamer names names like Grey Flannel and Polo. This is the scent she wants me to wear? He put the box to his nose, trying to get a whiff through the packaging, but put it down quickly when he remembered she was watching him.

"I have to think about this," he said, hesitating. "I have to think about whether I can accept a present from you." He was flattered, he wanted to accept it, but he just didn't know. Then he went into a mini panic. If he didn't accept it, he would be rejecting her. Here she had made this peace offering, fully expecting rejection. Wasn't it his job as her analyst to accept her? Already he knew he had spoken too much. He should have just said thank you and set it down noncommittally on his table and put an end to any great meaning it could have had. He put the box down and decided to affirm her act.

"How did it remind me of you?" he blurted out. "I mean, what does this cologne mean to you? In your fantasies, of course." He tried to recover by making his question sound clinical.

Kate looked shy. "Well, it's a dark, mysterious scent. Like you." She paused, searching for words. "It's commanding. Sort of like the way you sit in that chair, waiting for me to speak. Yes, that's it—it's a scent that makes me come to you, makes me do all the work, like I do in here."

Silence. Then, "It was a mistake to bring you this cologne." She told him she had a bottle of this very same cologne on her bathroom shelf and how she liked to splash it onto her breasts after a hot shower and sashay around the apartment. It was a scent she had discovered and it made her feel desirable, slinky and a little bit wild. And she wanted to smell it on him.

Frank thought, Wow, this session was going incredibly well.

They sat silently for a while until she broke down and told him the following. She began by saying she was exhausted from her own deception, lying was very tiring, but she didn't want to hurt his feelings. She didn't love him anymore. Perhaps he might have guessed; instead, she had fallen desperately (her word) in love with Boris.

Frank reconsidered. Maybe this session wasn't going so well.

"I've made a big decision," she announced, and left him hanging with a theatrical pause.

Uh-oh, Frank thought, hold on to your hats. She was looking at him as meaningfully as she could. God, she liked to be dramatic. He assumed the look of "Well?" by crooking his eyebrows and tilting his head. He didn't like to answer her teasers directly.

"I'm changing my name. I mean I have changed my name. I want to be called by my Russian name. So no more Kate. I'm Katia now."

Frank's heart started pounding. He hoped his agitation didn't show. This was bad, very bad. He had lost control of the therapy. She had gone over the edge. What was he going to tell his supervisor tonight? His palms were sweaty and he started to run his hands through his hair, he hoped casually. "And what brought this on?" he asked, making an effort to keep his voice calm.

"No, I want you to say it, say Katia, right now. Call me Katia, I want to see how it feels." She leaned back in the chair and closed her eyes in anticipation of the word coming out of his mouth.

He shifted uneasily in his chair. Now what? Should he give in to this little game? If he did call her Katia, would that mean she was getting her way with him, manipulating him as if she could order him about and thus set a precedent for the future? And if he didn't call her Katia, would that mean he was inflexible, not allowing his patient to have her fantasy? He decided all he could do was trust himself and to enter the fantasy with her to see where it would take them. Maybe it would set them both free.

He looked deeply in the eyes. "Okay, Katia." The syllables were uncomfortable for him to say.

"No. Ka-ti-a," she said, correcting his pronunciation.

"Katia," he repeated. He felt silly, not getting the Russian softness of the vowels the way she had said it.

"This isn't just for today, you know. In your notes you must start referring to me as Katia, and if you call my office to change an appointment or whatever, you must ask for Katia. It's the only way it will happen, if I insist people call me that."

"Okay, Katia."

"Don't humor me."

"I'm not humoring you. Katia."

"You see." She started bouncing in the chair. "Katia is me, it is who I *really* am. I feel good being Katia."

"Whose idea was this?" he asked.

She looked away and sighed as if he were being impossible. "My idea, of course." Then she was silent. She drew herself up. "Okay, now that we've got that settled, I want to talk about my trip to Bordeaux."

She prattled on about cognac and he watched her as she pretended to forget the earlier conversation. He tried to flow with her thoughts but all the time felt he really must press her. Finally he couldn't stand it anymore.

"Why are you being so difficult?" he interrupted.

"I am not being difficult," she said, knowing exactly what he was referring to.

"Look, I just think that if you're going to change your name, which is a very big step, that we must look into the reasons why. There are many things to consider—for instance, what are you going to tell your friends and the people at work?"

"Well, I have it all figured out," she gushed, and settled back into the chair, ready to enlist him in her cozy conspiracy. "I'm going to go home tonight and change the name on my résumé and then start looking for a new job, change advertising agencies. Everyone does that, you know. It's how you get more money and more appreciation. So when I go to work, they will never have known me as Kate. I'll be Katia from day one. Isn't that great? So that takes care of that. And besides, even if I don't get a new job right away, I'll tell everyone at work that I've repositioned myself, given myself a new concept and a new name. Believe me, that they'll understand. I mean, in advertising we're always repositioning products."

He made a face.

She rolled her eyes as if he were such a dummy. "Okay, I can see we're back in Advertising 101 here. When light beer first came out, it was called diet beer, remember Gablinger's? But the big he-men didn't want to be seen drinking "sissy" beer, so it died on the shelves. Miller got the brilliant idea of changing the name and concept to Lite Beer and told men that it was light so *you could drink more!* They turned its virtue into a nice vice. It was a brilliant marketing move, don't you think?"

Being a fan of light beer, he had to agree. Even though he drank it for its lower calorie content.

"Besides, in advertising, people like you if you're a bit off. They don't like safe people, they go more for zany. They think you're more creative when you're off the wall. Actually, my name change will appeal to them a great deal."

When she saw he wasn't convinced, she continued. "You see, I've done my homework." She rummaged once again through her satchel and handed him a neatly typed page. The heading read, "STATEMENT OF OBJECTIVES AND STRATEGIES" and the client was Kate, or rather, the product was Kate. She told him this document was drawn up on every assignment before the creative team set to work so they knew exactly what their TV commercial or print ad had to accomplish.

KATE

CRITICAL FACTS: Client is unsatisfied living as an American woman. Client feels great grief over the loss of her Russian heritage.

KEY AUDIENCE: The world at large.

OBJECTIVE: To reclaim client's heritage and the richness, therefore, of her life as a sensual Russian woman, thus adding value to her life.

STRATEGY: To reposition client as a Russian-American woman.

KEY PROMISE: Client will feel better, be happier as a Russian woman.

COPY POINTS: Client to change her name back to its Russian (original) version: Katia. Client to seep herself in her Russian heritage.

Katie told him he could keep it, that she had posted a copy of it on her refrigerator. Then she stood up as if to leave.

"Where are you going?" he said.

"Our time is up."

He looked at his watch, miffed that she had stolen his job of informing her that it was time to go.

Later that night when he was home reviewing his notes of the day, he
studied her document and then drafted another version of it in longhand
on a yellow legal pad.

KATE/ANALYST'S VERSION

CRITICAL FACTS: Kate is unable to buffalo her Russian boyfriend. Secondary: More importantly, she has no idea who she really is as a person.

KEY AUDIENCE: Boris Zimoy.

OBJECTIVE: To get her boyfriend (if you can call someone that who lives
across the Atlantic Ocean and whom she barely sees and knows) to love
her.

STRATEGY: To become Russian so she will evoke the feelings he left
behind.

KEY PROMISE: If client is Russian, she feels Russian boyfriend will fall
in love with her. Secondary: To exhaust analyst.

COPY POINTS: Same.

Frank stared at it until he didn't know what to think anymore. All this
name-changing business made him nervous. How was he going to handle this analytically? Should he get involved and try to put a stop to it?
This was all happening too fast. He got up and made himself a gin
gimlet then settled back down in his reading chair, stuffing a tiny pillow
under his back to ease the pain. He opened her folder with all his notes,
scanning slowly through the pages scribbled with his handwriting. It was
as if he were holding her life in his hands. The whole story. He sipped at
the drink and leaned his head back, closing his eyes, letting the gin seep
through his body and dull his overactive mind.

The image he had was of a drowning woman throwing her arms
around a man to save her. Man as life preserver. And he, not wanting to
go down with her, tries to throw her off. But the only way he can loosen
her grip is by strangling her. Which only makes her grip him tighter.
And so we have this dance of misunderstanding, a drunken waltz of
passion, which is, of course, death.

Frank felt that Boris had dropped into Katia's life like one of those magic bottles from *Alice in Wonderland*. He was labeled, "Obsession. Drink me." It doesn't take two people to make an obsession, just one. What is this desire of a woman's to surrender to a man, to lose herself, to melt into his being, to become him? I mean, he thought, you live your life with all its ups and downs, minor and major annoyances, pleasures, and then you meet a certain person and suddenly you can't live without them? Where a few moments ago you had been doing quite nicely. Is it a random shift in the universe? Particles bumping into each other? What is this curious piece missing in all of us that drives us to find the person who either soothes us like a drug or injects us with the divine nectar of life? What does it mean to want to be with that person, soaking them in, sucking up their essence? How hungry we are! We are all lost and we are looking.

Frank felt Katia had been sleepwalking in a depression that made her blind to all the kindred spirits she could have connected with over the years. And now she was hysterical because she felt the bloom was gone. She was used goods, slightly rumpled. She had lost that silkiness of personality, that element of surprise in her eyes. She was puffy, rounder and sadder and knew her life could have been different.

"I'm going to marry Boris," she triumphantly told Frank. "I just know it, it's some gut feeling I have inside."

"You mean you have the fantasy that you'll marry him," he said sarcastically.

"What a nasty tone of voice."

"You're right." He paused. "I'm sorry." He tried again. "It's a fantasy you have," he said softly.

"No!" She became angry. "This is it! He is the one for me! You know how people say, 'I knew the moment I saw him that we'd get married; you know how people say that? Well, this is it, this is the man I'm going to marry. I just know."

"Yes, yes. But did you ever stop to consider that the only people who say that are married people? So of course it happened to them and they can look back and say it. You don't hear that from the people who didn't marry the person they felt they would marry."

Frank thought it was very sad how most every woman he met and especially those in his practice had such tremendous fantasies about marriage and weddings, how they thought all their lives about the day they would marry. It was pap they had been fed from the time they were little girls: to be a beautiful bride, that a wedding day was the most important day in her life, the day she could look forward to, the day her life would really begin. It was pathetic.

What about men? They didn't seem to long for this day. They didn't have a picture they carried in their hearts of their ideal wedding fantasy. Most men did not relish the idea of standing up in front of a crowd of people as a groom and admitting in front of a bunch of strangers that he loved her, that he could not live without her. Whereas women found this very easy; they could just toss it off. Why was it that men could be men and be considered adults and be complete without a woman? Whereas a woman was treated as a child for as long as she was alone, because there was no one to "take care" of her.

Reality, according to Frank, was that a woman changed a man's life for the better but she became worse off. Off the pedestal and into the frying pan, that's how he viewed a woman's fall from grace and loss of power when she married. Perhaps that is why women were fed the stuff of dreams about marriage. It efficiently got them into what would be bondage and servitude to the undeveloped emotional needs of men. He felt a woman could have a rich emotional life alone; her nesting instinct would always make a home for herself. But a man needed a woman to provide all this. On the whole, he felt most men were not really up to dealing with a woman as she should be dealt with. Rare was the man, in Frank's experience, who was open enough emotionally to receive a woman truly, in all her deepest womanliness. A woman was extremely powerful, and instead of embracing and accepting this power, most men tended to belittle it, so frightened were they of it, and this set off a cycle of anger and frustration for both parties. The angry, castrating female and the confused, frustrated male. What a split this caused for him. He couldn't very well tell his patients this, and yet it was to him they turned with all their longings and anxieties. What could he do? What could he say? In the end, what did he know?

He had asked Katia, "What will your parents say?"

Oh, she dismissed his question with a wave of her hand. No problem. They'd breathe a sigh of relief. She told Frank that when she was a "young thing," her parents had set high standards about the man they imagined would marry her. He would be a doctor or a lawyer or extremely handsome, rich, brilliant, all of these things, and nothing less than an unbelievable guy. It disgusted her how their standards had edged downward as she grew older. Now that she had reached this precarious age, any man would do, as long as he had arms, legs, two eyes and didn't drool when he ate. Frank and Katia had a good laugh over that one.

He was on his third gimlet by now, getting soggy in his thinking. He had a crisis on his hands. What was he going to do?

Frank on Frank

THE REASON WHY Frank was so upset by Kate changing her name to Katia was that he had changed his name. Frank Manne was really Francesco Mangiapanne. He had gotten his Ph.D. in psychology and started his therapy practice only to discover that his patients found it amusing that their shrink was Italian. They couldn't understand, what was an Italian doing, as a therapist? What angst could he have possibly experienced in his life? Italians were supposed to be given to gratifying the senses, not repressing them, their sex drive was supposed to be healthy and joyous, not guilt-ridden and filled with dirty secrets. His patients told him the reactions of their friends when they mentioned they were seeing a Dr. Mangiapanne. "An Italian therapist?" They'd hoot and shake with laughter.

So when Francesco Mangiapanne moved to New York after slaving away on the psych ward of the county hospital in Bloomington, Indiana, he changed his name to Frank Manne. He loved it. Such freedom! He walked down Manhattan streets giggling, he was so happy. He loved finally being indistinguishable, one of the guys, an all-American male; why, he could be as insensitive as the rest of them, he could jam his tongue down some girl's throat as boorishly as his college roommate Fred Harris. He felt that as a born-again American he could be less responsible for his actions; he could raise his hands when accused of insensitive behavior and say, "Hey, I'm just a guy, what do you want?"

"Hey, Frank!" his colleagues called out at the institute, where they were the incoming class of Ph.D. psychologists studying to become psychoanalysts. He loved the idea of wearing gray flannels and boxy blue blazers with Bass Weejuns.

Only Dr. Janet knew about all this because Frank went over and over this material with her for months. "If they find out at the institute that I changed my name, they'll think I'm a nut case!" he cried. She was inclined to agree, so it was to be their secret. She also knew that Frank's intensely Italian name was somewhat hard to take seriously in the precious world of psychoanalysts. But she didn't want to tell Frank that, so she was just very positive and encouraged him to do what felt right.

That's why he panicked when Kate told him she wanted to become Katia. It was the exact opposite of what he had done. Over the past few months she had become more and more beautiful as she came closer to her Russian heritage and he was becoming more like a slice of white bread as he left his Italian roots behind.

Francesco versus Frank. Maybe he had been wrong to change his name. Well, what could he do now? Change it back? But then everyone would know what he had done and he would really suffer. Dr. Francesco Mangiapanne. Suddenly, miraculously, it sounded gorgeous to him. He called Dr. Janet immediately and asked for an emergency session. Naturally she was alarmed, but suddenly she saw lying on her couch, this extraordinarily handsome, dark, Italian doctor, so elegant, so sensual. He was in touch with a European "je ne sais quoi," and he had the most commanding name: Dr. Francesco Mangiapanne. Now that would be someone you'd want to tell all your secrets to!

"You must do whatever you think is best, Frank," she said. She paused. "Or should I say, Francesco?"

When Frank stepped out into the street, he stood up a bit higher. He hailed a taxicab and with great authority said, "Giorgio Armani, Madison Avenue, please." The driver snapped to and whisked him there effortlessly, weaving expertly through the congested midday traffic, zipping crosstown and pulling to a delicate stop outside the smoky glass boutique. It was Frank Manne who had gotten into the taxi but Francesco Mangiapanne who stepped out.

In the boutique he blanched when he saw the prices of the clothing, but once he started fingering the beautiful Italian garbardine, he knew there was no turning back. This was his heritage. He belonged in these clothes. A salesman was hovering discreetly nearby, trying to gauge who this customer might be. He had never seen him before. To judge from what he was wearing, he didn't seem to be an Armani customer.

"I'd like to try this on," Francesco said.

"As you wish, Mr.?"

"Dr. Mangiapanne."

"Ah, Dr. Mangiapanne, but of course." The salesman rubbed his hands in delight; an eminent Italian specialist, no doubt, who would spend huge sums of money, no doubt.

Francesco selected a blazer in an Italian Prince of Wales pattern. It was so soft and fell beautifully on his body. He felt the mirror was a picture frame and he was the picture. He preened for a while and felt like a better analyst already.

Two suits and a sweater later, he paid for his purchases with his American Express card. When the salesman looked at the name on the card—Frank Manne—and then at him, Francesco mumbled something about something and waved him away impatiently with his hand. When he stepped out with his Giorgio Armani bag with the tissue rustling so invitingly inside, wearing his new blazer, he felt like a million lira. He walked briskly to S'ant Ambroeus, the Italian espresso bar up the street and ordered a double espresso with grappa. As the thick coffee trickled nicely down his throat, he felt desirable and sexy. He could hear a woman's voice crooning, "Francesco, Francesco." He saw himself cooking dinner with tremendous flair, placing a plate of steaming pasta al dente topped with a biting Gorgonzola sauce in front of her as she gazed up at him with adoring eyes. Later, he would make love to her with such Latin finesse that she would do anything for him, so enraptured she would be by her Italian Francesco.

Oh my God! How was he going to pay for his $5,600 worth of new clothing; what, was he crazy? What would he tell his patients? Maybe he could be just as honest and forthright as Katia had been with him. Reclaiming your heritage was a great and proud act after all. They didn't have to know about his first name change. That's why New York was such a hell of a town. You could do anything here, get away with murder. And what a nice touch it would be if he wrote a professional article discussing his name change. Why, he could even become a specialist on name changing! Patients would come to him especially to work out this most personal of traumas and claim a new identity in his very own office.

He made a list on the napkin: change credit cards, call phone company, get new business cards and invoices, call the bank, driver's license

. . . Of course he knew all about this, he had done it all before. As he downed the last of the grappa he thought this must be how a transvestite feels, only they feel ten million times worse. He figured he was in for six months of hell, then it would blow over.

As the weeks passed by he noticed his patients becoming more emotional with him. The women wept more readily and proclaimed their love faster. "You're a man who understands!" they shouted desperately through their tears, where only a few months before, as Dr. Manne, they berated him endlessly with, "You're a brute. A typical, insensitive American man!" His male patients, who previously felt they had a comrade in arms when they confided in him, now felt his sexuality in a different way. "You bastard, you're fucking your brains out all the time! I can smell it! How can you possibly understand how horny and miserable I am?" they cried. Oh, they hated him bitterly. And throughout all of this, Dr. Mangiapanne lifted his eyes to the bust of Freud sitting on his bookshelf. You little genius, you, he thought laughingly. Here I am, the same guy, and I put on an expensive Italian suit and change my name and suddenly I'm the most sensual man in the world. Sometimes he had to hold on to his seat, so thick and fast came all the different accusations from his confused patients.

Buzz! Frank rolled over and shut off the stupid alarm clock. Damn! Morning had come too fast. What a horrible dream! He shook the ridiculous memories away and headed for the shower.

Katia Becomes Russian

Dear Katia,

How are you, tough little cookie? There's a bitter taste in mouth from letter I just wrote you and tore up. Maybe it would make a good pudding with raisins and cinnamon?

Grandfather Beethoven on radio. Windows full of ice. All Europe frozen. Minus 13 in Paris for last week now. All my window plants dead. What's happening in my life now? Chair cracked, answering machine stopped, Walkman, typewriter broken. Teapot and Scotch on strike! Even Frisbee refuses to fly.

Today I finally saw something horrible about my life. I will never be happy in West. Unhappy if in U.S.S.R. under bastard commies, unhappy if out of U.S.S.R. What a shock! I had no idea! I can't enjoy life in West because I translate everything first into my Russian soul. It gives no peace. I thought I could start over here, relax, feel in new ways, but no! But I'll take Versailles over Lefortovo anyday, thank you.

Let me say this. There are only a few people who can make this equation work: real person = his/her image. You are no different. I understand. You've seen me now in New York and Paris, and still, your knowledge is overwhelmed by some idea of me you have. Don't pout. Just take that Russian lacquer spoon in your kitchen and stir into the pudding all other ingredients of Boris: my money problems, writing problems, zany life of mine, brooding, Scotch—and add big pinch of salt. How your rotten shrink would probably love to get hands on our letters.

If you can send me some dollars, it would help. American Express best

way because so fast. Like a cable. I am sinking. Big kiss and thanks for the
life preserver of your thoughts.

Ciao, Boris

During the winter, letters from Boris would come drifting in from
time to time like snowflakes from some foreign outpost. They would
melt on her tongue and then be gone. He inhabited some version of
Paris, a Paris in Siberia, that was incomprehensible to her. True, she
knew the streets he walked on, the boîtes he spoke of, the names of the
parks he sat in, but he moved about in a demimonde she could only
dream of. Although his letters became increasingly remote and spoke of
some infinite suffering, her only thoughts were that everything would be
all right if only he let her love him.

He was a lone wolf howling in the night, that plaintive cry striking
terror in the heart of whoever might be awake to hear it. But who was
awake at that time of night? Katia happened to be and she knew you
could no more go out and help a wolf than you could help Boris. His
suffering became him, *became* as in "that dress is becoming on you." He
worshiped his own pain; it's what made him feel alive.

In order to understand him better, to empathize with his plight and to
become something, *someone* familiar to him, Katia set about her Russification task with the same gusto with which she did everything in her
life. Just changing her name wouldn't do, she wanted to *feel* like a Katia.

The most obvious physical change was that she stopped wearing
makeup. "The better to understand my Slavic face," she said after
spending hours in front of the bathroom mirror, wondering if she had
the nerve to actually do it. But after several staring sessions, she came to
appreciate her unadorned features and proudly showed her real face to
the world. She grew out her bangs and started wearing her hair pulled
back off her face in a bun. It goes without saying that she took to tying
flowered kerchiefs on her head. She took off all her jewelry, just another
bourgeois conceit, and put on the gold Russian Orthodox cross that had
been given to her by her godparents when she was christened. As she
predicted, the people at the agency were charmed. "Our Katia is on a
new binge," they said, and chuckled, and soon magazine and newspaper
clippings of Soviet and Russian interest were routed to her as a gesture of
their support in the reclaiming of her heritage.

She went to the library and lugged home six at a time, books such as

Life In Russia, The History of Russia, The Russians, How to Survive in Russia, The Magic That Is Russia, Peter the Great, and *Russian Life.*

She bought a balalaika from a pawnshop on the Lower East Side and enrolled at the New School for lessons. What a picture she made, sitting for hours in her apartment, strumming furiously and perspiring while tiny, breathless sounds floated up from the instrument. She served tea in a glass, burning her fingers every time she tried to drink it. Instead of sugar, she stirred jam into it or she practiced holding a cube of sugar between her teeth and sipping the tea through it. She haunted antique shops in the East Village until she found an old samovar, hauled it home and cleaned it up. When she tried brewing tea in it, she made a mess instead; burning coals in her apartment was not a good idea. Not to worry, she turned it into a lamp.

She researched as many Russian cookbooks as she could get her hands on and found the Time-Life book had the most authentic recipes. For weeks she enticed her friends with zakuski galore: marinated mushrooms, piroshki filled with meat or cabbage, eggplant caviar, salade olivet. She pickled baby cucumbers in dill and vinegar to perfect the traditional Russian pickles that Boris loved so much and served them with sour black bread. She stayed up all night to make yeasted buckwheat blini, which she served up with sour cream and caviar, washed down with hits of icy vodka. Vodka! To be a good Russian she had to drink vodka in excess and suffer from hangovers. She flavored various bottles of it with pepper, lemon, onion grass, raspberries, and left them to soak in her freezer. She urged her guests to drink their vodka in shot glasses, downing the contents in one swoop after wishing them "Na zdaroviye!"

She decided it was important to be overly sentimental and demonstrative with her friends and began having Russian sit-down farewells every time one of them would leave the apartment. She accompanied them to the elevator and made the sign of the cross on their foreheads with her right hand as the doors slid closed.

Occasionally she visited the Russian nightclubs in Brighton Beach to practice her Russian with the waiters and soak up the doleful, tacky atmosphere of the recent émigrés who frequented them.

In tribute to the present Soviet system she took to hiding books under her bed to see what it might feel like to be a dissident. Twice a week after work she made herself stand on the longest movie line she could find to experience how line standing really felt, and then, when she got up to the box office, she got out of line. The better to understand what waiting long hours for nothing was like. The Moscow correspondents who had written books about their stays in Russia all referred to trudging Muscovites, so she took to trudging the streets of New York. She translated everything she did into Soviet terms. For instance, she trudged from store to store in Manhattan, looking for black high-top Reeboks. It was impossible to find them since they were so popular and always sold out. But Katia didn't mind; she felt this experience brought her an intimate understanding of the hunt for inaccessible goods. In the end all she could find were red high-top Reeboks. But there was meaning in having been forced to choose red: it was so . . . communist.

She had to switch her food philosophy when the books on Soviet life discussed the chronic scarcity or nonexistence of most food items in the Soviet Union. And here she had been cooking prerevolutionary haute cuisine! No more blini and caviar for her! She lived on a diet of cabbage, potatoes, bread and vodka. No green vegetables. Not a salad passed her lips. If she did buy meat, it was the toughest, oldest cut she could persuade the butcher to give her. When she had a date for dinner at Le Cygne, she shocked the haughty French headwaiter by ordering nothing but potatoes—plain, boiled potatoes—and a glass of watered-down vodka, house brand please.

Every day she bought the *New Russian Word* which Boris had referred to as the "Hobo Clobo." She binged on Solzhenitsyn's accounts of Stalin's purges in the *Gulag Archipelago* and tossed and turned with Raskolnikov in *Crime and Punishment.* "The crime was his punishment," she liked to say.

She played the records of the martyred folksinger, Vladimir Vysotsky, letting him wail late into the night. On the piano, she concentrated on pieces by Scriabin and Rachmaninoff, but it was on Tchaikovsky she overdosed because Boris had once told her how every Russian was sick to death of Tchaikovsky, since his was the only music approved by the Soviet regime and it played constantly over the State radio. "I never want to hear Tchaikovsky again," he said. So Katia was determined to feel the same way.

Dear Sweet Cookie,
   A dream boutique. That's what's needed to fight the fucking life back. I will have Boris's Boutique of Dreams. Perfect for people who cannot remember theirs or who cannot dream the dream they need to live. Friendly

service. Happy customers. Price? Not too cher. Cash, checks, all credit cards, too. You like? Better to get work on it right away.

Bye for now.

Boris

She had the dream. It was the dream of their life together. But how to make him see it?

Katie walked the streets of New York, embracing this new life she had given herself. Yes, that was exactly it, she decided, you give yourself a life, you must find out who you are and then own it. She felt she had come full circle, having come from Russian roots, and now, falling in love with a Russian émigré. Loving Boris was perfect; no, more than that, it was her beautiful destiny. She breathed in her obsession like a divine gift and started writing Boris complicated letters about love.

She imagined how she would sell everything in her New York apartment; of course, they would live in Paris. No, on second thought, she would keep her New York apartment; he would want to have two homes. Her wedding announcement in the *Times* would say that the couple planned to live in New York and Paris. She imagined apartment hunting with him. Would they choose a charming, rambling old flat or go for something ultrastark in that particular style of French modernism? She knew she wanted a Japanese bedroom with a futon close to the floor, to sleep enveloped in poufs of down, "luxe, calme et volupté," as Baudelaire said. She imagined how she would choose a couch for the living room, how they would set up their ménage. A writing room for him, a study for her. And she would become international, adopting the best qualities of a European woman, but with the ease and expansiveness that only an American could possess.

They would be a fascinating couple, the toast of Paris and New York, Boris and Katia, the Russian émigré poet and his lovely American wife. She would dabble in French advertising, setting new trends in Europe. She would dress in Comme des Garçons and Kenzo. Boris would dress her; they would spend hours shopping and he would decide what was best. Photographs of them attending parties would appear in *Paris Match*; there would be feature stories in French *Vogue*. Their whereabouts would always be news, with Boris giving interviews for his new books from their vacation homes in Fréjus in the south of France. Of course, when he married her, his writing career would take off; there would be talk of a Prix Goncourt and even a Nobel.

Dear Trooper,

Paris is so gray. A famous, expensive gray, though. When I feel great, it is the best revenge on life. You too. Feel great. You'll see. I understand you want to be with someone, give yourself to another. But I am completely the wrong man. You make big mistake wanting me. I'm a parachute trooper, falling through air without parachute. I thought you knew this. I'm a marathon runner in biggest race of my life. If you catch me, you'll lose. You'll fall, too.

I'm obsessed with my new freedom in life. Jealous about it, even. You seem to want to lose yours. If you take mine away, you won't have Boris, but someone else. Because you met me in West, you think of me as Western person. But I'm not. I can never ignore my past. It hurts, my private pain, but it's part of me, too.

You know, you haven't read any of my books. You haven't even known me for a month! How can you think you know me?

Don't be so American, cookie. Sex is nothing. Just skin madness. Eros and life are bigger. People aren't very good at these in modern society.

I am poisoning myself with this life in Paris. Killing my writer's soul. Listening now to Bobbie Dylan and sipping velvet Scotch. It's at least a comfortable hell.

Big kiss, Yankee Stadium size.

                                                                    Boris

As the winter melted into spring Katia got tired of being so very Russian and slowly drifted back to being her usual crisp and cheerful self. It was just something she needed to go through, that's all, she told Frank. It hadn't been a useless exercise, it had enriched her life greatly, "sort of like a thaw between the two cultures waging a cold war within me," she explained. "And now, I'm a new and improved version of my Russian-American self."

Frank nodded. "Sounds good," he said, pursing his lips, trying to keep a sigh of relief out of his voice.

"But the name I'm going to keep," she said. "It's ever so much more lovely to be a Katia than a Kate, don't you think?"

Frank Falls

THROUGHOUT WHAT seemed like a very long year, Frank began to view Katia's life as a novel whose plot was unfolding right in front of him. He would have been the first to admit that in the beginning she had driven him crazy with her stories. But something had changed for him, and now she made an alluring Scheherazade, seducing him with the fiction of her days. It was in the way she drew out the words; she painted such pictures. It didn't just rain; no, it "drizzled teasingly." She didn't drink tea; no, she "stopped for a cup of steaming hot, comfortable tea."

Earlier, he had felt this was part of her problem in living. She was so caught up in the puffery of advertising that she never saw the reality of her own life or of the people in it. But now he had to admit that hers was an engaging way of living, for it added a certain corny richness and romance missing from so many of his patients' lives. Maybe even his own.

So, while she complained about her life to him (she was lonely in "a primal sort of way," she said), she managed to experience an extraordinary heightening of her days. For instance, she would describe to him how she loved lying naked on her all-cotton futon, it was very important for it to be one hundred percent cotton, she emphasized, on all-cotton French sheets, and how her Givenchy floral drapes simply "cascaded" to the floor, a sense of extravagance in the bedroom was important, didn't he think? And her room was not celery green, but celadon, much more translucent a color, yet milky, she said. She had black lacquer night tables with Japanese paper lamps on each one, one in the shape of a pyramid and one in the shape of a lopsided oval. This asymmetry was very important, didn't he agree? Don't forget the coral linen love seat. A love seat in the bedroom was such an important gesture, didn't he agree, so intimate . . . and linen was such a pure fabric, didn't he think? He could see, she said, that her room was very lush, that it was a place where you could empty your mind, yet a room that could incite great abandon, too. Here she lifted her eyebrows suggestively. Then she would describe lying naked on her futon, feeling the cool morning air softly caressing her shoulders, and how she would "plunge" into a hot, hot shower with a glass of freshly squeezed, frosty-cold orange juice. Did he understand that sensation, of being in a steamy, dreamy shower, sipping a glass of moist nectar? Then how lovely it was to step out and slip on a fluffy, clean, white cotton terrycloth robe. Yes, these were her words, all of them. And how she would fix herself a tray of tea and take it into the bedroom and sit on her love seat and read a few pages of a novel and sip tea. Tea from a little shop in Paris—Hediard, of course— they made the finest teas in all the world, and why shouldn't only the finest things in life pass your lips? she argued. Her favorite? "Thé aro-matisé aux fruits de la passion," she said, and then stopped to translate. "Tea, aromatized with passion fruit." He nodded. Of course.

When their sessions were over, he stood up and opened the door for her, then closed it immediately, delighted to be starkly alone after her lush outpourings. He found them intoxicating but frightening. That one could live in such a state of sensual gratification—it was exhausting to think about. In the few minutes before the next patient arrived he would write down his observations. They were typically notes like, "patient complains we are getting nowhere," or "patient distinctly uncomfortable talking about her father." But lately, with Katia, his notes on her therapy were increasingly concerned with the rules of her living. He found him-self jotting down names of restaurants she described, walks she had taken, books she was reading. When she talked about food, he became so aroused he felt like she was talking dirty to him. He coveted her recipe for Parmesan popcorn. His mouth watered over her description of making a "plump plum tarte glazed with a brandied black-currant jam and popped under the broiler to crunch it up a bit." He scribbled down her Thanksgiving menu: cranberries Grand Marnier with orange zest and black walnuts; a stuffing seasoned with fresh fennel and dried apri-cots; haricots verts with trompettes de mort (mushrooms called trumpets of death!) radicchio and arugula salad with raspberry vinaigrette; tiny pumpkin tartlets for desert.

He flipped through his notes on her and became distressed. Was it normal to be so interested in a patient? What was the fine line between professional listening and sheer curiosity about her life? He resolved to talk to Dr. Janet about it very soon, but for now, he was too embarrassed. He decided to be analytical about it, to live with his interest and discomfort and see where it took him. There, that let him off the hook. Temporarily.

Today after she left he had scribbled furiously, "There is only one café on the Place des Vosges, you can't miss it, have breakfast there, it is the most beautiful place in all of Paris." Lord, how he was addicted to her chirping about Paris. Her trip to France last summer had awakened something deep inside her that he hadn't seen before. Her eyes burned; she was alive with a silkiness of style that left him bewildered. She was smoldering with sensual stories. In her words Paris breathed and shimmered, it beckoned to him. He could taste those hot, flaky croissants and the thick, creamy French coffee. He soaked up the vision of her sitting in a café in the sun, lazily smoking a French cigarette and reading French *Vogue*. He could imagine her sitting on a bench, staring at a painting in the Orangerie or trying on a "key fashion item," as she called it, "chez Kenzo. You know . . . Place des Victoires?" She modeled it for him in his office. "It's a must," she said. "An entire wardrobe can be built around this one piece; why, it can go from day to date!" She whirled around, then plopped down in the chair laughing at herself.

Lately he found that it was Boris who interested him more and more. Through Katia's rumblings, this larger-than-life man had come to have a curious, almost seductive hold over him. But he wanted to find out for himself what he was really like, for he couldn't tell from Katia's stories what was real and what was her fantasy.

He studied Katia's snapshots of Boris when she brought them in. He remembers holding Boris's first novel, not being able to read a word because it was in French. But still, gripping it was proof of this seemingly impossible man. His ears would perk up when Katia mentioned, "Oh, Boris called me from Paris yesterday." He especially liked reading Boris's letters to her. Occasionally she would bring one in to discuss with him, reading little bits aloud. He couldn't ask her to hand it over, but he loved it when she did. They were typed in broken English with French and Russian words sprinkled heavily throughout. He liked holding the crinkly airmail paper filled such such clever Parisian and literary gossip. Boris's sensuality jumped off the paper.

Unfortunately, Katia found him out and zoomed in on his interest. For months she had been teasing Frank about an English translation she had of Boris's latest short story. She made references to the story and from time to time she asked if he would like to read it, and he always said yes, but she didn't take his answer seriously or maybe she thought he was just being polite. It was a story about a Russian émigré doctor who killed one of his female patients because he suspected she was a KGB agent. Now this made Frank very nervous, because from what she had told him of Boris's fiction, he realized that Boris always killed the women in his stories. Either that or they died of some grisly disease. Frank began pestering her to bring in the story.

"Why do you want to read it?" she asked warily.

Frank assumed the contemplative pose he usually retreated into when she was on the attack. "Because it will be good for your therapy if I read it."

Katia was silent. This didn't sound right. She leaned forward in her chair as if she was groping for some understanding. Then it dawned on her and she plunged in the knife.

"No"—she smiled—"you want to read it for yourself. You're interested in Boris." She sat back in the light of her discovery.

During her Russification year, Katia started, as she put it sotto voce, "dating m-e-n," although she was too involved in her fantasy life to pay much attention to any of them. She led a private life with Boris in her mind, waiting for his phone calls, engineering the scheme of how she would finally join him. Whenever she received one of his charming "communiqués," as she called them ("Art is a fountain on a rainy day: a triumph of uselessness and a vital necessity," and "I'm afraid of this coming winter. It looks for me like a troublesome gray froggy kiss on the forehead. Sorry, it must be the ink of night pouring in from the open window.") their poetry just served to inflame her imagination even further.

Frank was surprised to find he was torn about Katia's social life; he didn't know what he wanted for her. That he even thought such a thing disgusted him—after all, who was he to decide what was best for her?

Boris was appealing but deadly; and yet he was safe because he was so
unrealistic. The therapist in Frank tried to encourage Katia to find a
man in New York, but every time she met someone new, the man in
Frank held his breath, hoping she wouldn't fall in love. Just yet.

There was her bizarre interlude with Harry Halston. He was black and
she didn't know what to think. She had never considered him a possibility, but was intrigued as to why he was hanging around her. They met at
a house party on Long Island one Sunday afternoon and he offered to
drive her back to the city in his snazzy green Mazda coupe. Katia hated
the Long Island Railroad and she jumped at the invitation. Harry had
just installed a CB radio in his car and they played with it all the way
home, laughing and fumbling with the mike as if it was a hot potato,
passing it back and forth between them with Katia squealing, "You talk!"
She told Frank that Harry was the only man she knew who could roll
joints and drive a car at the same time. Frank didn't know whether he
should act impressed or reprove her for such wild behavior. He thought
what a curious combination they made, a cool black dude with a nervous white chick. When she and Harry had pulled up in front of her
apartment building, she got out of the car very quickly and ran up to her
apartment, vowing never to see him again.

Despite her initial resistance they became friends. She felt he liked
her—plain and simple. Perhaps it was because she was so afraid of him
that she was totally unaffected around him. And she had to admit Harry
was a dream machine, a walking pleasure palace. He would show up at
her place at odd hours bearing gifts like the three wise men. One night
he breezed in her door just after midnight and set down a bottle of
Tanqueray gin, some fresh limes and a bottle of Schweppes tonic. From
one coat pocket he pulled out some gourmet marijuana and rolling
papers, and out of the other pocket, a vial of cocaine and a miniature
vacuum cleaner to snort it up with. The pièce de résistance was a one-
pound box of David's fresh-from-the-oven, chocolate-chip cookies.
Then he stood back from the still life he had created on her coffee table
and waited for her reaction. "What is this," she hooted, "a new game
called Choose Your Poison?"

Frank was beside himself when she told him this.

They had ended up doing everything. They smoked dope and cooled
their throats with gin and tonic. When they got hungry, they ate the
cookies, and when they got sleepy, they sniffed cocaine. Katia had never
tried cocaine before and tried to protest. "Really, you shouldn't waste

this on me, it's too expensive. Give it to someone who would really appreciate it." But Harry cajoled her into trying it, and by daybreak she understood why Freud loved cocaine. They stayed up all night talking nonstop, examining their lives in great detail. It wasn't the silly marijuana-like-wow rambling free association. Cocaine rapping was cogent and intelligent. She felt so good, so clever, so interesting. Eventually they covered every topic under the sun and regressed to early childhood memories. She couldn't believe it when the gray-pink morning filtered in the windows.

They both agreed that the proper way to end this evening would be to find a McDonald's and have an Egg McMuffin. They were so pop, "an incredible concept," Katia said as she twirled the muffin around in her hand. By now they were sitting on a bench in Central Park. They sipped their coffee and watched the sunrise until they both dozed off. An hour later they decided their date was over, and each went home to crash.

Katia had several such experiences with Harry until one day he simply disappeared from her life. They never had sex. She wondered about this, but it didn't trouble her. "He was just the devil dropping into my life for a few weeks," she told Frank, "sent to teach me mindless indulgence."

Then there was Sam, the Dutch carpenter. "Every woman loves a carpenter," she said to Frank, trying to keep a straight face, "every woman loves a man who drills holes." She even said this to Sam, but it was lost on him. Poor Sam, he never understood half of what came out of her mouth. At first that bothered Katia, but then she decided to make him her Lady Chatterley's lover. And how her apartment improved while they dated! Before she would allow him to make love to her, she made him put up shelves in the bathroom, hang curtain rods, design a wall unit, cut legs down from a coffee table. One thing that bothered her was how he always wore a pencil behind his ear, even when he sat down to dinner. She knew it was a sign of a good carpenter, to have the pencil ever ready for a measurement, but it was the final straw when one day he wore it to bed. Besides, their lovemaking didn't really satisfy her, because she couldn't enjoy sex with someone she couldn't treat as a soul mate.

Thank God for small favors, thought Frank.

And then there was Clint. He fell into the category that a girlfriend of Katia's had named "the shock troops." These were the men a woman kept around her to save her from feeling bad. A man in the shock troops was sexless, but steadfast and true. He was the man who always called her magically when she most needed a friend, who was there when she needed rescuing on a lonely Friday night, thrilled by the impromptu invitation to come on over and cook spaghetti.

Katia had a wonderful friend in Clint. He took her to elegant restaurants, drove her around town in his BMW with the sun roof; he took her to gala balls where the seats cost a thousand dollars each. They went to Philharmonic concerts at Lincoln Center and bohemian dance recitals in the Village. They went camping together in the Adirondacks, sharing the same tent, sleeping side by side in two separate sleeping bags.

Clint was wonderful. He was kind, sharing, generous. He was smart, handsome, funny. But she didn't love him. She couldn't love him. How this tortured her! She tried and tried in her heart to love him, and her friends urged her to marry him. "But then I would have to kiss him!" she squealed. And that was the problem. They had been been friends for three years and had never even kissed. When she came home from an evening with Clint, she always had a headache. It wasn't from the tension of sexual attraction, it was from the tension of sexual avoidance.

Katia finally told Frank that evenings like this she ended in the way many evenings had ended this year—in the living room, dancing alone in the dark.

Paris

Boris Doesn't Love Katia

ON HER THIRD day in Paris, Katia decided it was time to take her diaphragm out of her handbag. Wandering around the city with it was ridiculous. Every time she opened her purse to take out some francs for the metro or a sorbet, or to look for her sunglasses or check on something in her Guide Michelin, there it was, staring her in the face, mocking her, underlining her failure like a bad joke.

I mean, it's not as if I'm some chick looking for trouble, she said to herself in a fit of pique as she paid for the balon of Beaujolais that the garçon had just brought her. She quickly snapped her purse shut. Au contraire, I'm a responsible adult woman, a "nice girl," she laughed sarcastically, I hate one night stands. The sex was always a comedy of errors—what goes into what hole, when should it go there, who should put it there, oh God, you either had to be drunk enough or unselfconscious enough or just plain selfish enough to enjoy it. Anyway, she thought sex was something very, very intimate and it took a while to have great, really great sex with a man.

So how did the diaphragm end up there? When she had packed for her trip, she was about to put it in her suitcase and then decided against it. What if the suitcase got lost? Then she'd really be in a pickle. If men only knew what women had to think about! So she packed it in her purse like a girl scout, or maybe it was the boy-scout motto, "Be prepared." In New York, Boris told her he had never slept with a woman who used a diaphragm, so in this way, Katia was pleased she was a first for him. When he asked her why she used one, she thought about it for a moment and said, "I'm thirty-three years old, I don't want to be constantly infertile on some pill. I must be ready to have a child at any time.'" Boris stared at her and nodded. "Yes," he said solemnly, "you are absolutely right."

But Dr. Manne had been unable to hide his surprise. "There are other, more modern, things you could use," he said when she told him. She let him have it. It was none of his business and how dare he make such a value judgment. "I suppose you find it disgusting. Well, you know what? It is. It's primitive and ugly looking."

All he could do was sit there meekly.

"Imagine how I feel," she continued, "having to jam this flying saucer into me with cream dripping out of me all day!"

It was a beautiful August day in Paris and Katia had just sat down in a café after getting off the Bateaux Mouches. How pleasant it had been to sit on the amphibious-looking tourist boat bobbing around the Seine. Now she was annoyed at the arrogant way the waiter treated her. Why did the French have to act this way? Boris had warned her that she was too friendly to the French, that the friendlier she was, the nastier they would be to her. "Baby," he lectured her, "you must treat them like shit, then they will respect you. It will show to them that you are discerning. Very simple."

He was always coaching her about how to behave in Paris. For instance, he was very annoyed at her when they had dinner the first evening she arrived. Apparently she swooned over the pâté after her first bite. In a scathing whisper he reprimanded her, "Katia, please. You are embarrassing me. You must not make any show. To you, this food should be normal, an everyday experience." And when she entered a boutique, he told her she must look around with her nose in the air and act disgusted. "Then say to the vendeuse, 'Is this all you have?' You see? Then they will respect you."

Paris in August was just like she had always heard. Empty. Even the air was vacant. There was no doubt that absolutely nothing of importance was going on or would take place during this month. The French had willed it this way so they could all leave and not fear missing a thing. All the interesting shops and restaurants were locked up tight, the theatre was straggling along with tourist junk, the painters and writers were absent, the soul of the city had gone to the mountains or the beach. But the monuments were still there, so the tourists continued to swarm the place, busloads of them whirling around the Place de la Concorde. The few Parisians who had stayed behind to earn money were exhausted, not to mention grouchy at this point in the long tourist season.

Katia sipped her wine and analyzed the two Frenchwomen sitting at the table in front of her. She studied every item of clothing down to the bangles on their wrists. Amazing! A Frenchwomen could be wearing nothing more than jeans and a white tee, yet she looked fabulous, she oozed style. How did they do it?

She sighed. She reminded herself that she was definitely over Boris and felt both proud and relieved to be liberated from her obsession. They were just good friends now. So what was she doing in Paris? Her last visit so whetted her appetite for all things French that she decided to return for her vacation. It mattered not that he happened to live there; if he wanted to see her, well, that would be fine, but she wasn't counting on it. She had phoned him, as she would any friend, to tell him she was coming. So why the diaphragm in her purse?

Well, any responsible woman would take care to protect herself. You never know and it's better to be safe than sorry. There was always the possibility that when she arrived, and kept totally to her lovely New York self that Boris would be attracted to her once again. That's the way men were. Now she understood that before, she had been one of those women who loved too much, she had pursued him too hard, had been too available and perhaps that put him off. This time it was going to be different. She was going to be Miss Cool Cucumber, a gal about town, all on her alluring own. But on this third day of strolling around by herself she felt defeated. This simply will not do, she decided, and that night when she returned to the apartment where she was staying, she took the diaphragm out of her purse and put it in the suitcase, out of her sight.

She had dreamed about this vacation for months. It had now been over a year since she had taken any time off. All summer long she worked hard at the agency, helping to win a major new account, Presto Plastic Wrap. She spent three weeks flying to six cities, sitting in the dark behind smoky one-way mirrors at focus groups, munching on M&M's and caramel popcorn, watching middle-class housewives, aged twenty-one to forty-five discuss "the wrap category." Hundreds of thousands of dollars were spent on the research, "Because, let's face it," her boss said in his rallying cry to the creative team, "everybody wraps, it's a big category." She still remembered every word of the presentation that clinched the twenty-million-dollar account.

"People want cling," she said gaily. It was her socko opening. "The hard, sad truth is that people really want two things in a plastic wrap: they want it to cling *and* they want it to be easy to handle.

"But the reality? *They can't have both!* The properties that make a plastic wrap cling are the same properties that make it hard to handle. Now, through testing, we have found that Presto is not the easiest to handle, but it does cling the best. *And you know what?* When people were forced to choose, *they wanted cling!*

"We found that an individual's wrapping habits are traditional: she, or he"—polite smile—"will do what Mom did, and use what Mom used. By the way, there's a large group of double wrappers out there. They simply won't use it in the freezer unless they double-wrap it.

"I must inform you that after sitting in on these focus groups, it's clear that plastic wrap is an overpromised category. There's an incredibly high level of consumer anger out there: they're promised something that just isn't delivered."

With the account won, Katia spent the rest of the summer in a dark, air-conditioned studio making the agency's first commercial for Presto. Her idea was to construct a trampoline out of plastic wrap and have actors portraying a happy American family (two blond parents and their two blond children and a bouncing dog!) holding things wrapped in plastic wrap, (sandwiches, fruit, leftover casserole), flipping, jumping, twisting on the plastic-wrap trampoline, delirious with the joy of New! Presto Plastic Wrap. The message imparted in those thirty seconds was simply that Presto clings the best. What she didn't tell the client was how she had almost lost her life over plastic wrap. She had been sitting in a rental car outside a toll plaza on the Pennsylvania Turnpike trying to figure out how to open the window of this totally computerized compact. As she sat there fidgeting with various buttons, an out-of-control truck missed the car by inches, careened through the alley next door and zoomed through the tollbooth, flipping the entire booth over! With the collector sliding out of the bottom of the booth! She started screaming and babbling incoherently to her art director. "I mean, one minute I'm talking about plastic wrap with my art director and the next minute I'm dead? I've had it!" she said, and the next day she made plane reservations for France.

Now she was ready to rediscover Paris, thirteen years after her junior year abroad when she had lived on the rue de Fleurus near the Jardin du Luxembourg. She was always proud that she had lived on the same street as Gertrude Stein. She was ready to daydream in cafés, get drunk on fabulous wine ("It's a crime, baby, a crime, not to drink wine in France," Boris told her), stroll the lazy back streets and march up those grand boulevards. She had two glorious weeks to buy beautiful French clothes, try new perfumes and makeup, invest in some drop-dead silk lingerie, eat excellent food, look at art and let Paris bathe her in special, musty moments.

But just now in the café, she felt annoyed at the waiter and annoyed at herself for letting him make her feel so self-conscious and dowdy. She was angry with herself because she was unable to find her equilibrium, all because of Boris. He was not only ignoring her, but he was even being a bit nasty. Now what? Usually she was good at being self-sufficient, traveling alone and having adventures, but for the moment she was lost.

It had started out nicely. She had a beautiful flight. It was smooth and serene, almost a dream the way the plane gently carried her away from the meanness of New York, from the filthy stench of the summer subways, where all she saw was men's spit on the steps as she navigated her way up into the sweltering street. The 747 whisked her away to a gentler culture, where cheese mattered, where perfume mattered, where the eyes were constantly rewarded with beauty.

Katia arrived at aéroport Charles de Gaulle feeling positively refreshed. For weeks she had planned the moment of her arrival, the exact picture of herself that she would present to Boris when he set eyes on her for the first time. She didn't ask him to meet her; he offered.

"Katia à la japonaise," was the first thing he said when he saw her at the baggage claim. Indeed. He had guessed her new look on the nose. She was wearing a gray Japanese dress with a black sweater and black sandals with white socks. Her hair was in braids, coiled around her head. Only she knew, and with some embarrassment to herself, that she had grown her hair especially for this moment. It was a Russian hairstyle, innocent yet worldly, and very soft. As they waited for the bus to take them to the metro she moved her hands as if to take her hair down.

"Leave it," he said, surveying her with a critical eye. "Leave it."

Boris had caught her off guard at the airport. She hadn't seen him when she came out of passport control. She looked and looked for him as she walked in a queue with the other passengers, trying to keep the disappointment off her face. She kept walking, pretending nothing was wrong, and stood waiting for her baggage, watching nervously for her suitcase to appear on the conveyor belt, when she turned around and there he was, walking slowly toward her. She gulped, suddenly realizing how tough this visit was going to be.

Frank had tried to warn her. He was suspicious of her motives and made sure to let her know about his concerns. "Are you sure you're over him? Maybe you shouldn't go to Paris. How about Venice?" No, she assured him, she felt nothing for Boris anymore, it really was Paris she was interested in.

"Well . . ." He continued his probing, not wanting to let her off so easily. "Let's imagine you are there. What are your expectations about him? How do you think he'll treat you? How are you going to feel if he's . . . not so nice?" he put it delicately.

She really tried to wrap her mind around his questions. She agreed it might be difficult but she viewed this trip as a test, to see if she really was over him, out from under his spell. She wanted to resume her life afresh and needed to recover her self-respect. She couldn't help it if it might be surprisingly wonderful, that Boris might take one look at her and realize he had been foolish, that it was really she he loved, and they would run into each other's arms at the airport. . . . But she didn't tell Frank this, she didn't want to give him any openings for discussion. She hoped that if she acted strong, she would feel strong. Besides, she was over him, she kept telling herself.

All Boris said was, "Katia à la japonaise," and kissed her à la française, once on each cheek. She fell silent, suddenly shy and scared. He had changed. He looked so mean and challenging. What had happened in a year?

He looked his usual unusual, extraordinary self. There was a curious air of something homosexual about him, the way he was so studiously, so beautifully dressed, outfitted and elegant in the most fantastic leather pants—Jean-Paul Gaultier, he told her—and a blouson jacket, from Girbaud, he said. He looked like one of those sexy gruff men photographed in American fashion advertisements, men just out of the shower, hair still a bit damp, displaying that certain rough-and-tumble masculinity that appealed to women as well as men. You never saw men like that in real life, only in the advertisements. But Boris looked just like this.

They sat on the aéroport bus without saying a word and then switched to the train that would take them into Paris. The look on Boris's face was one of bored suffering. He didn't seem at all delighted to have her there. She stared out the window at the ugly banlieue as they sped by.

"Why are you sad?" Boris said.

"No, I'm fine," she said, and forced a smile. He looked so aggravated she was afraid to say anything. Damn! Why did she feel so nervous?

A New York acquaintance had arranged through friends for her to stay in an empty apartment in the sixteenth arrondissement, also known as Passy. Katia was not particularly thrilled to be in such a nouveau riche quartier, but who was she to turn down a free apartment in Paris? Besides, there had never been any question of her staying with Boris. He hadn't offered and she knew better than to ask. His letters for the past few months constantly complained about the tiny size of his studio. Even so, wasn't it true that if a man loved you, he would want you to stay with him? That no space would be too small for lovers? In fact, lovers loved small spaces where they would never be more than a kiss away from each other.

They wandered down the rue des Belles Feuilles past the Place du Mexique, with Boris struggling with her suitcase, and her lagging behind. At one point she looked up and gasped. Boris stopped and put the suitcase down.

"What is it?"

She pointed to the Eiffel Tower looming hugely just down the street. "It's so kitsch!" She laughed.

"Yes, baby, this is Paaa-ris," he crooned in a bored tone. He wanted to hurry up and see this place of hers for himself.

They finally found the building. She was so nervous with him hoving over her that she fumbled with the keys until he finally took them from her hand with a disgusted air and opened the door easily himself.

They were struck by a blast of mustiness. A pile of canes and crutches stood in the entrance-hall corner. The depressing one-room apartment reeked of death. It told of the life of a decrepit widower eeking out his last days before being taken to the hospital to die. It was decorated in the old, démodé French provincial style with heavy gold tasseled drapes encrusted in dust, ugly, uncomfortable-looking chairs with their stuffing sagging out the bottom, stains on the bare mattress that stood nakedly in the middle of the room, lamps with yellowed shades that were too small.

Katia swallowed. Boris immediately went over to the windows and flung them open. The two of them explored the tiny room, not saying anything to each other. She heard him go into the bathroom and flush the toilet to see if it worked. It was only when she was back in New York, months later, that she realized she should have walked out right then and there, just stamped her foot down and turned right around to check into some adorable little hotel on the Île St. Louis. Une chambre sympathique where she would have bought a bouquet of flowers and put them in a vase on her windowsill in the sun. A cozy room that she would have decorated with a box of French chocolates and a French *Vogue*, a scented candle; a room where she could have lain in bed at night with the moonlight coming through the window, sipping wine and smoking Gitanes.

But it didn't occur to her just then. She was overwhelmed. She had no control of her mind, so thrown off was she by Boris's coolness. In the kitchen she opened a cupboard and saw a dozen bottles, stacked on their side, of the cheapest vinegary wine that she remembered from her student days; "Grapes Jolies," the labels said. Meanwhile, Boris opened a closet and saw an old man's clothing, heavy black coats, worn jackets, frayed white shirts, now yellowed. Katia was so horribly disappointed with the place, she felt she had to pretend that she found it all charming. Boris didn't say much. He found a radio and flipped it on, turning the dial until he found some music. They stood listening to an unbearably sad piano concerto.

"Do you know this piece?" he asked her, trying to place it in his mind.

She knew it. It was Chopin's Concerto no. 2. He had written only two piano concertos in his life and she knew both of them. This was the saddest movement, the music he had written when he thought he was dying of a broken heart.

Katie looked at the bed standing there in the middle of the room and wondered whether they would ever make love there. In a fit of fantasy she imagined Boris suddenly overcome with desire in this decrepit place. It would have been just what the room needed, a fit of frenzied, animal fucking in the midst of the death smell. It would have been deliciously desperate and life affirming.

Now what? There was another uneasy silence, so Katia brought out the bag of presents she had so carefully selected for him. She recalled how with great happiness she had chased all over New York buying the things he had asked for, adding surprises of her own. She unzipped a red *Life* magazine bag and started presenting him with these things, hoping they would please him, hoping they would break the ice.

But now he just took them, accepting them only after a cool inspection, as if they were something due him. She was at first puzzled by his ingratitude, but then realized he was acting indifferent and cruel because these things she brought him from New York mattered so much.

"Here is some scotch from Duty Free," she said gaily, knowing he loved scotch. Boris looked at it and mumbled that it wasn't single-malt. "Keep it here, baby, keep it for your guests," he said, putting the bottle down on a table.

She gave him three bottles of vitamins, which he held in his hand and, after inspecting them, told her they weren't the brand he had asked for. He had this tremendous belief in American vitamins. He felt the French just didn't make good ones. He would often write to her, begging her to send him vitamins because his health was slipping away and he needed them desperately.

She gave him five books, three he had requested and a two he hadn't, and he went through them, checking them over and shrugging his shoulders. She pulled out a royal blue Frisbee with white stars and a pair of cotton sweat pants and tried to be enthusiastic and jolly. "Look, lipstick red, just like you asked for!" He held the Frisbee, judging its weight, and said okay under his breath. American Frisbees were the only kind to have. He held up the sweat pants and commented that they looked too big for him.

"No, you have to buy them big because when you put them in the dryer, they'll shrink down to your size."

He told her sarcastically that this was France and they didn't use dryers here.

There were two windup toys, "the rage of New York!" she said like a woman in the know. She selected for him a walking monster that spewed sparks and a pair of sneakers that walked by themselves. "You put them on your desk when you are writing and play with them when you are stuck or when you are thinking," she explained. These he liked and pocketed immediately. A bit of Magritte, he told her, a bit of whimsy.

She gave him three American toothbrushes, each in its own little cardboard box with cellophane wrapping. Did he remember how he asked her for those a year ago when she was in Paris? It happened one afternoon after their siesta when they were both in the bathroom. He was brushing his teeth with her toothbrush when he turned to her and asked if she would leave it behind for him when she went back to New York. Katia remembers how poignant this request had seemed; she was touched. It turned out, he told her that he hated French toothbrushes, that American ones were softer and, well, better.

As she gave him each thing, as if making an offering, he would inspect it, grunt and put it quickly away into the red nylon *Life* magazine bag, like a squirrel storing away winter nuts. Finally she brought out the major present. In New York he had loved her sheets with their wild patterns and deep, unusual colors.

"Arabian Nights. By Martex," she said. "I hope you like them."

"Génial," he said, smiling broadly. He held them up for an instant and then tucked them quickly into the bag.

At a loss she added, "You really must take the Scotch, I don't drink it, and besides," she sighed, "I bought it for you."

"Well, if you insist," he said, and put it in the bag.

They went out to what would be her local café for the next two weeks, where he ordered deux café crèmes et un croissant. She wasn't hungry. He dipped the croissant into the hot coffee and held it to her mouth. She took a bite like a dutiful child. It was a warm and buttery, straight from the oven.

"Relax, baby. This is Paaa-ris," he said again. He wound up the walking sneakers and put them on the table and everyone in the café stared as they clattered across the marble tabletop. Boris smiled proudly as the owner of this heretofore unseen gadget in Paris, France. But he still looked like he couldn't wait to get away.

"You can leave now," she said, and gave him a pale smile. "I'm okay." He got up immediately and tried to give her a kiss on the mouth, but she moved her face so it landed on her cheek. He clucked at her and shook his head as if she were misbehaving.

"Go take a nap. Come tonight for dinner."

She watched him as he disappeared down the street, walking very fast with his big red *Life* magazine bag, bulging with American goodies, over his shoulder.

Katia sat and sipped her café in a daze. She couldn't figure out what was jet lag and what was Boris, but she felt as rotten as she had at the agency's Fourth of July office party, where she had gotten smashed out of some vague unhappiness. Without noticing, she gulped down several vodka gimlets like they were glasses of water. A few hours later her boss wandered down the hall and found her throwing up out the window of her sixteenth-floor office. "This is a perfect comment on life in advertising," she recalls her boss said. "One of my copywriters throwing up onto Madison Avenue." Then she hailed a taxi and helped her back home.

Now look at me. She could be a Manet painting: *Femme misérable in a Parisian Café.* For the briefest moment she considered the possibility of being charmed with a poignant interpretation of her own sad self on a gray August morning in Paris. But it didn't help. After a few minutes more, she paid the addition and asked the garçon where the marché for this quartier was located.

She found out that the rue de Belles Feuilles, her very own street, but a few blocks down, was one of the most famous food streets in all of Paris. Now she felt like she was back! How deprived Americans are, she thought as she surveyed the tempting shops and stalls filled to overflowing with incredible food. Where to begin first?

At the fromagerie she found herself surrounded with hundreds of cheeses, of which she didn't know the names or tastes of ninety-nine percent. The impatient, bitchy vendeuse stared at her, waiting to see what stupid decisions she, an American, would make. The look on all the shopgirls' faces was "Hurry up, hurry up!" Katia wanted to sit quietly on a stool in the shop for about fifteen minutes and stare at all the cheeses until she could begin to make sense of what categories they were arranged in and how they might taste. She tried to make her choices, but instead kept whirling around in a circle, so overwhelmed was she. The glaring stares of the shopgirls won out and finally she just pointed and said, "ça, ça et ça," selecting three cheeses she had never eaten before. Her purchase was wrapped in filigree tissue and tied with a delicate yellow ribbon. "Au revoir, mademoiselle," they cooed after her as she left their domain.

On to the épicerie, where again, the fruits and vegetables were displayed like rare works of art. Fraises de bois, white peaches, black currants, all beckoned to her, saying, "Choose me, choose me!" She had the same hard time choosing fruits as she did the cheese. Thank God she knew you weren't supposed to pick out the fruits yourself like she did in the Korean groceries in New York. No sniffing or pinching here. She pitied the poor, unsuspecting tourist who didn't know that it was death to touch a fruit or vegetable in France. She resolved to write a letter to Arthur Frommer to tell him to include that little fact in his guidebook. A somewhat nicer, but still gestapo-like shopboy watched her with a paper bag poised, ready to fulfill her slightest whim. That's just it, it was

too easy to start pointing at everything in a total loss of control. Italian
tomatoes, buttery lamb's lettuce, slender, authentic haricots verts. Yes to
all of it!

The same thing happened when she went into the wine shop and was
confronted by hundreds of bottles of fine French wine, wine she could
never afford back home, which was actually sensibly priced here. And
then on to the boulangerie, where impeccable loaves of bread beckoned
to her, saying, "Eat me, eat me!" Katia enjoyed struggling down the
street under the awkward balance of her purchases, juggling the wine
and bread, shifting the peaches and the cheeses. I am more French than
the French, she thought, and laughed.

Her spirits lifted, she made her way back to the apartment, where she
put away the groceries and made up the bed. She slept deeply, and when
she woke up, it was to the sound of church bells pealing. She counted
six. That meant it was five o'clock. She got up, groggy and disoriented,
and wandered around. She missed her meowing cat. She washed her
face and dunked her head into the sink to wash her hair, then dressed
very carefully, again planning her outfit for maximum effect. A different
gray dress this time, with a black sweater tied just so around her hips as
part of the look. Black sandals, smoky blue-gray around her eyes, an
apricot mouth. She looked at herself in the mirror, squinting her eyes.
Who did she see?

Katia walked slowly up the ultrawide Avenue Kléber, to what would
be her metro stop for the next two weeks, Trocadero, located smack in
front of the Eiffel Tower. In the early evening light, the place de Trocadero looked like a corny Hollywood stage set for Paris, complete with
newspaper kiosk and art deco metro grille. There was a café with fringed
umbrellas twittering in the breeze, filled with lazy couples and tired
businessmen who were ending their day, or rather beginning their evenings, with a drink. Tourists milled around, taking snapshots of the
magnificent view. Continuing in this Hollywood mode, she felt like an
extra. The air was so sweet. Did these people know how exhilarated she
felt, or how scared? Did she look French or American? She skipped
down into the metro and watched how everyone slipped their tickets in
the machine in order to get through the automatic turnstile. She bought
herself a carnet and did the same, slipping the canceled ticket under her
watchband like Boris had taught her in case she needed to show it to the
contrôle on her way out. As she sat down in the metro she felt twenty
years old again and let her mind wander back to memories of her stu-

dent days in Paris. The city was in her blood like an old friend, and not even the French could take that away from her.

She watched with disgust as an American hippie made his way slowly through the car, begging for money in broken French for his baby daughter asleep in a snugli on his back. Katia was embarrassed for America, and she was upset that he was using his daughter like this. She was happy when the train pulled into Montparnasse-Bienvenue and she made her correspondance for the train to St. Sulpice.

She found Boris's street easily enough and laughed when she walked past the firehouse he had complained about in his letters. How he hated those young, horny firemen, partying until all hours of the morning, staging drunken brawls in front of his windows in the middle of the night. "J'en ai marre des pompiers!" he wrote. She found his ancient apartment building and stood in front, looking up at all the open windows, listening to the many sounds that floated down to her. Rock and roll was blaring from a boutique next door, someone was typing, a woman was practicing an aria a cappella, a baby was crying, the TV news was on. Delicious dinner smells drifted from all directions. She loved this moment and wished she could hold it forever. She pushed open the heavy door and entered a dark, cool stone courtyard with mailboxes lining one wall. According to his mailbox, Boris lived with two other people, one Roland Campbell, and a Lady Sarah Bradshaw, both very English looking when seen alongside the Slavic name of Boris Zimoy. She knew he had put extra names on his mailbox for protection, to make the KGB think he didn't live alone. They never stopped hounding poor Boris, raiding his apartment and taking nothing, just roughing it up to shake him up a bit. She climbed the three flights to his studio, which she knew from his description to be one room facing the street.

"Door is open," he called out when she knocked. The reason he didn't answer the door himself was that he refused to disrupt any part of his daily routine, and now was the sacred time for his bath. He had written her how every day he spent the morning writing, then after lunch he played tennis in the Luxembourg to work out all the excess energy and tension from having been so cooped up. At five o'clock he performed his favorite ritual, which began with returning home and climbing the stairs of his building. Exhausted and sweaty, he would strip off his tennis clothes immediately, and while the water was running for his bath, he would make a pot of hot Russian tea, splash a shot of Scotch in the cup and finally settle into the steaming tub. No doubt about it, this was the high point of his day. In the bath he would lie back, read magazines or letters from friends, think about his writing, sip his tea and relax. Boris was a water bug. "I'm an Aquarius, this is correct," he said proudly.

Katia walked straight into the bathroom, where Boris was holding court in the tub. He looked totally happy. His bathroom was a most extraordinary world—unusual for a man, she thought, nicer even than most women's bathrooms. It was a sanctuary filled with different colorful soaps, shampoos, bath oils, shower gels, a variety of sponges, loofahs, washclothes and a huge stack of fluffy towels ready to be plucked. There were several choices of finely scented talcs in such exotic scents as patchouli and guava resting on a shelf along with colognes and an array of tortoise shell combs and hairbrushes of varying shapes, all of fine natural bristles, of course.

"I hope you feel better," he said. "You look better."

"I am much better," she said, and spun around so he could admire her dress. She was going to keep a grip this time and not let him get to her.

"You look great, baby. Your dress is by, hmmm, Agnès B," he guessed.

"Wrong. Comme des Garçons." She knew he hated Agnes B; he called her a salope. He was a great admirer of women's clothes. Once he had called her from Paris on a Sunday afternoon and told her how he had stood in front of Comme des Garçons, staring at the most beautiful silk dress in the window. "Oh, baby! Right then I wanted to be a woman so badly to be able to wear that dress!" he said to her.

Katia put down the toilet-seat cover so she could sit down. But then Boris seemed to be embarrassed and covered himself with his hands as though she had never seen him naked before. His unusual shyness made her uncomfortable, so she decided to let him bathe in peace and stood up to leave. "Take your time. I'll wait inside," she said. As she passed the medicine cabinet she saw the three American toothbrushes hung neatly in a row in a special plastic holder.

For some reason she felt like a spy when she entered his mysterious domain. Beautiful classical music was playing. So this was his private world. The room was peaceful and masterful, and totally masculine. No woman was allowed here, yet it was graced with feminine touches. A large glass bowl was filled with fruit, a vase held a sumptuous bouquet of wildflowers, the flower boxes outside his windows overflowed with the blooms of red-hot geraniums.

"You have a green thumb," she shouted over the music.

"Green thumb, what is this?"

She took a piece of chalk and printed the words on a green blackboard that hung by his desk. She looked at all his dictionaries lined up in a row on his desk, French–Russian, French–English, Russian–English. She studied the Russian typewriter with its Cyrillic letters and looked at the tortured manuscript paper stacked up next to it, fiercely crossed out and penciled in. She thought a moment more and also printed "gag me with a spoon" on the chalkboard, thinking he would like to learn American slang. She ran her finger against the Russian scarf hanging on the wall and studied the row of books in three languages tucked into the shelves. She looked at the postcards he had tacked up, and saw one from the Frick collection she had sent him. She was just about to take it down and read what she had written when she turned around and saw her sheets on his bed and the writing toys on the floor next to the bed. The Scotch was in a fine crystal decanter on a black lacquer tray, the new books stacked neatly on the desk, the vitamins displayed prominently on the dining table. The Frisbee hung proudly by the door like a trophy.

She slumped down into the only chair, suddenly feeling very weak and weary. And used. She understood just then that this was all he wanted. She had served her purpose, but worse than that, she was to expect nothing in return.

Katia Hates Paris

PARIS WAS A fickle city; she could turn on you at any moment. Sometimes she was a sweet temptress, whispering into your ear, making you ooze with your own goodness. Other times she could be a nasty bitch, flouncing her skirt right into your face like an impossible woman. Perhaps it was because Paris was a city of such high-flown style. If you woke up feeling not quite sure about yourself, those soaring and graceful vistas, or even those wistful little window treatments of lace curtains and flowers fluttering from behind some grillwork, could make you feel awkward and unspontaneous.

By contrast, New York was the perfect place to feel rotten. The city was driven by the energy of people feeling bad, dusting themselves off and trying again. It was a city filled with harshly lit coffee shops and dejected individuals with greasy hair and stained clothes sitting at counters eating breakfast specials. There was nowhere to hide from your sadness in New York, it smacked you right back in the face and said, "Toughen up, kid." The no-pity city: ride the New York City subway when you're sad and you'll feel even more like shit. What made it bearable was that underneath all the grittiness was the elusive, intoxicating possibility that your life could change at any moment.

But, Katia understood, when you're sad in Paris, you're a spoilsport. On the outside it seemed as if the city soothed your sadness, romancing you, coaxing it from you. "There, there, let me hear all about it," the Seine pretends to croon if you walk by feeling windswept and lonely.

She quickly learned the truth: there are no feelings in Paris; it is a city of illusion and stylish displays of surface emotion. Everything must be lovely there; it cannot tolerate the guts and pain of living. In this way, Paris turned on Katia and made her feel pathetic, unequal to the graceful and elegant feelings she thought she should feel there.

For Katia, these two weeks passed slowly like a Chinese water torture, her dream vacation turned into a nightmare. She tried to turn the situation around, but somehow it got away from her. She let herself be treated rudely by shopgirls, she stumbled on her French, she got confused in the metro, drank too much wine, couldn't enjoy the museums, sit in gardens or even read a book. She was tentative and unsure. It was like going to a French movie where the audience was laughing and she didn't understand what was going on. Oh, if only she could have taken hold of herself and the city like an unruly horse and given it a few swift, strong kicks to establish who was boss. If only she could have lunched smartly in cafés after a morning at the Orangerie and then, in the afternoons, scoured the important French collections, taken tea at a little boîte on the Left Bank. To be followed by a shower, a change of clothes, cocktails, then theater and a midnight supper with some urbane and witty acquaintance.

The problem, of course, was Boris. He was not behaving as Katia had hoped. He begrudgingly consented to have dinner with her every third night—if she was lucky. If she was good and left him in peace, she could meet him at his place for a drink when he would emerge from his bath, dressed in a beautifully casual French style. His appearing so complete and perfect left Katia feeling dumpy and démodé. On one occasion she arrived too early, following a dusty afternoon of walking, and having no place to go, she waited for him on the steps of his apartment. When he arrived from his tennis game, he looked at her and tsked in disapproval. Didn't she know that's what cafés were for, he said, places to dally so as not to impose on your friends?

What had gotten into him? She tried to please him, and when she did, he seemed to think less of her, shaking her off like some insistent fly buzzing around his head. They would go out to some understated, Parisian restaurant he had heard about and had always wanted to try, and have an uncomfortable dinner. It was the type of clubby, bourgeois enclave that no tourists would dare enter even if they could have found it. Over dinner he would criticize the movies she had gone to see, the shops and museums she had visited, the appetizer she had selected, the way she picked up a cornichon with her fingers or the way she didn't sniff her wine before drinking it. The dinner ended when she would pay for it over his polite but insincere protests. She could see the look of relief in his eyes when her American Express card clicked onto the table. Afterward, he would walk her to the St. Sulpice metro and she would go home alone in the dark. At Montparnasse-Bienvenue, instead of switching trains, she would get out and wander down the hugely impersonal boulevards, staring up at the grand edifices, feeling small and unimportant, wondering about the carefree, bourgeois lives taking place behind those soaring windows, underneath those crystal chandeliers, all the while clutching the date of her next, precious meeting with him, three nights from then.

Her days were restless and tiresome. Endless walking with no destinations and no reward at the end of her journeys. She was really in search of the peace in herself but, of course, couldn't find it anywhere. She made the hot trek up to Montmartre, getting lost at every turn, unable to appreciate the exquisite little houses and charming streets. Then she stared impatiently at the basilica and wondered, "What am I doing here? Exhausted, she turned to go back down immediately. She stopped awhile in a filthy café but felt conspicuous and uncomfortable sitting next to a boisterous group of young people. Another day she waited on line for an hour to get into the Louvre, and when she finally got in, there was nothing she really wanted to see, and besides, she was suddenly too tired to look at anything. At least look at the Winged Victory for a moment, she chided herself, but even that was unpleasant, so chaotic was the hall with the press of noisy tourists. The Louvre is a stupid museum, she decided, too big and filled with tourists milling about not really seeing anything at all, wanting only to be able to say they had been to the Louvre.

One afternoon she decided to sit on the quay of the Île St. Louis and write in her journal. She longed to be one of those lovely creatures she saw from her carnival perch in the Bateaux Mouches, the person she always assumed was a Parisian, sitting on the quay, enjoying the beauty of the island. She found the perfect empty park bench and settled down, staring back at the tourists as the tour boats floated by. Just as she began to write in her journal, a clochard sat down next to her. Ah well, this was Paris after all. She tried to concentrate on her diary, but felt ill at ease. She wasn't sure but she had the distinct sense that he was staring at her and masturbating. She sat absolutely still. Is that really what he was doing? But she didn't want to look and find out. She snapped the book shut and got up abruptly. Not even a few moments of peace. Well, since she was here, she should at least go to Bertillon for some sorbet. But, of course, it was closed for August. So she went to have a manicure instead. It chipped away an hour. Going back to that musty apartment of death didn't make things any easier. She tried to spend as little time there as possible, but even sleeping there was a torture. She lay in bed nights, listening to French radio, trying to imagine she was an old man.

Then, on August 31, the city changed gears with the Parisians miraculously pouring back into the city from their vacances. The rentrée was truly comical. On August 30, all had been quiet. The next morning when she went out for her coffee, there appeared millions of cheerful, spunky, sprite Parisians, looking rested and delighted to be back in the city. Cafés that had been closed the day before were now in full swing, with patrons greeting each other and comparing notes on their vacations. Overnight, shops were unshingled and new displays of the latest fall fashions were unveiled. Mothers were shopping for school clothes with their children; maids were furiously cleaning apartments and chatting with each other in the streets as they wrung out their mops. Of course it made Katia feel cheated and in the wrong place at the wrong time. She had come in August when Paris was empty, and just as the city was coming to life, she was leaving for New York.

On one of her last days, Katia found herself strolling nostalgically through the Jardin du Luxembourg. She looked at her watch and it occurred to her that it was the time of day when Boris might be playing tennis. She decided to peek in on his life, to see just how he looked and acted every day when he came here after his writing. She ambled slowly, hoping to disappear into the crowd. But she had the uncomfortable sensation that all eyes were aimed on her because of the secret plan clearly written on her face. Slowly, around the fountain, through the arbor of trees, to the direction of the tennis courts, she was drawn. The park was a festival of French people enjoying themselves, sunning, reading, playing Frisbee, kissing, strolling and discoursing. There were elegant old couples sitting in the shade and teenagers flirting with each other around the fountain. Children were riding ponies, sailing toy boats or being chased by their nannies.

She considered the Lux her park, for she had lived only a block away when she was an exchange student in '72. She thought fondly about all the time she had spent in the Lux, meeting friends, going out for a smoke or just walking through it several times a day on her way to and from classes at the Sorbonne. She especially remembered clunking in here one Saturday morning, painfully hung over, lugging seven empty wine bottles and depositing them in the large wire garbage bin by the rue d'Assas gate. She and her two roommates had entertained some boys the night before and had gotten a bit carried away and they didn't want their landlady to find the bottles in their garbage. That night they made up a game that was a cross between spin the bottle and strip poker. At the time they all thought it was so clever and inventive, but really, Katia laughed as the memory surfaced, what a dumb game, because there was no skill involved. Someone spun the bottle, and if it landed on you, you had to take off a piece of clothing. It would only be a matter of time before everyone was naked. She looked back on it fondly and thought it sweet that they needed a foil for how young and awkward they were. The evening ended when one of the boys insisted on running around the block in his underpants and, unfortunately ran past the police station and the French gendarmes chased him until he lost them and snuck back into the apartment for his clothes.

There he was. Her handsome nemesis, the source of all her unhappiness. For the first time she saw a meanness in him. He was duly decked out in his red American sweat pants and white T shirt, a navy sweatband on his forehead. He had just finished playing with her blue Frisbee with the white stars and put it into the *Life* magazine bag. He was a man proud and haughty in all his Made in the U.S.A. gear as he wended his way across the sidewalk to the courts. He did some exaggerated, show-off stretches and then took his place on the court opposite a blue jean–clad young guy whom she pegged immediately to be a teenage tennis hustler.

Katia approached the courts and slipped on her sunglasses, hoping Boris wouldn't recognize her in the crowd. She took a seat and tried to become just another one of the many people watching the match. Around her were tennis groupies waiting for courts and the wives and girlfriends of the players lounging casually, reading intellectual-looking paperbacks and sipping from plastic liter bottles of water. She noticed there were only men on the courts. Katia became miffed. It was a male tennis Mafia. The courts were hogged by asshole, macho Frenchmen who had fantasies about themselves as they played. They pretended they were tennis champs in the French Open; she could just see it on their faces. Brave was the woman who dared to set foot on a court. No wonder Boris had scoffed at her when she suggested they play together; he would have been embarrassed to show his face.

Katia was very clear today. Her mind buzzed. What good is a man who won't play tennis with a woman? Even just once? Is it that painful an ordeal? Isn't the company of a good woman fun enough, game enough? It's the charm of the game, after all, that makes it. When a man and a woman play tennis, it's a seduction, a delightful bantering, a me-Tarzan-you-Jane kind of thing. But when two men played, it turned into some sort of primal jungle banana contest, and when playtime was over, it was, "now who's got the biggest banana?"

As she watched Boris play she understood things about him for the first time, it was all there in his game. First of all, he was at a loss because of his size. Although he could move quickly, he lacked the long arms and legs to make it easier for him. He played tennis like a little dirty rat, scuttling about the court. His serve lacked grace and style, so instead, he delivered stealthy cannonballs with lots of spin. It was painfully clear he had not grown up with tennis, for he was behaving like a crazed, deprived person who was finally being allowed to play. There was a painfully secretive grin of determination of his face, as if he were just waiting for someone to find him out and order him off the court.

The teenage hustler had Boris hustling all over the court while he stood perfectly still and controlled the game with brilliant, economical strokes. Boris fell for his setups every time. But more important, he lost points by his own sloppiness. And then it dawned on her that this is why Boris couldn't win at tennis, nor could he win at life: too many unforced errors. He wanted only to be a winner, to have won, *but he didn't want to play the game.* One of the things he was most proud of was not compromising; in fact, to Boris, "compromise" was the ugliest word in any language. She knew he was a supremely talented writer but he wouldn't play the game of human relations. Canceled journalist trips, lost freelance jobs, undelivered promised advances for books, stories rejected by magazines—all the situations he lost were due to his own unforced errors and yet he blamed the world for being stupid.

Unconsciously she cried out. She realized this was how he made love, too. He didn't like the act of making love, he liked to *have made* love. Suddenly she saw it all—his short, abrupt movements, the flurry of his rushing her. What she had first taken for animal abandon, she now understood as insensitivity. Life was a one-way street for him. He made love one way: his way. He never cared how she wanted to be touched or asked her what she would like. And if she did not respond to his touch, it was her fault, not his.

Katia stared dully at the match, hypnotized by the rhythm of the ball, and with each bounce she became more distressed with her own blindness. Why had it taken her this long to realize she didn't enjoy their lovemaking? She thought now with distaste of how he clamped his mouth to her cunt and gnawed away. He never searched her out or reveled in her body or lost himself in it. Boris fucked women. It was just another match to be savored when it was over. When he made a woman come, he had won.

Then she remembered how he was pleased that she could come so effortlessly. He told her that most women didn't have orgasms. Katia was shocked at such a piece of information. "They don't?" She found it extraordinary that most women were frigid, but figured he must know because he was a man with lots of women under his belt. Of course, the reason he could say such a thing was not because women were frigid, but because he was such a bad lover. There at the tennis court she understood that she would rather have the tentative hands of an inexperienced man ravishing her body, abandoning himself, discovering and delighting in her, than the sexual technician that Boris claimed to be.

Katia shuffled out of the Lux in a daze. How could she have been so stupid? Where had she been all this time? She walked slowly like a wounded puppy through the streets of her old arrondissement, lost in the despair of her revelation. Her awakening, she called it. Finally she got on the metro and rode around for a while, spontaneously getting out at Concorde. She was walking up the Champs Élysées when she noticed that the Élysée Palais was showing Joseph Losey's *Don Giovanni*. Big frozen letters announced it was air-conditioned inside. She was in luck, it was starting right now, so she bought a ticket and dashed inside just as the lights were going down. As the titles rolled and the music swelled, the little old lady with the basket of treats came swishing by for her final round. Katia bought herself a Grand Marnier ice-cream bar and hunkered down protectively in her seat, letting Mozart soothe her for the rest of the afternoon.

Katia Leaves Boris

ON HER LAST night in Paris, Katia made the final trip to Boris's studio for her farewell dinner. She dressed very carefully, wearing the same dress she had worn for their first dinner together. When she walked into his cozy room, she looked like a bag lady, carrying all the items he had lent her during her stay—a typewriter, a sweater, a jacket, an umbrella and a bag of leftover groceries that she hadn't used. He scolded her for lugging it all by herself (but what other choice had there been, he hadn't offered to help, she thought dryly) and continued in his disapproving vein as he unpacked the bag of food. "This will kill you, it is poison," he said waving a tiny jar of instant coffee at her. Then, holding a jar of jam, "This is merde, these commercial preserves." She noticed however, how he put everything away very quickly in his cupboards.

By now, she was used to his ranting and paid him no attention. Despite his criticisms, he was in a jovial mood, suddenly feeling very sentimental about her leaving. He started talking about how she was part of his family, like a sister. Then he started flurrying nervously about the studio, looking for presents to give her, holding up a Limoges teacup, tiny crocks of rare spices, a Russian scarf.

"Here, do you want this?" He came out from rummaging in his closet holding a ratty old sport jacket. "It's very gamine for a woman to wear." She shook her head, annoyed by his trying to be nice to her after these two miserable weeks. "How about my sweater?" He pointed to a sweater lying on the chair. Again, she shook her head. He was like a salesman who couldn't even give anything away. He was determined, so finally, to put an end to this silly reverse bargaining, she accepted two records of piano music by a Russian pianist and a book on French wine. But before they left for dinner, he asked if she could leave him the book, because it was his only reference and he knew for a fact that the book was available in the States, so could she just pick up a copy there?

To complete her visit, as if drawing a circle, they went back to the same restaurant they had dined in her first night in Paris. The gay waiter remembered them and flirted with Boris. When that didn't work, he flirted with Katia. "You see," Boris whispered, "these pédés are very clever. When they want a man, they flirt with his woman." They had, surprisingly, a sweet dinner. There was candlelight and he attended to her wineglass and buttered her bread. He held her fingertips and kissed them. He poked his fork intimately onto her plate and his, searching for choice morsels to feed her. They talked of what she would do when she got back to New York and what his upcoming days looked like. Ironically, that evening she felt that Boris was relaxed in her company for the first time.

Afterward, he took her on a final walk of "his Paris," accompanied by a running commentary of what he saw, how he felt about the buildings, rating the various boutiques, recounting the history of certain charming streets. They ended up in the deserted garden courtyard of the Palais Royal, which Katia had always jokingly referred to as Richelieu's place. Richelieu had built it originally, and after his death, Louis XIV moved out of the cold and drafty Louvre to take up residence in this more intimate abode. The square was so perfectly beautiful and still that Katia felt she was standing in an outdoor chapel. "Colette lived in those rooms over there," Boris purred coyly in her ear. Then he looked around and became disgusted. In a loud voice that echoed off the walls, he said, "Unbelievable! Stupid French! Look at this! Absolutely empty! The Parisians don't care, they just walk right by, tara tara tara." He mimicked a nose-in-the-air walk. Then he spun around and spread his arms, displaying the history, the elegance, the soul of eighteenth-century Paris in one sweep. "But ees fan-taaas-tic," he crooned.

The silence and mystery were intoxicating, and for a few precious seconds Katia was able to step out of herself and imagine Molière dying as he performed *Le Malade Imaginaire* in this open-air theater. Then much later, Colette had come along, and Katia thought, I am sharing the same view Colette might have had, peeking out of her window for a breath of fresh night air. This is what Paris is about, she thought with chagrin. Living history, yours for a look, a touch, a moment. It was precisely this that had eluded her during her stay, only to find it now, on her last night.

They continued walking on back streets, on their way, Katia thought, to the metro. She didn't have much to say, so exhausted was she by her own confusion, so instead she enjoyed the bittersweet September evening air and kept quiet.

"See that woman over there?" Boris said.

"Which one?"

"That old lady, leaning against the wall." He pointed.

"Yes."

"She's the oldest whore in Paris."

"No." Katia looked at her. Why, she looked like a New York City bag lady. "I can't imagine any man . . ." When she looked again, she saw the woman was indeed strolling the street aimlessly, yet in total control, like she was an old hand at this routine.

"It's true. There is someone for everyone in Paris," he said. "It's different here, you know." He sounded very wistful. "Some men go to the same prostitute for years."

They continued walking until she realized she was seeing more and more girls on the streets. Katia turned to Boris and gave him a what's-going-on-here look. He had steered her to one of his favorite insomnia haunts, the red-light district of Les Halles.

"Every quartier has its own streets for girls. You never even have to leave your arrondissement. It's very polite the way the French do this, don't you think?" He told her to look, but not stare, at the girls. He pulled her close and held her hand sternly. "They don't like that. And they don't like that you're here with me because they know you're just looking at them. They're just trying to do their job. So be very nice."

She could see that Boris felt comfortable here; he had an affinity for these hardworking women, these noble souls, he called them. But she was nervous. How should she look? What could she say? But she was also excited, for this was an unknown world to her. She usually read about red-light districts in books or saw them re-created in the movies. No men she knew ever went to prostitutes, so she never heard about it firsthand. Now was her chance to experience this for herself and she was grateful to Boris for showing her something she never would have seen otherwise.

She was surprised to find the atmosphere of the street totally unthreatening, not at all like the vulgar, sleazy feeling she had expected. In fact, it was a sweet and gentle place. The girls were ultrafeminine, and Katia felt she had entered a secret world of cats, who were rubbing their backs on lampposts or simply crouched by twos or threes in the darkened doorways. Smoke was drifting up alluringly from their cigarettes, and there was the seductive, melodious lilt of female voices, murmuring, laughing, sharing confidences as solitary men walked up and down the street looking at the girls while the girls looked back. Who are these women? she wondered. Could they be just like me? She was surprised to find herself a bit in awe of them. Was she even a tiny bit jealous perhaps, for they seemed to have the keys to some secrets that Katia felt sure had eluded her. That was it—they knew something she didn't—but what, exactly?

"You will not get any disease here," he told her proudly. "It is all government-regulated. The girls go to the doctor four times a year for shots; they are very clean."

The words A *Spy in the House of Love* flashed in her mind. It was a title of a book by Anaïs Nin. Yes, that's exactly how she felt. Then she looked at Boris and wondered if he had ever gone to one of these girls. She tried to imagine him, but no, she couldn't. He was too poor, and besides, he wouldn't have to pay for sex, he could get it for free. She noticed that he was intrigued by the girls, too. The fact that sex was for sale when you could get it for free made it different somehow, but she couldn't quite understand how.

She turned her attention to watching the men on the street, observing their tense, uncertain faces as they shopped for a woman. She looked for a sign, a twitch of some sort, when they found the right one, the one who appealed. There seemed to be a light that flickered in their eyes, a quick flash of recognition that returned quickly back to their hunger and fear of rejection, for in the end, a man had to do the approaching, as always. All the fantasies one could hope for were represented here. You could choose a girl by her dress, her age or her height. There were blondes, brunettes, redheads. You like long hair, short hair, or maybe a wig? How about a young Lolita with a pouty smile and silly red glasses, or a motherly type? A schoolgirl with navy pinafore and braids? Slim? A chubby girl perhaps. A lady with a poodle on a leash or a girl in a business suit or nurse's uniform. Of course there were the usual prostitute types in tight sweaters and miniskirts, and the cocktail-dress and garter-belt girls.

Katia watched as some young boys ogled and teased the girls. She could see that they were doing it out of adolescent frustration and embarrassment in the presence of such overpowering womanliness. The girls just mocked them skillfully, wanting to get rid of them because they had real customers with money to look out for.

"Little pencils," Boris said.

"What?"

"In Russia the whores called young boys little pencils because of their little pricks. Come here, little pencil," he mimicked a Russian prostitute, and laughed at the memory.

"Were you a little pencil?" she asked, trying to imagine him as a little boy chasing after Russian whores.

Katia noticed a nice-looking man wandering back and forth on the street and watched how he finally chose a girl and walked up to her. She couldn't hear the exact transaction, but it sounded like pleasantries, hello, smiles, a little flirtation about the weather perhaps, possibly a "how much?" uttered under his breath and a "what do you want exactly?" under hers, and a quick deal was politely reached. The girl tilted her head and said, "On y va?" with an incredibly warm smile. So smooth, even classy. The two of them walked off together, and a second later they looked just like Katia and Boris, just another man and woman together on the street, enjoying each other's company. Katia suddenly felt jealous; she wanted to follow them, go right into the room with them and watch. She was sure they would do the most delicious things together, things she had probably never done before. Ah, the mystery of it all. The sex that those two were going to have would be real sex, no games about love, just an acknowledgment of animal needs. Sure, love had its place, but then, so did this. Only most people didn't look at it that way, preferring to forget the animal origin of fucking, choosing instead to sugarcoat it with frilly talk about love. It was an easier pill to swallow.

Boris turned to her and gave her a long, hard look. His eyes seemed to melt from some hardness to a tenderness as he looked deep into her. She wondered what he was looking at. He caressed her hand with his hand, then startled her by pinching her cheek so hard she cried out and pushed him away.

"Choose one," he said.

"What?"

"Choose a girl," he said coldly with a flourish of his hand.

Katia's heart pounded. What was going on here? Not only would he not sleep with her, he wanted her to choose a girl for him! She shook her head in shame.

"Live, baby. Live! Turn off your mind and just live. It is very simple," he said, and gave her a kiss on the cheek.

She knew there was some truth to his words, but she was too lost to make any sense of what was happening. She felt manipulated. What was right and what was wrong? What was he trying to do? She was engulfed by white noise pounding in her ears.

Boris took her hand and they walked up and down the street again, slowly this time, and Katia looked at the girls in a new light with the idea of actually selecting one. All right, she thought grimly, two could play this game.

"That one," she said finally, pointing.

He looked. "Okay. Wait here," he said, and walked up to the girl Katia had chosen. She seemed to be about her own age or maybe a few years older, very healthy looking, with clear blue eyes and shiny black hair. She was wearing a black dress that outlined her body perfectly, a pair of heels and black lace stockings, which Katia assumed were held up by the ubiquitous garter belt. She looked sort of like a street-smart Louise Brooks. Katia wondered why she had been drawn to her. Perhaps it was because she looked so sure of herself; she looked like Katia herself wanted to look: at ease and in control. Katia watched as she chatted with Boris. Then Boris pointed to Katia, and the girl looked in her direction and nodded.

He wants to fuck her and make me watch it. Or maybe he wants a threesome. Or maybe he wants to watch two women play with each other? She tried to run through all the possible combinations and realized how little she knew about this sort of thing. So what was it going to be? She just hoped she wouldn't make a fool of herself.

Boris came over and, taking her by the hand, introduced her to Chantal, who smiled at her with such grace and confidence she felt even worse. This is really getting weird, she thought; some people play bridge, others play golf, we are going to play sex games. But on top of her fear was a raging curiosity. Isn't this what she had wanted? Exactly what was she really capable of? What hidden things would she find out about herself that evening?

Chantal led the two of them down the block and around the corner to a nondescript building that looked just like an apartment house. Good, she thought, no sordid hotel to deal with. That made her feel a little more calm. They climbed two flights silently, then Chantal stopped in front of a door and took out her keys. She opened the door and motioned for Katia to enter. By now Katia was a wreck, her heart pounding; she felt suffocated and couldn't draw a decent breath. She turned and saw Boris still standing outside in the hall.

"I'll wait for you downstairs," he said.

The moment froze. Katia looked at him, uncomprehending. "What?" she croaked, barely able to speak.

"You should experience everything in life, baby, everything. You know the old saying: 'Once a philosopher, twice a pervert'? Try to enjoy, baby," and with that he walked away.

Katia was speechless; she felt like she had been hit. Chantal had watched this exchange and then closed the door quietly, realizing instantly that Katia hadn't been let in on the deal. Katia looked at Chantal with panic and then anger. There was no way anything was going to happen in this room. This was all a disgusting joke.

The room held a large bed, a bureau and an overstuffed chair into which Katia slumped down to think about what this all meant and what she would do next. Chantal flipped on a small lamp, sat down on the bed and lit a cigarette. Not a word passed between them.

Katia tried to calm herself. That bastard! Now, I am just going to sit here and after a decent interval I will go downstairs and tell him it was fabulous. No! I am going to leave right now and hit him, beat him. No, I will just disappear and never see him again. She put her head back; she was a little tipsy with all the wine she had drunk at dinner. She was utterly paralyzed in her confusion. What should she do? What had she gotten herself into? Why was he doing this to her?

She looked at Chantal, who was just sitting on the bed calmly, smoking a cigarette in the sexy way that Frenchwomen had. Was she bored? She seemed unconcerned and, strangely, rather benign. Katia sighed. Oh well, this girl's seen it all, hasn't she? Katia needed to figure this out before she left the room. Boris had not made love to her during the entire two weeks she had been in Paris. What was he trying to tell her by this act? What was the message in all of this? This was how he would send her back to New York? Was this an insult? A mockery of her? All these questions and no answers. She had a splitting headache.

"Vous avez un aspirin?" Katia asked her, not remembering that the French for aspirin was aspirine. Chantal nodded and went over to the cabinet above the sink and pulled out a tin box, which she brought to Katia with bottle of Vittel. "Merci," Katia said, and helped herself.

"Do you want to lie down?" Chantal said in nicely accented English.

"Ah, you must have American customers. Your English is very good." Katia was hesitant about going anywhere near the bed, but then decided, what the hell. She needed to lie down to appease her pounding head. "Thank you. Yes, I will lie down."

She closed her eyes, and before she knew it, Chantal had prepared a cold washcloth and put it on her forehead. It felt excellent.

"How old are you?"

"Twenty-seven," Chantal said.

"Hmmm," Katia mused. She looked older. A life on the street added years.

"Maybe you would feel more comfortable if you took your clothes off?" Chantal asked kindly.

"Look." Katia sat up, clutching the cloth to her head. "You are very nice, but I don't want to do anything. I don't want to touch you. I have no desire to touch you and I don't want you to touch me. I am not a—comment dit-on en français—lesbian? It is men I like. If you don't mind, I'll just lie here until my headache goes away and decide what to do, okay?"

"Okay," Chantal said. "No problem." There was silence for a few minutes and then she sat down on the bed opposite Katia. "But at least let me massage your head to send your headache away. You don't have to do anything. I'll do it. You can just relax."

Katia thought about it. She loved massages, but she was torn. She didn't want this woman near her. But surely a massage wouldn't hurt. In fact, it would feel good. "Well, okay," she said suspiciously. After all, the woman had been paid.

Chantal took her shoes off and climbed over to her, settling Katia's head in her lap. Katia felt gentle fingers rubbing her temples and scalp. God, it felt great to be touched. Chantal didn't stop, she just kept caressing her face slowly in long circular motions. Then she massaged her scalp. Ooh, scalp massages were the best. Katia loved giving a man a head massage; it rendered him silly every time. This whole experience reminded her of getting a facial back home. She sighed. Home. She felt pampered and woozy. Then Chantal's hands started rubbing her shoulders and neck. Katia was surprised at how she was actually able to relax and that she was being turned on by this strange woman's hands on her. She tried to stop slipping, but instead, her resistance turned her on even more and she started purring inside. She was embarrassed and determined to hide that it felt good. Her mind rambled. A gift to myself. This is for me. Totally for me. I don't have to do anything.

"Won't you let me give you a nice massage?" Chantal asked in an oozing voice. It was as if she had felt Katia relent.

Katia thought about it. If this felt good, that would be even better. Against her own better judgment she nodded. She knew full well what happened when you offered to give a man a harmless massage. Well, that wouldn't happen here. It's all happening because Chantal wants it, not me, she told herself. But at the same time she knew she wanted to be carried away by these forbidden, sweet touches. That's it. It could be a game. It would be okay. Maybe.

Katia sat up and started undressing. "Let me help you," Chantal said, and helped slide the clothes off her body, exploring her with teasingly gentle hands all the while. She had never quite been undressed like that before, even by a man. When a man undressed her, there was more urgency. This was more playful and sexy because both of them knew what was underneath her clothes. Chantal kept admiring the different parts of her body, running her hands along each newly undressed part, delighting in it, telling her how beautiful she was. Katia lay down on her stomach and felt Chantal's hands, now slippery with some pleasantly scented oil, glide expertly on her back. She felt the tension of her trip slipping away from her body as she entered into the most intensely private reverie she ever had. She took a long, slow, deep breath. This feels so good it should be illegal. Then she realized, it is.

In her dream state she thought how she had never been touched by a woman, and under Chantal's hands she was experiencing her body in a new way. Here was this kind lady showing her the secrets of her own body, pointing her to new ways of understanding. Katia was lost in a lush jungle of amazing feelings. Only a woman knows exactly how to touch another woman, she thought. A man's touch was learned; he appreciated a woman's body from an entirely different point of view.

By now, Chantal had gently rolled Katia over onto her back and was massaging her breasts and stomach. It was a party, a celebration of herself. She is giving me to myself, Katia said to herself as Chantal started licking and lightly kissing her breasts, then sucking them, first gently, then harder. She seemed to do everying perfectly and with great delight. Katia felt Chantal's fingers slip into her. By now she had surrendered to a sweet and sticky state of the most intense happiness. I am being ravished for the first time in my life. Her whole body was humming at a pitch that she never imagined was possible. She was soaring like a beautiful bird, with nothing supporting her but these currents of sweetness whooshing around her and finally in her and through her. She was out of her body! It was an inhuman feeling. She felt totally, a beautifully savage and cried out as she came, amazed at the primitive sound she made, laughing and crying at the same time.

She floated like a lifeless doll as the currents drifted her slowly back into her body on the bed. With her eyes closed, she didn't care where she was or who she was with, all she knew was, if this could be sex, she wanted more. Katia was shocked at her own need. She felt humiliated and high at the same time. But her humiliation turned her on even more. She didn't have to ask, because before she knew it, there was a soft touch on her cunt, a flirtation of the mouth. She gasped as Chantal started kissing the life from her, urging her to act in ways previously unimaginable. Chantal played her like an instrument, changing the tempos of the music, bringing her to a certain pitch, then slowing her down, arousing her to such a state that she found herself crying, yes, yes, yes.

Oh my God, I'm a lesbian, Katia thought as she walked slowly back down the two flights of stairs an hour later. She pushed open the heavy door and felt the cool night air on her face. Boris was standing across the street, leaning in a doorway; his head nodded as she emerged. He came up to her and put his arms around her, and they stood there, silently rocking gently back and forth.

"So?" he said.

"Am I a lesbian?"

"No, baby." He smiled and held her. "You are my sweet American tough cookie." He kissed her on both cheeks. "And you are the sexiest woman in the world."

He walked her for the last time to the metro and said, "Sleep tight." She felt drugged as she rode dutifully home, switching trains at Montparnasse, arriving finally at Trocadéro, confused as usual, but for a whole new set of reasons this time. Every time she thought she had hit the rock bottom of confusion, she fell even deeper.

The next morning had that neither-here-nor-there quality. She was still physically in Paris, but her mind had switched to the life she would resume in New York that evening. She got up early and went to have her last French breakfast in her café where she eavesdropped on the local gossip, dipping her last croissant into her last, thick, café crème. Katia laughed at how she made a melodramatic big deal of everything—this is my last metro ride, this is my last purchase of *Marie Claire* magazine. . . . She scolded herself for being such a cornball. Then she went up to the apartment for the last time to wait for Boris to come for her. He was late, and she became concerned about getting to the airport on time. She paced the room and got angry with herself for not having thought about getting to the airport herself. She tried to remember where to catch the special metro that went out to Charles de Gaulle.

The buzzer rang abruptly, and instead of waiting for him to come up, she struggled downstairs with her luggage. Boris was agitated. He had waited an hour for a bus and finally jumped into a taxi. This was upsetting his day and cost him precious francs that he really didn't have. But mostly he was in a bad mood because he hated good-byes; they were such a waste of time.

They settled into the taxi and Katia found herself suddenly hysterical about leaving him. A wave of panic engulfed her and she felt like she was going to throw up. Damn! After all his nasty behavior, after all her revelations about his personality, why were the tears spilling down her face?

"You started already," he berated her, "and we're only in the taxicab?" He turned away from her in disgust and ignored her by keeping up a conversation with the driver. Katia took his hand to see if he would comfort her, but he wouldn't. He left his hand limp in hers. He had turned off completely. It just made her cry harder.

They waited on the platform for the train to the airport, and when it arrived, he helped her on with her luggage and agreed to sit with her for a few stops until the train pulled into Montparnasse, at which point he would jump off.

"Now don't worry, you've got plenty of time when the train arrives. The aéroport bus will wait for you, so don't rush. The system is all set up for tourism," he lectured. Huge, burning teardrops rolled down her face. If only he could have put his arms around her and hugged her until she laughed, or held her tight and kissed her cheeks, it would have been all right. Instead, she felt ashamed of herself. He had humiliated her to nothingness.

As the train pulled into Montparnasse he stood up. Katia looked up at him and then, embarrassed by her bloated face, looked away. He bent down and quickly kissed her on both cheeks, then on the mouth. "Ciao, baby. Take the famous care," he said. He stood in the doorway and stared at her for the slightest second. His eyes at that moment were a camera, taking a final souvenir, snapshot memory, freezing on this frame: Katia, sitting and crying in her traveling clothes, the luggage piled up next to her. When she looked at him, she saw his clearness, the intensity in his eyes. She understood why he called good-byes "mini morts." Then he turned and left. She saw him jump off the train and disappear quickly into the crowd.

The train pulled out of the station and the tears rolled down her face even harder. To the few French people on the train, those who were leaving happily on some long-awaited vacation, or going to the airport to greet returning family, she knew she must seem a poignant sight. What had they just witnessed? A woman in love having just left her lover.

But now Katia was crying for a new reason. She was lost, she had lost. She was as alone as she had always been; only now she knew it.

New York

Frank Loves Bloomie's

Frank sat on the couch at Jo Anne's pondering the question she had just asked him.

"What's gotten into you, Frank?" She stood with her hands on her hips. "Think about it while I go to the bathroom." She swished out of the room, tsking and shaking her head.

He didn't want to think about it. He felt perfectly fine, thank you. And he didn't like being treated like a naughty little boy just because he skipped out of work that day and went shopping at Bloomingdale's instead. Give me a break, he thought as he rubbed the couch arm with his palm. It's the first time he had played hooky since he arrived in New York. He was always so diligent.

He leaned back on the couch to savor the experience. The store was pure New York, it was show business, it was jazz, it was a shot in the arm, good for whatever ailed you. He was probably the last person in the city to discover its pleasures, just like he was the last person on Earth to buy Michael Jackson's *Thriller* album. One of his patients had mentioned in passing that it was the top-selling album of all time, and he thought, Well then, I guess I should have one if it's that popular. He went to Tower Records and spied a punky salesclerk.

"Uh, excuse me. Do you have the album *Thriller?* It's by Michael Jackson." From the look on the clerk's face he realized his question was akin to walking into any newspaper kiosk in New York City and asking if they carried *The New York Times*.

Ah, Bloomingdale's. He had gotten caught up in the excitement of it, that's all. Instead of going to the hospital that morning, he had bolted. No big deal. As the downtown subway train went *clackety-clack*, he had a vision of his life going *clackety-clack* right by him. People poured in and out of the train with dour expressions, and his mouth went dry as he thought about the ruts they were in and the rut he was in. I just can't do this today. Why do I have to follow all the rules? Why do I always have to be so good? Why can't I rebel, too, like normal people? Aren't I a normal person? Don't analysts deserve an occasional mental-health day, too? He started laughing. That's something Katia did. Every so often when she felt stuck in her routine, she declared a mental-health day. She would call her office and say, "Hi, I'm sick. Sick and tired." It was her day to get out of all the confines of the office and onto the street, to see life from different angles and time periods, to poke around and feel alive again. She was quite adamant about it and reported her escapades to him with great relish.

He got out of the train and called the hospital. He didn't feel at all bad or guilty when he told the floor nurse who answered the phone that he simply wouldn't be in today. Then, alone in the midst of a sidewalk teeming with people scurrying to work, he pondered what to do with his day. He started giggling, he felt so free, released from his jail of a life. He was amazed that it could take so little, just a little day off, to make him feel so giddy. You have a lot to learn, Frank old buddy. He picked up a copy of the *Village Voice* and sat down in a Greek coffee shop and ordered a cup of coffee and a bran muffin and watched life take place around him. It was when a chic woman came in with a Bloomie's Big Brown Bag that he hit upon the brilliant idea of spending the morning there.

As he strolled through the first floor he thought, So this is what goes on every day while I am sitting at the hospital counseling nervous residents about their patients. He was buffeted by the slickly dressed women charging through the store with incredible purpose. Who are these women? Why aren't they working? Who are they married to and where do they get this money? Do they like their lives? Some of them were interesting, but most were empty in the eyes, wearing too much makeup, and had these controlled haircuts that looked too self-conscious. "I have chicly styled hair," their heads announced. Everything about them was too perfect, nothing was left to the imagination or to chance. They reeked of perfume. This must be the New York Woman that Katia rechristened the New Amazon, in a disparaging tone.

He strolled through Bway, where they were buying makeup with such seriousness that he had to stop and watch. They seemed to know exactly what they wanted, the way they compared lipstick shades, swatching colors on their hands and then holding their hands to the light. They dabbed their eyes with different colors and shifted their weight while looking in the mirrors, trying to decide on a color. Didn't these women have anything better to do? How could you even kiss a woman who wore all this paint? He watched how the salesgirls spoke so convincingly to the women about different creams and lotions and how they drank in their words like gospel.

He rode up the escalator, following the traffic of women. They all seemed to get off at the third floor, where he found himself on a street of boutiques, each bearing the name of a different designer. He thought how complicated it was to be a woman and sort through each designer's different style. Did she want to be the Anne Klein woman or the Calvin Klein woman? What if she felt Ralph Lauren-y one day and Chanel-ish another? Just as on the first floor, like homing pigeons, the women all seemed to know exactly where they were going. Up ahead, a salesgirl was spraying perfume on women as they passed by. He watched how the girl announced the name of the perfume and held it just so, poised, and then how the woman either nodded yes and held out her wrist, or ignored her completely and walked past.

When he came up to her, she didn't reach out with her atomizer or tell him the name of the perfume. He stopped and held out his wrist. "May I try some?"

"Of course, sir, but it's for women."

"That's okay," and he nudged his wrist in her direction and smiled broadly. She smiled back and spritzed him.

"What's it called?" he asked, bringing his wrist up to his nose. He closed his eyes and smelled roses. Roses and what? The word *dreams* came into his mind.

"It's a new perfume that's just arrived in the States. Paris, by Yves St. Laurent. We have a special today. See this umbrella? You get one for only seventeen-fifty with any Paris purchase." She twirled the pink-and-black-flowered parasol for him to admire.

Paris. Of course. No wonder it smelled familiar; that's what Katia had been wearing for over a year. She had picked it up in Paris on her first Cognac/Boris trip. She explained to Frank how Yves had captured the essence of Paris in a new parfum and the city was absolutely drunk on it. She smelled it on practically every woman who swooshed by her. "A new perfume in France is an event," she had boasted.

He thought about how he smelled Katia's perfume only when he stood up to open the door for her and she passed him. It was a parting flourish that said, "Who, me?" That was the proper way to smell perfume on a woman... only if you could get close enough to her. He didn't like it when a perfume announced a woman before she came into a room. No, perfume should be an intimate sensation.

The salesgirl was standing there impatiently, waiting for him to either buy some or move on.

"Okay. I'll take some. And the umbrella, too," he said. They stepped over to the counter where she proceeded to show him the different-size bottles and sprays, parfum or eau de parfum or eau de toilette. More choices to be made. Jo Anne will just love this, he thought as he paid with his American Express card. He asked the salesgirl to give him an application for a Bloomingdale's charge card, which she put into the shopping bag. Good, now I, too, have a shopping bag, he thought as he walked away. It was a morning already filled with surprises.

He continued strolling and found himself walking toward a display of mannequins wearing silk robes. This boutique was called Intimacies. Silks, laces, teddies, tap pants, sheer silk nightshirts, extravagant lacy nightgowns, slips, bikinis, body suits. He thought of how society's mores were structured so that women were encouraged to enjoy these acceptable sexual fetishes. I mean, when you came right down to it, there was no difference between a leather whip and a sexy silk teddy. He fingered a black silk gown and looked at the price. Three hundred and seventy-five dollars for something to sleep in? Oh my. And the matching robe was six hundred? He backed off. This was serious.

"May I help you?" He turned around. A kindly, older saleswoman had snuck up on him.

"Oh. Yes. I'm looking for something for my girlfriend."

"Did you have anything special in mind?"

He said he didn't know, but maybe a robe would be what she would like. He ran down his list of patients to confirm for himself that they would all be at work right now, tucked safely away into their various offices, and then reassured himself that the chances of them playing hooky in the lingerie department of Bloomingdale's were incalculable. Then he wondered if when a man bought lingerie for his girlfriend, did it mean he was really buying something for himself? This is ridiculous; he wished he could turn off his mind. He made a note in his mind to return to this subject in the future, but for now, he could live with the idea of a robe. Everyone did wear robes, after all.

He decided on a royal blue silk kimono. He remembered a phrase Katia used when she described her kimono as "something to throw on and dash around the apartment in." Sitting across from her, he had wondered who the hell had a New York apartment big enough to "dash around" in? Still, the idea was appealing. Then, as if Katia had read his mind, she said that the airiness and fluttering of the silk make it seem like you were dashing, even if you weren't. If Jo Anne had such a robe as this, would she dash about? Taille unique, the label said, one size fits all.

"Kimonos are all there are," Katia had said in her usual definitive manner. He laughed. No other patient of his could have sat there with a straight face and delivered such a compelling monologue about bathrobes. She seemed to be talking to herself. "Oh, and maybe a caramel-colored viyella robe for the deepest, coldest winter nights when you visit your friends in the country and sit by the fire."

"Sipping hot cocoa or camomile tea," Frank had added.

"What?"

"Nothing," he said, hoping she hadn't heard the sarcasm in his voice.

He fished out his American Express card once again and watched the saleswoman wrap the robe in tissue. She told him if he wanted a box, he'd have to go to the wrap desk just around the corner.

He stepped out of the lingerie boutique and walked down the central aisle of boutique row. He could not get over the decisions a woman had to make. Every single aspect of her wardrobe was an opportunity for choice, for style, for statement. He passed by a handbag counter. Day bags, evening bags, clutches, totes, shoulder bags, jeweled, minaudières, quilted, pouched, structured, leather. Then, hats. Rainhats, sunhats, cocktail hats, fur hats, winter hats, berets, scarves, square, oblong, silk, wool, challais, mohair. Jewels! He looked at the glittering beads, necklaces, pins, earrings, bracelets, bangles, studs, hoops, hair clips, hair bands. Then shoes, stockings, coats! How did they put it all together? Everything looked so alluring and seemed to shout, "Buy me, buy me, if you don't own me, you won't be happy, only I can make your life perfect, I'll be just the little thing that will make you feel better and look great!"

He walked out of the store three hours later, laden with four shopping bags. It was time for Jo Anne to stop wearing her corduroy pants. He watched what other women were choosing and trying on, and using snippets of information that Katia had mentioned, he made his choices.

He waved down a cab, shoved in the bags, then himself. He rode back uptown supremely content, feeling he had truly refreshed his life on this, his day of personal hooky. When he got to his office, he stashed everything into the closet and checked his watch. Good, he still had a few luxurious hours to himself before his afternoon patients. He set his alarm clock and stretched out on his couch for a nice, long nap. Afternoon naps were such a stolen pleasure. Later on, he noticed how well he listened to his patients; he felt like he was able to receive their information with a new light in his eyes. At 7:30, he waited for an appropriate interval after his last patient left and then strolled up to Jo Anne's with the shopping bags.

He pressed the buzzer downstairs and she let him in without even asking who it was. He would have to talk to her about that; she should always talk into the intercom because in this city you never knew. The excitement of his day was bubbling up inside of him as he rode up in the elevator. What delight he would cause her in just a few seconds! He rang the doorbell and couldn't keep the smile off his face.

She scrunched up her face when she opened the door. "I can't imagine you in Bloomingdale's pawing through the racks," was the first thing she said as she stood aside to let him in.

He was taken aback at her mood. "Why do you have to be so negative? Most women would be pleased to have a man bring them presents." He wasn't going to let her dampen his good spirits. "Besides, I had such fun shopping for you today."

"I guess I'm supposed to say, 'Oh Frank, you shouldn't have,'" she mimicked.

"Well, I did. So let's take a look."

He told her all about his day and about how complicated it must be to be a woman. She picked the clothes out of the bags, one by one, holding them up with her fingertips as if they were contaminated. She couldn't imagine herself wearing these.

"Oh, come on, Jo Anne, that's just the point. That's what today was about for me. And you too. Try them on!" he goaded.

"Okay," she said with a weary voice.

"And let's have some enthusiasm here!" he said.

She held up a black Japanese top, the shape of which she couldn't figure out. "Where are the armholes on this thing?" She turned it around searching for which way was up.

"Here, it goes like this. The salesgirl showed me. You see, it doesn't look like anything until you put it on! You know, the old shapeless-on-the-hanger-but-just-wait-till-you-try-it-on deal." He adjusted it on her body, twisting and turning it until he believed it was just right, then stepped back to admire his fashion expertise. She looked at herself in the mirror while he continued prattling.

"Spin around, Jo Anne, let's see," he said gaily. "This is a key item, you could build an entire wardrobe around this one piece."

She looked at him as if he was a child who had been learning naughty words that were chalked on the sidewalk. "I don't know. . . ." she said, turning around slowly. "Well, it is interesting, that I will say. Before I do anything else, let's send out. Chinese. I'm starving and I can see I'm going to need fortification to get through this event." She rummaged through the telephone-table drawer and found a menu. "Here, choose what you want and order me a moo shu."

She was in a slightly better mood when the food arrived and she turned on the television. That's when she was really happy, eating Chinese food in front of the TV. With "Dallas" on as background noise, she proceeded to try everything on, model it for him and discuss when she would ever wear such a thing. It was after "Dallas" and a bit into "Falcon Crest" that she turned to him and said, "What's gotten into you, Frank?"

She returned from the bathroom and sat down next to him on the couch. He looked at her. The clothes hadn't transformed her. She was still Jo Anne. Jo Anne dressed in a kimono and smelling of Paris.

"Well," she said, "talk to me."

"I . . . have nothing to say."

"Okay then, I'll start. I get the feeling that you're not happy with me the way I am. You want me to be someone I'm not. The question is, who? And, more importantly, why?"

He couldn't answer. He sat quietly, so she continued slowly, groping for her thoughts. "You're exhibiting all the signs of a man turned inside out in love, except something is terribly off." She tapped her fingers on her arm and mused, "It's not me you're loving."

Frank stared glumly into the middle distance. At that moment he felt utterly miserable. He sighed and ran his hands through his hair. A tremendous wave of sadness flowed over him and he had to struggle to keep his tears back. What was this all about?

She was right. His heart absolutely ached. There was a hunger that he feared would never be fed. What an awful feeling. He felt defeated and open, tender and raw. He felt wounded yet, at the same time, alive and vital. He was both clear and muddled, it was at once painful and wonderful. It was how he had felt looking into his dog's eyes when he was a boy, connecting in a profound way, but aching with the knowledge that he could never get closer to knowing him, because he was a boy and his dog was a dog.

"I have a broken heart," he said, and looked as surprised as she was at these words that had just came out of him. He didn't know what he meant, but it seemed to be exactly it. But who had broken his heart? Certainly it was not Jo Anne. It felt like he had broken his own heart. Katia? He couldn't bring himself to say it much less think it.

"Katia," she said, and then moved to the couch opposite from where he sat as if she didn't want to be so close to him.

He couldn't believe what was happening to him, or rather, what had happened to him. "I've fallen in love. I am in love." He spoke very slowly, forming the words as they came into his mind. "It happened *to* me. I didn't want it. And even though in this situation it is supposed to be wrong . . . how can falling in love be wrong? Falling in love is holy. It is rare." He shook his head in frustration. "God, I can't believe this is me talking." He lost himself in his thoughts.

After a few moments he continued talking in a dreamlike voice. "I am a failure. I have failed Katia. All this time I had been trying to be so good and so correct, and instead, I have screwed up totally as a doctor. I have failed the patient! But how is loving someone a failure? What I feel for her seems so normal." He sighed.

"It's so ironic," he said. "There she sits in my office talking about trying to find love and where are all the men, and I'm sitting right across from her! I feel like saying, 'It's me, right here. What about me?'" He buried his face in his hands. "It's a tragic comedy, all right. One in the repertoire of God's dirty-tricks campaign. Mr. Right is sitting right across from Ms. Right and never the twain shall meet."

He looked at Jo Anne sitting across from him. He could see it was a strain for her. This surprised him because it was an indication that she cared for him. He had often wondered about this. She pursed her lips.

"What makes you feel she's Ms. Right? Haven't you considered your countertransference? That just as she fell in love with the idea of you, you are in love with the idea of her?" She tried to keep her voice neutral as she spoke. "Do you really think you would be good together?"

"I don't know," he sighed, and wrung his hands. "How do you separate a woman from her qualities? The fact from the fantasy?" The television droned on. He didn't want to talk anymore, it was too frightening. "I better go," he said abruptly.

"Yes. I think that would be a good idea," Jo Anne said softly.

As he rode down the elevator he decided maybe he shouldn't see Jo Anne until he figured out some things about his life. But where to start exactly? She had raised some interesting points, but he couldn't add it all up. How could he even presume to help other people when he was so out of touch with himself? He walked slowly back to his place in the drizzle and spent an hour sitting in his chair, staring into the darkness. No understanding came; his mind was numb. He thought about Katia and wondered what had happened to her in Paris. How would it be to see her this week? The thought of her now made him nervous and excited. How would he act? Ooh, it was going to be difficult. Maybe he should resign. . . . With thoughts like this clouding his mind, he realized he should put everything on hold. But he couldn't go to sleep, he was too wound up. Suddenly he decided that what he missed was running. He hadn't run since college! He rummaged through the closet and found his old Nikes. Pretty old and dusty, but they would do. He put on his sweat pants and set out for a trial run on Columbus Avenue. The park was too dangerous at this hour.

Columbus Avenue looked like an electric birthday cake as he streamed past the boutiques with their colorful neon lights flashing in the soft September rain. The street was one big party. He looked at the parading couples walking hand in hand, eating ice-cream cones. This is what he wanted! He wanted to roller-skate with his girlfriend and buy silly things from the street vendors who spread their wares out on blankets on the sidewalk. He wanted to have brunches on weekends at these "all the champagne or Bloody Marys you can drink" places, or take a bottle of wine into Central Park on a clear afternoon and drink it lying on a blanket on the grass. While he ran, he made up a wish list and felt better admitting these things to himself. It also felt so great to stretch his muscles again.

When he got home, he took a shower and put on his tatty robe. Out of nervous habit he decided to check his office answering machine before he went to bed. He took the answering-machine beeper out of his briefcase and dialed his number, waiting with a paper and pencil at hand. He heard the tape rewind and timed it, guessing at about three messages. One appointment change for next week. One colleague asking for a patient referral. Then, Katia.

"Hi," was all she said.

He recognized her voice immediately. Thank God she was back safely. There was a long pause. Something was wrong.

"It's Katia." Another pause. "Well. I'm back from Paris. . . ."

About thirty seconds passed. A sigh. He felt turmoil in her silence. "Look, I just can't do this anymore. Therapy, I mean." Her words floated in slow motion.

A deep breath. He felt her searching for her thoughts. "I'm burned out. I can't take being in the presence of someone I love. . . . and not being loved back. First you. Then Boris. No more. I've had it.

"You've been helpful. But things are getting more confusing than clear. I feel worse when I come out of a session with you than when I go in, and I don't think this is right." A pause. "Do you?

"So . . . I won't be coming to see you again. It's finished." .

She cleared her throat. "Thank you for everything."

The longest pause. "Good-bye."

A few days later at the hospital his beeper beeped in the middle of midmorning rounds with the interns. When he called the operator, he was surprised to find it was Jo Anne who had left a message to call her. He dialed her immediately, expecting to get her machine, but she actually picked up the phone.

She didn't waste any time on chitchat. "Frank, let's go away. You and me. I think we both need a change of scene and I'm willing to do it."

He didn't know what to say.

"Well. What do you think?" she said.

"But it's only September." He stumbled over the words.

"So . . . we'll wait until—April. Seven months. Perfect."

Her voice had an urgency he had never heard before. He was stunned at her offer, considering she didn't leave her apartment, much less leave town. But it seemed like an interesting idea. They would discover their relationship, if there was anything there, in a new place, a place foreign to both of them. Leave it to Jo Anne to come up with something this good.

"How does April in Paris sound?" she asked.

"Paris?"

"Well. I've never been to Paris . . . and you were there very many years ago. Too long ago. Everyone should see Paris, don't you think?"

He was silent.

"Frank?"

"Well, I don't know about Paris."

Jo Anne paid no attention and rattled on. "Anyway, we can go and be together and . . . visit the Lacan institute and . . . it will be splendid."

"Give me some time to think about it," he said. "Like a few months." They both laughed.

That afternoon on his way uptown from the hospital, he stopped at Val's Travel and asked for brochures about Paris. Then he popped into Shakespeare and Co. and bought a Michelin Green Guide and *The Food Lover's Guide to Paris*. Just in case.

Katia Loves Herself

KATIA ARRIVED IN New York late Friday night and resolved to forget about Boris. It was going to be hard. She knew it sounded sick, but even after all she had been through, the idea of American men and New York City paled beside the thought of Boris and Paris. But it was time she faced reality. This man did not love her. This man was not even nice to her. She walked through the door of her apartment and thunked down her luggage with a tentative new authority. Boo the cat sashayed up to see who it was. Boris would have translated the nonchalant flick of her tail as, "Oh you bitch, you've been to Paris without me." Katia scooped her up and petted her fiercely. "Did Uncle Clint take good care of you?" she crooned.

It was when she was unpacking and sorting out clean clothes from dirty that her thoughts turned to Frank. Having just gotten rid of Boris, perhaps now would be a good time to get rid of another problem man in her life. Start fresh. That meant Frank would have to go.

It was strange, because until this moment, Katia could not have imagined a life without Frank. Even though theirs was a tortured relationship, she believed they were fated to be together for the rest of their lives. Why, they would grow old together; he would forever be the witness of her life. She had tried on occasion to imagine saying good-bye to him, but it was not possible. She could be riding the crosstown bus or sitting in the dark of a movie theater and without fail her eyes would well up at the mere thought of parting.

216

So she was quite surprised when she picked up the phone and dialed his office number. She listened intently to his voice telling her he could not answer this call right now, but to please leave a message at the sound of the tone. Then she hung up. She asked herself, Are you sure you really want to do this? She paced the living room nervously. She took a shower. She went into the kitchen and made a pot of tea.

Yes. Something was terribly wrong with her therapy. Things weren't getting any clearer. She felt like a little mouse scampering feverishly on a treadmill. It was scary. If she left Frank, wouldn't that mean she was a failure?

But she was burned out on men and confusion. She wanted to live in a sterile void for a while and purify her mind and her heart. Enough of all this questioning, this overanalyzing. Maybe down the road she would see a new therapist and figure out what had been happening all this time, but for now she wanted a break. She heard Boris's words echo through her: "Live, baby. Just live." That's it, she would stop thinking and start feeling. And most of all, she would try to love herself. She smiled sadly. She had come full circle: she didn't want any men in her life.

Her heart was pounding as she dialed his number again and in a clear but quiet voice, left her message and gently put the receiver back into its cradle.

On her first day back at the office everyone crowded around her. "How was Paris?" they asked. "Great!" she gushed, giving a brilliant smile. By the end of the day all she could muster up was an "Interesting..." which she delivered with a raise of the eyebrows and hoped it suggested something decadent and luscious. She wanted to let the whole matter drop and be forgotten as quickly as possible, and resolved right then and there to find a man in New York—no, make that Manhattan, preferably on the East Side, maybe even on her block or in her apartment building; so much the better. Enough of this transatlantic bullshit. What good was love if it wasn't right there, warm, lying next to you and reaching for you in the middle of the night?

She limped through the following weeks mechanically, feeling like a sad sack. Her wound was deep, a gash in her heart that hurt every time she had to breathe. It was all she could do to get up every morning and show up for life. She knew she was really in trouble when she was too weak to even think about putting her head in the oven. So she decided to suspend all thoughts and emotions for the time being. For now, going through the motions would have to do. Time would have to do its part and heal her. Katia just concentrated on getting up each morning and going smartly off to work. So detached from everything was she that her advertising concepts were quite inspired. Planters Honey Roasted Nuts. Cabbage Patch Kids. Oil of Olay. Freed from the tyranny of having to fall in love with every product she had to write about, she flourished. Her newest client was *Seventeen*, whose line, appropriately enough was, "It's where the girl ends and the woman begins."

The leftover Indian summer turned mercifully into a brisk autumn. Fall in New York was a brilliant concept. The city was awash in clichés, complete with a certain bite in the air, a contagious excitement and the charge of the high social season. The season's newest sweaters that you couldn't live without filled every store window. People actually walked with a bounce in their step, and there was that bittersweet quality of the days growing shorter. Katia decorated her apartment with pots of orange- and rust-colored chrysanthemums and went apple picking in Dutchess County. She made apple crisp, apple tartes, apple butter and apple sauce. She knit herself a new sweater, read mystery novels, and suddenly it was Thanksgiving.

She decided this year to celebrate on her own. She didn't want to go home to her parents' house and play the part of the unmarried daughter; she wanted to be mistress of her own home. So she billed the holiday as "a quintessentially American day of excess, devoted to the giving of thanks" and invited a few friends over who were orphaned by choice or in fact. "I'm starting a tradition," she told them, "Katia's salon des refusés." She assured them that in the years to come, her Thanksgiving salon would become the hottest ticket in town. And sure enough, it turned out to be a witty, brilliant occasion, and Katia thought it fine proof of the fact that it was the most interesting people who had nowhere to go.

The morning started for her alone as she dressed the turkey and put it in the oven, then marched across Central Park to take her rightful place on Central Park West, just across from The Dakota, for the Macy's Thanksgiving Day Parade. When she was fully chilled and frostbitten, she hopped the crosstown bus back to her apartment, which by now was filled with the smell of roasting turkey. A few hours later her friends entered an autumnal heaven filled with bowls of nuts, polished lady apples and fresh kumquats and persimmons. There were plates of tiny cranberry-and-pumpkin finger tarts, and vases filled with branches of bittersweet. That year's Beaujolais Nouveau was the drink of choice. Some old movies on TV attracted a certain crowd in the bedroom, while others chose the friendly banter of too many cooks in the kitchen. Grace was said elaborately at the table by a poet who read a verse she had especially created for the occasion. There was, of course, turkey for Boo and leftovers for everyone to take home in waxed paper at the end of the day because Katia felt part of Thanksgiving was having a turkey sand-wich on Pepperidge Farm white bread with mayo and a glass of milk before you went to bed. After the meal, everyone begged Katia to play the piano, and loving the attention, she took her place with great relish, treating them to "a private salon musicale." It was so provincial; they all felt so Chekhovian.

Then suddenly it was Christmas, which, at chez Katia, meant a few glorious weeks of reverence and magic. She walked up and down the streets looking for the perfect bushy evergreen and decorated it with a generous splay of tiny white lights and ornaments that friends had given her over the years. When she stood back to look at her handiwork, she realized the tree was a diary of her life. She placed a family of teddy bears under it, and there they sat, quite content to be guarding the crinkly packages that Boo kept poking with her nose and testing with her paws. There were white pillar candles in every room and plum puddings soaking in rum, lined up in a row on the credenza. Luciano Pavarotti crooned "O Holy Night" and Bing Crosby sang "White Christmas." She was always torn about the music, for it made some guests feel euphoric and others morose. In the end she played it anyway, loud and strong. Katia, cornball extraordinaire, filling out Christmas cards, drinking vin chaud with the *Messiah* blaring. Christmas Eve was a night of great solemnity because she felt it was the holiest night of the year. A simple but elegant dinner and a walk through the freezing night air to the midnight caroling service was her call. On Christmas morning her par-ents and grandmother arrived, and she produced a festive brunch of extravagant delicacies that she had shopped for a few days earlier at Balducci's. After a walk down Madison and up Fifth to admire the street and shop decorations, she set out a simple early-evening buffet of baked ham and macaroni and cheese. A good time was had by all.

New Year's she spent alone. That holiday never bothered her the way it did most single women she knew who walked around with gritted teeth days before, threatening with fierce determination, "I'm not going to spend it alone." They considered spending New Year's Eve alone the ultimate admission of failure and would rather die. But Katia always felt it was a forced holiday and never made a big deal out of it. It was an arbitrary new start, when really, you had the opportunity for a fresh start any day of the year. She ushered in the new year in a contemplative manner, which she considered appropriate for the new direction she wanted her life to take. She lit candles all over her apartment and stayed up late reading P. D. James. At midnight she "supped" on a dish of scrambled eggs doppled with caviar, accompanied by a split of very good champagne. She got up very early on New Year's Day and took a healthy walk through Central Park while all of New York slept.

After this year's holiday glitz, Katia appreciated the bleak, white, frozen expanse of January. Instead of being glum, she rather looked forward to the deep dead of winter. It was a stunning time of sparseness, and this year especially, the perfect complement to the delicate state of her psyche. It was a time for introspection, for holing up, for making soup and reading good books. She slogged through the nasty ice and slush, to and from work, like a metronome.

She stopped going to client lunches and went to the NYU pool instead, reappearing at the office afterward with the calm, glazed eyes of a swimmer. She loved swimming; it was such a slinky form of exercise. She began to appreciate the new body that emerged from these workouts, the soft but angular shapes, the fluid muscles in her well-defined arms and back. Swimming became her. In fact, her fantasy had often been to swim with a dolphin or a seal, to grab hold of that playful, slippery muscle of a fish and glide along with it under the water. She loved to hear stories about the kindness of dolphins who saved drowning sailors by pulling them ashore. Oh, to frolic on the cliffs of Big Sur in the early morning while the sun burned off the mist and bark happily with the seal pups! Being a mermaid did have its attractions—you got to be ultrabeautiful and you got to hang out with the dolphins.

Of course that pedantic Frank would have interpreted this most lyrical and generous of fantasies as her desire to grab hold of the biggest, most delicious penis in the world. When she went to the zoo, she was always drawn to the seal pond, fascinated with the chic, black seals sunbathing on the high-tech sundecks of their man-made pool patios. She waited patiently until they decided to dive in for a dip, and watched with glee as they zoomed through the water, making those careening turns, diving and flipping expertly over one another. So strong was her urge to join them that she had to grip her fingers on the railing to stop herself, because any minute she might turn to the man standing next to her and say, "Sorry, do you mind?" smile half apologetically, hand him her pocketbook and dive in to frolic with the fellas.

She swam alone instead. But before she swam, she liked to step into a sauna for a good long bake. Most women at the gym took a sauna after they swam, but not Katia. She went in before, as a present to herself for even having gotten that far, letting the heat relax her muscles and stretch them out before she plunged into the icy pool and swam like hell to warm up. She loved entering the tiny, cedar room and having it all to herself. She did her best thinking there. The world slipped away in that parched light as she sat naked and dripping, delighted to be devastated by such heat. The sauna aroused her; it woke up the tips of her senses and put her in a catlike mood. She purred and felt like the most special woman on Earth. She particularly enjoyed her body there, running her hands along her sweating, glistening curves. But too often, her erotic trance was spoiled by the entrance of whiny, complaining women who chattered away nonsensically in this sacred temple of femaleness.

As she opened her eyes and saw the other female forms splayed around the tiny room, all that womanhood seemed grotesque instead of escalating her own desirability times five. No, she preferred to think of her body alone, a single, sun-sweetened pear that would quench the thirst of the man who had been driven to take a bite, making him wild for more until he devoured her completely. Instead, there in the sauna with her body multiplied into grotesque shapes, dangly, odd breasts, sausage legs, flappy bottoms, she felt devalued and unspecial, like one in a bunch of odd vases sitting on a shelf in the Pottery Barn's stockroom. She looked at the women and tried to imagine them taking their pleasure, and it disgusted her. They seemed insatiable and ugly in the dim yellow light. She hated femaleness exposed to this degree; it was so cloying and overdone. Men had good reason to be so afraid of women.

From this state of fallen grace, she would plunge into the freezing pool and exorcise the heat frenzy into which she had worked herself. On this white January day, as she swam in a rocking rhythm that could take her miles, two realizations floated uninvited into her empty, meditating mind. Suddenly she understood the synergy of the two incomplete men in her recent past. There was the intimate and emotionally erotic relationship with Frank, which meshed perfectly with the trumped-up, "real" physical (hah!) relationship with Boris. Each man offered her a part of the whole and admonished her to go find the rest in another. She had been set up—no, she had set herself up for failure in an impossible situation: Frank would never give her his body and Boris would never give her his soul. But now she wanted everything in one man, and this realization spawned a second. The sad fact was she had been living her life in her mind instead of in her life. She had succumbed to the devastating, paralyzing power of female fantasy.

She climbed out of the pool and walked slowly down to the locker room dazed—all this clearness after months of not seeing anything. She sat down on the bench, finding comfort in the flurry of activity around her. Lockers slammed, showers were running, hair was being blown dry, the air was filled with the sweet smell of talcum powder, mingling with all the different perfumes being sprayed onto wrists and bosoms and necks. Women were in various states of wet and dry, dressed and undressed.

She noticed for the first time how women didn't stand in front of their lockers and just get dressed. No, they put on a grand performance for themselves: dressing as a ritual of female self-adoration. She found it fascinating and pathetic. Each woman staked out her personal territory of mirror and stared at herself as if hypnotized, examining virtually every inch of her body, lifting, adjusting, pinching, bending, running her hands along herself, watching the show of her body and the effect as piece after piece of clothing went on. It was a corps de ballet of twisting and turning, accompanied by ridiculous preening and pouting. Katia became contemptuous of all of them.

A woman with long blond hair was dressing nearby. She slid a slip over her head, then smoothed it repeatedly over her hips. Then she turned: how did it look from here, from there, from the side, then from the back? She tried holding in her stomach. She held her arms over her head and stretched, the better to see her torso. Even that wasn't enough. She stepped up on the bench to get her knees in the picture, then back down again. Next she considered the effect of her naked breasts complementing the half-slip. She flung her long hair to the front, studied herself, then held it on top of her head, then tried it in a ponytail. Finally she snapped a bra into place and studied her breasts from all angles as she repeated the same actions.

Every woman in the room had an intuitive understanding of her body as fetish and was totally caught up in some personal fiction starring herself. Katia watched as each woman revealed, through her ritual, her own particular brand of sexuality or her neurotic feelings about her body. There were the tit ladies and the leg ladies, the lacy ladies and the jock ladies, the self-conscious ladies and the parading ladies. There was a woman who was so pleased with herself, thinking she was the most delicious thing in the world. It was easy to pick out the women who felt uncomfortable with their bodies.

It was when she looked at their faces that she realized there were very few women at "home;" there seemed to be a "vacancy" sign flashing in their eyes. All these empty faces staring at themselves in the mirror, each woman a prisoner of her own fantasy, her own misunderstanding, dressing for some real or imaginary man with critical eyes that observed every bulge, every wrinkle, every misplaced ounce. In their minds, they transformed their bodies into their own idea of the perfect body.

She looked at all these Daddy's little girls—for that is what they all had been—and wondered at which point each had stopped being Daddy's little girl. It came for each woman at a different time, following what seemed like a lifetime of trying to be a good girl for Daddy. ("Are you Daddy's little girl?" Katia would run squealing with delight into Daddy's arms.) Lucky was the girl who got it in high school, when she realized that kissing that cute boy over there will make her Daddy's little girl no more, but she must do it anyway. She casts out Daddy and becomes her own woman.

There were the women who needed marriage to feel like an adult. And for others it happened not when they married, but when they got pregnant. There could be no doubt then that they are no longer Daddy's little girl. But, Katia felt, most women never stopped being Daddy's little girl, going from father to husband in some stupefied, infantile state, wanting to please, always.

She got up abruptly and went to the steamy shower room. She stood for a long time under the streaming water, letting it purify her as if it was a baptism. Today a new self had emerged. When she returned to her locker and began dressing, more questions filled her mind. So where do I fit in? What is the sexuality of a single woman in her thirties? Hmm . . . she would either be considered gay, or a pathetic, horny, incomplete creature to be pitied. Or, she was out stealing other women's misunderstood husbands. But it was the men who came to her; she did no stealing. Supposedly the sex she had as a single woman was sexier, because it was pure sex, not tied up with relationship or responsibilities, or will you take out the garbage, dear? But she knew better. It was a catch-as-catch-can sex, sex on the run, illicit, to be grabbed whenever it came her way. Such an unsteady diet was not good for anyone. This raised another question. Why was sexuality and desire in a man considered by society to be normal and attractive, but in a woman it seemed somehow voracious and unappealing? A man was excused from his lusty behavior because it was, after all, only his "nature." whereas the woman who longed for the press of human flesh was unnatural.

By now Katia was dressing absentmindedly in front of her locker, trying to make up some new rules for living. She bent down to pick up her socks and looked up to find the woman at the locker next to hers staring at her. She looked away and then caught another woman glancing at her from the corner of her eye, and yet another, who was bending over and brushing her hair, watching her upside down. Katia looked down and continued dressing. She put on her oversized white shirt and flicked up the collar, then finger-dried her hair, letting it fall in an appealing disarray. She pulled on her jeans and slipped into her loafers. She went up to the mirror to put on her makeup, and as she was sweeping on some mascara she noticed pairs of eyes studying her from all sides of the room. No matter where she looked in the mirror, there were eyes dashing furtively away when she caught them in her own. What was going on here? She tried to brush on some smoky eye shadow but couldn't continue. These eyes were in some way sapping her, draining her of all her knowledge. What was this, "The Twilight Zone"? She turned around quickly and caught them all staring at her, and suddenly it was as if their eyes were her own personal mirror. It was a frozen moment. Unsettled, she walked back to her locker in the now silent room with all eyes following her. She tried to pretend that nothing was happening. But it *was* happening. By now, quite self-conscious, she snapped the lock shut on her locker, spritzed herself with Chanel from the atomizer in her satchel and turned to leave. On her way out of the locker room she caught the glance of a woman passing by a mirror. Who's that? Katia gasped. She stopped. Is that? Could that? Really be?

Me.

That evening Katia sat in her living room with a glass of Irish whiskey contemplating her life. It slipped down her throat like liquid gold and she began to feel delightfully woozy. The skyline of New York was frozen and the city was still. No one was on the streets unless they had to be.

She watched with horror as Boo stalked a moth that had miraculously managed to appear in her apartment. Boo waited patiently, flicking her tail, and then, with a guttural cry rumbling in her throat, she pounced. Holding the live, fluttering moth in her mouth, she let herself enjoy the tickling sensation for a good half minute, then she spat it out and played with it a little until she finally ate it. When she finished, she came up to Katia. She was supremely content and proud of herself and tried to snuggle in Katia's lap.

"No, get away, get away!" Katia tried to shoo Boo away. "How could you kill that innocent moth; I thought you were nice!"

Boo looked at her blankly and didn't budge.

"No, get away, you have butterfly on your breath! I don't want you near me!" The cat jumped away before Katia could give her a swat with her hand. Now Boo looked back at her, confused and uncertain.

Katia stayed up thinking until about midnight and then got ready for bed. It was when she was dabbing some perfume on her neck and under the curve of her breasts that she realized she had tried to punish her cat because she was . . . a cat. Because when she was eating the moth, Boo had reverted from being Katia's sweet pet into the wild feline she really was. Katia took a deep breath. This day was getting to be too much.

She lay down on her futon, happy to be so cozy under the down duvet, and listened to the fierce wind rattling the windows. She let her hands roam all over her body and thought, once again, how nice it would be to be a man touching her. She closed her eyes and sighed, and in time, she gave herself the most deep and rocking orgasm. She hated the word masturbate, it was such an ugly-sounding word for such a nice thing. It had been five months since she had left Frank, but for some reason, she summoned up his image. She fantasized that she was on his couch and he was watching as she came in front of him. When she was still, she opened her eyes and saw Boo lying on the coral linen love seat watching her.

"So, what are you looking at?" Katia mumbled. They had a staring contest. It was a standoff. Then Boo decided it was boring. She stretched her paws and went to sleep, delighting in her butterfly dreams.

Katia dreamed she was the bride at her wedding, but there was no groom. She wandered around in a worried daze, distressed about what the guests might think. Her mother worried only about the hors d'oeuvres. Then she dreamed she went to see Frank, except instead of going to his office, she went to a Catholic church, and stepped into a confessional instead of sitting in his chair. She was relieved to find a prostitute sitting on the side where the priest was supposed to be. "Good," she said thankfully. "You, I can talk to."

Paris

Frank Doesn't Love Jo Anne

FROM THE MOMENT they slid into their seats on the special airport bus bound for Kennedy, Frank had a sinking feeling. Perhaps this would not be the trip he had fantasized about. Too late, he remembered the old travel maxim about how you could know someone really well, but traveling with them was a completely different story. Poor Jo Anne. She had been calm and enthusiastic when they planned the trip in the safety of her apartment, discussing what clothes they'd pack, reading guidebooks aloud to each other, practicing their French accents in front of the mirror and laughing, but she became hysterical the minute she got on the bus.

"We're going to miss the plane, Frank. This bus driver stinks. He doesn't know about the traffic on the way to JFK. We should have taken a cab. Or that helicopter they have."

"Jo Anne, relax. They do this every day. They take into account the traffic. Besides"—he looked at his watch—"we've got three hours till check-in." He tried to be understanding. He explained to her how traveling took away your sense of control, that it exposed you to an entirely different set of anxieties. "You must deliver yourself into the hands of the 'traveling spirit,' otherwise you'll be a wreck the entire time," he said, taking her hand and rubbing it between his.

"The traveling spirit?" she snorted.

He was unnerved by the time they got to JFK and started snapping at her. Damn! He wanted to be excited and enjoy his dream haze about

229

going back to Europe after all these years. What happened to his nice, mild-mannered personality? Jo Anne, who hadn't been out of her apartment for practically a year, was now leaving the country and was trying to hold on to something, but there was nothing familiar for her to grab hold of except him.

On the plane, she was okay until it finally dawned on her that Air Pakistan was Muslim, which meant there would be no liquor served on board. She became furious. "Now, this is really a bad joke!"

"Jo Anne, relax." He quickly understood that he would be saying this a lot in the week to come.

"How can I, with no booze on an eight-hour flight? You know the only time I really need a drink is on a plane."

He wanted to wait awhile before surprising her, but it was clear the time had come. "Surprise!" He pulled a bottle of Adair Vineyards Chardonnay from his Channel thirteen bag. "We'll drink Hudson River Valley going over and Loire Valley coming back."

"Frank, you devil. How did you know?" She giggled.

"You're dealing with a professional here. I look into these kinds of things," he said. "But let's wait a bit before we open it, okay? And don't worry. I brought a corkscrew." He pulled it out and waved it at her. She leaned back, content. Until the next crisis.

While he was planning this trip, he read through all his clinical notes on Katia. She flew Air Pakistan because it was one of the cheapest ways to get to Paris. "But not many people know that. It's wonderful," she said, relishing the memory of her flight. "They wear saris and speak in soft, accented voices and are always salaaming to you. You get your choice of Indian or English food. But remember, no liquor on board! You've got to bring your own." She waggled her finger in warning. He also thought about what she had told him about the French. "They are a very unhappy people right now, what with Mitterrand, socialism and the dollar being so high. They want and need our money, but hate us for being able to spend it. So you must be prepared for shenanigans and nastiness on their part." At the time, she had been speaking to no one in particular, offering advice to the air. But now, her words rang in his ears and comforted him.

The wine did the trick. They drank the entire bottle and nuzzled for the rest of the flight, passing up the movie and trying to sleep. In the safety of the hurtling plane, they were just another lovey-dovey couple. He tried not to, but he kept thinking about flying over vast expanses of dark, cold ocean and how the plane was staying afloat merely by consuming tons of fuel per minute. Better not think about that. He wondered about crashing. Would he get hysterical? Would he tell Jo Anne he loved her just as they went under? Would his body be recognized? Would he cry? Don't think about that, either. He got up and went to get an Alka-Seltzer from the flight attendant; the Indian food had upset his stomach.

It seemed that in no time preparations for landing at Orly were announced over the sound system. "Orly?" Jo Anne jolted up in a panic. "Why not Charles de Gaulle?"

"Because this is a"—he quickly searched for a reason—"third-world airline and they get shunted to Orly." It sounded good.

"Well, why didn't I know about this?" she demanded.

Frank continued to be valiant on the ground, shepherding Jo Anne through passport control, baggage claim and customs. Now, what was this about the airport bus that takes you to the metro? He tried to remember what Katia had said. All the buses looked alike. He wished he could open his mouth and have beautiful French come out. But it wasn't going to happen. He began to feel helpless and he hated it and they were only in the airport—imagine an entire week of this ahead of him! Then Jo Anne insisted they take a taxi. But within minutes after settling into the car, she began complaining about what seemed like an overly long ride, that the driver must be taking them on the rip-off route. Frank asked her how she could possibly know, since she had never been to Paris before. Finally they pulled up in front of their hotel, the Hotel Printemps (one of Katia's) on the rue Madame, just down the street from the entrance to the Jardin du Luxembourg.

"Look, there's the Lux." Frank pointed, trying to be nonchalant, using the slang name Katia called it. He wanted to try the words in his mouth and feel like he, too, was on familiar terms with Paris.

When they got into their room, the first thing Jo Anne wanted to do was take a shower. Frank tried the bed and then looked out the windows, which faced the Lux. "I'm throwing open the French windows," he yelled, and laughed. He breathed deep the French air and then joined her in the shower. "April in Paris," he crooned, trying to be playful with her. But she wouldn't have any part of his amorous advances and got out, leaving him alone with his bar of soap. He had no choice but to lather himself up, and he almost lost his balance in the tiny, slippery stall.

When they stepped out of the hotel, Frank plunged into painful self-consciousness. What was it about the French that made him feel so unimportant? In New York he felt just fine walking down the street. As they strolled in their jet-lag haze the new sounds seemed particularly loud: the cars with their zippy engines and their claxon horns, the tripping French voices; even his own voice sounded strangely hollow to him. He looked at Jo Anne and became embarrassed with her looking so dowdy in her wide-wale corduroy pants, gripping the Michelin Green Guide. He tried to grasp the new smells and rhythm of the street: the cafés, bureaux de tabac, fruit stands, pâtisseries. He understood immediately that New York was for the neurotic, and Paris for the carefree.

"Okay. Well. Let's go into the Lux," he said stiffly.

As if it didn't exist unless it was in the Guide Michelin, Jo Anne stopped and looked up the Lux in her book, making people detour around her on the sidewalk. They entered through the magnificent gates with Jo Anne reading aloud that they must observe the château, the fountains, the arbres.

"The what?" Frank said.

"The arbres. Trees, I think."

Frank hadn't been a tourist in so many years that he felt conspicuous as he tried to be appreciative of everything the book mentioned.

Finally Jo Anne said, "You go walk around. I will sit down here and read the guidebook and tell you later about the jardins." She pointed to the bench she intended to sit on and then walked over to it, nodded to him and sat down very properly. They had been reduced to speaking slowly, in overly polite tones, since they arrived in Paris.

The moment he left her, the Lux became a beautiful and gentle place. Suddenly the air was soft and luxurious and he felt ripe with pleasure. The sunlight dappled appealingly through the ancient plane trees and made lovely shadow patterns on the walks. Children's laughter caressed him as he watched them enjoy the marionette show, the pony rides, float their boats in the fountain, or be chased by their nannies. The Frenchwomen around him were angels, magical with grace and charm. He felt like an adolescent, so taken was he by their seductive energy and their lilting voices.

In the distance he spotted some tennis courts and started walking toward them. Were these the courts Katia said Boris played on every afternoon? As he got closer he felt his body tighten up. He approached the mesh fencing and searched among the French tennis players for the

Russian face he had come to know from the photographs Katia brought to her sessions. He didn't see him. Well, really, what did he expect? This was Paris the way New York was New York—a major metropolis where people disappeared into their lives. He stood there a few minutes more, then as he started to walk away chimes rang from a nearby bell tower. It was now two o'clock. The matches stopped and the courts switched over in an orderly manner as the old players left and the new players walked on.

Unbelievable. There he was. Boris Zimoy himself, snapping open a new can of tennis balls, chatting with his opponent before they took the court, slipping off bright red sweat pants to reveal white tennis shorts underneath. On top he wore a blue polo shirt with a pair of white sweatbands around his wrists. He looked much more striking than Frank could have imagined, a swarthy but manicured masculine presence whose seductive charm he could feel even from a distance. He found an empty chair and pulled it closer to the mesh fence so he could watch him warm up. Boris practiced serves and net volleys and then spun the racket for the first serve.

The play was swift and uneventful. At times it seemed as if Boris were looking right at him. Boris and his opponent switched sides with serious expressions on their faces and resumed playing. And then, the ball flew over the enclosure. Boris watched it fly and then ran over to the wire mesh and unleashed a barrage of French.

Frank had no idea what he said and looked around him to see if Boris was talking to someone else.

"Le bal, monsieur, c'est juste par là. Merci bien."

"Me?" Frank stood up abruptly. "The ball?"

"Yes, if you please," Boris said in a thickly accented English.

He retrieved the ball and threw it over the fence, then sat back down. He had to calm his pounding heart. There was no way Boris could know who he was.

"Frank!" yelled Jo Anne, who had come up behind him.

"Jesus!" Frank jumped in his chair. Her voice sounded so New Yorky.

"Since when did you like tennis?" she said, surveying the scene. They stood there, both unsure of why they were in Paris watching tennis in the Jardin du Luxembourg.

"Oh, I don't know. I was just wandering around and I wanted to get a feel for French leisure-time activities."

"He's cute."

Cute? Frank jumped on her words. *Cute* was not a word Jo Anne normally used. "Who's cute?" he asked suspiciously.

"The blue-and-white. The little man there with the beard."

He should have known. Nothing should surprise him anymore. It was as if she had a sixth sense and zoomed straight for him. He tried to sound nonchalant. "Oh. That's Boris Zimoy, the Russian émigré writer," he said dully, wanting to impress her.

"Since when are you up on émigré literature?"

"Well, he's rather well known," Frank said.

"Boris Zimoy," she said, drawing out the sound of his name, trying to place it. "Never heard of him." She dismissed him. "He must be a minor émigré."

"He is not!" he retorted, as if insulted. Then he lowered his voice. "He's published three books. Well, they are in French; that's why you've probably never heard of him. I understand that he will be translated into English soon."

They stood watching the game. The patter of tennis balls from the six courts was like modern music. "Actually, one of my patients used to read him," he said without thinking, and then quickly wished he hadn't said that.

"Oh. Could that have been . . . Katia?" she asked.

"Jo Anne, you promised. We promised not to discuss that. This vacation is about you and me. I'm here to get away from all that."

"Okay, okay, okay. So this is what jet lag feels like. Come on, let's go." She took his hand and turned as they left. "But he does look interesting," she added.

"Where to next, oh great tour guide?" he asked, and they strolled out of the Lux.

When Jo Anne started reading aloud from the Guide Michelin at breakfast in the hotel the next morning, Frank knew he was in trouble.

"'To get the 'feel,' the atmosphere, of Paris, besides seeing the sights described on pages twenty-seven to one hundred seventy-three, you will want to sit at a café table on the pavement, sipping a drink, go in one of the boats on the Seine, which enables you to see many of the major buildings from an unusual angle and rest at the same time, and go one weekend to the flea market.'"

The trip unfolded like this, day by day, and Frank continued to experience Paris in two ways. Whenever he was with Jo Anne, he felt like a fool. Nothing was fun, Paris was a place to be dealt with. Meals were a trial, getting lost was a pain in the neck instead of an adventure. He felt inadequate when he tried to speak French and he was constantly mortified at the Parisians' rudeness. Throughout all of this he tried to love Jo Anne; after all, he was here with her, and in his own way, he did love her, she was his girlfriend, his colleague, his confidante. But instead of a restful, dreamy week together, she put them on a forced march, an assault on the monuments and museums of Paris. The city, in turn, seemed mean and unforgiving.

But every afternoon after lunch, Jo Anne went back to the hotel to take a nap and he was free to explore the city alone. He felt like a prince, smoky and sultry as he wandered the streets without a map, getting lost, losing himself. As London was a man's world, Paris was a woman's paradise, filled with sensual temptations, and he was under her spell. He steeped himself in the windows of charcuteries, pâtisseries, bonbonneries. He strolled through the marchés and studied all the fascinating bottles in the wine shops. He looked at clothes and sprayed himself with colognes. Whatever was missing in his spirit, Paris supplied. One afternoon he went into Thierry Mugler and bought himself a silk shirt. Next door to Mugler was the Girbaud boutique. He had seen people in New York wearing these baggy pants, and he thought, Never in a million years. But here—well, it was different in Paris. He chose several styles to try on, smiling his way through the transaction, standing with his arms away from his body so the salesgirl could guess at his French size. When he came out of the dressing room to look in the mirror, the girl clucked at him, so handsome was he.

Katia's spirit pervaded the city. Now her style made complete sense to him and he understood why she was so drawn to Paris and how the city became her. He started seeing her all over. The first time, he was strolling on the rue du Bac and he could have sworn he heard her laughter. Two beautifully dressed women were walking ahead of him with their arms linked casually when they stopped to look at a photograph that one had taken out of her wallet. The other had to be Katia, bending over the picture, cooing and laughing. She lifted her head to look at him quizzically when he stared at her as he passed by.

Later that afternoon he saw her in a café, lazily smoking a French cigarette in the sun, sipping now and then at a tall, cool glass of something bright green. He crossed the street and sat down like a zombie who had no control of his actions and ordered the same drink by pointing to her glass.

"C'est du menthe," she said to him matter-of-factly and the waiter nodded.

Strolling up the rue de Rivoli one afternoon, he saw the Sonia Rykiel boutique and remembered it was a name Katia had often mentioned. He put his face close to the glass, and there she was, trying on a soft two-piece knit dress, looking at herself in the mirror. The sunlight filtering through the darkened glass made her look like a grainy photograph from another era. The shopgirl was fussing over her, arranging the pleats of her skirt, and then held up a hat. Would she like to try it on? Katia nodded yes and the girl placed the hat on her head as they both stared at the mirror. Then Katia spun around with glee and caught his eye. The shopgirl and Katia stood there looking at him for a minute until she turned to go back into the dressing room.

That evening he gripped Jo Anne's hand in the bistro just off St. Germain because the waiter led them to a table next to which Katia was having dinner with a handsome Frenchman. They were lost in each other's eyes, engaged in deep conversation. Katia was very animated and the man was sensuously stroking her hand. As he and Jo Anne sat down Katia turned her face up to see who was intruding on her private moment.

She was in the Jeu de Paume, sitting on a bench, leaning back on her elbows, staring at a painting. She was in the metro, dashing through a turnstile and disappearing in the correspondances for Château Vincennes. From the Bateaux Mouches he saw her sitting on a bench on the quay of the Île St. Louis, writing in her diary. When he and Jo Anne stood on line for a sorbet at Bertillon, she had just gotten her cone and was licking the drips as she walked by. It was a double: cassis and citron vert.

It was his private torture, a sweet hell. When he stopped with Jo Anne to study the beautifully sculpted pastries in a pâtisserie window, she sniffed, "They probably look better than they taste." He made her select one, a sort of apple tart, and when they went inside to purchase it, he asked the girl behind the counter what it was called. "Une jalousie," she replied.

"What?" asked Jo Anne.

"Jealousy," said Frank.

Trudging through the streets with her, he silently wished Katia was there to make it alive for him, to help him become a part of Paris, to hold his hand and laugh him into happiness. He had to drag Jo Anne anywhere that wasn't in the Green Guide. He insisted they go into Kenzo on the Place des Victoires, where he urged her to try some things on. But she just looked silly. He had to drag her into a parfumerie ("What's Paris without a new bottle of perfume?"), where he gazed with confusion at all the glowing bottles. If only Katia were there to counsel him, she would know what was new, what was fun, what was a "must-have." He asked for Yatagan by Caron, but when the girl handed him the bottle, it was the same one he had sitting at home on his ugly brown bureau. It had a vicious smell. He shook his head and handed it back to the salesgirl, who sneered at him, as if to say, "silly man."

He couldn't get away from Boris either. One afternoon after they had a choucroute garnie in the Brasserie Lipp (recommended by Michelin, of course), they were strolling toward the Musée de Cluny for a look at the famous Unicorn tapestries when they passed a librairie. One section of the window display was devoted to Boris's latest book, stacked in multiples around a large photograph of him and a slew of miniature French and Soviet flags. He felt so frustrated that he didn't know French because he wanted to read the book. *Les Baisers à la Russe* was the title. "Russian Kisses," he supposed it meant, although he seemed to recall that Katia had mentioned the verb *baiser*, "to kiss" in French, was also slang for "fuck."

"There you are," Jo Anne said, breaking into his reverie. "I thought you had disappeared. What's up?" She looked in the window and saw the books. "Hey! It's that tennis player who writes."

"It's the writer who plays tennis," Frank corrected. "Yeah."

"Hmm . . . " she said, studying the display.

That evening they returned to their small hotel, exhausted after a day that included a march up the Champs Élysées, a visit to the Rodin Museum and a whirlwind spin through the Galleries Lafayette. Oh, yes, and a stop at the opera to pick up some tickets for the next night. The clerk had been very rude to Frank, pretending not to understand what he wanted, and gave him terrible seats.

"I'm going to take a hot, hot bath," he said to Jo Anne. At home he never took a bath, he took showers, but in Paris a bath seemed perfect.

He was beginning to sound like Katia. He waited for Jo Anne in the hotel's tiny sitting room while she picked up the room key and discussed the situation of the bad opera seats with the concierge. The TV was on, and who should come on the screen but Boris Zimoy, speaking French a mile a minute!

Frank strained to understand. It was some sort of talk show. The other hotel guests in the lounge were ignoring the TV and he wanted to shush them all. He studied Boris, the way he gestured wtih his hands, the way he smiled coyly at the female interviewer, (who was charmed,) the way a sweater was tied just so around his shoulders. Frank looked around and saw a girl who had to be French from the way she was dressed, smoking a Gauloise and watching the TV intently. He gestured to her, first pointing to the TV and then raising his hands in frustration. "Can you tell me what he's saying?" he tried in English.

"Américain?" she asked in a thick accent.

He nodded.

She searched for the words. The show was called "Apostrophes." She continued, "Um. Every Friday. It is a literature hour. For writers. And super intellectuals," she said. "It is very important. Um . . . It can make your career if you get on this show with your book," she finished proudly.

It was over too quickly. He turned around only to find Jo Anne had been standing behind him all this time, watching both him and the TV. She inclined her head and smiled at him.

"This Boris character seems to be everywhere," she said.

"Where's the key?" he grunted.

Up in the room, he sat at the edge of the bed and bent down to pull off his shoes. He noticed the Parisian telephone directory on the bottom shelf of the little nightstand. Jo Anne was in the bathroom. He took the book out and started looking up Boris's name. What was he doing? He flipped the pages to B and then said, "You dummy," and went to the Z's. He found it. Boris Zimoy, 24 rue des Honorés Chevaliers, 6e. He sat there with the book open on his lap, tapping it with his fingertips. What would he say? "Hi, I'm a former doctor of Katia's and I saw you on TV tonight?" He stared at the name. What was he doing? Why would he even think of calling Boris? Fingers shaking, he dialed the number and listened to the French rings.

"Allo?"

Frank didn't say a word.

"Allo? Qui est à l'appareil?"

Frank hung up. "Sorry, wrong number," he mumbled to himself.

"Your bath's ready," called Jo Anne from the bathroom. She opened the door and a puff of steam came out. He snapped the book shut.

"Thanks, you're sweet," he said, and took off his clothes. Paris was making him horny as hell. "Jo Anne?" he said in his sweetest voice. "Will you give me a bath?" He pouted coyly. She looked at him and shook her head.

That night, after dinner, they were browsing in an antiquaires when he came across a small pyramid of sienna marble. The shape was so pleasing in his hands, the marble so cool when he pressed it against his cheek. It reminded him of the stillness of cathedrals and the hours he had spent in church as a boy. The echoes, chants and footsteps, the comfort and the misery. Then he recalled that a pyramid was a feminine symbol. It reminded him of Katia. It would be the kind of "quintessential" present for her.

"What did you find?" Jo Anne asked.

"I'm going to buy this pyramid," he said, displaying it in the palm of his hand. "It will look excellent in my office."

When they got back to the hotel room that night, he unwrapped the pyramid that the little old man had put so carefully into a tiny box and tied with a tiny ribbon. He held it to his cheek once more, then put it on the night table next to the bed. Later, with Jo Anne asleep beside him, he lay awake staring into the darkness with a dreadful feeling that something was slipping away.

Frank Loves Paris

FRANK THOUGHT he heard sirens and sat up. No, wait, he already was sitting up. Were the sirens the police kind or the fire-engine kind? His heart pounded wildly. He shook himself and grabbed the edge of the bed, but there wasn't any bed. He was sitting in his seat on Air Pakistan, flying back to New York. In the darkened cabin filled with the white noise from the engines, he glanced around at the other sleeping passengers. They were mostly Pakistanis in their colorful dress, exhausted, lying sprawled out on each other, mothers, fathers and children, having survived thus far the arduous eighteen-hour flight from Karachi, with stops in Cairo, Frankfurt, Paris, and now on to New York.

His watch with the luminous dial said two o'clock. Was that New York time or Paris time? He settled back in his seat and pushed the little button to lower the back down. Two tears rolled down his face; he wiped them with his hand, spreading the wetness over his parched face. A flight attendant walked through the cabin and he waved at her.

"May I have some aspirin?" he whispered.

"Is there anything wrong?" she said.

"No, just a headache." He felt the onset of a whopper, for he had opened a bottle of Côtes du Rhone the minute the plane took off. He was shocked that he could down a bottle of wine so effortlessly. That was probably the result of spending a week in Paris.

He felt better the minute he took the aspirin, then realized he was cold and stood up, opened the overhead bin and rummaged around for a

240

blanket. He was in luck; he also found a pillow. He tried to shut it quietly so as not to disturb the other passengers. He settled himself back in his seat, arranging the blanket and pillow until it suited him.

I'm in a plane back to New York, he said to himself in the most rational voice he could muster. I was just having a nightmare. He lifted up the little shade in the window and was startled by the bright stillness outside. He lowered it immediately, preferring the intimacy of the darkened plane hurtling through time and space. In this plane he was safe because he was in transit, not here and not there. Hmmm . . . the nightmare had sirens, that meant trouble. It meant, help! It meant a crime was being committed? Or, it meant fire. He felt burned.

Amazing how life could happen just like that! Suddenly the week in Paris was over and he was going home. Alone. Jo Anne had jumped ship. She was staying in Paris another week to be with Boris. That was exactly how she told him, in words as simple and flat as those. As he sat there in the humming, vibrating plane he realized he wouldn't understand what really happened for quite a while, but whatever it was, it happened quickly.

With Jo Anne's defection to Boris, Frank realized he had lost two women to the Russian. Although he couldn't really count Katia, could he? After all, she was entitled to fall in love with whomever she pleased. It was the mingling of his personal life and his professional life that was too much for him to bear. He of all people, good old conscientious Frank, had crossed that very fine line, mixing two worlds together. Was he going to be excommunicated from the institute? On top of that it raised the more ontological issue of what was real and what wasn't. There really is no such thing as reality, he thought, it's just something each person makes up. And pretty badly, too.

He was tired of being an analyst and supposedly having the ability to figure life out. Nothing figures. He was only human, wasn't he allowed to fuck up, too? Well, he had his wish. Everything seemed harmless enough when it was all happening, but then it sped up like a bad, old movie. One morning, the fifth morning of their stay, they had woken up very early, and while they were lying in bed talking, he suggested they skip breakfast in the hotel and go out to a café instead.

"Okay. But where shall we go?"

"Let's go . . . to the Place des Vosges. In the Marais. It's Paris's oldest square," he said. "I read about it in the Guide," he added. There, that would validate the experience for her.

"Let me see," she said, as if his word was not enough. She picked up the by-now worn book lying on the night table, and after a few minutes of sleepy reading she said, "Okay. Metro St. Paul or Bastille, with a correspondance at Châtelet. I'm getting pretty good at this metro, don't you think?"

It was eight o'clock when they left the hotel. They hopped on the metro with all the Parisians on their way to work. Parisian commuting looked so much more civilized than New York commuting. People spoke in hushed morning voices and there was no unpleasantness, no graffiti, no ghetto blasters, no rowdy teenagers passing joints, roughing their way through the crowds. They managed to find their correspondance and ended up at St. Paul without a hitch. From there they would walk north a few blocks in order to find the square that Katia had called her favorite and the most beautiful in all of Paris.

Frank would never forget that morning. Even at the moment it was happening he was saying to himself, I am being born. He was mesmerized by the beauty of the charming old hotels as he and Jo Anne wound their way through the ancient streets of the Marais. Patisseries sent fumes of baking pastry onto the street; the boulangeries were doing a brisk trade in crackly fresh bread, picked up by uniformed maids and little old ladies on their way home from morning Mass; the fishmongers were setting the day's catch out over mounds of freshly chipped ice; flower vendors were arranging their tubs of bouquets. From the cafés, the smell of fresh café au lait mingled delightfully with the crinkly snapping of the patrons' morning newspapers. The freshness in the air rose up from the recently watered-down streets to the baby, apple green leaves of spring's new trees. Concierges were sweeping the sidewalks in front of their domaines and children were walking to school in their navy blue uniforms with their little backpacks perched dutifully on their delicate backs.

That life could be this sweet! He shuddered at all the tenderness he felt. Then, in slipped the nasty thought of his life in New York, that noisy, filthy, vulgar city! He could feel himself being dragged into an internal tirade about the outrage of it, but then stopped himself. I must live in this moment, here in the Marais, now. And so they walked, Frank, basking in his new world of the senses, and Jo Anne, following the street map, dictating every turn, confirming every street they passed, expressing delight that the city conformed so well to her map.

"Place des Vosges should be right up there," she said, as if in warning.

He had no idea what he would find when they stepped through the ancient arches, the "Pavillon du Roi," she said they were called, that loomed up ahead.

As they stepped into the silent square he wondered, How was it possible that a place could be so beautiful? The interplay of sky, space and architecture had reached a zenith here: the massive yet delicate buildings, so orderly, yet flowing and graceful, arranged around a perfectly natural yet manicured park. It was entirely pleasing to look at and to stand in. Never before had he been so physically affected by an outside space.

"Number six is where Victor Hugo lived from 1833 to 1848," intoned Jo Anne, her head still buried in the Guide.

Frank didn't hear her. He was lost in the sleepiness of the square, the dewy trees filled with twittering birds. From the houses and apartments that lined the park, he could hear appealing domestic sounds filtering out from the open windows. His eyes followed the sound of high heels clicking along the pavement and echoing back up to the facades and beyond. A huge door snapped shut behind a young woman wheeling her bicycle out. As they walked through the park, Frank kept spinning around like a thirsty man, trying to drink in the Place with his eyes, as if one more spin would explain everything.

"There's no café here," Jo Anne said, breaking into his reverie.

"Yes, there is. Apparently. . ." He spoke vaguely, groping for Katia's words to float up. "There is one café here, on the northwest corner."

He knew it would be there. Katia wouldn't be wrong about such a thing. As they veered over to the left and walked the length of the Place, sure enough, hiding under the porticos, was the tiny Café Louis XIV. He imagined in the summer it would be jammed with tourists, but now, on this cool April morning, it was a neighborhood café, empty save for the few locals who chose to have their petit déjeuner there.

It was a cozy and inviting place with the doors of the café thrown open so the fresh air collided magically with the steam from the coffee machines, the smell of fresh baguettes and the Gitanes fumes. They seated themselves, and as they had come to expect, a surly-looking garçon walked over to see what these two stupid Americans could possibly want.

"Deux cafés au lait et croissants, s'il vous plaît?" Frank asked hopefully. He immediately realized his mistake in spite of Katia's coaching. He should have demanded, not asked. The garçon remained expressionless and walked off, giving no sign he had heard anything.

"I'll be right back," Jo Anne said, pushing back her chair. "I want to find a newstand. Un kiosk." She laughed with a flourish of her hand. She walked like a galumphing puppy. He watched as she stood outside for a minute, deciding whether to go left or right, then disappeared.

Seated there alone, in Katia's favorite café, he knew he was living out his curious destiny. It was one of those rare times in life when the reality of something matched up with the fantasy of it. He was having exactly the experience she had had, and the experience that she would have wanted him to have. He sat back and listened to the barman's banter with his daily patrons as he steamed milk and poured coffee. The waiter came back and set down two cups of café with the creamy lait foaming beautifully on top and a basket of croissants.

"De la confiture?"

"Pardon?" Frank said.

"De la confiture," he repeated, loudly this time, as if that might make him understand.

Frank shook his head, indicating he didn't understand.

"Jam?" the waiter drawled sarcastically.

"Yes. I mean, oui, merci, s'il vous plaît," Frank said, nodding his head vigorously up and down.

Frank reached for a croissant, thrilled to discover they were still warm from the oven. Right then and there he promised himself he would go to Zabar's as often as he could for cappuccino and fresh croissants. Wasn't it Katia who told him that Zabar's had the best croissants in the city? Back then he had paid no mind. He dipped the croissant into the café au lait as he had seen other Frenchmen do and then bent his head down so he could slip it into his mouth without making too much of a mess. Lord, if he did this in the United States, he would be considered a lout, but here, it was the elegant thing to do.

"Look what I found!" Jo Anne said, flopping down across from him just at the moment he stuffed the croissant in his mouth. He looked up at her, chewing contentedly, wiping coffee off his chin.

In addition to the *International Herald Tribune*, which she bought every day of their vacation, she had an oversized magazine with a color photograph of a woman in a long evening gown on the cover. It was *Passion. The Magazine of Paris.*

"It's in English," she said with glee, "a magazine for Americans in Paris! It's all about Paris. Isn't it a great idea? I wish we had known about it when we arrived. Now it's almost too late." They had only two days left.

He took the *Tribune* and skimmed the front page while Jo Anne rattled off what was in the magazine. "The best American bars in Paris. Where to buy knockoff couture. The jewelry of the streets. A new look at Americans in Paris." Then she lapsed into silence. "And look. An article on Boris Zimoy, that tennis player."

Frank had not been listening, but at the mention of Boris he looked up. "Let me see," he said, snatching *Passion* from her. Sure enough, under the heading "Paris ♥ Les Écrivains ♥ Paris" there was a tiny subhead: "Émigré of the Month." The headline proper, in large letters was, "For Soviet Exile Boris Zimoy, Paris is Siberia." To Frank, it seemed that this rather strong headline clashed ironically with the photograph of Boris smiling and waving from a café table on the Left Bank. Before he could read a word, Jo Anne took it away from him.

"I found it, so I get to read it first," she said, and gave him back the newspaper. She took her time reading the article, slurping her café au lait and scattering croissant crumbs on the table. After fifteen minutes of silence she said, "It says here that he will be reading from his works, in English, at the Big Apple Bookstore on the rue de Petits Choux, on Friday evening at twenty hours." She paused and looked at her watch. "That's tonight. At eight. Let's go."

Frank sat there, entirely unsure of what to say. He didn't know how he really felt about the idea. He was curious and wary.

"Oh let's. I mean, he's been with us one way or another since the day we arrived and you spotted him in the jardin. Don't you think it will add something unusual to our trip? A real Russian poet, here in Paris."

Frank was intrigued but felt a sense of dread. Bumping into Boris coincidentally was one thing, but going out of his way to see him— well, that was a different matter. It would be too eerie; after all, he had read this man's correspondence and he even knew what he said when he came. It was secondhand intimacy, bordering on voyeurism, that's what.

"Well, let's see how we feel tonight," he said in a cautious tone. "We have a long day ahead of us." But even as he spoke, he could see she wasn't going to give in on this one.

She nodded. "So what's on our agenda for today?"

"Montmartre," he said. "We can't leave Paris without seeing Montmartre."

"Oh, that's right." By now they were both getting a bit weary from their touristic exertions, mixing up place names and historical facts, kings, centuries, streets, museums. Jo Anne turned to the Montmartre walk in the Michelin guide and read, "'There is more of Montmartre in Paris, than of Paris in Montmartre.' Now what the hell is that supposed to mean?"

Frank laughed. He paid their addition and hoisted his day pack on his back. "What metro, oh great tour guide?"

"Clichy, of course." They walked back through the Place and Frank felt an evil thrill run through his body as he thought about going to Boris's reading at the Big Apple Bookshop. He reluctantly admitted to himself that he was dying for an opportunity to see Boris, that snake, up close.

Where just an hour ago Frank had been at one with the universe, having been given the key to life by Paris herself, now, on the hike up to Sacré Coeur, he felt expunged. As they made their way up the tiny winding streets, following the Michelin walk as interpreted by Jo Anne, he felt left out. How could this be? With only two precious days left in Paris, he had the uncomfortable feeling that the city was mocking him and his pauvre existence in New York. He gazed at the elegant terraced houses perched on the hills of Montmartre and the people walking with their baguettes under their arms; he strained to hear the maids chattering with each other across the walled gardens. Everything seemed to say, "You will never have any of this, you will always be an outsider." How could he have shifted so quickly from trembling with love for his own life to feeling so utterly miserable and heartsick? Nor would the mysterious street names reveal their centuries-old secrets. There was the rue Yvonne Le Tac (she must have been something to get a street named after her), the Place des Abbesses, (sounded so powerful and beautiful), the rue Le Lapin Agile (what clever fonctionnaire received permission to name a street like this), rue des Trois Frères (just who were these extraordinary brothers).

By now they were both hot and sweaty from the climb. It was only 10:30 and Frank wanted to stop for a quick bière panaché. "I'm so parched," he said, surprised that he used that word instead of, *thirsty*. *Thirsty* was American, *parched* was French. Parched was Katia.

"Beer this early in the day?" Jo Anne said, disgusted. She perched her hands on her hips and was breathing heavily from her unaccustomed exertion.

"One thing I've learned on this trip," he said, panting, turning around to her, "is that there are no rules in life."

Who said that? They both looked around, stunned at these words that seemed to have come from nowhere. They were so profound that they even rendered Jo Anne speechless.

The Place du Tertre was exactly like the description in the guidebook; a pseudo-bohemian carnival in which the artists were hawking their paintings to the milling tourists. They stopped long enough for Frank to have his beer and limonade. Jo Anne took a sip and grudgingly admitted that it was refreshing, then ordered one for herself.

They made the final ascent to Sacré Coeur, climbing the steps carefully as Jo Anne read aloud. After she had fully described the edifice, they entered. The cathedral was refreshingly cool and dark inside, the perfect solace after the morning's climb. They walked slowly around the perimeter of the basilica.

"Let's light some candles," Frank said.

"I'm Jewish and this is a Catholic church," Jo Anne said.

"That doesn't matter, we can light them for symbolic, cosmic reasons."

"You light one for me," she said, and sat in a pew while Frank made another tour of the tiny chapels, trying to decide on a saint for whom to light a candle. He stopped in two different chapels, slipped some francs into the boxes and lit candles. He stood silently as if saying a little prayer and came back to her.

"Well?" she said.

"I lit one for each of us in the chapel of St. Raphael, the healer. That's appropriate, don't you think? And then I lit one candle for St. Michel, the warrior against evil. He's also the patron saint of Paris."

"If you say so," Jo Anne said.

They spent some time outside on the terrace, admiring the view of the city. The cathedral grounds were turning into a circus, with mimes performing, busloads of tourists pulling up, souvenir vendors selling plastic replicas of the basilica. It was time to go. They continued their march on Paris, and before they knew it, they were back at the hotel, showering and changing for dinner.

They were well fed and a little drunk as they found their way to the Big Apple Bookshop. The rue de Petits Choux was a winding street, so they didn't spot the shop until they turned a corner and were practically on top of it. They sign was in the shape of an apple, painted red with only the word—"Bookshop"—on it and underneath, "Established 1981." According to *Passion* magazine, which Frank read while Jo Anne was in the shower, the Big Apple was the only English-language bookstore on the Left Bank and it had quickly become the favored hangout of a new generation of expatriate writers. An article, "Where Writers Like to Read," said that Paris was experiencing a minirenaissance, with writers possibly as strong and talented as Ernest Hemingway and Gertrude Stein. The magazine awarded Big Apple a rating of four Eiffel Towers, "for its generosity toward writers,"—they could buy on credit—for its excellent selection of contemporary English-language literature, and for its rafraîchissant customer attitude, which encouraged browsing and conversation."

There was a crowd of people standing outside the shop, enjoying the evening air. Frank heard lots of English mixed in with American French and French French. He thought he heard some Russian, too, but wasn't sure. He felt as if he and Jo Anne were the only tourists; everyone else seemed to know each other from the way they all waved and greeted each other. He supposed they were mostly writers who had crawled out from their literary dens for an evening of chitchat and wine. There were girls with no makeup who kissed each other on the cheek twice; there were sexy, artiste-type men with funky Japanese clothes and cigarettes dangling from their lips. There were preppy types—"bon chic, bon genre," as they were called—who could have been editors in French publishing houses, along with some older, very well-dressed people who exuded an air of accomplishment.

"Well, shall we?" Jo Anne asked him, and pointed to the door.

"Okay," Frank said agreeably.

When they entered the shop, he could understand why writers liked the place. It was a real book lover's paradise, designed to make you want to buy every book in the store. There were Persian rugs on the blond wood floors and the books were housed in antique pine shelves. Spotlights created intimate pockets of lighting. There were wicker chairs and love seats, quilted in Provençal fabric, tucked into the oddest places so you could sit and read if you liked. Tables overflowed with books and there was a magazine rack filled with such American publications as *American Photographer, Esquire, Interview, Yankee,* and the *New Yorker.*

There was a superb sound system with classical music playing, and the scent of potpourri filled the air.

The place filled up quickly and Frank and Jo Anne managed to claim a love seat in the corner. People sat on the floor or leaned against bookshelves. At 8:15 the music was turned off and a young woman with round, black glasses stood up in front of the shop.

"Welcome to the Big Apple," she said. "My name is Mia McCormick. I'm coordinator for the Big Apple reading series"—she scanned the room—"and I'm really happy to see such a large group tonight." The crowd started settling down. "I just want to remind you that there's no smoking in here. Also, I'd like to start by thanking the Big Apple and especially, Tyler Kass, the dedicated founder and owner of this marvelous place." She turned her head and gestured to a warm, bookish woman with a thick braid of brown hair standing behind the cash register. There was an enthusiastic round of applause, to which Tyler Kass responded with her hands raised in applause for the audience.

Mia continued. "Big Apple has added so much to the Parisian literary scene, don't you agree?" Smattering of applause. "We can live in Paris and have a place to come and meet each other and keep up with the state of English-language literature." More applause.

"What a love fest," Frank whispered.

"Shhh." Jo Anne nudged him.

"To introduce our reader for the evening, I pass the microphone." Mia made an imaginary motion as if she was holding one—"to Grisha Lobek, himself a rather famous Russian émigré writer, who knew our featured reader, Boris Zimoy, when they both lived in Moscow.

"Today, Grisha is world famous for his poetry, his essays and his conscience. There's even talk of a Nobel, right, Grisha?" She looked coyly to her right then continued, "But to us, he's just our Grisha. Ladies and gentlemen, Grisha Lobek."

There was applause again and Frank looked at Jo Anne, who was sitting rapt but with the usual sneer that had become a part of her face.

"An introducer to introduce the introducer of our reader," Frank whispered.

"Shush!" Jo Anne really elbowed him this time.

A balding, out-of-shape man with bushy blond eyebrows stood up and began speaking in a high-pitched voice without waiting for the room to

quiet down. He had an impatience about him that made it seem as if he
was yelling at the audience.

"My name is Grisha Lobek," he intoned in a bored manner, and was
immediately interrupted by applause, which he brushed away with his
hands and an annoyed look on his face. In his thick Russian accent he
continued, "I promised to Boris ten years ago when we were in Moscow
that such a night as this would take place." As he spoke his eyes didn't
connect with any others' in the room. It was clear from his demeanor
that he did not particularly want to be in the Big Apple Bookshop that
evening and that he had no use for literary groupies or events that took
time away from his writing.

He spoke slowly, emphasizing each word as if the audience was stupid. "Back then, it was our fantasies that kept us alive. You, here, filled
with your coq au vin and Beaujolais, cannot imagine. To have such
fantasies in a frozen gulag! Of course, we had no idea we would be
forced to live in exile.

"The West. This word floated from our lips. It was an imaginary place
of mythic proportions, filled with sweetness and dangers we could only
piece together from quick conversations with tourists on Red Square or
seeing whatever Western films were smuggled in. I understand these
days, from friends in Moscow, that *Tootsie* is a good one for seeing the
streets of New York."

Everyone laughed.

"Boris Zimoy would rather write than live. He is now in Paris to
continue the literary tradition from which he came—the tradition of
Pushkin, Chekhov, Lermontov, Gogol, Dostoyevski, Tolstoy. He wanted
to continue this tradition in his homeland. But this was not possible.
You must never forget: he is not here for the pleasure of Paris, as many
of you are! No, Boris is here in exile, just as if he were in Siberia. He
will always be a prisoner of his past, of his motherland and of his Russian soul. He is exiled from his people! And it is his people who need
their literary tradition, not you!" He paused for a dramatic moment. "It
is important for you to know that he would go back if he could. And it is
on this serious note that I introduce my friend to you, Boris Zimoy."

On this moving note, the applause started up again, but fervently this
time, as Grisha held out his hand for Boris. The audience started looking around to see from where Boris would emerge. Finally, it was a terse
Boris who stood up in the back row and made his way to the front of the

room, stepping over people who were sitting on the floor. They shifted their bodies to give him room.

Frank's heart started pounding wildly and his hands wouldn't keep still. He clapped, then clasped his hands, then ran them through his hair. He felt like one big fidget about to burst. Boris looked as alluring and electric as Katia had always described. But he had changed since that first day in the Lux. He looked leaner and meaner. He had shaved off his beard and wore a super-short, stylish haircut, slicked back with gel. His dark eyes pierced through everything. He was trying to keep a solemn expression on his face, but Frank could see under the veneer of toughness to a little boy who was pleased as the breeze with all the attention. Occasionally he would smile as he said, "Pardon, pardon," climbing over people. He was immaculately groomed, with a sweater tied around his shoulders just as it was that night on the television.

When he got up to the front of the room, he and Grisha embraced and Grisha sat down on the floor in the front row. Boris squinted and asked that the spotlight be adjusted, for otherwise he would not be able to read a thing and that was why they had all come, no? Frank saw immediately that his thick Russian accent charmed all the women in the audience, who giggled.

"Thank you, thank you, Grisha. Yes, and here I am, living in Paris and giving a reading in English. You never know how life will turn out. Never." A camera flashed. "Please, no flash," he said, indicating he couldn't see because of the light.

"I would like to read to you a story of mine that has just been translated into English by Dr. Anne Santos of McGill University, Montreal, Canada. I write in Russian, then it can go into French or English, sometimes French first, then English. So you see it is very difficult. You are always a prisoner—of your publisher, of your translator, of your agent." He shook his head at this, then he remembered that he was standing in front of a group of people and collected himself.

"This story is called 'Lana,'" he said, and cleared his throat. "Lana is the familiar version of the Russian name Svetlana," he explained.

"When I met Lana on my first trip to New York City, I had no idea I would fall in love with her. It was the farthest thing from my mind." His voice droned on seductively.

Frank felt a dread coming over him as Boris read deeper and deeper into the story. It was a story about an American Lana he met in New

York who seemed to be a reincarnation of a Russian Lana he had loved in Moscow. She lived a typically American life in her Manhattan apartment with her cat and her job, but strangely enough, he felt she had a Russian soul trapped in her body. He suspected it was some KGB trick, that she was an operative whose orders were to tease and torture him. She would speak perfect New Yorkese, but then shock him with her doleful Slavic looks and interpretations of life. What really sent him over the edge was when she was at work and he tried speaking Russian to the cat (who, it turns out, already spoke French) and the cat understood every word he said!

In the end they were riding the subway when he pulled out a gun, and with people all around watching, yet uninvolved in that typically New York way, he shot her. It was the perfect anonymous crime for which New York was famous. She looked at him and softly said, "Po-chemu?—why?—" and then slumped over. He bolted up the stairs, shouting and pointing, "Stop that man! Murderer!" as if he was chasing the killer. He grabbed a taxi for JFK and flew back to Paris, where he now stood before you, telling this tale. The End.

"So here I am, ladies and gentlemen. That is all." He smiled and raised his eyebrows mysteriously at the audience. "Thank you very much."

Frank wasn't surprised. The story was true to form. In his stories Boris always killed the girl or she died some grisly death. Of course this one was all about Katia. While the plot had been somewhat heightened for fictional purposes, all the details of their ill-fated romance were there. Boris had written a superb psychological persecution drama à la russe, superimposing Slavic melodrama onto a gritty New York setting.

Frank looked at Jo Anne sitting there enthralled. What a child she was! For all her adult understanding of other people's pain, she was a little girl, stuck in some early stage of development. He could see she had enjoyed being read to. Well, he had, too, for that matter. He saw something about her that he had never seen before, yet for some reason he didn't feel compelled to comment or do anything about it, as he was wont to do as a psychologist. Mr. Fix-It, he sometimes called himself, "Come here, Daddy will make you better." He was weary of being a saviour, of constantly trying to please. I've got to look out for myself, he kept repeating to himself.

"So? What'd you think?" Jo Anne asked him. From her bubbly tone she had obviously enjoyed it.

"So?" he mimicked her. He tilted his head. "I thought it was okay."

"Well, I thought it was great. He is fabulous. Such a simple story and so well written."

He shrugged.

"I thought that Lana sounded suspiciously like one of your former patients."

"Oh really?" He yawned. "Which one?"

"You know which one."

"Don't be ridiculous," he hissed.

"Well then, don't you find it interesting how art imitates life?" she said.

He didn't reply.

"And the part about how this Lana in the story had a psychiatrist, and that the only person who could possibly identify him as the murderer was the doctor because he knew the most intimate details of her life?"

"Are you quite ready to go?" Frank said. He wanted to scram. No way did he want to come face-to-face with Boris.

"Not yet. I want to hang around a little. Maybe buy some books." And with that she got up and left. She knew. Jo Anne was not dumb. He had told her about Katia back in New York when he was feeling overwhelmed by the mess of her therapy.

By now everyone was milling around, sipping wine out of paper cups, trying to get a word in with Boris or Grisha, who were holding court in one corner of the store, posing for pictures together and autographing books. The classical music had been turned back on and the cash register was ringing merrily as people made purchases. Frank inched his way around the room, eavesdropping on conversations, looking at the various books people selected. He was intrigued by *Interview with the Vampire* by Anne Rice and was paging through it, thinking about female infatuation with vampires, when to his horror, he looked up and saw Jo Anne talking to Boris!

Instead of the usual polite banter Boris had been having with the women who came up to him, he and Jo Anne seemed to be having a serious tête-à-tête. Frank moved a little closer and strained to overhear their conversation.

"You're bogged down in trashy and, if I might add, bourgeois, common-grade paranoia." She sneered at him. Her nostrils flared; there was joy in her eyes. Jo Anne on the attack.

"And you, a bloody shrink, know better?" He threw his head back and laughed.

"If it's pyschological dramas you want to write . . . I could be of great help to you," she countered.

Was that a lilt of flirtation he detected in her voice? He felt a chill run through his body. Now he understood. This was their flirtation, their way of making love. Of course. It was perfect. Jo Anne and Boris, two tigers poised for the kill. He moved away and ended up at the cash register, where Tyler Kass, proprietress, stood with a pleased look on her face.

"Oh, you've picked a good one there," she said warmly, taking the book from him and turning it over to find the price. He smiled back. From what he read on the back cover, the book's themes appealed to him: feeling left out of life; ever being the outsider; looking for one who understands. He wondered how the hell he would signal to Jo Anne that it was time to leave? He was fumbling with his traveler's checks when she came up to him instead.

"*Interview with the Vampire,*" she noted his purchase.

"Yes, that's just what you were having," he said testily.

She didn't know how to reply to that and stood there fidgeting. "So here's the story. Boris has invited me to join him at a café," she blurted, waiting to see his reaction.

The bomb had dropped. He looked away from her and tried to count how many traveler's checks he had left.

She put her hands on her hips. "I said yes. I mean, here I have this chance to meet a famous Russian writer and—"

"A few days ago he was a 'minor émigré,' if I recall correctly," Frank interjected sarcastically. He turned to Tyler Kass and asked sweetly, "Can you change fifty dollars U.S.? Good. And what will the rate be?" He turned back to Jo Anne and softened his tone. "I'm just very tired, that's all. It's been a long day. Really, you go, I'll be fine. I'm going back to the hotel. Tomorrow is our last day in Paris. I'll leave the door unlocked."

It was clear to him that Jo Anne was pleased with his reply, but pretended that she would miss him. "Okay," she said heavily, but then turned away briskly and bounced out of the store. Boris was waiting outside the shop with friends and nodded at Jo Anne when she joined them.

Frank stood around for a decent interval in order to give them enough time to get away before he left the bookstore. Finally he walked out into the chilly April evening. Jo Anne and Boris. He was stunned with what had just happened. It was a nightmare! He made a pact with himself not to think anymore about them. Whatever was going to happen was out of his control. The balance of power between he and Jo Anne had shifted. She was on her own now. Paris seemed to have awakened her, too.

Strange city this is, he mused as he strolled down the Boul' Mich' with his book under his arm, staring at the people who were sitting in cafés watching him. He was struck by this situation—who's watching whom? Who is living and who is the observer? Suddenly he wanted to be in one of those cafés, sitting under the bright lights amid laughing crowds, watching the street life, just as the Parisians were watching him. He spied an empty table in the back and maneuvered his way to it and sat down.

"Un cognac," he said to the garçon with the most assurance he had during his trip. He looked at the table next to him, where a woman was also sipping cognac along with a small bottle of mineral water. She smiled at him. "Et un Perrier, aussi," he added, again with authority. The garçon barely nodded and disappeared, having already caught sight of the newest customer.

Things must change! They must! This is the Frank I want to be, the Frank in his Girbaud pants, sitting in a café, sipping a cognac. The Frank in the Place des Vosges. Tomorrow is my last day in Paris. Vacations really are a bitch. You felt under such pressure to have a good time in your little allotted week, and if you didn't have a perfect, incredible time you felt as though you had failed. Finally he understood his patients when they returned from their vacations complaining that they needed another vacation to recover from their vacation.

He looked over at the girl sitting at the table next to him and she smiled at him again. This time he smiled back. She was so pretty, so French, with her fluffy short dark hair tied with a pink pouf, a wrist full of bangles, a simple navy skirt and sweater, which she wore with white ankle socks. This must be the gamine look that Katia was always talking about. She raised her glass and toasted him. "Merci," he said, and then looked away shyly.

Supposing he got tired of being an analyst, what would he do? He closed his eyes and all he could come up with was grooming horses at the Claremont Riding Academy or being a park ranger in Central Park. They were both outdoorsy, physical jobs, jobs you didn't take home with you at night, just an honest day's labor and your life was your own. Also, you could wear a uniform. The simplicity of it appealed to him. He resented having to be on the ball all the time.

He didn't know how it happened, it just did. At one point she—her name was Faustine—joined him at his table. She spoke some English and he ordered more cognacs and she took his hand and played with it. It was wonderful. Then she started rearranging his hair and playing with his ear and suddenly he started breathing funny and her mouth was near his and it was so sexy to be sitting at a café table in Paris, kissing a French girl... a girl he knew nothing about—who wouldn't spend the night telling him her life story—or if she did—he wouldn't know—or care.

Jo Anne Loves Paris and Boris

HE HAD NO idea how long he slept but was aware that someone had turned the light on. "Jo Anne?" he mumbled with his eyes still closed. He felt a hand gently touching his shoulder.

"Would you like a little snack?" she said.

Frank nodded yes.

"Sir?"

He opened his eyes. It was the flight attendant leaning down and holding out a little beige tray covered with plastic wrap. Damn! He hated being caught with his mouth open, drooling in his sleep. He wiped his mouth and sat up. His fellow passengers were stirring uncertainly, stretching their legs and freshening up. If it was snack time, that must mean they would be landing in the real Big Apple fairly soon. He waited for the drinks cart to come around and asked for two glasses of orange juice, then he unwrapped his snack. It was cheese and crackers, a brownie and an apple. Not bad. He couldn't wait to get home and have his first hamburger. Oh yes, and . . . chocolate-chip-mint ice cream.

He wondered what Jo Anne was doing now. Taking a bath with Boris? Taking a walk with Boris? Sitting in a café with Boris? Making love with Boris? He shuddered at the thought. Oooh, his head hurt. He had been hung over for the past two days. Barely did he get over a hangover than he got drunk again, and this last bottle of wine he had polished off on the flight sure didn't help any.

257

Jo Anne and Boris, what a match. At last, Boris had met a woman who had the ability to be not nice to him, a woman who could curl up her nose and dish it out as well as he could. Finally, a woman who didn't love him, a woman who wouldn't buy him yet another bottle of Yatagan. And for Jo Anne, let's see, Boris was a man who could treat her as meanly as she could treat him. And from what Frank knew about him, Boris was more interested in a life of the mind than of the body. Perfect for Jo Anne. Oh, this is a sad world, he thought. If a person such as Jo Anne, who lived an ascetic life solely in her apartment, could fall prey to such foolishness as Boris's and stay in Paris, then who am I to make any judgments about anything or anyone? Life seems to happen without us; we are just dragged along for the ride.

He remembered how even in his cognac-induced sleep he heard the hotel-room door open. She must have been trying to open it quietly, but in that morning silence, the calm after that storm, everything sounded loud. In his hangover haze he thought he heard her whisper, "You wait downstairs, I'll be right there." He heard the rustling of clothes, the rummaging of drawers and the sound of a suitcase being unzipped.

Still keeping his eyes shut and not moving, he said, "Jo Anne?"

"Good. You're awake," she said in a loud voice, and came over. "We have to talk."

"Shhh." He winced. "So early in the morning? Can't it wait?" he murmured. He still hadn't opened his eyes.

"Frank!" she said sternly, and sat on the bed.

"What?" He opened his eyes and looked at her. Oh my God, she looked different. Her cheeks were flushed, her eyes were wild and bright.

"I know this is going to come as a big shock to you, but..." She stopped, leaving him on a precipice. "I'm staying in Paris for another week."

"What?" He sat up. "Owww! Give me those aspirin will you?" Knives were slashing through his head. She handed him the bottle and watched while he popped two of them in his mouth and sloshed them around with some Evian.

She took a deep breath and shrugged her shoulders. "I know there's no rational explanation for this."

"Jo Anne, this is crazy. What about—"

She interrupted him. "It is the weirdest thing I've ever done. And you know something? I like it. Most of my adult life I've spent sitting in my apartment watching other people live. Now it's my turn. I'm tired of patching up other people's mistakes. I want to make my own mistakes," she said very matter-of-factly.

He could see it was no use. She hadn't come to discuss anything with him, she came merely to inform him. What he thought or said did not matter in the least. They were two consenting adults. The horrible, funny, sad thing was, when he really thought about it, he didn't care either.

"What has happened to you?" He felt he should at least try to talk some sense into her.

"What happened is that I met Boris Zimoy," she sighed.

"Oh, that's just great, Jo Anne," he said sarcastically. "You're just another one of his literary groupies. Pretty soon you're going to be buying him perfume just like the rest of them."

She ignored his last words, pursuing her own tack. "You really put on quite a show. I'm impressed in an annoyed sort of way," she said.

"What do you mean?" he said.

"About Boris. Pretending to know nothing about him," she said.

"What are you talking about?" he said, trying to hide his nervousness and stall for some time to figure out exactly what she had learned from her evening with Boris.

"Frank. I was with him all night. We talked. The minute he found out I was from New York, that's all he wanted to talk about. He told me about a woman named Katia. . . ." She left it at that.

"Jo Anne, he hates shrinks," he said, groping, trying to grab on to something, anything.

"What does that mean? What does that have to do with anything? Look. I'm going to spend the week with him. Not at his atelier—he told me there wasn't enough room—but in a hotel right down the street from his place. He wants me to correct an English translation of his new book. And I want to do it."

"He's just using you," he warned.

"Boris is an extraordinary person. He's trying to do something with his life. His whole life is his art. He's in a marathon against death and politics. I believe in him. And I can help him better than any other woman can. I understand him. He needs me."

Frank realized she was beyond help.

"This is different! I know it is!" She sounded like a young girl, desperate, in love. "Then I'll come back to New York and decide what to do next," she said thoughtfully, implying that this was so big, it could change her life.

"I can't believe you're doing this," he moaned.

She rushed around the room, throwing her clothes into the canvas bag, and collected her toilet articles from the bathroom. She didn't have much stuff, so it didn't take very long. She zipped up her bag and announced, "Well, I'm ready."

"You're in way over your head, Jo Anne," he warbled. But lying there devastated, naked, hung over in bed, he was in no shape to shake any sense into her. He decided to give up. "Good luck," he said quietly.

She picked up her canvas bag and her tote bag and left. Frank found his watch on the night table and checked the time. Ten-thirty on his last full day in Paris. He went to open the window and saw Boris waiting on the street, looking impatient and annoyed. When Jo Anne came out of the hotel, she handed her bag to him so he could carry it. He heard Boris say, "I can't. My elbow is sprained. From tennis. If I use it, I will need an operation. Sorry."

"Of course. Yes. Better if I carry it," Jo Anne said.

Frank rolled his eyes.

He got up and took a shower, hoping the steam would clear his head. As he stood unsteadily under the beneficent spray, he thought, If my patients could only see him now. Mr. Perfect. Wait a minute. Did he really do what he thought he did last night? Leaving the café with Faustine and going into the Bois de Boulogne to a secluded spot and...? Jesus Christ! He held on to the towel rack for support. Suddenly it all came back to him and he blushed in shame.

He shaved carefully and put on his soft French clothes. He packed his bags so that he wouldn't have to do it tomorrow. Then he went out for breakfast because the hotel would have stopped serving by now.

Paris seemed its usual chipper self this morning, unconcerned with his pain, not caring that it was his last day. It would continue jauntily without him. He stepped gingerly across the Lux, trying not to aggravate his head as he walked, and went into the first café he saw on the Boul' Mich'. Now what was this Katia had told him about French hangovers? The people you saw drinking beer in the morning were treating their sore heads. Un demi, she had called it, and explained it was the collo-quial expression for a half liter of cold beer.

He stepped up to the bar and said "Un demi?" The barman gave him a conspiratorial nod as if he understood perfectly. Frank looked at the two other men standing there nursing their glasses of beer. When Frank was about to lift his glass to his lips, one of the men raised his in a salute. Frank acknowledged his little toast and took a long drink. The cold bubbles tumbled down his throat and he felt better immediately.

Feeling a whole lot better, he ambled back into the Lux and sat down on one of the wrought-iron chairs surrounding the fountain. He watched tourists take pictures and overheard them say silly things. He felt like an old-timer, like he belonged. He decided to spend the day in the back streets of the Latin Quarter, just walking and smelling and looking. He felt sentimental, as if he were leaving a good friend.

Tomorrow at this time . . . he mused. He got a flash of himself walking through JFK, and it reminded him that he would be going home alone. By now he had wandered onto the rue Mouffetard and was being carried along by the cheerful crowds of this popular market street. He spied a wine store and remembered that he would need wine for the plane. Ooof, the thought of wine made him sick, but he knew that tomorrow, he'd probably appreciate it. He bought himself a nice bottle of Côtes du Rhone and put it in the French string bag he bought a few days earlier for a few francs. He walked out of the store and caught sight of himself in a window when the crowd thinned out. Was that really him? Why, he looked almost French.

He put on his earphones and listened to a soaring symphony as the aircraft glided down the eastern seaboard. God, nature was beautiful! He felt suddenly patriotic and loving toward America as he spied Massachusetts, the Cape, the Connecticut shoreline and finally the tawny arm of Long Island, sparkling in the setting sun. The cocoon of this flight was ending. He looked fondly at his fellow passengers who had made this plane a traveling country all its own. He wondered where all the Pakistanis would go once they reached New York. The touchdown was gentle and everyone clapped for the pilot.

Frank breezed through passport control by simply waving his American passport at the U.S. official who was letting all U.S. citizens on Air Pakistan flight 002 from Paris right through the gate. The immigration line, however, was another story, stretching down long corridors. He felt sorry for the foreigners if this had to be their first taste of America. His bags were among the first off the plane and he was waved through customs, too. He couldn't believe it. It seemed pretty lax, but that was okay with him. He got his French unpasteurized cheeses and sausages through without a hitch.

He pushed through the frosted glass doors and for a split second was excited by the crowd peering expectantly at him, but deflated quickly, knowing there was no one waiting for him. He tried to smile as he walked with his suitcase bumping his legs, stepping around family re-unions, hugging and kissing, until the smile slowly faded off his face.

The cabdriver tried to strike up a conversation, but Frank didn't feel like talking. "I'm a bit spaced out," he said apologetically.

"That's okay, mahn," the driver said with a thick Jamaican accent. When he dropped Frank off at his apartment building, he said, "Take care, mahn."

Frank looked up at his building and sighed. I'm home. He opened the heavy outer door and searched for his keys to unlock the inner door into the lobby. He checked his mailbox and was pleased to see that the super had emptied it just like he had asked him to. You never knew with these supers, they were so temperamental. As it was when he had first arrived in Paris, everything was heightened for him: the musty smell in the lobby, the sound of his keys clicking into his own door, the creaks under his feet as he let himself into his apartment, the stuffiness of the room from being closed up. He felt as if he was seeing his own life for the very first time.

He threw his bag down and picked up the pile of mail that had been placed neatly just inside the door. He walked around and flicked on some lights. What to do first? Unpack? Do laundry? Go grocery shop-ping? A shower? He opened the refrigerator door and saw three bottles of Amstel and some moldy fruit. He opened a beer and settled into his armchair with the mail. He flipped on the all-news station to find out the exact time. It was ten o'clock in the evening, which meant three in the morning, Paris time, his time. He was too enervated to go to bed right then. The silence around him was huge, it enveloped him. He could hear himself swallow.

After a few minutes he got up and went to his filing cabinet, rum-maged around and finally found what he had been looking for. It was a tape cassette dated over two and a half years ago. He popped it into the Toshiba, sat back down in his armchair and turned off the light. He took another slug of beer and leaned back, stretching his legs out in front of him comfortably.

In the darkness he heard her voice. "So what am I supposed to do?

Talk and tell you things? This is a joke, right? I can't believe you're going to be my doctor. What I think is that we should smoke a joint and go out dancing, that's what."

"Just start from the beginning," he heard his own voice echo coolly.

"Well, I do like my job. I'm a copywriter in an advertising agency. Say, did you know that people hate it when you say you love your job? It makes them terribly uncomfortable because most people hate their jobs. But I love mine, I really do."

Silence. Her attempt to be upbeat ran out of steam. He heard a sigh. Her voice changed into a slow lament. "I'm totally depressed. And lonely. I haven't had a date in two years. All I want to do is meet some nice guy. . . ."

New York

Katia Still Loves No One

"You could have married him," her friend clucked in a singsong tone.

"Dolly, please!" Katia turned to her with an exasperated look. "You're not helping matters!" She returned to twisting and turning in the mirror, adjusting the straps of her camisole underneath the black Romeo Gigli she had just slipped over her head.

Dolly was sitting on the love seat in her bedroom, sipping herbal tea, while Katia dressed for Clint and Carla's wedding. She had invited Dolly over for moral support, and instead she was turning out to be torture in disguise.

She turned around once again from the mirror and gave her a good, hard look to warn her not to do any more damage to her already-frail psyche. "I'm going to his wedding and that's that," Katia said emphatically. "And besides, you know I never loved him."

"Yes, you're right," Dolly said, and took a sip of tea. She sighed and crossed her legs. "I'm very sorry, Katia, dearest."

"It's okay. You're upset for me. I know." She patted Dolly's arm and turned back to the mirror. "Now which eye shadow do you think? I say . . . *Gold!*" she yelled extravagantly, trying to change the mood in the room. They both laughed over her enthusiasm.

Of course she couldn't have been more surprised that Saturday morning six weeks ago when she went down to her mailbox and found a heavy, creamy envelope with her name handwritten in an elegant calligraphy. Who could it be this time? Everyone she knew was married.

267

She remembers exactly how she felt when she slit open the envelope and read the invitation. First she was shocked, then surprised, then hurt, confused and finally happy for Clint. But what a way to find out. Of course she was genuinely happy for him, but why couldn't he at least have told her himself? Surely if she and Clint were the kind of friends she thought they were, he would have confided in her that he was in love with another woman. After all, she liked to think of herself as his confidante. Sadly, she realized she hadn't been that at all.

Gone was her one-man fan club, the last member of her personal clique. Now who would there be to appease and distract her, spoil her when depression set in? Clint was moving on; he had graduated from being one of her shock troops to another woman's knight in shining armor, from being the extra man in Katia's life to the man who mattered most in Carla's.

When she accepted the invitation by dutifully filling out the little ivory card and sending it to the bride's mother, she realized she had never been the guest of a groom before. She thought about that and decided she liked it; it appealed to her sense of drama. Then she called Clint to congratulate him. She was so nervous, she gushed all over the phone. "I'm so happy for you! When did this happen? All this time! And you never said a word! When did you realize she was 'the one?' Incredible!" And she was genuinely happy for him. Deep down she felt happiness was for other people, not for her.

His voice was polite and formal on the phone. "Thank you, Katia. We have decided on Mustique for our honeymoon," he said. "We've already started looking at houses in Connecticut. As a matter of fact, we put a bid on one this morning." We this and we that, he said.

Katia went through all the motions of being the perfect wedding guest. She bought a new black cocktail dress for the wedding, which was a formal affair. Oh dear, was it correct to wear black to a wedding? To Katia black was the only color there was. Except for white in the summer. So black it would have to be. She found out where Carla was registered—Bloomingdales—and went to the bridal registry where she spelled the bride's name and a lady tapped it into the computer and handed her an entire computer printout of their selections. Goodness, times had certainly changed. Instead of being shown around personally by a bridal consultant, she was left to wander the store alone with the printout, six pages long, hunting for the things they had chosen. She finally decided on a set of crystal candlesticks.

The six weeks passed quickly and suddenly it was June. As she sat in the church and listened to the woodwind quintet play "loving" music, she tried to feel sorry for herself. She went through her litany of how she always felt left behind at weddings, that people were moving ahead two by two, as God intended, and she was standing still, alone. And how weddings seemed to be love fests for all of the other invited couples, because it was their chance to walk down memory lane. She noticed how they nodded approvingly as another two people took the same jump off the precipice and leapt into the unknown.

But try though she did, she couldn't feel sorry for herself. She felt marvelous and full of love. It made her nervous. This day was about Clint and Carla and all she could muster up was genuine joy for them, that they had found each other. She listened seriously to the vows they had memorized and spoke as if they were their own words. She saw the couple next to her grasp hands lovingly. She looked down at her own hands and clasped them in her lap.

She gushed her way through the receiving line, telling all the bridesmaids how beautiful they looked, kissing Clint and congratulating Carla, then introduced herself to the ushers that Clint had dug up from somewhere. Did they have wedding bands on? Oh well, they would be busy dancing with the bridesmaids. She spotted someone she knew from Clint's office and shared a cab to the reception, which was held in a private club across town. She checked her coat and wandered through the various rooms during the elaborate cocktail hour. She poked around the tables of hors d'oeuvres, trying to look deeply occupied as she nibbled fried zucchini sticks and crab cakes. She hung out at the bar for a while and downed two Campari and sodas because she didn't know what else to do. She had no one to talk to. She surveyed everyone who acted as if they knew each other, standing around in small groups, chattering animatedly. But she knew this was not true. It was the illusion of cocktail parties that everyone seemed to be having such a grand time and mingling with new people, when in fact they were talking only to the people they knew, people who by now bored them. What they were saying were things like, "Nice place, isn't it," "When is dinner going to start," "Get me one of those crab cakes, will you," or "Where *are* the bride and groom?"

She tried standing still, hoping her solitude would inspire someone to come up and talk to her. It didn't work. The waiters were good sources of conversation, though. Hors d'oeuvres had gotten so complicated these days that you always had to ask, "And what do we have here?" when they paused in front of you with a tray. You could count on a lengthy reply. "Duck pâté perched on the tips of blanched Belgian endive, dipped into a coating of crushed, roasted pignoli nuts," or, "chicken seviche, that's raw chicken marinated in Florida Key lime juice and cilantro, wrapped in an Italian roasted red pepper."

As she looked around the roomful of expensive people who were badly dressed, she was surprised that she didn't know any of them. This indicated to her how really peripheral she had been in Clint's life, but back then, she had felt she was his only distraction. Then she spied Ricky. She had always liked Ricky—Eric he was called by everyone else. But he was so difficult. Well, maybe he wasn't difficult, it was just that he wouldn't flirt back. He looked so debonair in his well-cut dark suit, talking to some friends of Clint's parents, flashing his elegant smile that opened so many doors for him. Good, Ricky would be her savior.

"Ricky!" she cried dramatically as she swept up to him.

"Oh, hello, Kate," he said, and stepped forward to squeeze her hand and kiss her cheek. Ricky had never gone in for calling her Katia. "You look mahvelous tonight."

"Thank you," she said, reveling in this small bit of attention. "Nice wedding."

"Wonderful, wonderful," he said, looking around.

"And Carla looks so gorgeous," she said.

"Gorgeous, just gorgeous," he said.

Stupid cocktail chatter. Why was everyone so ill at ease? She looked at him and he was his usual cool and distant self. Poor thing, he hadn't yet figured out who he was. She had always fancied herself to be the perfect woman for him and then realized that many women probably did. He was that kind of a guy, the archetypal good catch. The *idea* of him appealed greatly: the urbane, handsome, filthy-rich eldest son, heir to a family fortune. Who he needs is me, Katia always thought, instead of those ridiculous women who tagged doggedly after him. She looked at him holding a Scotch and soda in one hand and nodding away the hors d'oeuvres being offered to him by waiters. Some men had to chase waiters to grab an hors d'oeuvre, Ricky stood still and the waiters flocked to him.

He made no attempt to introduce Katia to the people he was talking to or bring her into the conversation. Bastard, she thought. She felt awkward standing there, feeling extra again. "Will you dance with me later, Ricky?" she asked coyly.

"Of course, Kate. I wouldn't miss it for the world."

"I'm counting on you!" she said sweetly, but she could see, to no avail. Oh well, sweet wasn't her style anyway.

By now a steel band had set up and was starting to play. The evening theme was Caribbean—why, she had no idea, since Clint was from Oklahoma and Carla was German. She got another drink and walked over to watch the musicians play, and then she noticed the photographer snapping pictures of the wedding party. She wandered over and stood there with her drink melting in her hands, twisting her head this way and that to consider the scene in front of her. She started giggling. How silly and how sublime, this lineup with every possible permutation of the wedding party captured for posterity: the couple; the bridesmaids with the couple; bridesmaids with the bride alone; the ushers with the groom; the ushers with the couple; sister of the groom with the couple; sister with just the groom. This went on until the newlyweds had missed the entire cocktail party and the guests were well on their way to being drunk.

A waiter was now circulating and inviting everyone in to dinner. He directed Katia to a tiny round table where she would find a card with her name and seat assignment. She waited until a small party of people had found their names and then stepped up and searched for hers. There, Miss Katia Odinokov, Table 17. She picked up the card. Okay. She went into the ballroom and searched among the tables for number 17. The Caribbean theme was in full force, with centerpieces of pineapples and birds of paradise rising high above each table that was set with a hot pink tablecloth and orange napkins. She had to admit it was very festive, with the steel band pummeling away and the ladies standing around in their vulgar, spangly evening clothes so that everyone could get a good look at them. It looked like a dinner on a cruise ship. However, she appreciated the effort made to entertain, even if it did not come off in the best of taste.

When she finally located Table 17, her heart sank. It was in Siberia, not only the table farthest away from the bridal table, but tucked in next to the swinging kitchen door where the waiters huddled. This must be the reject table, she thought as she sat down to await the other table companions who would soon find themselves exiled to number 17. She knew from helping her friends plan their weddings that there was that point in the seating arrangements when you had accumulated enough odds and ends of people who didn't "go" anywhere to form an entire table of them. Now, Katia, she scolded herself for thinking such a nasty thought, this is very amusing and you are having a great time! She leaned back in her chair and enjoyed the spectacle of the room slowly filling up with the tipsy guests, ambling about, looking for their tables. She decided that she had the most beautiful dress. There, that must count for something.

Her table filled up with—she was right—a few distant cousins, a couple from out of town, an older woman, also without an escort. There were still two empty seats, one on either side of Katia. Let's see who my lucky seat mates will be. The dinner was starting, with the waiters bringing out the first course, an appetizer of sliced papaya and chunks of fresh coconut, swimming in port. She was right again. Her strategy when it came to catered parties was: eat the hors d'oeuvres, skip the dinner. As she shook her head and smiled no at the waiter she was struck by the sight of a couple strolling toward the table.

He looked like Gatsby coming out of the mist, holding an open bottle of champagne by the neck with one hand and escorting a blonde with his other. His tuxedo was open at the neck, giving him a rakish air. He looked as though he never went anywhere without a bottle of champagne and a blonde. The fact that the woman was older than he simply made him a more interesting creature, no matter that her glittery orange dress was a disaster area. Orange was a color? He had dark hair and deep blue eyes and reeked of bored money and stuffy upper crust. Katia had to close her mouth when she realized they had stopped at her table. Since there was one empty seat on either side of her, she moved so that they could sit together.

"May I join you? Do you mind terribly?" he said rhetorically to Katia as he pulled the chair out.

"Oh. No. Please, go right ahead," she said.

He sat down and looked at his dish of papaya and coconut and then at her empty place setting.

"You're not having any?" he asked her.

She shook her head and smiled. She watched as he put a forkful in his mouth and chewed thoughtfully. He put the fork down and pushed the plate away. "How right you are," he said. "More champagne then?" Katia nodded and held out her glass. She told him her party maxim about eating hors d'oeuvres, to which he again said, "How right you are," and then turned his attention to the woman in the orange dress on the other side of him.

The whole table had introduced themselves when they took their seats, but she had already forgotten his name. The woman he was with, she remembered, was Carol, who had smiled warmly at her. She didn't try to make conversation but was pleasant enough when she was spoken to. Where was Ricky sitting? She craned her head. Ah, there. He was at a table filled with women who were giving him their rapt attention. Why hadn't she been assigned to that table?

It was now time for the first dance and toast. In a thick Jamaican accent, the band leader announced, "And now, ladies and gentlemen, Mr. and Mrs. Clint Kalanty will dance their first dance to the song they selected, 'I Love You Just the Way You Are.'" The steel band started playing the tune as Clint and Carla swept in with foolish grins and danced. It was all so lovely and mushy that Katia started laughing uncontrollably while everyone else sighed at this vision of pure bliss, unbeset, as yet, by the trauma and boredom of daily living.

Within moments, people were starting to get up and join the dancing. Ricky wasn't dancing; it was clear he was not going to participate this evening. Everyone at her table had gotten up to dance and she sat alone as the waiters cleared the appetizer plates for the next course. Well, there were just too many extra women at the wedding, that's all. What a bore. Mr. Nameless had asked Carol to dance and Katia watched him escort her to the dance floor and start in among the swirling couples. He was a terrible dancer—no, worse than that. He had no sense of rhythm, he stepped on her feet. How indelicate. Wasn't he embarrassed? No, he kept right on tromping, having a grand old time.

Clint and Carla were now being passed on to the guests who wanted to have a dance with the bride or groom. Carol was on her way back to the table and Mr. Nameless was dancing with Carla, proving to be a no better dancer than before. Carla just tried to keep up with him, but she looked perfect because a bride could do no wrong.

The dinner progressed at the caterer's perfectly choreographed pace. Adding coconut to every dish was this chef's interpretation of Caribbean cooking. The main course was bits of beef and shredded coconut in a brown sauce over rice. Salad was oranges and bananas on a lettuce leaf in a coconut vinaigrette. Dessert was coconut sorbet, and the wedding cake was chocolate with coconut frosting. Katia sat amused throughout the dinner and was, in her own way, having a wonderful time. Mr. Nameless had been dancing all evening long with the women at the table and women at other tables, and she found it curious that he had not asked her to dance.

She decided to take matters in her own hand and dashed up to Clint as soon as one dance ended and said, "May I have a dance with the groom?" Clint was in a fog, this being his big day, and would never have gotten around to finding her or asking her to dance. He was only too happy to oblige.

It was her farewell dance with Clint, and she hoped it would be a sweet reminder of all the time they had spent together. But whatever they had was gone, he was lifeless in her arms, he had given himself to another. But still, she reveled in the private sentimentality of her act and she enjoyed the attention she knew they were getting from people looking to see who was dancing with the groom now. "It's me!" Katia wanted to yell.

The dance ended and Clint said, "Thank you, Katia. Now, where are you sitting?" He was going to walk her back to her table, but was intercepted by yet another young lovely who wanted a dance with the groom. He smiled a helpless smile at Katia and she walked back to her seat alone.

By now, everyone at the table had given up trying to make small talk with each other. Chairs were pushed back, cigarettes were being smoked, and people were visiting other tables. It was the disarray after the perfection that had been plotted out by the bride and her mother for months.

Katia sat down from her dance with Clint. She took out her compact and powdered her nose.

"Are you a friend of the bride?" Mr. Nameless had turned his chair toward her.

"No," Katia said.

He hadn't expected that answer. "The groom?" he tried, for who else was left.

"Yes," she said, and gave him a smile.

"Oh, I see." He seemed to be at a loss for words and paused to consider what this could mean. He looked her up and down, trying to determine something.

"Are you . . . ? Well, what I mean is . . . did you and Clint . . . ?" He groped for words, he was trying to be subtle.

"We were friends, yes," she replied subtly, trying to be vague and complicated.

"Oh, I see," he said again.

Was that agitation she noticed he was trying to hide? Would this information make her more interesting to him? Perhaps now he'll ask me to dance. But no. That was the end of their conversation. The evening clipped by at a rapid pace with the dances getting more frenzied as couples got drunker and drunker. Mr. Nameless danced some more with Carol and one of the giggling cousins at the table. He did offer to get Katia a drink from the bar, which she accepted.

After she finished the drink she decided it was time to go. She gathered her fuchsia silk shawl from the back of her chair and picked up the souvenir matches that said "Clint and Carla." She bid good-bye to the few remaining people at the table, and when she turned to say good-bye to him, he stood up, which she found terribly polite. "We didn't get a chance to dance, did we?" he said.

She looked at him. What a curious remark! What she really wanted to say would not at all have been polite. Instead, she looked at him demurely, as if she were trying to recollect. "No, I guess we didn't," she murmured icily. She turned and clicked rapidly away in her black heels, navigating her way across the crowded dance floor, hoping her Romeo Gigli swished as she walked. Just as she was about to exit the ballroom she turned around to look at him once more, but he had disappeared.

Frank Loves Katia

BEFORE KATIA, everything had been fine. Frank had liked his life, the way he had set it up, the way it was turning out. He liked his decision to lead a life of the mind. Then *she* entered the picture, driving him crazy with her overdramatizations and her sensual approach to la vie quoti- dienne. He had had no patience for her and told her that she never saw things as they were. And now? Now he knew nothing. All that time he was denouncing her, she had been showing him a way to live.

Since his return from Paris he had gone through his days like an automaton, showing up for his prescribed duties, present in body but not in spirit. Curiously enough, he did notice his patients getting better, which was ironic since he felt so much worse. Perhaps it was because he was so detached from the process, he became more accepting, less de- manding. He hadn't talked with Jo Anne, although she sent a postcard informing him of her decision to take a few months off from her New York life and live in Paris. There had been lots of wild gossip about her at the meetings he attended at the institute, but he never said a word.

It wasn't until June that he felt recovered enough from his trip to start thinking about how he was going to change his life. He would do it little by little. He would start with his leisure activities first. He sent for the New School catalog and pored over it. He had a hard time choosing between a gourmet cooking class and singing lessons. In the end he decided on the cooking class. What better place to meet women? Sing- ing lessons he could take in the fall. He went crisply off to Zabar's with his list of required equipment and picked up a nice blue-and-white striped apron to wear in class and selected his first two Wusthof cooking knives. Goodness, they were expensive. But they were the only ones worth owning, according to you-know-who. As he was standing in the checkout line he noticed a pretty woman looking at him rather wistfully, and he decided there was nothing sexier than a man who cooked superbly.

He joined Les Amis de Vin and loved telling his colleagues at the institute that he was a friend of wine. He always made sure to dress impeccably for the weekly wine-tasting seminars. So far he had attended, "Les Grands Crus de Bordeaux" and "Hudson River Valley Ho!" He was especially looking forward to "Burgundies Galore" and "Ooh La La Champagne." What fun it was to walk about the tasting room with his special tasting card and pencil, sipping the different wines and wearing a look of deep consideration on his face as he tried to discriminate between an oaky wine with a kiss of blackberry, and a young, impertinent wine with an aftertaste of smoky birch.

He threw out most of his clothes and haunted the sales at the Columbus Avenue boutiques, building a new wardrobe based on textures and colors. He started experimenting with new ways to mix prints and fabrics. He rearranged his office for a more pleasing look and bought fresh flowers for it every Monday. He put down his Freudian textbooks and picked up Henry James and John Irving, to name but two, and felt that he was learning more about human nature than ever before.

But try as he might to stay busy and occupy his mind with new thoughts and experiences, he couldn't get rid of the specter of Katia. There was unfinished business here. He woke up every morning and went to sleep every night thinking of her. He searched for the answer to the question that nagged him: what was he going to do about Katia? Finally, he couldn't stand it anymore. He loved her. He had to see her, to tell her, to resolve something one way or the other. He didn't care what the facts were, he felt alive with these feelings and wanted to share them. But how to see her? He couldn't very well call and ask her to come see him in his office, she'd never do that. But he didn't feel comfortable calling her up out of the blue and asking her out for a drink or dinner, either. For some reason he thought that would be tacky, and besides, she wouldn't know it was the "new and improved" Frank speaking. After mulling over the possibilities, he decided it would have to look like a chance meeting, yes, something natural and effortless.

And so it was on a brilliant Saturday afternoon at the end of June that Frank came upon the perfect scheme. He was sitting in his armchair in front of the fan wearing nothing but underpants and a T-shirt that said "Je' ♥ Paris," flipping through the *New Yorker*, scanning the "About Town" listings. Of course. A poetry reading at the 92nd Street Y! Katia had a membership to the Poetry Center, and this Monday night, Milan Kundera would be the final guest of the season. She was a big fan of his, having read all his novels. She would definitely be there. He barely got through the weekend thinking about their meeting, a mere two days hence.

When he arrived at the ticket window Monday night, there were no tickets left. It never occurred to him. "It was sold out weeks ago," the lady said. "But you could sign up for next year." She pushed a flyer under the grate. He said that wouldn't help, it was tonight that he wanted to attend. Then she told him if he stood in the lobby, someone might be trying to sell an extra ticket, but not to pay more for it than the allotted price because the 92nd Street Y didn't believe in scalping. He thanked her and roamed the buzzing lobby anxiously.

"Dr. Manne!" said a female voice.

Katia! He turned around and it was Rose Bruno, one of his newest patients. Damn!

"Oh, hello, Rose," he said amiably, and smiled.

"I didn't know you like Milan Kundera," she said coyly.

He thought, There are a lot of things you don't know about me, but said instead, "Oh, I do. I adore him."

Rose giggled uncomfortably and said, "Well, see you Thursday."

He nodded and turned to walk away, but God must have wanted him to go to this reading because he bumped into someone trying to get rid of an extra ticket and bought it on the spot.

People were pouring into the auditorium and he walked down the aisle feeling very self-conscious. He looked left to right, trying nonchalantly to find two empty seats—the better for her to spot him.

The sold-out hall was purring with anticipation on this special evening, for Milan Kundera was a literary superstar. Frank leafed through the program and felt like he had been here before, a result of Katia's excellent descriptions of the readings she attended. He was getting anxious. Where was she? Would he recognize her? The room was almost full and he kept having to turn people away who kept asking, "Is that seat taken?" "Sorry," he would say, laying his hand over it, "it is."

Then he saw her striding down the other aisle to the front of the auditorium. True to form, she was coming in late to find an empty seat next to the most interesting-looking man she could find. He wanted to stand up and wave his arms. How different she looked. How could one woman affect so many different looks? She was a chameleon, growing and changing into new definitions of her self. But this evening, she had arrived; she was at her most beautiful, so elegant in a simple eggplant-colored dress, with her hair long now, pulled off her face into a low braid at the base of her neck, accenting her subtly made-up eyes. She wore chunky black sandals and carried a black sailor bag draped casually over one shoulder, a study in style. That's my Katia! He was so proud of her. He looked around to see if anyone else was admiring her.

She gazed into the crowd as she walked, surveying the situation. "I'm over here," he felt like yelling. He watched tensely as she continued to scan the audience. Now, after his trip to Paris, he was able to understand how really French she looked. He loved it. She was the most beautiful woman in the room. There was a new calm in her face, a clearness that was striking. She looked softer, more approachable than she had during her time with him. Back then she had been anxious, often angry and uncomfortable. What had happened to her? She must have met some-one in order to look so great. He knew he should be happy for her, but instead he was alarmed. What if he was too late? Not to worry. He would deal with that when they came to it. Maybe they would go to a café after the reading and he would tell her how much he loved Paris.

Katia started back up the aisle, apparently having spotted an empty seat. Oh my God, she was coming right toward him! His heart fluttered. He tried to sink down into his chair. He didn't know where to look. Oh no! What would he say? It was exactly what he wanted to happen and now he was petrified. He tried to calm himself. He had every right to be there, this was a public reading. He cleared his throat and froze a smile on his face.

She swished right by him, leaving a trail of Paris in her wake.

He turned around to see her sliding into a row just two behind his, setting calmly between two men. What? He couldn't believe it. Didn't she see him? Wasn't he interesting looking enough? Then he realized, of course, why sit next to one man when you can be between two.

The lights in the hall began to dim and the audience started settling down. Damn, why did she have to sit behind him! He couldn't keep turning around to look at her. A wave of unhappiness drifted over him.

The atmosphere reminded him of Boris's reading in Paris. He thought, My God, what other dramas are going on in this hall at this very moment? He had visions of all sorts of trumped-up liaisons, broken affairs, literary spats and jealousies churning around him. He relished his anonymity when the lights finally went out all the way.

The head of the Poetry Center came out to make the introductions. As he had guessed, she was there to introduce the person who would introduce Milan Kundera. He slumped down into his seat, aware of the empty one next to him. After making several announcements about upcoming readers for the next season, changes in the schedule and the usual plea for donations, she was now going to turn the podium over.

"And now, ladies and gentlemen, I have a delicious surprise for you this evening. Someone very special is here to introduce our special guest. It is my pleasure to introduce once again—for he read to us last year from his own work—a writer who's on everyone's lips as the next Nobel Prize winner." A thrill ran through the crowd. "Grisha Lobek." Audience murmurs. "Fortunately for us, Grisha, who lives in Paris, had to be in New York tonight and has graciously agreed to introduce his friend, Milan Kundera. And so, without further ado, please welcome Grisha Lobek."

There was enthusiastic applause as Grisha dramatically lumbered onto the darkened stage and into the spotlight. Frank's mouth dropped open. What was this, some sort of joke? Reality was simply too weird, with all its themes and replays. Grisha looked his same tense self, once again slightly annoyed with the audience for being there and looking as if he had better things to do. Who exactly was this Grisha Lobek, Frank wanted to know, and why did he seem to be the king of émigrés?

Since Milan Kundera was a major émigré, Grisha had prepared an elaborate introduction. Frank knew from reading the Sunday *Times Book Review* that Grisha had written reviews of Kundera books. Since he had first seen Grisha in Paris, Frank had tried to read some of Grisha's works but had found them opaque. He couldn't follow much of what he was saying now either, so he turned instead to look at Katia.

Oh my God! Frank's mouth dropped open. His mind ground down to slow motion. Was this a dream? A perfect Katia fantasy come true? The man sitting next to Katia, with whom she was now chatting, was Mikhail Baryshnikov! What was this, a Russian émigré Mafia? A poor American guy didn't have a chance!

No doubt both Grisha and Misha were friends of Kundera and had come to hear him read and probably go to a party with him to celebrate afterward. And now, if Katia worked her charm, she would be included in this little soirée. But didn't she understand? It would be all over for her! She didn't have a chance in the hands of these master womanizers! Frank had read all about them in *People* magazine! She was as good as chewed up and spit out with Misha, or Grisha for that matter. Women simply could not resist his deadly charm. What was it about him? he wondered. Every one of his female patients included Misha in the fantasies he was able to wring out of them. "Those eyes," the women said, drooling. Even his male patients wanted to be Misha. When he asked them why, one of them said, "Well, just look at all those moving parts!"

Katia looked self-possessed and lovely as she exchanged a few words with him. It seems Misha had noticed the tiny gold Russian Orthodox cross she was wearing and struck up the conversation. She was holding it in her fingertips and he was smiling at her. Frank tried to imagine how she would be feeling right now. She would be burning up at this fantasy of fantasies come true. To have Misha, the ultimate émigré, in the seat next to her; now this was like dying and going to heaven. Why a woman couldn't do any better than this! He could just hear it now: this would forever be the night that Baryshnikov sat next to her at Milan Kundera's reading.

Frank reluctantly turned back toward the stage, where Grisha was still droning on in his whiny voice. He felt utterly defeated. How could he, Frank Manne, Indiana psychotherapist, possibly compete with Mikhail Baryshnikov, Russian émigré ballet superstar? He realized it was all over. His timing just plain sucked. Just when he was finally able to deal with her, to understand that he loved her, she had slipped away from his grasp. In her own life-affirming way, she left him behind. She evolved to a higher sphere, a place of personal power, where other women's fantasies became her own reality.

His attention was shot. There was no way he could sit there and listen to the reading. Grisha had just finished and everyone was wildly clapping for Milan Kundera. This would be the time to escape, during the din of applause. He started coughing and got up as if he needed water desperately, covering his mouth with his hand, and ran out of the darkened auditorium.

He stepped out into the calm, dark night and walked slowly down Lexington Avenue, filled with the sadness of surrender. At Seventy-seventh Street he decided to take his chances and walk home across the park. He rounded the boat pond and was taken by the lovely sight of the moonlight dabbling the water. He sat down on a bench and listened to the sound of water lapping against the concrete edges of the pool. He felt surprisingly peaceful for the first time in ages. The tension was gone from his body. Some karmic lesson was finished. Katia and Jo Anne and Boris had been placed in his path to put him through his paces, to teach him things about himself and then depart. And tonight, with a gentle, dull thud, it was all over.

How strange it was to have a broken heart and at the same time feel freed, finally, to go on with his life. He juggled these two feelings, alternating between sadness and peace. When he realized he probably would feel like this for days to come, he got up and continued his walk through the park. Back on the West Side he stopped at Baskin Robbins and bought a chocolate raspberry truffle cone and licked it thoughtfully the rest of the way home. He slept better that night than he had in years, with no dreams. Just thick nourishing sleep.

Boris Loves Katia—In His Own Way

It was about ten o'clock on Saturday night of Labor Day weekend when Katia went out to pick up the Sunday *New York Times*. She bought herself a gelato, which she licked contentedly while strolling around the neighborhood with the bulky paper under her arm, observing her local nightlife. The Upper East Side was quiet. Everyone but everyone was out of town, at the beach or in the mountains, for the final fling with summer. She finished the cone and walked home, looking forward to spending a contemplative, stimulating evening with the paper. She wanted also to think about some new autumnal resolutions.

Like a good New Yorker, the first thing she did when she got home was weed through the paper, taking out the sections she never read. She glanced at the sports section for news of the U.S Open, then put aside the week in review, the classifieds, most of the business section and, regretfully, the real-estate pages. "Sorry, Boo, we can't afford a house this week," she said to the cat, who was waiting to sit on whatever section she was going to read. It didn't leave much of the paper, but what was left was prime: the news pages, arts and leisure, the magazine, which she always leafed through first to see how her ads looked, travel (where did people get all the money not to mention time for those adventurous excursions?) and finally, the book review. It was her favorite, so she always saved it for last, better to read it slowly and savor it. When she

283

was a girl, she had thought the book review was for lazy people. Why would you want to read a review of a book instead of the book itself? Now that she was older she appreciated the concept of books being reviewed for her reading pleasure. How considerate. She especially enjoyed it when literary feuds boiled up in the pages right in front of her, as writers bickered with each other over some misunderstanding or interpretation. She got a kick out of the picky brouhaha, the he-said, she-said, wait-a-minute, take-that-back, I-will-not, drama of it all.

Because it was such a sultry night, Katia decided to change into her Brazilian pareo. She was feeling sexy and good and the sarong made her feel like a luscious lady in a Gauguin painting. Since Labor Day marked the end of the gin season, "Might as well live big," she said to Boo and whipped up a slush of peaches and gin in the blender and then slipped Boo some catnip, seeing as it seemed selfish to enjoy her gin alone. Two ladies lolling about, one a little tipsy, the other a little stoned. Sipping her tropical drink to the sound of the whirring fan, she methodically read her way through the paper, transferring each section from the unread pile to the read pile, which on Monday morning would become the trash pile. She went to bed about 1:30, leaving several sections to dawdle over with her morning coffee. She went to sleep wondering what she would do tomorrow. Bicycling in the park? An air-conditioned movie? Shopping in SoHo?

The next morning, having gotten up at 5:30 to feed a nagging Boo, who kept walking on her with elephant feet (Oh, excuse me, I'm just passing through, did I wake you?) Katia went back to bed for more sleep. She finally got up at what for her, the habitual early riser, was the decadent hour of eleven. My goodness, half the day gone, she exclaimed to Boo while she made her café au lait. She pulled out the book review from the pile on the floor, where it had been mistakenly buried inside the real-estate section, and settled down at her pine table with her café. Boo settled into her sphinx position at the far end of the table for her morning meditation. Katia took a sip of coffee and turned the book review over.

"Ow!" she screamed, spilling the scalding hot coffee on her hand. Boo jumped in alarm and glared at her with wide eyes. "Oh my God," she said, licking her hand as she stared at the front page of the book review. It featured a large picture of a windswept, gruff Boris, dressed in leather pants and leather jacket, perched like a nouveau coolster on a pile of construction junk at Les Halles. What bullshit French kitsch, she thought, as she peered at his brooding visage. She thought of all the thousands of women in New York staring at the same photograph, swooning over his drop-dead handsome face. How much did he pay a publicist to get him this space? she wondered sarcastically.

Then she saw the title of the book. *Katia in the Lex*, by Boris Zimoy. She screamed, "Oh my God, I can't believe this!" Was it about her? Was she going to be unfamous? Her heart started pounding wildly, and she couldn't contain herself. She scooped Boo up in her arms and ran around the apartment, giddy with laughter and fear until Boo started biting her arms, demanding to be released. Finally Katia sat down, gripped the paper in her hands and read.

The review was entitled "Look Ma, No Hands." It referred, according to the reviewer, Grisha Lobek, to how Zimoy liked to ride the New York subway (without holding on to anything) and to how Zimoy felt the book was written, with no hands. "It wrote itself," he was quoted, "just like that." No hands was also a metaphor for his life as an exile, Lobek pointed out, since with the past gone and the future uncertain, he was living with nothing to hold on to. And Katia interjected sarcastically, don't forget he doesn't want any woman's hand on him. Look but don't touch.

Katia skimmed the review in one wild sitting. She was more than numb, more than stunned. She didn't quite know how to feel. Her mouth was dry and her heart was pounding. She reread it again, this time slowly.

The title, *Katia in the Lex*, was a literary nod to the famous French avant-garde novel, *Zazie dans le Metro*, written by Raymond Queneau and published in the Paris of the 1950's. She was impressed. Well, she always knew he was clever. The Lex, of course, referred to her subway line, but surely he could at least have changed her name. It both flattered her and pissed her off. That was inconsiderate and lazy of him. But what did he care? Well, it's too late now, she groaned. Everyone will know it's me.

The next part she thought was just grand. Lobek wrote, "Katia is Zimoy's painstaking and loving portrait of a postfeminist heroine who will no doubt join the ranks of such lofty literary lionesses as Truman Capote's Holly Golightly and E. F. Benson's Lucia."

That made her feel good. Real good.

But then Lobek went on to say that Zimoy was "a shrewd observer of contemporary American life, capturing the stultifying anomie, the neurotic behavior and desperate hunger of the modern-day New York woman on the prowl for love in the big city."

At this she got furious. How dare he? How dare he take my pain, my life, and make a mockery of it? How dare he judge me? She wanted to kill him.

The novel's heartthrob is Alexei, a surly, brooding Russian poet living in Paris. Just as a Siberian hunter would dress in the skins from his kills, Alexei, clothed in the sumptuous leathers of Marithe ý François Girbaud or Kansai Yamamoto, stalks the streets of Paris and New York, letting women fall prey to his exotic, foreign charms. He discovers a strange phenomenon in his encounters with Western women. When they meet Alexei they profess to be self-sufficient, career types with satisfying lives of their own, but within weeks of dating him, they turn into crying, petulant, greedy souls, wanting only to marry him. His interest quickly turns to disdain and ultimately he discards them.

But enter the engaging spirited Katia Beck whom Alexei meets par hasard on a cold January in New York. At first she follows the pattern of his other women, and in the scene where she begs him not to leave her, he dismisses her icily. "Baby, every woman loves a Russian poet." She is stunned. Something clicks and she rises to the call of revenge. She knows that while claiming to abhor bourgeois values, Alexei conceals a desperate love of fine things and longs for the seductive life-style of the rich and famous. In a marvelously entertaining series of twists and turns Katia develops into a formidable foe, slaying Alexei in her own way.

Well, that was good. In the book, at least, she got some revenge. But what could she do in real life to get back at him? Hmph, this would require some real thought. . . . Later, later.

An Upper East Side woman, her psychiatrist and a Russian émigré, all set against the background of wintery New York. A simple tale brilliantly told. *Katia in the Lex* will no doubt bring Zimoy to the attention of a wide audience that has previously ignored him. *Katia* is his fifth novel and no doubt his most commercial. The book has already been optioned by Hollywood, and when this reviewer tried to telephone Zimoy in Paris, a woman, who declined to identify herself, answered the phone and said that he was unavailable. It turns out that Zimoy was on vacation. At Club Med.

She felt as though her life had been stolen out from right under her. He took my life and made it his. What do I get out of all this? she wanted to know. Bastard. The least he could have done is write to me and tell me. But no, I had to find out this way, like the rest of the world. What a prick. He couldn't even send me a copy of the book. But mostly she was feeling like shit because he had reduced their relationship to this. A book. She had been good material. That's all.

So Boris was finally going to hit the big time. Katia turned the pages of the book review absentmindedly and there on page five was an ad for the book. It showed yet another picture of him, this time leaning on the Christo-wrapped Pont Neuf, basking in the sun, his scavenger eyes staring into the distance. It was disgusting. It read:

Will the real Katia Beck please stand up?
All the men in New York are dying to meet you!

Katia in the Lex

The boisterous bestseller
by Boris Zimoy

Published by Siegel & Schwartz.   At fine bookstores everywhere.

Now she wanted revenge. What could she do? Write a letter to the book review? But what would she say? That she had been one of his poopsies and he was a real drag? She checked her watch. It was noon. Good. The bookstore would be open. She dashed in and out of the shower and threw on her jeans and a T. Her hair could dry by itself. Forget the makeup. She jogged the few blocks to Books & Co. on Madison Avenue. They were sure to have it since the store was into émigré authors. Besides, this was a boisterous best-seller.

She went into the shop and cruised once around the table of current hardcover fiction. It wouldn't be on "The Wall" yet; that was reserved for the owner's selects and certain timeless classics. She couldn't find it.

"Do you have *Katia in the Lex?*" she asked the hip-looking guy with the ponytail standing behind the huge arrangement of baroque flowers at the cash register. "It's by Boris Zimoy . . . in the book review today?" He ducked down below the counter and then reappeared with the book in his hands.

"I was just unpacking it," he said, passing it to her. "I sold out the first shipment last week on word of mouth alone. Good you came in early. With a review like that, it's going to go today."

"Have you read it?" she asked, flipping through the pages, two hundred and ninety-three of them.

"I read a reviewer's copy a few weeks ago. It's fun. Literature, it's not. It will make a better movie than it is a book." He went back to his work behind the counter. "He's supposed to do a book signing here in a few weeks," he said absentmindedly. "Are you on our mailing list?" He handed her a three-by-five card. But the minute she wrote "Katia Odinokov" she felt self-conscious and crumpled it up.

On the cover was a beautiful black-and-white platinum-print streaky photograph of a woman in motion, zooming through a subway turnstile. It was sensual and arresting. It struck Katia that it was such a feminine-looking cover for a male author. The whole back cover was a picture of—you guessed it. Jesus, you could tell just by looking at him that he was in love with his looks. The picture was taken at a dramatic angle; this time he was in his Parisian atelier, shirtless, displaying his furry Russian chest. What was this, a pinup? He looked swarthy and fresh, as if he had just gotten out of bed after a healthy tussle with a woman. That picture alone ought to sell a fair number of copies. Katia opened the book. It was dedicated to a Jo Anne. Who was Jo Anne; was she the one after me? Well, she's not French, that's for sure. Why wasn't the book dedicated to Katia herself? Then she reasoned, you don't get a book dedicated to you when it is about you. If, that is, it really was about her, which she had yet to find out. She handed the guy behind the counter a twenty-dollar bill and waited for the change from $16.95. Under normal circumstances she would have gone to "Barnes & Noble, Of Course! Of Course!" for the discount. But these weren't normal circumstances.

Frank rolled out of bed that Sunday morning rather late. He had been lying there for quite a while, considering whether he wanted to get up or spend the entire day in bed. He was so enjoying this new strain of self-indulgence. Lately he was leading a double life. At work he was ever the meticulous, caring therapist. But at home he indulged in the slovenly, sensual life he craved.

No, he decided, he would treat himself to a cappuccino breakfast at Zabar's café. A croissant warm from the oven wouldn't do any harm, and maybe he would meet a lone lovely who had the same idea. He tried to imagine who she might be, lying in her bed on this lost Labor Day Sunday thinking the very same thoughts. He headed for the shower and decided not to shave. He put on his softest chinos and a cotton shirt from The Gap. He loved that store, even the name; it was so sixties. He always felt "with it" when he wore his Gap clothes.

The sun blinded him when he stepped out of his building, so he went back in to get his sunglasses. A dog-day Sunday morning in Manhattan. Broadway was strangely quiet. Everyone's in the Hamptons. Tant mieux, he said, practicing his latest French lesson from the Alliance Française. As he passed Shakespeare & Co. he thought he would pop in and get himself something nouveau to read. He loved Shakespeare & Co., too. Besides being a superb bookstore, it was such a great pickup place. You could get high on the electricity just watching the boys look at the girls and the girls look at the boys, and even the boys looking at other boys, but all the while, everyone was pretending to be browsing for a good book. He liked to stand around looking at books while listening to the various come-ons.

He was blasted by the air-conditioning when he opened the door. Then he stopped short.

"Please step in and close the door, sir!" the man behind the cash register yelled amicably. "You're raising our electric bill!"

"Oh." He jumped in and closed the door. There, in front of him, on the hardcover best-seller table, was a display of books piled high between two paper sculptures of the Empire State Building and the Eiffel Tower. *Katia in the Lex* by Boris Zimoy. He stepped up to the table and stared at the books. Taped to a piece of cardboard was a review of the book by Grisha Lobek, which appeared in today's *Times Book Review.* He read the review quickly, standing there and with his hands shaking; he picked up a book and made a beeline to the cash register. White noise was rushing through his head. Did Katia know about this? Surely she must. As he waited on line to pay he opened the book. It was dedicated to Jo Anne.

Frank ordered two cappuccinos to go at Zabar's and went to the park. He sat on a bench near where the skateboarders and roller skaters whipped through their maze of soda cans and read quickly, skimming for plot.

By the time he finished the book late that afternoon, he knew he would reread it many times. He closed it and stretched out on the now empty bench. This wasn't entirely the work of Boris Zimoy, although he had been the one to actually put the words and story down. No, he saw the brilliant mind of the crafty Jo Anne at work. After all, who better than Jo Anne, with her finger on the pulse of today's women, to weave a story about the angst of urban living? *Katia in the Lex* was Boris's Katia transposed by Jo Anne into every woman who had ever sat before her, spilling the beans of her lonely soul. No wonder the book was so insightful in the matter of woman's psyche. As far as Jo Anne was concerned, "woman equaled loneliness." Every woman was lonely, it was her birthright, it was her burden. If she was alone, she was lonely for people and understanding. If she was surrounded by a family with never a moment alone, she was lonely for herself.

He got up and walked slowly home. It was now six o'clock and the weather had turned. No doubt there would be a thunderstorm within the hour. Frank welcomed the sky's angry rumbling and the cozy, closed-in feeling of the puffy gray clouds. People were starting to pour back into the city from their weekends away.

So how did it feel to see himself pop up as a character in fiction? To see himself make love in black letters on white pages; to see his trip to Paris recreated step by painful step. He had been analyzed and turned inside out in public, though he had been disguised well enough so that no one would know it was he, Frank Manne, masquerading as Joe Viggeano. But still. Incredible the way this Boris Zimoy swept into New York, turned three lives topsy turvy, then checked out to write it all up. Just. Like. That.

Then there was Katia. He couldn't begin to imagine what Katia would be thinking. He stopped at the deli for a bag of "Cool Ranch" flavored potato chips and a six-pack of Coors and made it to his building just as the big drops began to fall.

The media loved Boris Zimoy and put on the blitz. Not only had he written a book that touched the nerve of contemporary American pop society, but he was marketable, media-handsome in addition to being a Russian émigré. He was the Nureyev of letters, the Sakharov of suffering. His lusty face appeared on the covers of *People* and *GQ*. In one week he charmed Jane Pauley on the "Today Show" and Joan Lunden on "Good Morning America."

"How is it that you seem to know so much about women?" Jane Pauley asked him in that coy, probing way of hers.

"Ah, it is not easy. . . ." A sly shake of the head, a pause for effect. "Women are ve-ry, ve-ry com-pli-ca-ted," he said in his baby-talk, sing-song English. Everyone loved that answer, especially the millions of women out there.

The morning she saw him on "Today," Katia was so excited she could barely finish putting on her makeup. He was in New York! Oh good, today he'll call me! She hurried downtown to the agency, and when she walked into her office she told her secretary, "I'll answer my phone today, Raima. No need to screen calls." And every time the phone rang, she yelled excitedly, "I'll get it!" But it was never him. At the end of the day she was deflated. Maybe he didn't have her office number. Yes, that's it. And, probably, he had forgotten the name of her agency. Damn! She had left in such a rush for the office that she forgot to turn on the answering machine. That night she recorded a special message for him on it. "Bonjour, Paris. I'm in the Lex, so won't you please leave a number or call me at Drake Boucher? Ciao." For the next few days, the first thing she did when she came home at night was rush into the bedroom to play back the messages. Not a word.

At first she thought, Well, he's really busy right now with publicity and interviews and all. Things will settle down and he'll call. Then she thought, Maybe he's scared to call me, he feels guilty or he's afraid of my reaction. So she decided to make the first overture and called his publisher, Siegel & Schwartz, and left a message for him there. But still nothing. Maybe he never got the message. But then as he appeared on the early evening soft-news shows, "Live at Five" and "Eyewitness News," she began to feel hurt and angry. Why wasn't he calling her? What had she done to deserve this treatment? Weren't they friends? Hadn't he written a book about her? She knew that things had ended badly between them, but surely he would have the human courtesy to contact her. Especially given these extraordinary circumstances. Finally, when his picture started showing up in the society pages of the *Post* and *New York* magazine, at some soirée at the Palladium and at the Milk Bar at 3:00 A.M., she became furious. She had been the ticket to his success and now he had discarded her. She wasn't even worth a goddamn lousy phone call. She was more furious with herself. Once again, she had set herself up to be dumped. When would she learn? When would she get it into her head that he was a bastard, a not-nice person, a prick. Boris was now officially and forever on her shit list.

Vogue did a photo essay on "Boris Zimoy's Paris," complete with clothes and styling credits (photos by Fregatina; hair and grooming by Ziggy of Jean Louis David, Paris). Katia had a name for it: fashion porn. Boris's face under the spray of his shower (Clinique Clean Shave; Aramis shower gel) followed by Boris sitting at his typewriter with just a towel around his waist (IBM, Fieldcrest); Boris strolling alone, by the Seine, lost in Slavic memories (silk shirt by Thierry Mugler; jeans by Levi's); Boris (in Comme les Garçons) gazing at a Boul' Mich' bookstore window, sitting at a café, etc., until the final photograph: Boris in bed at night, naked, save for a splash of cologne (Yatagan by Caron) in the perfect muss of his linen sheets (Pratesi). It made her want to throw up.

Katia, Ms. Cornball Advertising Executive herself, knew the power of the publicity machine. She just sat back and watched the prophecy come true: every woman loves a Russian poet.

As the days drifted by she toughened up. Well Katia, what did you expect? He never was any different. He never promised you anything. In the weeks after she first read the book, she went through a multitude of emotions. At first she seesawed in a delightful confusion of shock and delight. But when she read it again more carefully, she was beside herself with rage and humiliation. He analyzed in the most sophisticated manner how she lived in an illusion, wanting only to jump into the future and grab a convenient fantasy in order to escape her manless state. But then her response grew into one of subdued and serious amazement. Boris had done what Frank had failed to do: make her see herself.

In the end, the most important thing happened when she read it a third time: she fell in love with her life. For that was her life he had painted, and it looked like a complicated, interesting and lovely life. Suddenly all the world wanted *her*, exactly who she was! She was a fascinating woman with a rich life all her own, a life people found charming and wanted to emulate. He showed her as human and vulnerable and, most importantly, desirable. Instead of feeling invaded and exposed, she understood that her life had been made into art. Best-selling art.

Of course everyone joked to her about her name. When she was introduced at cocktail parties or client meetings, she was invariably asked, "Oh, and do you ride the Lex?" Unwittingly, Boris added a new expression to the lexicon of American argot. "In the Lex" took on its own colloquial meaning of not knowing where someone was, because when you rode the New York City subway, you descended into a version of never-never-land, unreachable for the time being. The other meaning for "in the Lex" became out to lunch, dizzy, cuckoo.

Katia blossomed into her new, self-imposed reign of love and acceptance, bemused by all the furor, enjoying the speculation about the movie and Boris's whereabouts and liaisons as reported by *People* magazine. But curiously it didn't affect her or make her sad because none of it had anything to do with her. Boris was Boris; the book had a life of its own, and so did she.

When the phone jingled abusively in the middle of a breezy October night, even in her dream state, she knew it had to be him. Boo looked up from her post at the foot of the bed. Katia groped for the alarm clock. The illuminated dial said 3:09. She didn't turn on the light and reached for the phone in the dark. Her heart was pounding from fright.

"Hello?" she whispered.

"Hello, baby. It's me."

It had been so long since she heard his deep, liquid tones. His voice sounded muffled and far away. She was silent. Her mind went blank. Was this a dream?

"Where are you?" she asked suspiciously. She spoke very slowly; for some reason it felt like they were underwater.

"It doesn't matter."

Her body surged with a familiar, horrible feeling. He was doing it again! ushing her off! Her nerves were jangling, sending signals of danger. She went on alert, trying to navigate through this mine field of a phone call.

He sighed and then said, "I'm here. I'm nohere," in an exhausted, bored, dramatic tone.

"Are you sad? You sound sad," she said, giving him an opening. But she kept her voice cool and even. She wasn't going to let him get to her this time.

No reply.

"You should be thrilled. Aren't you?" she probed warily.

"It's fine, baby, everything's fine," he replied in an annoyed tone. "How are you?" he asked as a matter of form, and without waiting for a reply, he launched into, "Did you like the book? Look, I'm sorry about not telling you, but I was sure you'd get a kitschy kick out of it. We both know it's bullshit. Nabokov wrote his *Lolita* to find fame for his serious works, I write *Katia*. No difference."

Is this how he thought he could handle it, just toss off a little apology at three in the morning after months of ignoring her? He really was oblivious, she thought. A man without feelings, stuck in some childish, selfish, emotional state where he thought he could get away with anything, believing this charm, his righteous suffering would explain all.

"Why are you calling me?" she asked in an exasperated tone.

He grunted.

"It's after three in the morning," she said. "Don't you know it's rude to wake people up? And for nothing? You must have wanted something, so out with it. What? Or stop wasting my time."

"Don't be like this," he said.

"I'm not one of your literary groupies, Boris, who thinks everything you do or say is wonderful. I think you're pathetic. Unless you figure out some things about yourself, you're going to have a sad, miserable life, alone. Just you and your fancy bubblebaths."

"This is a stupid conversation," he said, dismissing her as if she was being foolish, going off the deep end like all women were wont to do.

But Katia was onto him. Clever, very clever the way he always made everything her fault, as if she were the one who was fucked up. She understood then, that there was no winning with him. She'd never make him see. Give up, Katia, she said to herself. She thought about what else she wanted to know. "So who's Jo Anne?"

"Ah, Katia. You still ask such silly questions? No one important. Jo Anne is just a woman who helped me a little with my book."

"Do you love her?"

"No, baby. She is like a secretary. She read the book and made comments."

"Are you still together?"

"No. She was in Paris for a while, but she is back in New York now."

Katia thought about what she wanted to know next. "Are you alone now?"

He laughed softly. "Of course, baby. You know me. I will always be alone."

"Are you kidding? I see your picture all the time with pretty girls."

"My struggle is gone, my libido is gone. Pouf! I could have any nineteen-year-old girl anytime and I just can't. You see, I don't want."

It was so eerie, lying in bed with Boo asleep at her feet talking to the now famous Boris Zimoy in the dark, calling from nowhere. What women would give to have Boris Zimoy call them in bed at three in the morning!

"What do you want, Boris? Why did you call me? Are you lonely? Do you feel guilty? What?" she said in a nasty tone.

He didn't like her questions and gave an exasperated laugh followed by another overly dramatic sigh. "If this is the way you're going to be," he threatened.

"Don't do this to me!" she cried.

"Listen, take care, baby. Take the famous care. I'll be in touch." Total condescension.

"No, wait!" she said, struggling to maintain control of her voice.

"Ciao baby, je t'embrasse." The click of the phone.

She slammed the receiver down, and much to her annoyance, silent big tears rolled down her cheeks. Damn! She was annoyed at herself for crying. She had been fine, not hearing from him, and now, why had she lost it? He still had the power to affect her.

She sat up and carressed Boo as if it were her cat who needed comforting. "He's an awful man, Boo," she said. She thought of how he told her he was calling from nowhere, a nowhere man. How sad for him. How could she ever have found him appealing? But then she thought, Boris had changed, he was not the man she met two years ago. That first freezing January he was a sweet, frightened and very soulful man who awakened new things in her. He had been nice to her in the ways he knew how to be nice. Now, he was achingly bitter and tough, a sad, lone survivor trying to get a foothold in the Western world.

Every woman loves a Russian poet. The words echoed in her mind. Every woman has a Boris in her life, she thought. Every woman loves a man once in her life who is totally wrong for her. In fact, many women succumbed to the misfortune of marrying their Russian poets. It was only through the trauma of divorce that they started on the painful road of self-discovery. Katia realized she had gotten off easy. Could it be that in order to recognize and love the right man, you had to go through the torture of loving the wrong man? That in the process of loving the wrong man, a woman really came to know herself?

Of course, the same thing applied to men, too. Why should they be any different? She thought of the men, married and single, who regularly came to sit in her office, confessing their woes about their love lives to her. They, too, had their infatuations, chasing after impossible women who didn't love them back.

She lay back down and tried to go to sleep. She tossed and turned fitfully and a while later noticed that Boo had jumped off the bed and was luxuriating on the celadon carpet in a pool of moonlight. Katia thought it was one of the most beautiful visions she had ever seen. "Are you taking a moonbath?" she crooned. It looked so inviting, sleeping in the eerie silver blue light of the moon. "I'm going to take a moonbath, too. It's a good idea," she whispered, and got down on the floor next to Boo. She stroked the cat and closed her eyes. "I don't want any men in my life like that, Boo. And neither do you. I want a man who loves me. Don't I deserve that? I think I do." She didn't remember falling asleep, but in the morning she awoke curiously refreshed. She decided the moonbath must have cleansed her soul.

Two days later she received a Federal Express envelope posted from the Beverly Hills hotel. Inside was a Wells Fargo Bank check for a thousand dollars payable to Katia Odinokov and a Hermès scarf from the Helsinki Duty Free shop.

So this was the final farewell. She fanned the check against her hand and recalled how she had wired him the money lovingly, back in the early days. He had called her up frantically, pleading with her to save him because the bank had closed down his credit and he was about to be evicted from his apartment. He had not a centime, not a sou to his name.

She was very happy to have the money back, even if he didn't add any interest. After all, a thousand dollars was a thousand dollars. She thought he had conveniently forgotten the loan. It would be just like him to consider the money a gift. She unfolded the scarf and looked at the pattern. He had picked out a good one, ancient keys in gold with navy tassels and braids. She ran her hands over the heavy silk. Yes, this she would wear. She was happy with it, but not because it had come from him. She was able to separate her pleasure in the object from the sender.

A feeling of euphoria welled up inside her. She let out a whoop. It dawned on her that she had cause to be thrilled for another reason, the biggest reason of all. The words emerged triumphantly as a smile slowly blossomed on her face. She was finally over him. Her feelings for Boris were dead. Truly, really, fabulously dead.

Frank and Katia

FRANK THOUGHT he was over Katia. The experience at the 92nd Street Y made him realize that she had truly left him behind and flown beautifully into her own life. But then *Katia in the Lex* came out and he was obsessed. All over again. He was desperate to talk to her. He wanted to know what she thought, how she felt. Perhaps she needed him. After all, Boris spared no compassion in his portrait of her; the book was fairly harsh at times, even though it ended on a complimentary note. And he wondered how she felt about him after reading the parts with analyst Joe Viggeano.

Then he said, Frank, stop kidding yourself. That's not what he wanted at all. He wanted to tell her how *he* felt, tell her he loved her, make her understand how she had changed his life.

He tried calling her but kept putting down the phone. He said to himself, This is ridiculous, over a year has gone by, we are no longer doctor and patient. Once he called when he knew she was at work so he could listen to the message on her answering machine. Her voice didn't sound angry; it seemed cheerful and clear as a bell. Then he decided a letter might be best, so every night for a week when he got home from work, he sat down and wrote out some sort of explanation, about the book, about himself... and went to bed, only to tear it up in the morning. The letters were either too detailed and boring, or cloudy with emotion and incomprehensible. He went through a whole box of stationery, not to mention all the stamps he had to steam off the envelopes.

When would he learn not to stamp and seal the letters he wrote at night? He wasn't sleeping well, tossing and turning with nightmares about what she might be doing and thinking. He was petrified of meeting her by accident so he steered clear of places like Zabar's and Fairway, where he knew she went to stock up once a week.

One Friday night in October he was sitting in his armchair reading when he remembered the grapes in his freezer would be frozen by now. This was a Katia recipe: "Freeze grapes and enjoy by dipping them into sour cream and brown sugar." He had forgotten the sour cream and brown sugar, so he skipped the last part. While he was eating them, a memory of Katia floated into his mind. It was when she had come into his office with a bag of grapes from the farmers' market and sat in the chair talking to him, plopping grapes, one by one, in her mouth. It was the way she ate them, that vision of her caressing the grapes with her fingertips as if they were precious drops of jade. . . .

He picked up the phone and dialed her number. He had it memorized by now. When she answered on the third ring, he hung up. Good, he thought, she's home. He checked his watch, it was seven o'clock. He bolted out of his armchair. He was just going to have to take his chances. He brushed his teeth and ran a comb through his hair. He decided his jeans were okay but changed into a white shirt and chose one of his new Italian sport jackets. Minutes later he was standing on Central Park West hailing a cab. Better to act fast before he had a chance to back out.

"East Side, please," he told the cabby as he slid into the backseat, "Seventy-eighth and Lex." He leaned back and saw himself in the rear-view mirror. Good Lord, I am possessed! He didn't care. Now was not the time for thinking. For the first time he was actually more excited than scared.

It was a very chilly October evening and the city seemed, somehow, quite pleased with its sparkling, Friday night self. The traffic was heavy and the cab bumped its way slowly through the Seventy-ninth Street crosstown. Still, it seemed as if one minute he was in his armchair, and the next, the cab was pulling over to one side of Lexington Avenue. Frank paid the fare, and as he hopped out he had the vision of himself as a handsome man, jumping out of a cab on a Saturday night on his way to pick up his date. He looked left and right on Seventy-eighth Street to determine which way the numbers went. As he approached her building he saw a doorman standing guard outside and lost his nerve.

He decided to walk around the block to collect himself. Just once around the block did it, and this time as he came up to her building his feet transported him inside without any problem. The doorman just looked up at him as he breezed right past him authoritatively.

"Katia Odinokov, she's expecting me," he said.

The doorman nodded and didn't budge. Frank supposed that he looked like a safe, normal person, probably just another of Katia's ad friends. He checked the listing at the entrance for her name and buzzed her. That was the polite thing to do, after all, one just didn't drop in without at least buzzing downstairs first. Who would answer a knock on a door in New York City?"

A few seconds passed. Then, "Hello?" Katia's voice came muffled through the speaker. "Hello?"

Frank mumbled something, not wanting to give himself away. These intercoms were usually fuzzy and you could never figure out who it was anyway.

"Who?" Another garbled attempt from Katia.

This time he mumbled "Frank Manne" and hoped she would buzz him in. A few awful seconds went by, and finally, the obnoxious buzz went off and he pushed open the heavy glass door. He headed for the open elevator and then realized he had forgotten to see what apartment she was in, so he dashed back, checked her number and then ran back to the elevator and punched eight. It was one of those ancient elevators that took its time creaking up the eight floors. Then suddenly the door opened and he stepped out as if he were in one of the dreams he had over the past few weeks. He found himself standing at her door, knocking gently, without any hesitation.

"Who is it?" she said at the same time that he saw the peephole open. He was being looked at. He had been discovered.

"Frank Manne."

She opened the door slowly and gave him a "what the hell are you doing here?" look, not making any move to let him in. She was surprised, all right. As they stood there looking at each other, they both knew it was *Katia in the Lex* that had brought him here.

God, she was beautiful! She looked like an exotic animal in her worn and soft-looking jeans, a hand-knit sweater, her hair pulled back in a casual sweep. Bare feet. Natural and womanly. He could tell she didn't have a bra on from the way the sweater outlined the shape of her breasts.

"What do you want?" Her voice was wary and ungiving.

"To talk." He was very nervous.

"About what?" she asked, shifting her weight onto one foot.

"Things," was the best he could muster. "The book," he added quickly.

"Why didn't you call first?"

"I was afraid you'd say no." She was giving him the third degree. "It's the truth," he said. The games were over. He wasn't going to say, "I was in the neighborhood and thought I'd drop in."

She continued to stand there and look at him. He sensed that under her seeming composure she was both frightened and angry. Well, he couldn't blame her.

"Please, can we talk? I know, I have a lot to explain."

She moved away from the door and motioned him in with a sweep of her hand.

"I promise I won't stay long," he added.

He stepped into her apartment and, strangely was momentarily stunned by the familiarity of it. Everything was just as she had described to him many times before. But to finally be here, in her environment, was intoxicating. He felt embraced by her being. No, it was more intense than that, it was like finally being inside of her. The living room was so cozy with its soft pools of light. The chairs looked comfortable and inviting. Books and magazines were strewn all over. There was a vase of freesia on the dining-room table. Chopin trickled dreamily from the stereo.

He stepped into the living room and watched her close and lock the door. Before he could say a word, she said, "Please, sit down." He sat down on the couch uneasily. She took the chair opposite him. "Now, what do you want to tell me?"

He looked at her sitting across from him and had a flash of how they used to sit like this in his office, only she was on the couch and he was in the chair. But suddenly he felt out of his element. This was not therapy anymore, this was life. He cleared his voice. "How are you?" he asked tentatively. He had to start somewhere.

"Fine," she replied, puzzled. "How are you?"

"Good. Fine." This was more awkward than he had imagined. He took a breath. His words came in fits and starts. "Well. I just wanted to tell you. I read the book. And the Katia, in the book? She is not you. You know that, don't you? You are better than that. And . . . I wanted to know how you felt about the Joe Viggeano scenes. That must be . . . me.

Of course. Don't you think?" Oh dear, she looked more confused than before. This was not at all going as he wanted it to.

"I'm fine about the book." She tossed the words off, shrugging her shoulders as if to say, "What's all the fuss about?"

He blundered on slowly, groping for words. "I wanted to say I'm sorry for whatever pain I caused you. I understand now why you had to break off seeing me. It was my fault, not yours. You were fine, you were doing exactly what someone is supposed to do in analysis—thrash around in a mire of feelings. My job was to figure them out and help you through it. And I didn't." Here he stopped and took a deep breath. "Because I was attracted to you and wouldn't admit it to myself. It was too scary. Remember that first day when you said, 'This is all a joke, right?'" They both smiled. "Well, you were right. You should have walked out of my office and we shouldn't have had therapy. So I came today to apologize and . . ."

"And what?"

"And tell you that I didn't know how I felt about you at the time, but now I do. And that I still am. Attracted to you. And I like you. I would like to see you. You made me think a lot and you changed my life."

She shifted uncomfortably in her chair and looked away. There was an awful silence. "You really are an asshole!" she said, and burst into tears.

He flew across the room and tried to put his arms around her. Her body stiffened immediately and she pushed him away. "No! No! Get away from me! How could you?" Tears streamed down her face. She pushed back loose strands of wet hair and started pummeling his shoulders with her fists.

"It's okay, it's okay," he kept repeating. He tried to hold on to her and absorb her blows. "It's okay."

"It's not okay!" she snarled at him. "Let go of me!" Then she walloped his face with her hand. It stunned him. He had never been slapped before. He put his hand to his face in disbelief and then felt foolish, recalling how men always did that in the movies and how silly it looked. He stepped back. She stood up and started pacing in front of the window.

"You think you can come barging into my life after a year and a half? Into a life that I've had to figure out on my own, and tell me *now* how you're feeling? *Now* you tell me that all that time I was feeling horrible, that it was you who screwed up, that it was your fault? One little 'I'm sorry' and you expect me to be thrilled about it? Well, that's just great, Frank."

She paced some more, fuming. "Why do I always cry when I'm angry? I hate it. And I hate you!"

"But . . . this is the new me," he said brokenly.

She stopped short and glared at him. "Oh, that's just great, 'new and improved.' Well, I hate to inform you, but I never knew the old you," she added sarcastically.

"What do you mean you never knew me?" he asked, offended.

She smirked. "How could I know you? All you ever did was sit there and say nothing."

"Please," he begged, moving closer to her with his outstretched arms.

"Get away from me! What do you want from me? Why did you come here?" she yelled.

"I just wanted to explain . . . I just want to comfort you." He moved closer and reached out his hand to her.

"Don't touch me!" she snapped, and stepped back. "I'm perfectly fine. I don't need your comforting."

"It's okay," he said.

"Why do you keep saying it's okay? It's not okay!" She was now backed up against the wall. This was all wrong, it wasn't how he wanted it to be. How could he turn this horrible situation around, how could he make her see?

"Now you can. Trust me, that is." He was at a loss for words. He shook his head and wrung his hands. "Because . . ." He stopped. Because why? He was defeated.

She continued, "*Now* you decide to love me. What did you think, that I was pining for you all this time? That you would come here and tell me you loved me and everything would be back where it was and I'd jump into your lap?"

She was right. His timing sucked. What was going on here, why had he come? He should just apologize and leave her alone. Go home. It had been a mistake. It was his loss for words that seemed to calm her down. She got up and went to the kitchen. He didn't know what to do, should he leave or what? He heard her blow her nose and then the sound of splashing water. She came back composed, holding two glasses of red wine, and handed him one.

"Thank you."

She sat back down. They sipped in silence for a few moments and then she started talking to the air. "You know, it's strange to find you speechless," she said, searching for her thoughts. "I used to think you had all the answers, only you weren't going to tell them to me, you wanted me to figure things out by myself. I thought you were so mean." She smiled at this memory of herself and sighed. "I guess you didn't have all the answers."

He nodded and took a gulp of wine.

She continued. "And I did figure some things out by myself. I was loving two of the most wrong men. I wasn't loving myself. I didn't believe that I was lovable. I was so afraid of being loved, I treated men terribly." She seemed to drift off into her own world. Then she turned to him. "Look, I don't know who you really are or what you want with me. . . ." Her voice was quavering as if his presence were making her nervous, as if he were a nut case in her own living room.

"What do you mean, you don't know who I am?" He became distraught and started trembling. He could see that she was being as polite, as gentle as she could be, but her words stung him. His mind went on a rampage, repeating the same thoughts over and over. *I'm here to tell you I love you, that you were right all along, I should never have been your doctor. Don't you see, we were meant to be together! It was a fluke of fate that we were thrown together at the institute. But at least we did get to this point. I'm sorry about the book. There was this woman Jo Anne. I saw Boris in Paris. I saw you that night at the Y. You've taught me how to live.*

His heart overflowed with his silent monologue. He couldn't bring himself to say any of it. Damn! Life was so much more complicated than it seemed when he was sitting in his analyst's chair. How easy it was to admonish his patients for not communicating with their lovers. He had often said things like, "Well, did you tell Tim (Tony, Beau) what you're telling me? Why not? How can you expect him to know what you're feeling if you don't *tell* him?" And here he was making a fine mess of it.

"Maybe you better go now," she said gently.

This was a nightmare!

"It's just too sad," she added.

"No!"

"Well, what then?"

"I want to know you," he said quietly.

"But you do. You know everything about me. I told you everything, twice a week for two years. You know more about me than any other person." She assumed a contemplative air as she weighed her own words.

"Well, now you can know me," he said. "It can be different now. Now we can have a real relationship."

"Back then, you always told me we had a 'real' relationship." She smiled at the memory. "Remember how I always complained to you that it wasn't real? And you said it was as real as it was ever going to get?"

He tried to smile and sipped some wine in order to let the stinging effect of her words melt away.

She said, "You know, I used to love you so much. And you would tell me it was transference—that it wasn't really *you* I loved, but some made-up ideal I had in my own mind. I remember how I refused to believe you. How I cried and cried. I really believed we were something special, that we could be something special, but that you weren't going to let it happen." She spoke very slowly as if dredging up these memories wearied her. She turned to him. "But I understand it now. You were right! I didn't love you. It was only some fantasy of you I loved. Just like you said. I don't even know who you are . . . I mean . . . I'm sure you're very nice. . . ."

A roar rose up in his body. He wanted to scream. His heart refused to believe her words; this couldn't be happening.

"There has been a big mistake," he whispered.

She tilted her head in confusion.

"All this time . . . I learned that I love you," he said.

She drew away, frightened, and shook her head. "No," she said. "You can't!"

Then it hit him with a dull thud. She was used to dealing with him as a figment of her own imagination. Maybe his being a real person having real emotions was scaring her. Maybe she didn't want him to be a real person with real feelings and real needs.

The tension in the air was shrieking in his ears. He stood up, took the wineglass out of her hand and put it on the table. He took her hands and pulled her up from the chair. He was very shy as he stood in front of her. Her body had an electric aura. Was she beckoning him? She moved closer to him as if she were presenting herself to him. He tentatively put his arms around her. He couldn't believe he finally had her in his arms. Holding her for the first time was a release. She felt wonderful. He rubbed his cheek against her soft face, which was cool from the water she had just splashed on it. Damn! He hadn't shaved and she drew back. He must be hurting her. But then, as if she liked the roughness, she became a cat, purring and subtly rubbing her body and face against his.

He became hard immediately and it made him self-conscious. Up until now he had been the cool, distant, untouchable doctor, but now he was a healthy, warm-blooded man. From the way she submitted to his caresses and melted her body into his, it was clear that she liked it. He breathed deeply. He was finally holding the woman who sat across from him for two years pouring out her soul, and now there was no stopping his hands from exploring her. He was drunk on his very own dream, having finally admitted to himself, and to her, his desire. As he touched her he recalled the words *brown and round* that she had used to mockingly describe herself.

She was enjoying being touched by him. Their faces nuzzled each other as he ran his hands along her body, trying to learn it. The neck, the shoulders, the arms. He felt the strength of her strong swimmer's back and then felt her breasts through her sweater. How he had longed to rub up against her body and feel her breasts through her clothes. He couldn't stand it anymore. He slid his hands up her sweater and felt the soft cotton camisole she was wearing. His hands traveled up and he caressed her breasts. He moaned. A cat meowed and brushed up against his legs as if saying, "Hey, what about me?" They both laughed.

She pulled off her sweater and he smiled. It was a man's undershirt she was wearing. She smiled back and calmly stared him in the eye. They still hadn't said a word. This was a silent ballet. He stepped forward and took her hands in his, then kissed her lightly, barely touching her lips with his. It was the kiss to start kissing, that exploratory kiss, followed by a cavalcade of kisses, the kind of kisses he had always wanted them to be. He couldn't believe how soft her lips were. Were lips ever this soft? No, never. Such exploring lips, lingering and playful. Kisses filled with a desire to connect, kisses that were offered, kisses that he took.

"I can't stand up," she said breathlessly, and led him to the couch, where they sank down and she pulled him close and without any self-consciousness drank in every kiss he gave her. His pleasure came in pleasing her. He was wild with the surprise of all this. With Jo Anne, kissing had been something she put up with and he had felt like a naughty, insatiable child. Now he saw how he had been deprived of the experience of truly ravishing a woman. Katia's mouth kept urging, more, more, more. She ran her hands through his hair, massaging his scalp, and he felt like he was going to explode. Their kisses were a conversation of all the words that they could never say.

He looked at her and admired her appealing disarray, her head back, her hair mussed, her eyes closed. His lips traveled to her shoulders and then, while her hands gently stroked his head, he unzipped her jeans and slipped his hand onto her belly, only to find she was not wearing any underpants. Then he found she was soft and wet. He was wild as he felt her move under his fingertips. "I want to feel you come in my fingers," he whispered. She was totally his. He looked at her faraway face; she had gone to another place.

And then, for the first time—everything seemed to be for the first time that evening—he truly felt the wave of a woman coming. Her hips began undulating ever so slightly and she started moaning until she gasped in surprise as if someone had hit her and knocked the air out of her. He moved his hand slowly to the motion of her body, staying with her.

Frank held her in his arms and looked at her languorous face as she breathed deeply, lost in her primal state. He, who could never satisfy her when she sat across from him in his office, he who made her cry, had finally been able to satisfy her. He thought of how close he was to her right now, how close and yet how far away. This strange thing called sex. It was a tremendous feeling to have taken her to this place. They sat like that, quietly for several moments, until Katia opened her eyes and looked at him. He tried to smile at her, but then he looked away. He suddenly felt lost. What would she say?

She zipped up her pants and then stood up slowly. Everything seemed to be in slow motion, as if they were drifting in outer space. "Come with me," she said, and took him by the hand through the hallway to the bathroom. The cat scampered after them. She caressed his face with her hand.

"What?" he said uncertainly. He was nervous.

"I want to shave you."

"What?" He couldn't believe what he heard.

"Can I shave you?" she said.

"Now?"

"I've never done that to a man . . . and I thought it might be a nice thing to do," she said. "Besides, you need a shave." She sounded perfectly serious.

He rubbed his face with his hand. Oh dear, the idea made him extremely nervous. Jesus Christ, it took years for a man to be able to shave his own face without totally botching it. He knew every bump and every contour and he still managed to cut himself even when he was careful. To submit his face to a woman with a razor in her hand... Maybe this was some sort of revenge fantasy?

"Uhhh..." he stalled. How could he say no as gently as possible? But as he spoke, it suddenly became the thing he wanted most, to have Katia shave him. "Okay, but..."

"I'll be very careful," she finished the sentence for him. "Let's see." She surveyed the situation for a moment. "Sit down here." She motioned for him to sit on the floor of the bathroom. He watched as she assembled a variety of creams and potions, cotton balls, a washcloth and pulled a fresh disposable razor from a plastic pack. The cat perched on one corner of the bathtub, watching all her preparations, too. Then Katia sat down and unbuttoned his shirt and took it off.

"Now, lie down on your back and put your head in my lap, like this," she said.

"You're going to shave me upside down?" he asked nervously.

"No, silly. First I'm going to give you a minifacial," she replied in that spunky way of hers, "to prepare your skin, of course," like he was a dummy.

"Of course." He laughed and lay down. He wanted to do whatever she said. So this is how she played. He was delighted; it was like they were children, but they were consenting adults.

He wanted to remember every minute of it. She started by steaming his face with a hot washcloth. Then she soaked a cotton ball in some wonderful-smelling lotion and stroked his skin with a soft touch. It felt as if a cloud of carnations were caressing his face. "This is a carnation toner," she said. "to cleanse your skin. Next, an apricot-honey facial scrub, to loosen the layer of dead skin."

He was embarrassed. "I have dead skin?"

"Everyone does." She scrubbed his face gently with this pleasantly scratchy cream that smelled so good he wanted to eat it and then rinsed it all off with a hot washcloth. Then she poured some white lotion on her hands. "This is a buttermilk moisturizer, from Switzerland. I'm going to give you a massage, just like when I get a facial. Are you comfortable?"

He nodded. He noticed how tense his body was and tried to relax.

"Okay. Now just close your eyes and relax." She started slowly stroking his face with the cream that she had warmed in her hands. Oh my God, it felt so good. So this is what women experienced when they got a facial. No wonder they loved it. If men only knew what they were missing. He could not believe how gently she touched his skin and how extraordinary it felt to have his very own face massaged, the same face that he usually treated so brusquely every morning. He had just discovered a new erogenous zone at this late age of thirty-six. How retarded he was . . . ah well, better late than never.

She massaged his temples and his brow in long sweeping motions, then she poured more lotion on her hands and swept up from his shoulders onto his neck. He was hard, wonderfully, pleasurably hard. He thought he would come right then and there. Then he became very sad because he had never experienced such sweetness before. This was her way of making love to him. He felt his entire body relax slowly, starting from his head down to his toes.

After what seemed like hours, she said, "Okay, now I think your face is ready. I guess you'd better sit up." They readjusted themselves and sat face-to-face, cross-legged, like children playing Indian chiefs. Had they been kindergarten playmates in another lifetime? The cat jumped from the bathtub to the sink. Katia spritzed some shaving cream onto her hand and very seriously applied it to his face. Once again he was mesmerized by her gentleness. Slapping on shaving cream was something he did every day of his life without even thinking and here she was being awkward and shy, doing it for the first time in her life. He liked being the man to be joining her in her fantasy. He was charmed by the sight of her leaning so earnestly toward him, getting shaving cream all over her hands and wiping it on her jeans. She was still wearing the man's undershirt and he reached out to touch her breasts and she pulled away laughing.

"I don't think you should do that right, now," she said. She picked up the fresh razor and tried holding it in various ways as she studied his face.

He swallowed nervously.

"Now what? Do I go up? Or down? Where do I start anyway?" She grimaced a little. He was glad to see she was nervous. She should be. It wasn't easy what she was going to do.

And so they sat on the bathroom floor, Frank coaching her, giving suggestions and advice about holding his skin and submitting totally to her hand with the razor. It was the most intimate thing he had ever done. And all it was—was shaving. No, it was being shaved. By Katia. He sat very still as she leaned toward him and relished being the object of her attention. He felt her delicate breath as she worked on him. Their silence was punctuated occasionally by her asking "here?" or "like this?" or "uh-oh." He didn't want it to end. She could shave him every day if she liked.

"There," she said, and sat back surveying his face. Satisfied with her work, she wiped him clean with a warm washcloth and gently smoothed on another wonderful-smelling cream. She smiled when he noticed it. "It's an almond cream from Caswell Massey," she said, leaning forward and kissing him on the lips. This time it was she who did the kissing and he who drank in her every kiss. By now he was long gone. He had surrendered way back when, during the facial massage. He was her slave, totally in awe of her gentle hands and mouth.

"Take off your pants," she murmured. And right there on the bathroom floor, she made love to him. Kissing him was not enough; she proceeded to taste his entire body. She swirled his ears and kissed his eyebrows, she licked his armpits and the inside of his elbows. What aroused him most was when she nibbled his toes. It was an unbelievable feeling. Then she poured a tiny bit of lotion onto her hands and started massaging his cock, staring into his eyes until he could look back at her no longer. He was wild. How was it that she knew exactly how to touch him? He had never even let himself imagine that a woman would caress him just as he had always wanted. Before he knew it, he lost control. "Stop, stop, wait!" His hands reached for her, but it was too late.

He felt a little self-conscious lying there without any pants on, totally exposed and vulnerable. There he was, Frank Manne, her former analyst, lying naked on her bathroom floor. They hadn't resolved anything. Instead they were acting out some primal scenario that didn't seem to require words or explanations. It was wonderful. It seemed so natural and uncomplicated. By now she was sitting up and leaning against the bathroom wall. After some time passed she looked at him and smiled.

"So?" she said.

"So," he said. Then, "The bedroom's in there?"

She nodded.

A half hour later they were lying in her bed with their glasses of red wine. An uneasy silence had descended upon them. How strange, Frank thought, just moments ago they had been lying on the bathroom floor together and now they were as uncomfortable as two strangers trying to make conversation at a cocktail party. He took her hand in his. "What are you thinking?" he asked.

She put her wineglass down on the floor next to the futon. "In the bathroom . . . that was . . . I don't know what that was about exactly," she said in a faraway voice. "But it seemed right. It seemed to finish something off, something from the past." She paused. "Don't you agree?"

He ran his hand along his cheek, feeling his freshly shaved face. "I don't know."

"This is very sad," she said, her voice tinged with despair. "Timing really is ninety-nine percent of life."

"I can't believe you're saying this," Frank said in alarm. "What is all this talk about the past and sadness? This is now. We are here. Together. There is a future."

"No! You don't see, do you?" She said, and pulled away. "This can never work. You and me. We are having this moment now, but that's all it is. For me, it's a fantasy of the past, and yes, it's nice. But what basis do we have for a relationship?"

He couldn't believe what he was hearing. It was all he could do to put his wineglass on the floor. "We can start over. New. Fresh."

She shook her head. "No, we can't. Because there was a past. And I've changed. I'm not the same Katia you knew. The Katia of today wants something more, something different, than"—she was trying not to hurt his feelings—"you," she said softly.

No! No! He had no words left to convince her. It was clear talking would get them nowhere. He was seized by the desperation of the moment. He would simply have to make her see how he felt. She would know everything in the way he would make love to her, at which point he took her in his arms and engulfed her with all the fury of his body, roaming and devouring every inch of her with his hands and mouth. He buried his face between her legs. It was the only place he wanted to be. He loved the taste of her, kissing her there until he felt the throbbing of her coming. Then he held her in his arms, gently stroking her all over. He wanted her to want him, and when she was still, he started kissing her again in another wave of assault. Finally he thrust himself inside her and gasped. He was swimming in the ocean of femaleness that he had craved his entire life and it was Katia he held in his arms, his Katia who received him with a deepness he had never known before. As he moved inside of her he wasn't Frank anymore. Some powerful masculine presence took over his body and he was thunderstruck by the majestic, primitive animal raging within. Her moans urged him on even more until they became too much for him. "No!" and "yes!" he cried out. The roar, the rush, the silence.

It was a long night filled with forbidden pleasures. A night of the most happiness he had ever known and the saddest night of his life. They were drunk, not on wine but on the heady abandon of this long-lost, misplaced passion for each other. As the darkness pressed slowly into dawn, he understood that this was their first and last time together. That he would leave her in the morning to her own life, to make her own decisions. He had made his case and could impose on her no longer.

Oh Eros the bittersweet! How he stepped in and played his hand so deftly, and with another light tap, he was gone.

Katia Says Yes

A FEW WEEKS later, Katia was sitting in her livingroom, sipping tea and as usual, contemplating her life. She was in a wistful mood as she wondered what to do with the beautiful Saturday afternoon that weighed heavily upon her. Winter had started closing in that week but today was a final, sunny day of glory before the grey skies of November firmly took over. Still alone, she sighed. She was full of sighs. Would she ever meet someone? Doubts started dancing around her. Had she made a mistake about Frank? Been too hasty perhaps? Had she thrown away her last chance for happiness? Should she? Call him?

No, she shook her head. Katia! Stop sabotaging yourself, she admonished and pushed the regrets away. Press on! Let's see. She could start knitting that Perry Ellis sweater she had just bought the wool for, or she could take her bike out for an invigorating spin in the park. She could practice the piano. That Scarlatti sonatina was giving her some trouble and could use the attention. She could write letters to friends abroad on her favorite wispy thin blue airmail paper and dream of foreign lands. Everything sounded good. That evening she would make herself a nice dinner, say, a Julia Child coq au vin, with no shortcuts. Cognac flambé, watch out.

Then the phone rang. It was Clint. She hadn't talked to him since the wedding four months ago. Once he got married, their friendship dropped off. It made her sad how he stopped calling her, and when she called him, he seemed uncomfortable, as if he was betraying Carla if he spoke to her. Oh, well, what could you do?

"So. How's marriage?" She tried to sound light and gay.

The question seemed to embarrass him. "Great," he said, and changed the subject. "Actually, I'm calling to ask if you'd do me a favor."

"If I can do it, I'd be happy to."

"Well, it's a friend of mine. He's moving to New York and he's here apartment hunting and there's been a mix-up and Carla and I have to dine with her mother, a small family matter has come up, you know, and we were supposed to see him for dinner and I feel terrible about leaving him alone, he doesn't know a soul. . . ."

"And you want me to have dinner with him," she finished.

"Yes. Please, Katia. Would you?"

"Sure. What's his name?" What the hell. She didn't particularly feel like going out, but her new philosophy was one of surrender. Like Dorothy in *The Wizard of Oz*, she had seen her fate written in the sky; "Surrender, Katia."

"Sterling. Sterling Lee Smith," said Clint. "You may have seen him at the wedding; he was one of my fraternity brothers. He's from an old Boston family."

Sterling Lee Smith. What was he doing north of the Mason–Dixon line with such a name? Sterling? The name didn't ring a bell. Had she met him at the wedding? Katia scrunched up her face. Surely a name like Sterling she'd remember. She tried to remember and realized she'd hardly met anybody at the wedding. Maybe he was one of those ushers in the receiving line.

"Maybe I saw him, but I don't know." There was a slight tinge of exasperation in her voice. She was feeling defensive and a little embarrassed that Clint was now playing matchmaker, so she said, "Sterling Smith?" in a mocking manner. The combination of such an elegant first name with such a common last name seemed a bit silly. "What kind of a name is that? And what do people call him? Surely not Sterling."

"Yes, as a matter of fact. Just plain Sterling," Clint said. "Now don't be like that. It's only dinner."

Oh dear, did she sound tiresome? She changed her tone. "Fine. I'd love to. Give him my address and tell him to come over . . . um . . . around eight, okay?" Sterling; it sounded stuffy. And if he was a friend of

Clint's, he couldn't possibly be her type. "What does he do anyway?"

"Computers," said Clint.

"Oh, great." She tried to inject a tinge of delighted approval into her voice. Computer jock, she thought. The more questions she asked, the worse he sounded. She decided to stop right there.

"Have a good time," Clint said. "And really, thank you. You're doing me, I mean us—Carla and me—a big favor."

"My pleasure. Really, thanks for calling and give my best to Carla; we really should all get together soon. It's been too long," she said, and hung up. Actually, the thought of a dinner date cheered her up. Yum! she thought, what delicious restaurant shall I suggest? She decided she needed some fresh air and exercise. She bundled herself up in layers of sweaters, put on her gloves and went for a breezy bike ride in the park with her Sony Walkman blaring rock and roll loud in her ears until she was laughing and singing along with the wind in her hair.

At 7:45 that evening when the doorbell rang, Katia was still in her kimono. "Shoot," she said, and looked at her watch. "It's just like a computer jock to be early, right, Boo?" She checked her face in the mirror to see if she shouldn't go to the door wearing half her makeup, but she decided she looked okay. When she opened the door, she had to control her face.

Oh my God! It was him! The man who had sat next to her at Clint's wedding and danced with everyone but her! How was she ever going to get through this evening? He looked just as he did the night of the wedding, elegantly and expensively dressed in a dark suit, with a bottle of champagne in one hand. What was missing was the blonde on his other arm.

She decided right then and there to make the best of it. "Hello. I'm Katia," she said cheerfully, extending her hand.

"Incredible! You were at my table at Clint's wedding."

She nodded and tried to smile.

"Katia," he repeated, "what kind of name is that?"

"Russian," she said.

He thought about it for a moment and then said, "Forgive me! Sterling. Sterling Smith." He offered his hand.

Katia exhaled slowly and tried to assume a pleasant look on her face. Yes, I'm the woman you ignored all night long.

"Fabulous wedding," he continued. "Say, it's a shame we didn't have a dance all night."

You never asked me. She shrugged her shoulders as if to say, "Oh well." "Well, as you can see, I'm not ready yet, so please come in and I'll just be a minute." She stood back and let him enter. He dropped his coat over a dining-room chair and turned to her.

"Say, I've brought some champagne to celebrate my new apartment. Can you believe it? I actually found one today—on my first day looking! I must say, I do have luck. My father always said so. And all I heard were horror stories about how impossible it would be. Shall we?" He started taking the foil off the bottle.

"How lovely," she said, and went to get her champagne flutes. She stood there holding them while he expertly pried the cork. As she watched him listen for the muffled pop she tried to see the label but couldn't. "What are we drinking?" she asked.

"Veuve Clicquot, 1979," he replied, showing her the bottle before pouring into the glasses she held.

At least he knew his champagne. "Vintage," she said approvingly, and smiled. They both waited for the foam to settle, then held their glasses up. "To your new apartment," she said.

"To our first dance," he countertoasted, and they both laughed and clinked glasses. "Hmmm, very nice," he said, analyzing the flavor in his mind.

She looked at him and thought how strange that he should have spoken her line. "Mmmm . . ." she agreed. "Well, I'm going to finish dressing. Here, let me put on some music for you." She flipped on the stereo as she left the living room.

Katia closed the door to her bedroom firmly behind her. It was a new sensation. She had never closed this door before, or any door for that matter, in her apartment. That's from living alone, she thought, there was never any need to shut doors when you lived alone. She took a long sip of champagne and put the glass down on the bureau and proceeded to finish with the mascara and the blush until she was satisfied with the effect. The final touch, red lips and a spritz of Jolie Madame. Next she looked through her closet. He was pretty elegant, so she might as well match. Which black dress would it be? Good, she could wear her Azzedine. After rummaging through her underwear drawer she found some sheer black pantyhose with gold glitter and checked them for runs. Satisfied, she slipped them on, twisting and turning until they felt right. Then she slid the dress over her head, adjusting it in the mirror. She liked what she saw. No muss, no fuss, just simple and bold. Her usual.

She sipped some more champagne. I'll need this to get through the evening, she thought, and stood there in front of the mirror, watching herself finish the entire glass. Not bad. Downright delicious. Both her and the champagne.

She loved the solitude of her warm, perfumy room just then. It seemed like such a haven, safe from the vagaries of the outside world. In a few seconds she would have to leave this cozy place and deal with that unknown man outside, have a dinner, make some conversation. She turned off her lights but couldn't make herself open the door. Not yet, she sighed. She went to gaze out the bedroom window for a few seconds more. She scanned the Saturday-night scene. It was still early. A man was walking his dog. Two teenagers sped by on their roller skates. A car was double-parked, waiting for someone. Her doorman was lounging against the awning post. A delivery man carrying a large white pizza box stopped to gain permission to enter, then disappeared under the awning.

She was about to turn away when her eye passed over the darkened, silent school windows across the street. Suddenly the street lamps flicked on and from the glint of the light on the shiny windowpanes she caught the reflection of the janitor, standing in his usual spot looking in her direction. She was disgusted. Oh, he's waiting for me to dance. "Well, sorry to disappoint you, mister," she said softly. He didn't budge. What could he be looking at? She wasn't dancing. But he kept his eyes riveted on her living-room window. He's pathetic, that horny creep. Probably imagining things. She turned away. It was time to leave.

When Katia opened the door of her bedroom, she was unprepared for the blast of music that hit her. Reggae cranked up higher than she had ever heard. Chills ran up and down her spine. All the lights were off. Who had turned them off? Was there a power failure? No, the music was on. What was going on here? She was frightened and her heart started pounding. Was he going to attack her? Rape her? What's happening? She couldn't see a thing. She felt her way against the dark hallway with all her nerves jangling. What she saw set off screaming in her head.

There was Sterling in her living room, with his jacket off, shoes off, tie slightly undone, dancing up a storm, in the dark.

Her mouth dropped open from the shock of recognition. He was lost in his own world, completely given up to the wailing music, lip-synching, mugging and emoting to the lyrics, leaping, twisting, swaying and singing it like it was. And he didn't see her standing there.

The screaming in her head moved down to become pounding in her heart. "Hey, that's my fantasy!" she wanted to yell, as if she felt he was taking something away from her. Her feelings flowed in a jumble. Was this really happening? Or was this a fantasy, too? Had she drunk that much champagne? She touched the table to make sure she was really standing there. Her hand found his glass and she gulped down the rest of the champagne in it. She became dizzy from the icy bubbles.

Now he was standing as if with an imaginary partner, spinning and accompanying her with extreme finesse. Except that he danced as badly as ever! How awful! How embarrassing! She was both attracted and repelled by the sight of him; one second she was intrigued and delighted, and the next she was in a panic because he was so clumsy.

What should she do? She would turn off the stereo immediately and stop him. No. She would go back into her room and pretend she hadn't seen any of this and come in when the music ended. No! She should flip the lights on to stop this foolishness immediately before another second passed. But then what would she say? Then she had the urge to get out of the apartment, just run away from this and slam the door.

By now the fast dance had segued into a romantic slow song. And so had Sterling. Breathing heavily from all his prancing around, he changed tempo and was gliding slowly around the room, dipping and swaying. He was so earnest, this dreamy-looking man dancing slowly with his eyes closed, striking poses. He didn't look scary anymore. He looked vulnerable and, yes, touchable.

Katia's heart ached. *This was her moment! The moment she had always dreamed of.* She wanted to enter the dance, but . . . with him? He can't possibly be . . . Finish the sentence, Katia, a voice inside her sternly ordered. He can't possibly be who? Mr. Right? Mr. Right . . . What a stupid concept that is. It was unfair to men, too. There's no such thing as Mr. Right, she thought, why those words should be banished from the language. Instead there should be a Mr. Okay, or a Mr. Why Not.

She looked at Sterling dancing. Now here is a real man, Katia, she said to herself, a real man with your fantasy. She smiled sadly. And what are you going to do about it? This is what you've been waiting for. She poured some more champagne into the glass and drank it down for courage.

Katia! This is the final call! If you don't act now, this moment will be lost. Forever. Her heart ached for all the moments such as this that she had let pass her by. *Now*, Katia. She took a deep breath and slipped off her shoes. She felt the soft carpet under her stockinged feet. At this moment Sterling turned and saw her looking at him. He froze with his arm in the air and tried to smile. The music played on.

"I don't know how to do reggae," she said shyly, and held out her hand. "I usually do ballet."

He looked relieved. "Well, I'll show you some of my steps" he said tentatively, taking her outstretched hand, "and then you can show me some ballet." At which point he swung her into his arms.

After a few awkward seconds during which they both struggled to understand each other's rhythm, he started gliding her around the room, quite well, actually. She was amazed. She thought how perfectly dreamy and romantic to be ballroom dancing in her own living room and with a stranger, no less. Why it was just like a Fred and Ginger movie. They were certainly dressed for the part. Vintage champagne too. Oops, he stepped on her toes and he drew back apologetically. She put her arms back on him and they began again, this time flowing even more smoothly, with a few whirls thrown in, and she wondered how could it be that they were dancing so well together when she had seen him dance so badly at the wedding? Suddenly he dipped her and she screamed but held on and they laughed. The next time he warned her playfully, "Here it comes!" and when he dipped her, he held her there for a second and she looked into his eyes and then had to look away. He brought her back up and she felt her body relax. He relaxed, too, and pulled her closer. How was it possible that she felt as if she had danced with him for years?

She liked the feeling of his back under her left arm, solid but light. She loved the way the sleeves of his shirt were rolled up, exposing his masculine forearms. Along with his slightly loosened tie, it made for a debonair look. His hand felt good, too, the way he held hers with just the right amount of pressure, sexy but not presuming. They seemed to be about the same height; maybe he was slightly taller. Freshly shaved face. His cologne was . . . she moved her face slightly toward his neck and breathed in. He caught her at her own game. "Good old Canoë," he said. They both laughed. But mostly, what she found appealing was how he felt comfortable with what he wanted, and what he wanted was her.

Her eyes glimpsed the shadow they made on the walls as they spun about the room. Instead of the usual solitary shape she was used to seeing, she saw a new silhouette, the curious melding of two separate bodies into a single form, both masculine and feminine. She tried to make out their separate parts, her legs, his arms, his legs, her arms, but it was no use. For now, they were one and she was happy.